THE LOST FLEET

BEYOND THE FRONTIER

GUARDIAN

JACK CAMPBELL

TITAN BOOKS

The Lost Fleet: Beyond the Frontier: Guardian
Print edition ISBN: 9781781164648
E-book edition ISBN: 9781781164655

Published by Titan Books
A division of Titan Publishing Group Ltd
144 Southwark Street, London SE1 0UP

First edition: May 2013
10 9 8 7 6 5 4 3 2 1

What did you think of this book? We love to hear from our readers. Please email us at: readerfeedback@titanemail.com, or write to us at the above address.

To receive advance information, news, competitions, and exclusive offers online, please sign up for the Titan newsletter on our website:
www.titanbooks.co.uk

A CIP catalogue record for this title is available from the British Library.

Printed and bound in Great Britain by CPI Group UK Ltd.

THE LOST FLEET

BEYOND THE FRONTIER

GUARDIAN

To Robert, my younger brother, who kept getting back up every time life knocked him down. He was the strongest of us. And to Debbie K., his wife, who gave him what he had always sought, stayed by him, and will always be family.

For S., as always.

THE FIRST FLEET OF THE ALLIANCE

ADMIRAL JOHN GEARY, COMMANDING

Second Battleship Division

Gallant
Indomitable
Glorious
Magnificent

Third Battleship Division

Dreadnaught
Orion
Dependable
Conqueror

Fourth Battleship Division

Warspite
Vengeance
Revenge
Guardian

Fifth Battleship Division

Fearless
Resolution
Redoubtable

Seventh Battleship Division

Colossus
Encroach
Amazon
Spartan

Eighth Battleship Division

Relentless
Reprisal
Superb
Splendid

First Battle Cruiser Division

Inspire
Formidable
Brilliant (lost at Honor)
Implacable

Second Battle Cruiser Division

Leviathan
Dragon
Steadfast
Valiant

Fourth Battle Cruiser Division

Dauntless (Flagship)
Daring
Victorious
Intemperate

Fifth Battle Cruiser Division

Adroit

Sixth Battle Cruiser Division

Illustrious
Incredible
Invincible (lost at
Pandora)

Fifth Assault Transport Division

Tsunami
Typhoon
Mistral
Haboob

First Auxiliaries Division

Titan
Tanuki
Kupua
Domovoi

Second Auxiliaries Division

Witch
Jinn
Alchemist
Cyclops

Thirty-one heavy cruisers in six divisions

First Heavy Cruiser Division
Third Heavy Cruiser Division
Fourth Heavy Cruiser Division
Fifth Heavy Cruiser Division
Eighth Heavy Cruiser Division
Tenth Heavy Cruiser Division
Emerald and **Hoplon** lost at Honor

Fifty-five light cruisers in ten squadrons

First Light Cruiser Squadron
Second Light Cruiser Squadron
Third Light Cruiser Squadron
Fifth Light Cruiser Squadron
Sixth Light Cruiser Squadron
Eighth Light Cruiser Squadron
Ninth Light Cruiser Squadron
Tenth Light Cruiser Squadron
Eleventh Light Cruiser Squadron
Fourteenth Light Cruiser Squadron
Balestra lost at Honor

One hundred sixty destroyers in eighteen squadrons

First Destroyer Squadron
Second Destroyer Squadron
Third Destroyer Squadron
Fourth Destroyer Squadron
Sixth Destroyer Squadron
Seventh Destroyer Squadron
Ninth Destroyer Squadron
Tenth Destroyer Squadron
Twelfth Destroyer Squadron
Fourteenth Destroyer Squadron
Sixteenth Destroyer Squadron
Seventeenth Destroyer Squadron

Twentieth Destroyer Squadron
Twenty-first Destroyer Squadron
Twenty-third Destroyer Squadron
Twenty-seventh Destroyer Squadron
Twenty-eighth Destroyer Squadron
Thirty-second Destroyer Squadron
Zaghnal lost at Pandora
Plumbatae, Bolo, Bangalore, and **Morningstar** lost at Honor
Musket lost at Midway

FIRST FLEET MARINE FORCE
MAJOR GENERAL CARABALI, COMMANDING

3,000 Marines on assault transports and divided into detachments on battle cruisers and battleships

1

The admiral was having a bad day, and when the admiral was having a bad day, no one wanted to attract his attention.

Almost no one.

"Is there anything wrong, Admiral?"

Admiral John "Black Jack" Geary, who had been slumped in the fleet command seat on the bridge of the Alliance battle cruiser *Dauntless*, straightened up and glared at Captain Tanya Desjani. "Are you serious? We're extremely far from the Alliance, the Syndics are still causing trouble for us, and the warships of this fleet are shot to hell after fighting our way through enigma- and Kick-controlled space, then fighting again here. The warship we took from the Kick alien race is valuable beyond measure but also a threat magnet and a drag on this fleet. We have no idea what's happening back in the Alliance but every reason to believe whatever is happening isn't good. Did I forget anything? Oh, yes, my flagship's commanding officer just asked me if anything was wrong!"

Sitting in her captain's seat next to him, Desjani nodded, eyeing him calmly. "But, aside from all that, you're good?"

"Aside from all that?" He could have exploded, but she knew him better than anyone else. If he hadn't had a sense of the absurd, his responsibilities would have driven him up the wall long before this. "Yeah. Aside from all that, I'm good. You're amazing, Captain Desjani."

"I do my best, Admiral Geary."

The bridge watch team could see them talking, and knew what the admiral's mood had been like, but couldn't hear what was being said. Which was why Lieutenant Castries sounded a bit wary as well as urgent when she called out her report to everyone else on the bridge of *Dauntless*. "A warship came out of the gate!"

Combat systems alerts were already sounding as Geary straightened in his seat, the frown he hadn't realized was riding his brow vanishing as he hastily focused his display on the hypernet gate that loomed at the edge of the Midway Star System, nearly two light-hours distant from where *Dauntless* and the rest of the Alliance fleet orbited.

"Another Syndic heavy cruiser," Tanya commented, sounding disappointed. "Nothing to get excited—" She broke off, narrowing her eyes at her own display. "Anomalies?"

Geary saw the same information popping up on his display as the fleet's sensors peered across light-hours of space to spot the tiniest visible detail on the newly arrived heavy cruiser. He felt keyed up despite knowing that he was viewing history. The heavy cruiser had arrived almost two hours ago, the light from that event just now reaching *Dauntless*, the flagship of the First Fleet of the Alliance.

Everything that was going to happen in the next two hours had already happened, yet viewing it still felt as if he were watching it occur right at this moment. "They've rigged extra cargo capacity with life support along their hull," he commented.

"That means a lot of passengers," Desjani murmured. "An assault force aimed at the facilities here?"

That was a real possibility. Midway had revolted months ago, casting off the heavy hand of the Syndicate Worlds and declaring independence. The Syndicate Worlds was crumbling in the wake of its defeat in the war with the Alliance, but even with star systems falling away in many other places, Midway was too valuable for the Syndic government to accept its loss. Geary had been wondering what the Syndics would try next to regain control.

But, before he could answer, Desjani's eyebrows shot up in surprise. "He's running."

Sure enough, the heavy cruiser had seen the small Syndic flotilla still hovering near the hypernet gate and, instead of altering course slightly to join up with them, had twisted about and accelerated away.

"They're not here on orders from the Syndics. It's another breakaway," Geary said. One more element of the armed forces of the Syndicate Worlds that was responding to the erratic fragmenting of the Syndic empire by taking off on its own, probably for the home star system of the crew. "Or does he belong to the authorities here at Midway?"

"Not if they told us the truth about how many warships they have." Desjani paused, grinned, then laughed with a mocking edge. "Did you hear what I said? I wondered if a bunch of Syndics had told us the truth."

The rest of the bridge watch team laughed along with her at the absurdity of the statement.

"Midway revolted against the Syndicate Worlds," Geary pointed out though he had to admit that Desjani's ridicule was justified. He had encountered a few Syndics who had dealt straight with him, but most of the Syndics he had met (especially Syndics at the CEO level) seemed to regard the truth as something to deal with only after all other possible alternatives had been tried and failed.

"So they painted over the stripe on their tails," Desjani replied. "Does that mean they aren't still skunks?"

He didn't answer, knowing that argument would resonate deeply among everyone in his fleet after a century spent fighting the Syndics in a war that had seen behavior on both sides spiral downward through the decades. But the Syndicate Worlds had always led the way down, their leaders hesitating at nothing to pursue a war they could not win but refused to lose until Geary himself had smashed their fleet.

The commander of the Syndicate flotilla, their old acquaintance CEO Boyens, had reacted to the heavy cruiser's arrival almost as soon as the flotilla had sighted it. The single battleship forming the core of the flotilla had not altered its orbit, but the majority of the escorts had rolled down and over and were accelerating on curving vectors, aimed at intercepting the new arrival.

Desjani shook her head. "He's sending all six of his heavy cruisers and all nine of his Hunter-Killers? Overkill."

"We know Boyens is usually cautious," Geary said. "He's not taking any chances, and he has to worry about the locals intervening."

"The locals can't get to that new heavy cruiser before Boyens's ships do," she pointed out. "If the cruiser wasn't burdened with that extra mass, he might get clear. But as it is, he's toast."

Geary stared at his display. The combat systems aboard *Dauntless* were presenting the same assessment that Desjani had made. The physics of the situation were not complex, just a matter of mass, acceleration, and distances. Curves through space projected courses, with the points where different weapons would be within range of their target clearly marked. The newly arrived heavy cruiser had only been going at point zero five light speed when it left the gate, a fairly sedate pace for a warship, probably intended to conserve fuel. Even though the new cruiser was now accelerating for all it was worth, it would be overtaken by Boyens's heavy cruisers well before any help could reach it. Those heavy cruisers were already pushing up toward point one light speed and would surely keep increasing velocity to at least point two light. "I wonder who the new cruiser is carrying with them that required the extra life support?"

"More Syndics," Desjani replied in an uncaring tone.

"More people fleeing the Syndics," Geary said. "Maybe families of the crew of that heavy cruiser."

She looked down, lips pressed tightly together, then glanced his way. "Maybe. The Syndics killed countless families during the war. They'll kill these, too. I had to stop thinking about things like that, especially because at times like this there wasn't a damned thing I could do to stop it."

He nodded heavily. Whatever had happened had already taken place hours ago. The families and crew of that heavy cruiser had probably been killed by the Syndic attackers before the light of the cruiser's arrival at Midway had reached *Dauntless*.

"We're seeing the Midway flotilla altering vectors," the operations watch-stander announced. The little flotilla belonging to Midway, made up of former Syndic warships, had been orbiting only five light-minutes distant from the hypernet gate. It had taken them only those few minutes to spot the events around the gate, and as they saw the new heavy cruiser flee, they had gotten involved as well.

"They can't get to that cruiser in time," Desjani said, her voice professionally detached. "And even if they did, the force Boyens sent after that cruiser outnumbers them nearly three to one."

"Why did they try? Kommodor Marphissa can run the data as well as we can. She must have known it was hopeless."

"Maybe she wanted to hit some of the Syndic heavy cruisers while they were off by themselves. She probably lost half of her ships if she tried, though." The emotional separation in Desjani's voice cracked slightly, letting through a sense of frustration and anger.

Geary watched the projected tracks of the different players altering as the Alliance fleet's automated systems estimated courses and speeds for the Syndic warships and the Midway flotilla. The lone heavy cruiser had started out at the hypernet gate and was now on a track curving outward toward one of the several jump points that had given the star Midway its name. CEO Boyens's Syndicate Worlds flotilla had been only a couple of light-minutes from the gate, closer to the star and slightly above the gate, and had kicked out its heavy cruisers and HuKs on flatter, faster curves, which intercepted the path of the fleeing cruiser long before it could reach safety.

And the flotilla consisting of two heavy cruisers, five light cruisers, and several small Hunter-Killer ships belonging to the "free and independent star system of Midway" had surged out of its own orbit five light-minutes down and starboard from the Syndic flotilla.

He understood Tanya's attempts to separate herself emotionally from what they were watching. They were much too distant to do anything to influence the events near the hypernet gate. Those who were to die were already dead. But it was very hard to pretend not to care about that.

Geary felt a temptation to shut off his display, to avoid watching the inevitable. The best he could hope for was that before it was destroyed, the fleeing cruiser would damage some of Boyens's ships, and that a portion of the Midway flotilla would survive their own attack on the much more powerful force of Syndic heavy cruisers and HuKs.

But he kept watching because that was his job, watching with a sick sensation in his gut as the unavoidable results played out.

"What the hell?"

He hadn't realized that he had said that until he heard Desjani laugh in reluctant admiration. "The Midway warships aren't trying to rescue that single cruiser. Their Kommodor is aiming for the Syndic battleship!"

"That's…" Geary studied the developing situation as the vector of the Midway force steadied out, aiming for an intercept with the orbit of Boyens's single battleship and the light cruisers still with it. "What is she doing? The Midway flotilla can't take on a battleship, even with so many of the battleship's escorts gone."

"Check the geometry, Admiral," Desjani advised. "They couldn't get to the lone cruiser before Boyens's own cruisers caught it. But they can get to the battleship before Boyens's cruisers can nail the lone cruiser and return to protect the battleship."

"Boyens still doesn't have much to worry about. He might lose some light cruisers, but the battleship—" A bright red symbol appeared on the Syndic formation. A collision warning, blinking steadily over the Syndic battleship. Geary followed the arcs of two projected, lethal vectors back to the ships that had settled on those courses. Two of the Midway HuKs. "Ancestors save us. Do you think they'll go through with it?"

Desjani was rubbing her chin, her eyes calculating as she studied her display. "It's the only way they could cripple or destroy Boyens's battleship. With the heavy cruisers and HuKs gone from the Syndic formation, and the rest of the Midway ships screening those two HuKs to make sure they can get through the remaining Syndic escorts, it could work. Crazy tactics, though."

"Kommodor Marphissa is an ex-Syndic," Geary observed. "Boyens might know something about her."

"You mean the fact that she mad hates Syndic CEOs?" Desjani asked. "And therefore might actually have two of her ships ram Boyens's battleship? Yeah. Boyens might know that."

Geary's gaze on his display was now horrified. Would he have to watch two ships destroy themselves in the hope of crippling the Syndic force in this star system? "Hold on. There's something about this that doesn't fit. Assume the Kommodor really intends to nail that battleship. Why would she set them on collision courses with the battleship that far out?"

"Unless she's an idiot, and I'm willing to admit she isn't, if she meant to ram that battleship, she wouldn't have broadcast her intentions that early." Desjani laughed again, low and admiring. "It's a bluff. Boyens can't afford to risk losing that battleship. But he can't be certain of stopping those HuKs with the escorts he's got. What's he going to do?"

"Hopefully, the only safe option," Geary said, his eyes back on the Syndic heavy cruisers and HuKs heading to intercept the lone cruiser still fleeing at the maximum acceleration it could achieve.

Because of the time delays involved in communicating across even such a relatively short distance as a few light-minutes, it took about ten minutes before the tracks of the six heavy cruisers and nine HuKs that Boyens had sent out began changing rapidly as the fifteen Syndic warships bent up and back, coming around and accelerating toward the battleship they had left not long before.

"The Syndics have abandoned their attempt to intercept the new cruiser," Lieutenant Castries reported, as if not believing what she was saying. "The Midway flotilla is continuing en route an intercept with the Syndic battleship."

"Maybe it wasn't a bluff," Desjani said, eyeing her display. "We'll know in twenty minutes."

"Captain?" Castries asked.

"If the Midway flotilla acted to ensure that lone cruiser got clear, they'll maintain their threatening vectors against the battleship until the Syndic cruiser force can't turn again and overtake the new ship."

Geary felt confident that Kommodor Marphissa had been bluffing, but he still watched, with increasing tension, as those twenty minutes crawled by. *Because Tanya is right. From all that we have learned of her, Marphissa does hate the Syndic CEOs who once controlled her life. Does she hate them enough to let that hatred override her responsibility to conserve her forces and use them wisely? Syndic commanders aren't taught to worry about casualties in carrying out their missions, and Marphissa learned her trade under the Syndic system.*

"It's been twenty minutes, Captain," Lieutenant Castries pointed out. "The single cruiser is now safe from intercept by the Syndic force."

Desjani nodded wordlessly in acknowledgment. If she was worried, she didn't let it show.

Not that she, or anyone, could change what had already happened two hours ago.

Twenty-one minutes after the Syndic heavy cruisers had turned back, the Midway flotilla pivoted and began a wide, sweeping turn back toward its previous orbit five light-minutes from the Syndicate flotilla.

Geary let out a breath he had been holding for a good portion of that last minute. "She kept her course longer just to mess with Boyens."

"Probably," Desjani agreed, smiling. "It's too bad that Kommodor is a Syndic."

"Ex-Syndic."

"Yeah. All right. She might make a decent ship driver someday."

It was Geary's turn to reply with just a nod. Coming from Desjani, that statement was a huge concession and considerable praise. But she wouldn't want anyone pointing that out. "After having Boyens taunt us with our inability to get him to leave, it was nice seeing him get shown up in such a public way. The whole star system will see what happened, how he got out-thought and outmaneuvered."

"That's good, sure, but it doesn't solve anything," Desjani grumbled.

"No." He knew what she meant. The presence of Geary's fleet here was the only thing preventing Boyens from using his flotilla to reconquer the Midway Star System for the Syndicate Worlds. Technically, Midway Star System was under the control of a so-called president and a so-called general who had formerly been Syndicate CEOs. In reality, the amount of firepower present in Geary's Alliance fleet made him the effective ruler here. But for all the power in his fleet, Geary's hands were tied when it came to dealing with the Syndics.

This fleet had to get back to the Alliance, far distant on the other side of Syndicate space. There had been other reasons, besides the Syndic flotilla, to linger here after fighting its way through alien space beyond the frontier of human expansion. The Alliance ships had faced repeated battles and taken a lot of damage. The auxiliary ships accompanying the fleet had restocked their raw materials by mining asteroids in this star system with the permission of the authorities on Midway, and had been busy using those materials to manufacture replacement parts for the battered warships. Everyone in every crew had been working to repair the damage they had sustained.

Nonetheless, they needed to get home. As Geary gazed glumly at his display, another collision warning popped up, this time on the captured superbattleship that had been christened *Invincible*. Dwarfing even the four massive battleships mated to it, *Invincible* was the work of an alien species nicknamed the Kicks, who had matched their adorable teddy bear/cow appearance with a ferocious refusal to interact with humanity in any way other than all-out attack. To the Kicks, humans were predators, and the evolved-from-herd-animals Kicks did not negotiate with predators. *Invincible* held within her countless clues and information about the Kicks and their technology, which made her by far the most valuable object in human space. The sooner *Invincible* was safely back in Alliance space, the better.

He didn't worry about the collision warning, though. It had been triggered by the movements of six ships, nearly featureless ovoids, which flitted among the human ships of this star system like graceful birds swooping around clumsy animals. "The Dancers are going to give our warning systems a heart attack," Geary commented. The Alliance sailors called these aliens Dancers because of the agile ease with which the aliens swung their ships through maneuvers that even the best human ship driver or human-built automated system could not match.

No one knew how long the Dancers would loiter here waiting for the human fleet to move, and as the only alien species that had shown any desire to speak with humans as well as the only alien species that had helped humans instead of attacking them, Geary had to get these representatives of the Dancers back to the Alliance government as quickly as he could.

Not every reason for leaving Midway and heading for Alliance space could be seen. An invisible and intangible element, morale among the men and women of the fleet, was very poor. They had fought long and hard, and they wanted some time to enjoy the peace that allegedly now existed. They wanted time at home. But home, or powerful factions of the government of the Alliance at least, was worried about those weary combatants. Worried about their loyalties, worried about the costs of keeping their ships going, worried about the huge numbers of veterans already dumped into the reeling economies of the Alliance's star systems after the strains of the war.

There were plots under way back home as well. How many, he didn't know. How many were aimed at him, he didn't know. How many would undermine the Alliance or cause it to break apart like the crumbling empire of the Syndicate Worlds, he also didn't know. But he couldn't deal with any of those plots while as far away from Alliance territory as it was possible to be and still be in human-occupied space.

If this was what victory had gained, then he hated to imagine what a mess defeat might have generated.

He watched the track of the fleeing heavy cruiser altering, probably in response to offers of assistance from the Midway flotilla. Geary still couldn't figure out how to get rid of the Syndic flotilla commanded by Boyens without blowing to shreds the peace agreement between the Alliance and the Syndicate Worlds. But if he left without dealing with Boyens, the potentially extremely valuable allies here at Midway might be lost to the Alliance, and if he lost access to Midway, he would also lose access to the regions of space beyond where the Dancers were.

Days later, his nerves jumpy, Geary watched a freighter belonging to Midway easing its boxy hull in among the shark shapes of the Alliance warships. His experiences with Syndic freighters during the war had usually involved cunning attempts to damage or destroy Alliance ships by means of hidden or improvised weapons. Seeing such a freighter gliding close to his warships, Geary had to fight the urge to target it and order it destroyed.

He glanced over at Desjani, whose glare told him that she was having an even harder time accepting the freighter's near presence.

"We need the food," Geary said. "We've eaten Syndic rations before, and Midway has some substantial stockpiles since they were a central supply node for this region of Syndic space."

"I know!" Desjani replied. "But the Syndic rations we picked up before had been abandoned in place when the installations holding them were vacated. We didn't have to worry too much about *those* rations being poisoned or otherwise sabotaged."

"The fleet physicians and Captain Smythe's engineers are going to check these rations with every test known to humanity to ensure they're safe, without poison, bacteria, viruses, nanoplagues, or other dirty tricks."

"Fine," she said. "Though given how bad Syndic rations taste, I wonder how hard it would be to tell if they had spoiled."

"At least Syndic rations make Alliance fleet food seem decent by comparison," Geary pointed out as he watched Alliance shuttles mating with the main hatches on the Syndic freighter to take on cargo. He didn't mention another advantage that easily aroused suspicions as well. The authorities on Midway were providing these rations for free rather than haggling over the highest possible price. He knew they were doing that because they desperately needed the good favor of the Alliance against the threat posed by the Syndicate Worlds, but it was still a very uncharacteristic action, a very peculiar action, compared to the usual behaviors inside Syndic space.

His display told him that fleet medical personnel and equipment, as well as engineers with their own scanning gear, were on every shuttle for what would be just the first safety check of the rations.

A soft tone drew Geary's attention to his comm display. *Why is Emissary of the Alliance government Victoria Rione calling me now?* He tapped the accept command and saw her image appear slightly to one side of the display.

Rione, calling from her stateroom on *Dauntless*, blinked weariness from her eyes and gestured in the direction of the Midway freighter. "There's something unexpected on that freighter."

"Now what?" He didn't bother trying to disguise his anger. If Midway was going to play games with him after all this fleet had done to defend the people here—

"Not a bad thing, I think. Two representatives from General Drakon. They used the private comm channel I've been talking with President Iceni on." Rione smiled crookedly. "I have already inquired whether they intended asking for your support for General Drakon against President Iceni. They insist that is not why they are here."

"Good. They wouldn't have gotten that support." He drummed his fingers on the side of his seat, giving Rione's image a skeptical look. She had every right to look tired, as she been negotiating for over a week with the authorities here, wrangling with CEO Boyens, and trying to develop better communications with the Dancers. "What do they want?" Geary asked. "What's so secret that they had to sneak up here in person?"

"Something they will only discuss with you. In person. You may safely assume it is a matter too sensitive to risk any chance at all of a message being intercepted."

"The hell." Geary glowered at the depiction of the freighter on his display. He had learned all too well how even the most secure communications channels could be penetrated, so he understood that aspect of the matter. But… "Me alone? No. There will be at least one other person in any meeting with me and those two."

"Not me," Rione said. "I can't give any implied endorsement by the Alliance government to whatever Drakon is proposing until I have some idea what it is about. Take your captain. She's equal in rank to the two representatives from Drakon, and she's sufficiently protective of you to give them pause if they wanted to try anything."

"It wouldn't hurt you to occasionally say Tanya Desjani's name," Geary pointed out.

"How do you know it wouldn't hurt?" Rione asked with a smile that carried a great many possible meanings, none of which he wanted to pursue further. "You'll have to give approval to a shuttle to bring Drakon's people to *Dauntless's* dock. Have fun."

After breaking the connection with Rione, Geary looked over at Desjani, who was pretending not to have noticed the conversation. "Did you hear any of that?"

She shook her head. "Your privacy field cut in. What did that woman want?"

"Is it so hard for you to say Victoria Rione's name?" he persisted against his better judgment.

"Yes. Yes, it is."

"All right." He would never win this argument, so instead Geary passed on what Rione had told him. "I'll tell one of the shuttles to bring those two here, and we'll see what they say."

"Ancestors help us," Desjani muttered, then turned to her watch team. "I need combat-configured Marine guards at the shuttle dock, secure conference room 4D576 cleared, and all passageways from the dock to that conference room kept empty of traffic until further notice."

"Yes, Captain," Lieutenant Castries replied immediately.

By the time Geary and Tanya reached the shuttle dock, the Marines were already there, fully outfitted in combat armor.

Desjani smiled at the sight of them. "Excellent. There's nothing like a few Marines when it comes to impressing Syndics face-to-face."

She led the way inside the dock, where the shuttle had come in and settled, its ramp still sealed. "Open up," Desjani ordered.

The ramp dropped, and Geary walked to the end of the shuttle's ramp to look inside.

It only took a few seconds before the two representatives sent by General Drakon appeared at the head of the ramp. Geary had seen both of them before, standing behind General Drakon during some of his messages. One man, one woman, both in uniform. He felt an indefinable sense of alarm as they walked toward him at a measured pace. These two did not look dangerous, but something inside Geary was nonetheless warning him not to underestimate them.

He noticed out of the corners of his eyes the Marine guards shifting positions slightly, preparing themselves to counter anything these two visitors might try.

It had not even occurred to Geary that he might face a personal threat of assassination from Drakon's representatives. An unpardonably careless failure on his part when meeting face-to-face with Syndics, or former Syndics, he realized. But at least Tanya had shown the foresight to have the Marines on hand.

"Colonel Morgan," the woman said, as if that name told him everything he would ever need to know about her. She said it like Geary could have said "I'm Black Jack." But he never did that, and he wondered at this woman who projected that kind of arrogant competence. She was undeniably attractive, in a way that once again disquieted Geary, and she moved with the unconscious grace of someone trained as a dancer or in lethal martial arts. Colonel Morgan was ignoring the presence of the Marines, as if they did not matter, and Geary had the unpleasant feeling that if she had been sent to kill him, the fact that the Marines were here would not have hindered her too much in carrying out that task.

"Colonel Malin," the man said, more formally, his attitude more reserved, deferential as a subordinate should sound but also conveying a sense that no task would be too difficult. He didn't seem nearly as dangerous as Morgan. And yet Geary's instincts warned him that Malin should not be discounted.

He had formed a broad opinion of General Drakon from the official conversations they had engaged in. There had been no unofficial conversations, of course. A professional, Geary had thought. Perhaps not too different from a senior officer in the Alliance.

But Drakon kept these two beside him as close aides. Was that because of the ways in which people operated in the Syndicate Worlds, or was it because Drakon personally was comfortable with such lethally competent individuals close at hand?

Trying not to let his expression reveal his thoughts, Geary nodded in reply to the two colonels' introductions. They surely knew who he was, so he simply gestured toward Tanya. "Captain Desjani."

He would have had to have been blind not to have seen the way Desjani, Malin, and Morgan wordlessly sized each other up after the very brief introductions. Tanya eyed the two like she would a force of enemy ships. She obviously also saw the threat in them.

The walk to the secure conference room was brief and silent. The Marines said nothing, and the passageways had been cleared, as Tanya had ordered.

Once inside the room, Geary waited while Tanya sealed the hatch, leaving the Marines outside against his better judgment, then he sat down and nodded to the two colonels without offering them a seat. "What is so important your general had to send two personal representatives? What couldn't be transmitted by even the most secure message?"

Instead of immediately answering, their eyes went to Desjani, Malin's look subtly questioning and Morgan's challenging. "The matter is for your attention only," Morgan said.

"Those are our orders," Malin added, with what might have been an annoyed glance at Morgan. "I hope you understand, Admiral."

Geary leaned back, deliberately emphasizing that he felt unthreatened and secure in his authority. "I hope you understand that I won't be dictated to on my own flagship. Captain Desjani is the commanding officer of this ship and my most trusted advisor. She will be present for any discussion."

Malin's pause was barely apparent, then he nodded in agreement.

Morgan's look this time was almost amused as it went from Geary to Desjani. "We understand... special relationships," she said in a way that made Tanya's jaw visibly tighten.

The implication didn't please Geary either, but he wasn't about to defensively explain his relationship with Desjani to these two. "Then get on with it."

Colonel Malin spoke with respectful formality again. "President Iceni asked us to forward her personal request for a meeting with the Dancers."

Geary shrugged. "We've already told President Iceni that the Dancers have turned down direct contact with her or anyone else from Midway. We don't know why. The Dancers haven't explained their reasons. I'll have them asked again, but I don't expect the Dancers to change their answer."

"Your president," Desjani added dryly, "might not want to the meet the Dancers personally."

"We have seen the pictures you provided," Colonel Malin said with a hint of a smile. "We know the Dancers are…"

"Hideous," Colonel Morgan said.

"They saved your butts," Desjani replied in a deceptively pleasant voice.

"We do wish to thank the Dancers for diverting the enigma bombardment aimed at our planet," Malin interjected before Morgan could speak again. "Ideally, we'd like to thank them in person, if you could tell them that."

"I'll pass that on," Geary said in noncommittal tones.

"General Drakon also sends his personal request that we be given access to the ship you call *Invincible*, Admiral. We understand that any access would be strictly limited—"

"No," Geary said. "There's too much we don't know about that ship. I've been told by your general that you are still very concerned about deep-cover Syndicate Worlds agents operating in this star system. I cannot risk what little we do know about *Invincible* ending up in the hands of the Syndicate Worlds. Colonel, I'll be blunt. Neither of the requests you have made justify the extreme concern for the security of your visit here. What's this really about?"

Malin nodded, with the look of a man admiring an adversary who has refused to be distracted or diverted. "An opportunity has presented itself, Admiral. An opportunity to resolve a matter which is of concern to you as well as to General Drakon and President Iceni. As long as CEO Boyens commands a Syndicate Worlds flotilla which is here and is stronger than our own mobile forces, we will not be secure. From your previous actions and discussions with our superiors, General Drakon and President Iceni believe that you would also like to see CEO Boyens and his flotilla depart this star system before you leave."

"Or, if you're in the mood for that, an opportunity to destroy that flotilla," Colonel Morgan added, this time with a slight smile, as if they were sharing a mutually understood joke.

"What is this opportunity?" Geary asked, not replying directly to Morgan. The more he was around her, the more she unsettled him. It wasn't just her attractiveness; it was the casual, pantherlike attitude of deadliness combined with allure. This was a very dangerous woman, in ways very different from Tanya, and it annoyed Geary that part of him found that danger fascinating.

It was hard to tell how much Tanya could sense of that. She was keeping her eyes on Malin, apparently not watching Morgan, but Geary had seen that sort of misdirection in Desjani before. Morgan probably sensed Tanya's attitude, too, and was reacting with thinly veiled amusement, which was simply provoking Tanya all the more.

But then Geary noticed Desjani visibly relaxing, a quiet smile appearing. A tactic. She had analyzed what Morgan was doing and altered her own approach.

Malin, pretending like Geary to be unaware of the byplay between Desjani and Morgan, continued speaking. "The opportunity involves the heavy cruiser that recently arrived in this star system. C-712 has declined our offer to remain here. We have offered one of our own heavy cruisers as an escort for C-712 to ensure they reach their home star safely."

"How kind of you," Desjani commented in a flat, insincere voice.

"Doing an important favor for someone is a way to gain a friend, and Midway needs all the friends we can get," Malin replied. "Friends with heavy cruisers could be particularly important once you leave here, Admiral. Those friends can, in fact, do us a service now without even realizing it. General Drakon and President Iceni are proposing a course of action involving our escort that would serve your interests as well as ours, Admiral. If we work together, we can deal with Boyens, as long as we make every effort to ensure he does not even suspect the trap we are laying for him."

Geary had no trouble assessing Desjani's unspoken reaction. *No. No deals with Syndics. No "working together" with Syndics.* But there was no harm in finding out exactly what was being proposed. "Tell me what you're suggesting," he ordered Malin.

They had escorted the two colonels back to the shuttle and seen it depart before Geary looked a question at Desjani.

"No."

"Because…?" he prompted.

"They can't be trusted." She waved toward where the shuttle had been. "What kind of sick, twisted mind comes up with a plan like that?"

"But it might well work and resolve our problem with Boyens."

Desjani frowned, then shrugged. "It might. What are you going to do?"

"We need at least one of the Alliance government emissaries to sign off on the idea, or it won't work. I'll show them the pitch Colonel Malin made and see what they say."

"That should be interesting. I'll want to know how they react to the suggestion that you use this plot as an excuse to actually destroy Boyens's battleship." Desjani gave him a wry look. "Speaking of which, you didn't seem to enjoy the attention Colonel Morgan was giving you."

"She wasn't—"

"Oh, yeah. Not at all. *Hey, Mr. Admiral. Want a bite of the apple? Just give me a wink.*"

"I didn't—"

"No, you didn't. You have more sense than that."

"Tanya, I'm sure she didn't know I was married."

"Ancestors preserve us! Do you really think *she* would have cared?" Desjani paused as she was about to head back to the bridge, her attitude that of someone fighting an internal struggle. "Before you make a decision on this, you need to come with me." She didn't say anything more as he followed, puzzled, until they reached her stateroom. "We'll risk gossip for a few minutes of privacy because we need that."

"Why?" He had rarely been inside her stateroom, maintaining that distance for the sake of discipline.

"Inside." Tanya waited until Geary had entered, then closed and sealed the hatch. She stood for a moment before speaking, running one hand through her hair. "Look, I know a lot of the things we've done, and by *we* I mean the people of this time, violate your sense of honor."

"You stopped—"

"Wait." She dropped her hand and looked at him with a frank expression. "If you want that Syndic battleship gone, there's a way to do it without leaving any fingerprints or cooperating with people who say they aren't Syndics anymore but still think like Syndics."

"And by gone you mean… ?"

"Destroyed." Tanya walked a few paces, turned, and walked back. "You know what it's like. Sometimes you have to do things. Things you've been ordered not to do. And you have to know how to do those things anyway, without leaving any records or traces of what was done."

Geary watched her, baffled. "Are you saying that, with all of the records automatically created and maintained on every single detail of what every ship in the Alliance fleet does for every moment of its existence, that there is a way to conduct an operation as major as destroying a Syndic battleship without leaving any indications of what was done?"

She gave an apologetic shrug. "Yes."

"But even if you could subvert fleet systems that much, so many people would know—"

"No one talks. No one." Tanya's gaze challenged him now. "It doesn't happen very often. But sometimes we had to. And because we had to, we figured out how to. If you need this badly enough, we can do it, and there will be no evidence."

"The systems belonging to the occupants of this star system will see everything!" he protested, still only half-believing her words.

"Oh, please, Admiral. If official records on the ships of the Alliance fleet say one thing and some systems belonging to people who were recently Syndics claim something else happened, what is going to be believed?"

Geary turned away from her, trying to think. *If the people of this fleet had been comfortable with acts like bombarding civilians from orbit and killing prisoners, what sort of actions would have required total concealment from official records? I can't even imagine—*

Desjani's voice cut through his increasingly dark thoughts. "It wasn't about atrocities, Admiral. We could do those above the board."

Her tone was scathing, bitter, but when he looked back at her, Geary could tell that Tanya was aiming those emotions at herself.

"It was about evading orders," she continued in a quieter voice. "Doing what needed to be done. Or not doing something stupid, and you know almost as well as I do how stupid things on the record could be, so just imagine what sort of orders motivated us to develop a way of acting invisibly to every official record."

"Tanya, I can't even picture something like that."

"Count your blessings." She said it even more harshly this time, then looked away. "You can't picture it. You didn't live it. Be glad for that."

"I'm sorry."

"*Don't be sorry for me!* For anyone in this fleet! We did what we had to do with what we were given!"

He stared at the deck, biting his lip hard enough to taste the tang of fresh blood. "All right. How do you make happen something of which there's no record?"

"I spread the word. Don't ask how. The groundwork gets laid. When it's ready, I tell you, and you order the op. After the last shot is fired, fleet records will say every ship involved was just engaging in routine operations, and no sailor or officer will contradict those records." She shook her head. "Don't look shocked. People have been doing that kind of thing ever since the first ones were sent out to kill other people. It takes more work now to keep the official record clean, but it's an old, old practice. You know that as well as I do."

His eyes went to the plaque by her hatch, the one listing a long line of names. Absent friends. The many dead companions whom Desjani had served with and wanted to be sure she never forgot. "Yes. I do know that. Tanya, here's the thing. If I go with your suggestion, we fight another battle and more die, quite possibly including some of our own. Battleships are damned hard to kill. If shots start flying, Boyens might even target the hypernet gate as a last bit of defiance. But if I go with the plan proposed by those colonels, I may not need to fight, and I'll still have your option available if necessary."

She took a while to respond. "Boyens might not react the way they hope."

"But his track record, what we know of him, makes it likely he will. And they know him better than we do."

"I… can't deny that," Tanya said with obvious reluctance.

"Tanya, if we start shooting, I don't care what the fleet's records show. The Syndics could take it as an excuse to go hot war again. And you know what the reaction in this fleet and in the Alliance would be if that war started once more."

"Yes." Desjani turned toward her desk and leaned on it with both arms, her body slumping. "By my ancestors, I am so tired, Jack. Tired of having to do things like this. But I will, if that's what needs to be. If you don't think we should, I'll accept your judgment. You've been right a lot more than I have."

"No, I haven't." He reached out, very carefully, and barely touched her arm. He ached to hold her, to wrap his arms tightly about Tanya and give all the comfort he could, but that could not happen. Not between an admiral and the commanding officer of his flagship. Aboard *Dauntless* they were always on duty. "Tanya, I'll keep your option in mind. But I don't want to do it."

"You and your damned honor." But she said it with a self-mocking tone this time and turned a rueful smile Geary's way. "As long as we're being honest, did you really not notice how that Colonel Morgan was looking at you?"

"I noticed." Geary rubbed the back of neck and grimaced. "And I thought she was one of the most dangerous things I'd ever seen."

"Right again." Tanya smiled a little more. "I guess I have taught you something." Her hand went to the hatch controls. "Let's get out of here before any rumors start, Admiral."

Geary called both of the Alliance government emissaries into the same secure conference room where he had listened to Colonel

Morgan and Colonel Malin, then played the record of the meeting, images of the two Midway officers appearing where they had stood.

After the recording ended, Victoria Rione canted a look toward Geary that was disturbingly like the one Tanya had given him. "She's a real piece of work, isn't she?"

"Colonel Morgan, you mean." He frowned at Rione. "If she so clearly provokes you and... other people, I have to wonder why she was sent along with Colonel Malin."

"Oh, that's easy." Rione smiled in amusement. "First of all, you might have been, shall we say, *intrigued* by what Colonel Morgan was offering. You wouldn't be the first powerful man to fall for that sort of bait, and if you did, it could open all sorts of possibilities for them to exploit. Including the possibility that you would accept their proposal in hopes of, how shall I put it, working *closer* with Colonel Morgan."

His anger at her words, Geary realized guiltily, was generated at least partly by the realization that some small part of him might well have pondered that idea. "I would not—"

"I didn't say you would, Admiral. But I suspect two other reasons also played a role in her presence. Did you notice how you and your captain reacted more positively toward Colonel Malin as you reacted negatively toward Colonel Morgan? She made you more accepting of him."

"Damn." Geary wanted to argue that point as well, but he realized it held a great deal of truth.

"That's not all. If I know anything about body language, those two trust each other about as much as we trust them. I believe it is safe to say that Colonel Morgan and Colonel Malin were keeping an eye on each other."

Emissary Charban was watching Rione with the expression of a man who was realizing how much he had to learn. "They're still operating like Syndics, aren't they?" Charban said. "There are a dozen different things going on at once, layers and layers and intertwining plots."

"It's what they know," Rione said. "And they are good at it, if 'good' is the right term to use." She tapped some controls. "Did you see this? The room's sensors picked it up."

On the recorded images of the two colonels, a bright object now glowed on one of Morgan's wrists, something so carefully matched to her skin that it was invisible to the naked eye. "What is it?" Geary asked.

Rione tapped a few more times, then glanced at him and Charban. "Not a threat, or you would have been alerted to it as soon as she entered here. It's a very sophisticated recording device. Unless I'm wrong, it's also sealed. Neither Morgan nor Malin could change anything on it."

"They're not trusted, either," Charban said.

"Maybe. It would certainly provide someone like President Iceni with a record of what was actually said and done here. That could be why she allowed two of Drakon's people to bring the proposal to you." Rione lowered her head into one palm, thinking. "Their plan could work."

"Do we dare trust them to carry through with it?" Charban asked.

"Drakon and Iceni? Or Morgan and Malin?"

"All of the above." Charban winked at Geary, who nodded back in recognition of the joke. At some point in the past, the fleet had decided that multiple choice questions on training exams almost always had a correct answer of "all of the above." Even though he was, like Rione, an emissary of the government, as a retired general of the ground forces, Charban had much more in common with Geary than he did with his fellow emissary.

Rione sighed in exaggerated fashion. "Drakon and Iceni would not have sent those two unless they trusted them. No. 'Trust' is the wrong word. I don't know what the right word is. Some Syndic concept that involves having a good idea of whether or not someone else will betray you. You do realize that this won't work without the full cooperation and assistance of me and Emissary Charban, right?"

"Yes," Geary said. "It surprised me that those colonels, or rather Drakon and Iceni, didn't also know that."

"It surprised you?" Rione gusted a small laugh. "Would it have surprised Captain Badaya?"

"No, because he thinks…"

"Because he thinks you're actually controlling the Alliance now, and the government is only a figurehead carrying out your orders." Rione smiled in an unpleasant way. "Naturally, these former Syndics think the same thing. Who could possibly fail to grasp such power if it beckoned? You refused the chance, but Drakon and Iceni surely assume you seized it."

Geary looked away, angry again. "All right. So they didn't think I'd have to talk to you, to get your approval. But I do. What do you think?"

"I recommend that we do it, Admiral. It is a risk. It involves putting our confidence in people whose understanding of concepts like keeping their word is extremely elastic. But it will solve our problem as well as theirs."

"Self-interest," Charban said. "They want this to work more than we do."

"Exactly. It would be unpleasant for us if we were to leave here with Boyens still holding superior firepower to the people of Midway, but it would be a disaster for Midway."

"All right," Geary repeated. "I'll send the agreed code word to the freighter, and we'll get this going. If it doesn't work, there might be hell to pay."

Rione shook her head, looking tired again. She had aged on this trip, and now seemed a decade older than when he had first met her.

"Hell is going to get paid no matter what we do. There are no painless options, Admiral. Have the authorities here accepted your offer to leave Captain Bradamont at Midway as a liaison officer for the Alliance?"

"Yes."

"Good. We can use that. CEO Boyens is about to catch a little hell himself."

2

It would require about two weeks for the plan proposed by the rulers of Midway to come to fruition. Two weeks during which the fleet should have been heading toward home. But scanning down the long, long list of repair work still required on many of his ships, Geary tried to make the best of it. "Whatever happened to those plans for fully automated nanobased repair systems on ships?" he asked Captain Smythe, commanding officer of the auxiliary ship *Tanuki* and senior engineer in the fleet.

Smythe mimicked choking. "The same thing that always happens. The last test, to my knowledge, was about five years ago. The second generation of nanos started attacking 'healthy' parts of the test ship, except for those nanos that developed into nanocancer and began replicating out of control and harming critical systems. It took about two days for the ship's repair system to turn it into a total wreck."

"The same problem as a hundred years ago," Geary agreed.

"And for long before that. We're still working on trying to keep the repair and immune systems in our own bodies from going haywire and killing us quickly or slowly," Smythe pointed out. "And those had who knows how many millions of years to develop. Making something that fixes anything that goes wrong but doesn't damage things that are fine is not a simple problem."

"What did they do with the last test ship?"

"An automated tug towed both test ship and itself into the nearest star. Good-bye nanos. Nobody wanted to risk them infecting other ships. You could lose a fleet that way before you knew what was happening."

"How long before we can leave?" Geary asked.

"Today. Or tomorrow. Or a few months from now. Admiral, there's only so much my auxiliaries can do. Some of the damage our ships have sustained requires a full repair dock. The longer we spend here, the better condition all of our ships will be in, but we'll never hit one hundred percent until we get home." Smythe cocked a questioning eyebrow at Geary. "Do you expect to face more fighting before then?"

"I have no idea. I hope not, but I don't know. We've got the biggest threat magnet in the human-occupied region of space with us."

"Ah, yes, *Invincible*." Smythe looked both unhappy and enticed. "Have you been aboard her? There are so many puzzles inside that ship. I wish we could dig into them."

"We can't risk it, Captain."

"I may be able to isolate something so we can at least try to figure out how it works," Smythe pleaded. "My people will work it up on their own time. They're itching to get their hands on that Kick equipment."

"Send me your proposal," Geary said reluctantly, "and I'll think about it."

Have you been aboard her? No, he hadn't. *The chance to visit a truly alien construction, to see the work of intelligent, nonhuman hands, and I've only seen as much of that superbattleship as could be seen through the views of numerous Marines during the capture of it.*

Once we get Invincible *home, odds are the ship will be completely isolated, only high-level researchers allowed aboard.* Invincible *will be taken far from any star system that I am likely to visit.*

He called Tanya. "I want to see *Invincible*."

In her command seat on the bridge of *Dauntless*, Desjani nodded absentmindedly. "They've got enough systems hooked up for you to do a virtual visit?"

"No. I figured I'd go in person."

She jerked in surprise, her lips moved as she visibly counted to ten, then Desjani recited her next words in resigned and mechanical tones. "I must advise you of the dangers involved in physically visiting an alien warship containing unknown threats including but not limited to possible pathogens capable of infecting human hosts, equipment which works in unknown ways and which could reactivate at any time with unknown consequences, and aliens who could have survived the battle and remained hidden from our security sweeps and could still emerge to strike at a sufficiently high-value target."

"Your concerns are noted," Geary replied.

"And you'll do it anyway."

"This will probably be my only chance to visit that ship, Tanya. Once we get back to Alliance space, *Invincible* is sure to be quarantined."

She put on a look of exaggerated wonder. "You don't suppose there's a *reason* they'll put that ship in quarantine, do you?"

Seeing that Desjani wasn't about to abandon her line of attack, and knowing that she indeed had a point, Geary played his last card. "Tanya, there are sailors and Marines aboard that ship by my command. I sent them there. Are you saying that I should avoid doing something I am willing to order those under my command to do?"

This time she gave him an aggravated look under a furrowed brow. "Using good leadership principles against me? That's low."

"If you really want me to be a bad leader..."

"Oh, knock it off!" She tapped some commands. "You'll be using one of *Dauntless's* shuttles." That came out as a statement of fact rather than a question.

"Of course." He knew better than to point out that she had given in. "Do you want any souvenirs?"

"From that thing?" Desjani's shudder didn't seem to be feigned. "No thanks."

Admiral Lagemann met him at the main air lock into the occupied area aboard *Invincible*. Lagemann saluted briskly, grinning at Geary. Next to him, a Marine major saluted as well, the Marine's gesture far more polished and precise. "Welcome aboard *Invincible*, Admiral Geary," Lagemann said. "This is the commander of my Marine detachment, Major Dietz. I have to confess the ship is not quite ready for inspection. There are a few discrepancies."

"Oh? Discrepancies?" Geary asked, picking up on Lagemann's joking tone of voice and trying himself to sound like certain self-important inspectors he had dealt with in the past.

"All ship systems are nonfunctional," Lagemann explained cheerfully. "There is extensive unrepaired battle damage in most areas. The ship cannot move under her own power, and in fact has no power except for portable emergency systems. Most of the ship is uninhabitable and requires survival suits or combat armor for access. The crew is a tiny fraction of that necessary for safety, security, and operation. As you can tell, there's no working gravity. And, um, the brightwork hasn't been shined."

"I can understand the rest," Geary said with mock severity, "but unshined brightwork? Where are your priorities?"

"My priorities have always been misplaced," Lagemann confessed. "I volunteered for duty on this ship when I could have stayed comfortable on *Mistral*. I did spend quite a few years in a Syndic prisoner-of-war camp, though, which wasn't all that comfortable, and at least *Invincible* doesn't have Syndic thugs watching my every move."

Geary finally smiled. "How are your crew holding up?"

"Could be worse. They volunteered, too, which I remind them of if the complaints get too loud."

"What about the Marines, Major Dietz?" Geary asked.

The Major made a gesture of nonchalance. "They've been in worse places, and they all volunteered, too, Admiral. Of course, the Marines did that volunteering the day they joined, so we didn't ask regarding this particular assignment."

Admiral Lagemann and Major Dietz led Geary through the compartments occupied by the human sailors and Marines, everyone pulling themselves along through zero gravity by means of handholds either put into place by the Kicks or fastened on by humans since they had moved in here. Temporary cable runs carrying power, communications relays, and sensor data were strung everywhere, as were larger tubes that provided ventilation, heating, cooling, and recycling of the air inside this small part of *Invincible*, so that the atmosphere remained breathable. As Lagemann had warned, there were a lot of places where overheads came down too far and threatened to dent skulls. Geary also found numerous spots where the accesses narrowed enough that he had to move through them with care, scraping slowly past the life-support tubes and cable runs that made the openings even tighter. "This brings home more than anything how much smaller the bear-cows are than us," Geary commented.

"Fortunately," Lagemann replied, "it's actually a little easier for us to get around without gravity. We can wriggle through some places up high that would be a pain to reach if we were walking. And the Kicks may be small, but this is a damned big ship. I've been on my share of human battleships and battle cruisers, including a Syndic battle cruiser that picked me up when I was captured by them. You know some passages on those seem to go on forever. But *Invincible*... I swear that sometimes it feels as if the bow is in one star system and the stern is in another."

The small group had paused at one of the temporary air locks leading into the rest of the ship. "How are you keeping an eye on things outside this area?" Geary asked.

"We've got sensors strung into some portions of the ship," Lagemann replied. "For the rest, patrols."

"That is," Major Dietz continued, "security patrols that follow paths worked out by our systems to cover every compartment and passageway at least every few days. Some of the patrols take more than half a day."

"How big are the patrol teams?"

"Full squads, plus one or two sailors. They do full safety and security scans."

Geary felt his eyebrows rising in surprise. "That's a lot of people for patrols of empty spaces. Has there been trouble?" One thing he had learned early on as a junior officer was that sailors could be counted on to seek out compartments where they could find privacy for various activities prohibited by rules and regulations. On most ships, compartments like that were hard to find, but on *Invincible* there was a remarkable number of them.

Major Dietz and Admiral Lagemann exchanged glances. "There hasn't been any problem with people wandering off on their own," Lagemann explained. "Not after the first few days."

"Why not? Even if people didn't plan doing something they didn't want to be caught at, I'd think there'd be an urge to explore."

"Not on this ship," the Major said. "They're out there. In the passageways."

"Who's out there?" Geary asked, feeling a slight chill.

"The Kicks," Lagemann said. "I don't think I'm particularly sensitive or superstitious, but I can feel them. Thousands of them died on this ship, and if you go out there in the rest of the ship, you can sense them crowding around you. They know we took their ship, and they don't like it."

Major Dietz nodded. "I've been in abandoned enemy installations before, the kinds of places where you keep feeling like whoever left will come back at any moment and be really unhappy to find you there. That's a little spooky. This ship is a lot worse. We send out squad-strength patrols because that's the smallest group that can keep from going buggy while they're out there. We tried fire teams for a while. A couple of Marines. They ended up firing randomly, running back to the occupied area with stories of hundreds of Kicks still aboard and alive, that sort of thing."

"Was it worse in jump space?" Geary asked.

"Now that you mention it, yes, sir. But even here, in normal space near a star, it's spooky. *Nobody* goes off on their own. Not more than once."

"That's strange. We'll get this ship back home and let the scientists and techs dispute control of it with whatever remains of the Kicks."

"We've speculated," Admiral Lagemann said, "that it might be some sort of side effect of some Kick equipment that's still running somehow. Like the way a high-pitched whistle can make a dog unhappy, only it's something that works on human nerves in an unpleasant way. Like virtual fingernails scraping on an imaginary chalkboard. Or it could be ghosts. Damned if I know."

"Be sure you put your speculation about Kick equipment into your report when you leave the ship," Geary directed. "Could it be some sort of last-ditch defense? Some means the Kicks could activate that would make occupancy of this ship untenable for their enemies?"

Dietz and Lagemann exchanged intrigued looks this time. "That's possible, too," Lagemann said. "But since it makes sense to us, it might not be the real reason."

"I understand," Geary said, thinking of what he had seen of Kick technology. Much of their equipment used methods totally foreign to the conventions of human thought and equipment. "Where should I see next?"

Lagemann pointed toward the temporary air lock. "Out there."

"You're kidding. I believe you about the ghosts. Or, at least, about something unnerving out there."

"It's not to show you that. It's something the Marines came up with in their spare time."

Another half dozen Marines had joined them, all in full combat armor. Geary's lingering suspicions that his leg was being pulled by Lagemann and Dietz dwindled away as he noticed the wary manner in which the Marines eased out into the unoccupied portions of *Invincible*.

Warnings flashed on the face display of Geary's survival suit as he pulled himself down the passageway with the others. *Poisonous atmosphere. Toxic trace elements. Temperature barely within human-survivability range.* Those factors alone would have discouraged explorers among the human prize crew.

But he could feel something else, something that didn't register on his suit's sensors. A feeling of something just behind him, ready to leap. Of other things moving just out of the range of his side vision. Shadows, brought to life by the lights on the human suits, that jumped around in ways those shadows should not.

And, with every meter farther away from the area occupied by humans, the sensation of being surrounded by something hostile grew.

Admiral Lagemann began speaking with forced casualness, his voice across the comm circuit between suits too obviously trying to sound relaxed. "We've had time to think, Major Dietz and I, and here's what we've been thinking. We're behind an awesome amount of armor, and we're linked to four battleships, which are towing us. Beyond that, you've got an impressive even if damaged fleet. That's good. But *Invincible*, as the first nonhuman artifact controlled by the human race, and an incredibly big artifact at that, packed with nonhuman technology, is the most valuable object in human history. Anyone who sees it, or knows about it, is going to want to get it for themselves or at the least destroy it to keep us from learning whatever we can from the ship."

"I can't argue with any of your points," Geary said.

"Correct me if I'm wrong, but the odds of encountering on our way home a force of warships capable of destroying the rest of the fleet and capturing *Invincible* are basically zero."

"Again, that's true. The Syndic shipyards have probably kept going to the best of their ability, so they might surprise us, but even if they do, we're certain to have vastly superior numbers."

"So," Lagemann continued, "how would someone try to attack and capture *Invincible*?"

As Geary paused to think, Major Dietz provided the answer. "Boarding party."

"Boarding party?" Geary repeated. "How?"

"With enough stealth suits, they could get a force aboard this ship," Dietz explained. "Hit us while we're transiting a star system."

"They know where we have to go," Lagemann pointed out. "They can plant stealth shuttles along the route from a hypernet gate to a jump point and just latch on as we pass."

"There wouldn't be much opportunity for that along the route from here to Varandal," Geary began, then stopped as a memory came to him. "CEO Boyens strongly implied that obstacles would be established to keep us from getting back easily."

"Any idea what or how?"

"No. What could a boarding party do?"

Major Dietz answered again. "Standard practice when boarding a ship is to head for the three vital control centers. The bridge, main engineering control, which also controls the power core on the ship, and weapons control."

"There isn't any main engineering control on this ship," Geary said, reaching for another grip and pulling himself farther along the passageway, "unless you found one and didn't tell me."

He could hear Lagemann's grin. "Nope. There are eight power cores, and eight control stations. Why? Our engineers say it's not efficient. Two big cores would have worked better. But that's what the Kicks did. All of the cores are fully shut down and none of the control stations are operational. At least, not by humans. Who knows what a Kick could do? And all main propulsion systems were blown to hell during the battle at Honor, so even with power, *Invincible* can't do any serious movement under her own propulsion."

"There are two operational weapons left," Major Dietz offered. "Particle beam projectors similar to our hell lances. But both lack power. They're useless even if someone could find the right control station for them."

"And the bridge is also useless," Geary said. "Right?"

"Right, sir. We still don't understand that stadium seating in the back of it, but none of the controls are powered and working. It's all dead." Dietz made an annoyed sound, as if unhappy that he had used that term while it felt like Kick ghosts were hovering around.

"Then what's the threat? I'm not discounting the impact on you if an attack force boards, but how can they take *Invincible*? All you have to do is hold out until we put reinforcements aboard."

Admiral Lagemann waved one hand around them. "The threat is to the most valuable thing in human history. What can you do to keep someone else from using it, from learning from it, from putting aboard new forces to contest your control of it?"

The ghosts felt like they were crowding closer as the answer came to Geary. "Threaten to destroy it?"

"Give that man a prize. If they bring nuclear weapons aboard and set them off inside, they could turn this invaluable alien artifact into a giant stubby tube of armor containing radioactive slag. What would we do to keep them from doing that?"

He hated to think of the compromises that situation might require. Perhaps even surrendering *Invincible* to keep her interior intact in the hopes that she could be recaptured. "You think this will happen?"

"We think," Major Dietz said, "that it's the only possible way to threaten our control of this ship. But they'd have to eliminate my Marines to prevent us from stopping them from carrying out that kind of threat."

Geary shrugged irritably, trying to ward off the ghosts his senses claimed were bunching around him as he moved. "Do you want reinforcements now?"

"We can't use them, Admiral," Dietz explained. "The safe area on *Invincible* can't support many more humans. We're better off with a smaller force that knows the ship fairly well and can hit attackers where they least expect it."

"And where would they least expect it?" Geary asked.

"If they come, they'll be Syndics. Or people who were trained as Syndics. That means they'll follow standard procedures in their planning."

Geary shook his head. "Surely they realize that the deck plan for this ship doesn't match anything built by them or the Alliance."

"Yes, sir," Major Dietz said, then continued in very diplomatic tones for a Marine. "These plans will be very important. They'll be drafted by the Syndic high command. Not by any field forces. By the highest-ranking CEOs in the Syndic military hierarchy."

"Which means," Admiral Lagemann added, "that any relationship between reality and those plans will be purely coincidental."

"That's the way it tends to work," Geary agreed. "Those high-ranking planners far from the scene of the operations will use standard assumptions, so any attack force will come in and try to locate the three critical areas. I have to admit I have trouble believing that they could manage a boarding operation without our spotting it."

"It is possible, sir." Major Dietz spoke with authority but no hint of boastfulness. "As I said, lurking at full stealth near the path they expect us to use, so they'd only have to use minimal power to bring about an intercept. I've done it to their ships. I'm force recon, Admiral."

"I see. That makes you a much bigger expert on the matter than I am." The group had reached another temporary air lock blocking their path. "What is this?" Geary asked.

"The fake main engineering control," Admiral Lagemann advised.

"You've made a fake main engineering control?"

Lagemann opened the air lock and stepped inside.

Geary blinked at the lack of clean atmosphere on the other side of the air lock. "A fake air lock, too?"

"Naturally." Lagemann waved around him. "This was some kind of Kick recreational area, we think. Mostly empty except for what looks like sport equipment sized for Kicks. General Carabali sent over two Persian Donkeys at the request of Major Dietz." Lagemann pointed to a squat device resting in the center of the space. "Here's one of them. Have you been briefed on what the Donkeys do, Admiral?"

"Yes. We used them at Heradao." Geary came closer to the device, which didn't look at all like a real donkey. "Marine deception gear. They can send out full-spectrum signals and signatures to mimic just about anything."

Major Dietz nodded. "Anything from a headquarters complex to a dispersed armored ground forces unit on the advance," he said. "Each Donkey isn't very big, but they each carry scores of little subdecoys that can be sent out and generate all kinds of signatures that someone is there. Communications, bits of spoken conversation, infrared signatures, seismic thumps to match steps or equipment moving, other sounds of weapons and other equipment, you name it. This particular Donkey has been set to generate fake indications that this compartment is full of power-core-control equipment and people operating that equipment."

"Nice," Geary approved. "Where's the other Donkey?"

"In the compartment a ways from here that will look like a bridge area to Syndic sensors," Dietz said a trifle smugly.

Geary smiled despite the sense of disapproving ghosts hovering nearby. "A fake bridge and a fake main engineering control. These Donkeys will lure anyone sneaking onto the ship toward a place where you aren't. Can you spot them moving here?"

"If they're in full stealth mode?" the Major asked. "Not easily, sir. That's why we've got all of the approaches to these areas laced with sensors to spot anyone coming in. We can't cover the whole ship with what we've got, but we can cover the two areas that are baited."

"Sensors can be defeated," Geary said, recalling some of the things he had seen Marines do during their operations. "Can the Syndics spot your sensors and disable them or spoof them?"

Major Dietz definitely sounded smug this time. "They can, Admiral. But we have a sergeant who's a bit of a tech genius in her spare time. She's always fiddling with stuff. Sergeant Lamarr came up with *decoy* sensors."

"Decoy sensors? Fakes?"

"No, sir. Much better than fakes. They look just like regular sensors of certain types. Externally, no matter how good you check them, they look like regular sensors, and if they're active, they send out the same indications. But inside, the guts aren't designed to do what that sensor would do. Instead, they're designed to detect all of the ways that type of sensor could be bypassed, spoofed, or disabled without alerting people."

Geary almost laughed. "They are designed to detect nothing but methods of defeating sensors? Methods which can usually be undetectable?"

"Exactly, sir. Normally, that sort of stuff is piggybacked onto the sensors, which means it has limited capabilities since it's a secondary function. But on a Lamarr sensor, it's the primary and only function. A Lamarr sensor can't spot anything *unless* someone messes with it."

"There's a risk with using those," Lagemann added. "If you put one of those Lamarr sensors on a hatch, and someone just opens the hatch, you don't get any warning. But if someone spots the sensor and tries to defeat it before opening the hatch, you are sure to know. Oh, actually there are two risks. They're unauthorized and unapproved modifications to existing equipment. We could get slapped on the wrists by fleet headquarters."

Geary let out an exasperated sigh. "Sergeant Lamarr's chain of command hasn't approved that type of sensor?"

"Up to a certain point," the Major said. "All field commands approved. But when it hit headquarters and the design-and-acquisition bureaucracy, it got shot down."

"Surprising, isn't it?" Admiral Lagemann murmured.

"Shocking," Geary agreed dryly, thinking of the problems he had been having with fleet headquarters. As much as he looked forward to getting this fleet home, he also dreaded having to deal with fleet headquarters again. "As fleet commander, I hereby officially authorize a field test of modified equipment required in light of unique circumstances. I can do that, can't I?"

"I think so, but you don't have to attract their wrath," Lagemann protested. "I'm retiring the day we get home, so I have no problem having my name attached to the sensors."

"I think Sergeant Lamarr has her name attached to the sensors."

"That's true. Rightly so. In any event, the good ship *Invincible*," Lagemann said, patting the nearest bulkhead affectionately, "is ready for any attempt to prevent her from reaching Alliance territory.

You'll keep warships away, and if the Syndics do the only thing that might work and come aboard by stealth, we'll handle them."

"Good job. Very good job." He hadn't considered the possibility of *Invincible* being boarded, hadn't had time or the leisure to think about such a threat, but that was why a commander needed good subordinates. And the effort of putting together these fake command nodes on top of the routine patrolling had kept Major Dietz's Marines occupied instead of bored. *There are two things that worry me the most*, one of Geary's former commanding officers had once said. *The first of those things is the great minds at fleet headquarters and whatever they might decide is a good idea. The second thing is bored Marines and what* they *might decide is a good idea.*

The zero-g swim/pull back to the human-occupied portion of *Invincible* seemed much longer than the trip to the fake main engineering control. Without Admiral Lagemann and Major Dietz explaining their concerns and plans, Geary had nothing to distract him from the strange feeling of invisible others gathering around. He had to repeatedly fight down an urge to spin and look behind him as the skin between his shoulders crawled. A sense of being unwelcome, an intruder, seemed to fill the toxic air about him. If this was some normal Kick equipment, they could endure things humans could not. If it was a countermeasure to keep enemies from enjoying their conquests, it was fiendishly effective.

Invincible was not a happy ship. Usually that referred to the morale of the crew, but in this case the sailors and Marines were doing well enough. It was the ship herself that felt surly and ill-tempered.

Shuttle pilots usually left their hatches open into the ship while waiting for passengers to return, often coming out to stretch their legs and chat with any personnel at the air lock, but this time the pilot had stayed inside the shuttle and sealed the inner and outer hatches. Geary had to wait a few moments for the hatches to reopen and spent that time talking with the squad of Marines on sentry duty here. Normally an air lock like this might have one or at most two Marines guarding it, but after moving through the passageways of *Invincible*, Geary didn't feel like questioning the number of sentries.

"Something about the air in the ship's lock didn't feel right," the pilot apologized by intercom to Geary as he took a seat in the passenger deck.

"Did your sensors spot contaminants?" Geary asked the pilot, already guessing the answer would be negative.

"No, sir. Readouts said everything was fine. But it didn't feel right," the pilot repeated. "I thought it was better to keep the hatches closed until you got back."

"You didn't feel like looking around an alien warship?" Geary pressed.

"No, sir. That is, yes, sir. I was thinking about that, and the Marines there urged me to go ahead and wander around a bit, but when I went close to the air lock leading into the ship I... uh... it didn't feel right. Especially since those Marines seemed real eager for me to go in on my own."

Bored Marines. Definitely something to worry about.

The number of people in the fleet who knew the precise reason why the fleet would remain at Midway for the next couple of weeks was limited to four—Geary, Desjani, Rione, and Charban. Continued repair work provided justification for the delay, but feedback to Geary from his commanding officers and the senior enlisted told him that his crews were getting increasingly restless.

That information had been chillingly confirmed by an incident on one of the assault transports.

Dr. Nasr looked worn-out, but then, he often did these days. "We have had an incident with one of the Marines that I wanted to be sure you were aware of."

"Corporal Ulanov," Geary said. "General Carabali already told me about it. Ulanov took a weapon and tried to shoot up his troop compartment but failed because his platoon leader had deactivated the weapons available to him."

"Yes. Corporal Ulanov." Nasr stared at nothing for a moment before refocusing on Geary. "I thought you would want to hear the results of the medical exams."

Geary sighed, making a helpless gesture. "He's faced too much combat, and he wants to get home."

"Yes. And no." Nasr smiled thinly. "He does want to get home. But the actual reason for the attempted rampage was that Corporal Ulanov is also afraid of getting home."

"Afraid?" When a piece of information was so different from what you expected, it took a while to absorb it. Geary found himself repeating the word. "Afraid? Of getting home?"

"We're seeing more cases like that, though Ulanov is the worst," Nasr observed. "Admiral, what will happen when we get home? What will happen to these ships and these Marines?"

"As far as I know, they'll remain under my command."

"But perhaps not."

"I don't know."

"That is the problem," Nasr said. "You don't know, I don't know, no one knows. Corporal Ulanov kept telling his medical interviewer that he was afraid. It took a while to realize that what Ulanov feared was uncertainty. He is comfortable being a Marine. He knows he can face combat, though the physical and mental stresses from the combat he has experienced have done damage that Corporal Ulanov does not acknowledge. But he fears being cast aside like a machine designed for a purpose that is no longer needed. He wants to get home, but he fears what might happen when he gets there. That internal conflict is what made him snap."

Geary slumped as he thought about Ulanov and the many others in this fleet who shared the same worries for their future. "I can get them home. We won't wait here much longer before leaving. But there's not much I can do about worries over the future. I don't have the answers to those."

"There is something you can do, Admiral. Tell them you will look after their welfare to the best of your ability. That may not seem like much to you, but to them it will mean a great deal." One corner of Dr. Nasr's mouth tilted in a small, sad smile. "As a doctor, it is all too easy to see people as a collection of parts that either work right or need to be replaced or repaired. You can forget the human those parts make up if you focus too much on the parts. I have seen those in command positions look upon people the same way, as parts in the organism they rule over. Parts that exist only to serve the organism. If a private fails or dies, the private is replaced by another. That's all. We all fear being seen as parts, expendable and replaceable, don't we?"

"We do, Doctor, because we've all seen it happen to others and sometimes felt it happen to us. All right. I'll find a way to let everyone know they won't just be cast aside."

He was reaching to end the call when the doctor spoke again. "Have you seen the reports from the ships of the Callas Republic and the Alliance?"

Geary nodded. "I've looked them over. There don't seem to be any problems on those ships. I know they want to be detached from this fleet when we get home, and I'll do all I can to make that happen."

"There don't *seem* to be problems," Nasr repeated. "But there are. Those men and women expected to go home when the war ended, to have their warships recalled to their republic and their federation. That didn't happen. At the moment, they are all outwardly doing fine. But do you know how a person can be just walking along, or working as usual, no signs of trouble, then suddenly they snap because of hidden stresses? That describes those ships. Be careful of them, Admiral."

"I will be, Doctor." He sat for a while after ending the call with Nasr. *There's nothing else I can do about the Callas Republic and Rift Federation ships, and I've already told all supervisors to watch their people carefully and refer for evaluation any who seemed marginal. I need to make the supervisors' job easier, though.* Geary straightened in his seat and tapped the record command on his comm software. "This is Admiral Geary. I want to give everyone a situation update. We *will* be departing Midway soon, returning home. We'll stay at home for an extended period because even though you have all put in amazing efforts to keep our ships going and repair the damage they've sustained, this fleet will still require a lot of work at the maintenance facilities at Varandal."

How do I say the rest? "I want to offer my personal assurances to all of you that I will make every effort to look out for you, to ensure that when we return home, you are treated as you deserve after your service to the Alliance." *That isn't enough. Of course I'm going to look out for all who have served under me. That's my responsibility. But I can't promise there will be no problems once we return. What else do I say to let them know I won't abandon them?*

Oh, hell. Just say that. "We did not leave anyone behind anywhere in alien space. No one will be left behind after we return home."

He ended the recording, then called the bridge. "Tanya, could you look over something for me?"

"You mean since I have nothing else to do but oversee a battle cruiser and her crew?" Desjani asked.

"It won't take much time," Geary promised.

"Gee, I've never heard that one before. All right, Admiral. Will you be coming to the bridge soon?" she added pointedly.

He glanced at the time. "I'll be up there in a while. There's no rush, is there?"

"No, of course not," Desjani agreed.

Neither of them knew exactly when things would begin happening. There were too many uncertainties about travel times within the other star systems a certain ship had been transiting. But sometime within the next twelve hours, the plan proposed by General Drakon's representatives would either succeed or fail.

Geary made a show of wandering up to the bridge of *Dauntless*. He stopped several times to talk with members of the crew. Most of them asked variations on "when are we leaving?" He replied with variations on "soon."

On the bridge, Desjani nodded to him, gesturing to her display. "Good update, Admiral. Do you want to send it?"

"You don't have any suggestions for improvements?" Geary asked as he took his seat and called up his own display showing the situation in this star system.

"Nope. This is one of those times when unedited words from the heart are best."

"Then please transmit it to the fleet, Captain."

"Certainly, Admiral."

"Anything new from CEO Boyens today?"

She made a gesture of indifference. "Just another complaint about provocative maneuvers on our part. He seems to feel threatened by the fact that you've moved so many warships to an orbit only ten light-minutes from the hypernet gate."

"And only eight light-minutes from his flotilla," Geary said. "Did we send him the standard response that the authorities at Midway have given us freedom to maneuver within this star system?"

"You'd have to ask our emissaries," Desjani said, now disdainful.

"I will," Geary said. His annoyance with Boyens had been growing, as the Syndic CEO had sent repeated messages supposedly about negotiations but mainly containing thinly veiled derision of Geary's inability to budge him from this star system.

But while the Syndic flotilla had stubbornly held its position near the hypernet gate, the Alliance presence near that gate had grown to include seven battleships and eleven battle cruisers, along with dozens of heavy and light cruisers and eighty destroyers. Few of those warships were in perfect condition, but all of them had the propulsion, shielding, and weapons if necessary to go on the attack. Geary had designated them Formation Alpha and arranged them into a single, giant fist aimed toward Boyens's Syndic flotilla.

As the Alliance warships took up position, Kommodor Marphissa had taken the remaining warships of the Midway flotilla out and around, forming a small pocket of defense that still blocked any movement by the Syndic flotilla toward the star and also further limited possible movement by the Syndics by threatening their route toward the nearest jump point.

"He's got to know what we're doing," Desjani commented, her posture and tone of voice now that of someone who did not expect anything to happen today that hadn't happened yesterday and the day before. "Boyens isn't stupid, even if he is a Syndic CEO."

"He thinks we're trying to bluff him into leaving," Geary said.

"Isn't that what we're doing?" she asked with exaggerated innocence.

If he had been drinking something, he might have choked on it at that moment. Fortunately, any need for a reply was eliminated a second later.

"Another ship has arrived at the gate," Lieutenant Castries said, her voice perking up as the identity of the new arrival became clear. "It's the heavy cruiser belonging to Midway that escorted that other cruiser out through the jump point for Kane."

"He came back through the gate?" Lieutenant Yuon blurted out. "That's—"

"Not very bright," Desjani said, still calm and composed. "They must have thought the Syndic flotilla would be gone. Look, they're coming around and heading for the rest of the Midway flotilla."

"Not very fast," Lieutenant Castries muttered. "Captain, fleet sensors estimate that the heavy cruiser has lost a main propulsion unit. No damage that we can see, so it might be an equipment failure."

"Syndic ships have much less onboard-repair capability than we do," Desjani replied.

"He's in trouble," Lieutenant Yuon confirmed. "Maneuvering systems estimate that with that much propulsion out, the Syndics will be able to catch him before the rest of the Midway flotilla can join with him."

"You sound perplexed, Lieutenant," Desjani said. "Why?"

"I…" Yuon licked his lips, then made a helpless gesture. "I sort of feel like they're on our side, Captain. Even though that's a Syndic cruiser. I mean, it used to be one."

"It's not a Syndic cruiser," Geary agreed. "The Syndics built it, but somebody else owns it now. And the cruisers that still answer to Syndic authority are going after it." He didn't need to rerun the maneuvering system's conclusions. Even judging the movement of the ships on the display by eye, he could tell that the heavy cruisers and HuKs leaping away from the Syndic battleship would get within weapons range of the lone Midway heavy cruiser at least half an hour before it reached the company of the rest of the Midway flotilla.

Geary tapped his comm controls. "All units in Formation Alpha, prepare for combat."

He could feel the startled stares of the rest of the bridge crew on him, even Desjani feigning surprise. With the exception of Desjani, they had no idea why he had given that order. *Not yet. We can't let the cat out of the bag quite yet.*

"Assume full combat readiness," Desjani ordered her watch team. Alarms blared, summoning the entire crew to action stations, while Geary watched the movements of the other ships and judged the right time for his next communication. "Captain Desjani, I see that the Syndic cruisers and HuKs aiming to intercept that newly arrived Midway cruiser will be within weapons range of their target in eight minutes."

"That's what our combat systems say," Desjani confirmed.

"Set me up for a transmission to the Syndic flagship."

The Syndic battleship with CEO Boyens aboard was eight light-minutes from *Dauntless*. The heavy cruisers and HuKs that had raced away from that battleship were now nearly a light-minute from the battleship and rapidly closing on the lone Midway cruiser at a high angle from above and behind. The Midway flotilla had surged into motion but was still several light-minutes away from where the Syndics were about to attack their lone comrade.

Now. Geary tapped his controls again, choosing the one prepared for sending a message to CEO Boyens. He had assumed a puzzled and angry expression and spoke with the same mix of emotions. "CEO Boyens, this is Admiral Geary of the First Fleet of the Alliance. You have sent forces to intercept a ship chartered by and operating under the authority of the government of the Alliance. You are to cease any actions aimed at an Alliance-flagged ship and withdraw your forces immediately. Geary, out." He deliberately left off the formal ending, giving the message an abrupt tone.

The bridge crew was staring at him again, but their gazes shifted as Emissaries Rione and Charban walked onto the bridge. "Admiral," Rione said, as if genuinely surprised, "we chartered that ship for Alliance government business. Why are Syndicate warships pursuing it?"

"I don't know, Madam Emissary," Geary replied. "I have informed the Syndics of the ship's status and told them to veer off."

Desjani once again pretended to be startled. "We chartered that Midway cruiser? The Alliance government?"

"That is correct," Charban said. "We judged it to be in the interest of the Alliance that we be on good terms with the home star of that heavy cruiser."

"But if it's under Alliance government charter, it is Alliance property during the period of the charter. If the Syndics attack it—"

"They will be attacking an *Alliance* ship," Geary broke in. "All units in Formation Alpha, immediate execute accelerate to point two light speed, come starboard three two degrees, up zero six degrees."

"You will have to act if they attack an Alliance ship," Rione agreed, sounding as upset as if this had not all been arranged in advance.

He had timed his message as well as possible. The Syndic heavy cruisers and HuKs had surely been sent out with orders to attack the lone Midway heavy cruiser. Having been humiliated once before, Boyens would be determined to ensure that this time his prey did not escape. They would launch that attack unless Boyens countermanded his earlier orders. But Geary had sent his message to Boyens so that it would arrive before the Syndic ships fired but too late for any message from Boyens to reach the Syndic attackers telling them not to fire. It was a simple matter of geometry, the three sides of the communications triangle adding up to less time than Boyens needed.

CEO Boyens would be realizing that right about now. Geary

found himself smiling at the thought of the Syndic CEO becoming very, very unhappy as he spotted, too late, the trap laid for him.

"The Syndic heavy cruisers have launched missiles!" Lieutenant Castries said, as alarms from *Dauntless's* combat systems accentuated her report.

"CEO Boyens must have received your message before those ships fired," Desjani said, the words going into the official record as she spoke them.

"That's right," Geary agreed. "We have to assume that he has deliberately attacked an Alliance ship, and we have to make sure the Syndics don't get away with such an act of aggression." He tapped his comm controls again, this time pretending only anger. "CEO Boyens! Your forces have fired on a ship *after* you were informed that ship was operating under the Alliance flag! This is a hostile act, a clear violation of the peace treaty the Syndicate Worlds pledged to observe. Under the terms of that treaty, I am authorized to take all necessary measures to protect Alliance life and property. I will now do so and eliminate any threats to the Alliance within this star system! Geary, out!"

Just to add to CEO Boyens's headaches, the apparently crippled main propulsion unit on the lone Midway heavy cruiser suddenly came to life at full power, dramatically boosting the acceleration of the warship. "That," Desjani observed, "will create some serious problems for the missiles the Syndics launched based on their earlier assumptions of the maximum acceleration that heavy cruiser could achieve."

"But they've still got two dozen missiles coming at them," Geary said.

"They'll be all right," Desjani said, her eyes on her display. "If they listen to Captain Bradamont. She's aboard that heavy cruiser, isn't she?"

"Yes." It had not been easy to arrange Bradamont's transfer to the Syndic ship without her movement being detected, but routine resupply operations could mask a great deal of nonroutine activity. "Her presence on the heavy cruiser establishes clearly and legally that the ship is temporarily Alliance property. The authorities on Midway," Geary added, "also assigned a Kapitan-Lieutenant Kontos to ride the cruiser while it was under Alliance charter."

"Kontos?" she asked. "Do we know him?"

"He's the one who thought up fastening the battleship to the mobile forces facility so it could tow that facility out of the path of the enigma bombardment," Geary said.

"Oh." Desjani smiled knowingly. "And now Captain Bradamont can provide us with detailed observations about this Kapitan-Lieutenant who is such a quick and innovative thinker?"

"That's right," Geary agreed.

"Well done, Admiral." She tapped her weapons controls. "We'll be within range of Boyens in forty-five minutes if you hold us at point two light speed."

Geary nodded, gazing at his own display again. *What will I do if Boyens doesn't run? If he stands his ground? I'll have to engage that battleship and take out the heavy cruisers, light cruisers, and HuKs escorting it. It'll be a massacre, but they could still inflict damage on some of my ships, and when I get home, it'll be a lot harder to explain annihilating a Syndic flotilla than it will be to explain chasing one away.*

Boyens had a limited period of time in which to act. Battleships excelled at firepower and armor, but not at acceleration. If Boyens wanted to avoid the Alliance attack, he would have to head for the hypernet gate soon enough to overcome the Alliance advantage in coming up to speed first.

"The gate's his only option," Desjani commented. "If Boyens heads toward the only jump point he could reach before we could catch him, he'll run right into that Midway flotilla."

"Isn't that a lucky coincidence," Geary said.

"We need to keep after him," Desjani added in a low voice. "Boyens isn't going to enter that gate if he has any doubts that we might veer off. We need to stay on a firing run, maintaining our velocity, until his flotilla leaves. If we bobble at all, if we slow down, if we give him any reason to doubt our intent, he'll veer away from the gate. Then we'll *have* to destroy him."

"You're right." He had been trying to estimate when he could order his attack force to break off, but Desjani was correct. "He'll cut it as fine as he possibly can, to see if we actually open fire."

"Count on having to open fire," she said.

"I hope you're not right about that."

But as the minutes went by, Boyens's flagship remained stubbornly in the same orbit. Geary checked the combat systems readouts, seeing the steady scrolling down to the time when the Syndic battleship would be within range of the weapons on the leading Alliance warships. One number for the specter missiles, another for hell-lance particle beams, a third time for the ball bearings called grapeshot used at close range, and finally a time for the very-close-range null-field generators carried by the Alliance battle cruisers and battleships.

Desjani shook her head as she studied her display. "If he doesn't start moving in the next five minutes, we'll catch him before he reaches the gate."

Rione spoke from where she had come to stand on the other side of Geary. "Why hasn't CEO Boyens tried to communicate with us?" she wondered. "Accused us of setting him up, tried to apologize, anything at all? Ah, I know."

"Do you feel like telling me?" Geary asked.

"Certainly, Admiral." Rione held out her open hand, palm up. "Syndic CEOs hold their positions through fear. Subordinates know they cannot cross their CEOs. But if a CEO is seen to be weak, subordinates will see wounded prey."

"And an apology, an attempt to deflect our attack, would make Boyens look weak."

"Extremely weak, as well as foolish." Rione closed her hand into a fist. "He knows we set him up. To openly admit that he fell into a trap we set might drive the last nail into his coffin."

"Do you think he'll stay and fight?"

"That would be suicide." She made an uncertain gesture. "But the price of failure here for him might be high, and his own anger at being humiliated might drive him to fight a hopeless battle. I don't know."

"Two minutes left for him to start running," Desjani said. "We need to see thrusters firing on those Syndics ships within the next thirty seconds to get them faced on a course for the gate."

Thirty seconds to wonder if the cunning and twisted plot dreamed up by the rulers of Midway would blow up in everyone's face. On the main inhabited world light-hours from the hypernet gate, President Iceni and General Drakon would not see what happened until a long time after it took place. Thirty seconds to wonder what they would think as they saw the same limited time rapidly running out. CEO Boyens must be angry, frustrated, knowing he was trapped, knowing that failure would be punished by his superiors in the Syndic hierarchy but knowing also that if he lost that battleship, the punishment would certainly be death. Thirty seconds to wonder if Boyens would choose to risk that rather than fail here.

Ten seconds.

Five.

3

"Maneuvering thrusters firing on all warships in the Syndic flotilla," Lieutenant Yuon called out. "Vectors changing toward hypernet gate."

"There you go," Desjani said approvingly. "He'll wait until the last possible second to cut in his main propulsion, too," she predicted.

"What if Boyens miscalculates?" Geary said.

"Then we punch some holes in the hide of that battleship to remind him that he should allow a little larger margin for error in the future." She smiled at him. "Right?"

"Yeah. Whoever is driving our 'chartered' heavy cruiser is doing a good job."

The lone heavy cruiser had kept accelerating all out away from the pursuing Syndic cruisers and HuKs while twisting slightly to one side and down in order to put the oncoming missiles into the most difficult possible stern chase. Geary's eyes went to where the Midway flotilla was swooping in from the side, aiming to intercept the heavy cruisers of the Syndic force that had gone after the lone cruiser. "They're not faking this at all. They're going to try to take out those Syndic warships."

Desjani gave him a sidelong glance. "The Midway ships are outnumbered three to six in heavy cruisers. Having a few light cruisers along won't compensate for that. If their Kommodor goes straight in, the Midway flotilla will get its butt kicked pretty hard."

"Probably," Geary agreed. "Let's hope she's smarter than that." Something else caught his attention, the Dancer ships swinging outward from their last orbit and heading this way. "I wonder what the Dancers are thinking while they watch this."

"If they've been secretly watching us as long as we suspect they have, then they're probably thinking *business as usual for those humans*."

Charban spoke in a thoughtful voice. "There must be many things they still don't know about us. I feel certain that the Dancers are watching all we do very closely."

By contrast, Rione sounded amused. "It would be interesting to know their interpretation of what they are seeing right now."

Geary didn't answer this time, his eyes once more on a time count scrolling downward. If the Syndic flotilla did not light off their main propulsion in another twenty seconds, Geary's fleet would be certain to get within firing range before the Syndics could use the hypernet gate to escape.

"He's not giving himself much margin for error," Desjani commented. "Even if he— All right. Finally." She sounded slightly disappointed.

"Main propulsion units have lit off on all Syndic warships," Lieutenant Castries declared. "They're accelerating at maximum."

"They're cutting it very close," Desjani said. "I wonder…"

"What?" Geary asked.

"Maybe this isn't about Boyens's pride. Maybe he's trying to tweak us one last time, by staying just barely out of reach and entering the gate just before we can hit him."

"It's still a dangerous game. If he cuts it that fine and misses by a hair, he could take a lot of hits."

His display rippled as a string of updates appeared. "What's this?"

"Tactical data link from the Midway flotilla," Desjani said. "I told my systems people not to pass it through in real time but to scrub it and let periodic updates through."

You're letting transmissions from a flotilla of former Syndic warships through at all? Geary wondered. But he could see that those tactical links provided some useful information on the readiness state of the Midway warships as well as the single heavy cruiser fleeing the Syndics. That lone heavy cruiser was now identified as the *Manticore*.

The missiles fired at the *Manticore* had shifted their own vectors to maintain intercepts after the *Manticore* accelerated and maneuvered. They were still closing, but the slow relative speed with which they were overtaking *Manticore* made them good targets for the heavy cruiser's armament. Geary watched as hell-lance shots slammed into the leading Syndic missiles, knocking out four. That left twenty incoming missiles, though.

Manticore's vector altered abruptly as the cruiser's main propulsion cut out, then her thrusters pitched her up and over, facing back the way she had come. Hell lances from *Manticore's* forward batteries fired on the still-pursuing missiles as the heavy cruiser's bow pointed toward them, but the ship's movement continued away from the missiles.

I know this maneuver. The next thing to happen will be…

Manticore's main propulsion flared to life at maximum, now braking the heavy cruiser's velocity. The oncoming missiles could not slow their own speed quickly enough, instead using maneuvering thrusters at maximum to try to claw around fast enough to still manage intercepts as their closing speed grew rapidly, and *Manticore* got closer a lot faster than the missiles had planned for.

Missile vectors swung wildly, sliding past the oncoming shape of *Manticore*, stresses on the missile structures causing many of the weapons to come apart in mid–vector change. The missiles that survived the radical change in course were burning their remaining fuel off trying to match *Manticore's* movement, which caused them to come to a near stop relative to *Manticore*. That made them perfect targets.

The six surviving missiles blew up as hell lances stabbed through them.

"You're not supposed to try that maneuver with anything bigger than a light cruiser," Geary commented.

"That must be prewar doctrine," Desjani said. "I've done it with a battle cruiser. So has Bradamont. She must be showing those former Syndics how to really drive ships."

With *Manticore* now slowing, the vectors of all the other forces near the hypernet gate were angling in toward the gate. Boyens, with his sole battleship and four light cruisers, was accelerating toward the gate at the lumbering pace which was the best a battleship could manage. Geary's much-larger formation was bearing down on

Boyens, but the projected intercept point with the Syndic flotilla was just past the gate. If Boyens kept accelerating at his current pace, he would get away just before Geary's force closed to firing range.

The six heavy cruisers and ten HuKs that Boyens had detached to chase *Kraken* had come over and about and were now angling back to meet up with the battleship a few minutes prior to the entire flotilla's reaching the gate.

And the Midway flotilla was coming in from almost the opposite side as Geary's formation, aiming to hit the Syndic heavy cruisers before they could join with the rest of Boyens's flotilla.

Not the simplest situation, with five different groupings of ships belonging to three different players near the gate, but far from being too complex to get his mind around. *As long as the Syndics keep their vectors steady, all I really need to worry about now is whether Kommodor Marphissa is going to stage a senseless charge into a force that outnumbers her two to one. Should I—*

Geary jerked in surprise as one of the Syndic light cruisers blew up. "What the hell happened?"

So surprised was everyone on the bridge that it took close to three seconds for anyone to reply.

"There have been no weapons fired at that light cruiser," Lieutenant Yuon said.

"It just blew up?" Desjani asked sharply.

"It wasn't hit by any weapon we could see," Lieutenant Yuon insisted. "They're still well out of range of us and the Midway flotilla, and none of the Syndic ships near it fired."

"Could it be something the Midway flotilla did? A drifting mine?" Desjani questioned.

Lieutenant Castries answered. "Our sensors indicate it was an internal explosion, Captain. Not external. It couldn't have been a mine."

"Captain," Lieutenant Yuon said, "we're picking up indications consistent with a power core overload. But our systems also say there weren't any warning indications, no signs that the power core on that ship was having problems. It just blew."

"No hits and no indications of problems," Desjani mused as she tapped an internal comm control. "Chief engineer, can a power core blow without sending out signs of instability that we could detect?"

"No way, Captain," the chief engineer replied. "We would have picked up something. This went from fine to critical as fast as a power core can overload. There's only one thing that could explain that."

Desjani waited for several seconds, then prompted her chief engineer. "And that would be?"

"Oh. Sorry, Captain. Someone blew it on purpose. That's the only thing that fits."

"A deliberate core overload?" Geary questioned. "Why would they do that?"

"Damned if I know, Admiral. Even Syndics don't usually do something that stupid."

"Admiral!" Lieutenant Iger's image had appeared in a virtual window near Geary. "If we're interpreting the data right, about three minutes before that Syndic light cruiser exploded, it severed its links to the Syndic flotilla command and control net."

"It cut its links to the Syndic net?" Geary looked over at Desjani and saw she was reaching the same conclusion he was. "Isn't that consistent with a mutiny?"

"Yes, Admiral," Iger agreed reluctantly. "It could mean that. We don't have nearly enough information to support or reject such a conclusion, though."

"Do you have an alternative explanation for a ship's suddenly blowing up? Did we pick up any unusual signals sent from the Syndic flagship to that light cruiser before its core exploded?"

"No, Admiral, but a burst transmission on a special frequency would be very difficult for us to spot. We'll have to comb through all of the signals we're intercepting to try to spot any strange transmissions."

"You think they blew up their own ship to keep mutineers from getting away?" Desjani asked Geary.

"I think," he replied, "that knowing what I do about Syndic leaders, and knowing how many ships of theirs have taken off on their own after killing any internal-security agents aboard them, that the Syndic leaders would have come up with some sort of additional fail-safe."

Lieutenant Iger had been listening, and nodded. "Admiral, we've got this entire star system seeded with collection and relay sats. If a signal was sent, and it's that important, we'll find it."

"It's important to the Syndics," Geary said. "Are you saying it's important to us, too?"

"Yes, sir. If we can find that message, we can analyze it, break it down, copy it, and perhaps use it ourselves if it should ever become necessary."

Desjani leaned over, grinning. "Blow up their ships using their own fail-safe? I like the way you think, Lieutenant."

"There's no guarantee we can do it, Captain. Even if we can locate the signal, there may be specific codes and authentication requirements for each Syndic warship. But if the Syndics cut corners to get the capability fielded fast, they may have left some large back doors open."

"Captain?" Lieutenant Castries said. "The Midway flotilla has altered vector."

Geary pulled his attention back to his display, seeing the Midway flotilla swinging wider now, pushing their track farther in toward the star and farther away from the Syndic heavy cruisers. As he watched that movement, an explanation suddenly came to him. "They weren't making an attack."

"What?" Desjani asked.

"The Midway flotilla. They weren't going to hit that heavy cruiser force. They were going to come close enough that if any of the heavy cruisers or HuKs decided to mutiny and veer off, the Midway flotilla would be able to screen them."

Rione laughed like a teacher whose favorite student had just guessed the right answer. "Yes, Admiral, that's probably exactly what they were doing. President Iceni has been frank with me that she and Drakon have been sending transmissions to the Syndic warships encouraging them to mutiny."

"But," Charban said, "when they saw that light cruiser blow up, they knew that the Syndics had a countermeasure in place that would keep any other Syndic warships from trying to mutiny and join them." He shook his head. "Haven't the Syndic leaders figured out yet that short-term solutions like that don't actually solve the underlying problem?"

"They stopped at least one mutiny," Desjani said.

"At the cost of a light cruiser," Charban said. "They still lost the ship. Crews on other ships will be trying to figure out how to stop that Syndic fail-safe from working. They *will* figure out how to do that because the enlisted always figure out ways around the brilliant schemes of their superiors, and the mutinies will again succeed. In the short haul, it's easier to blow something up than it is to fix what's wrong with it. But blowing it up isn't a solution. It's just a way of trying to forestall something without figuring out how to really fix it."

"Ten minutes until we're in range of the Syndic flotilla," Lieutenant Yuon cautioned.

Geary eyed the remaining distance, hoping that Boyens wouldn't develop a last-moment desire for a grand, suicidal gesture. The Alliance formation's combat systems were choosing targets, assigning weapons, preparing to fire when the Syndic warships were in range, and the order was given. He decided to send one more message. "CEO Boyens, if you or any other Syndicate Worlds formation enters this star system again without approval, you had better be ready to deal with the consequences. Geary, out."

"Not that I disapprove of threats aimed at Syndics," Desjani said, "but why do you think they'll pay attention to that?"

"Because of one other thing I've had Captain Smythe's engineers working on. The light from that event should be showing up right about now. I wanted it to be revealed earlier, but this will do."

The combat systems on *Dauntless* sounded an alert, highlighting on displays distant movement, the light of which had only just reached here. Far off, at the Midway facility orbiting a gas giant, the new battleship *Midway* was underway. To all appearances, as far as any sensor could tell, *Midway* was fully operational and ready to fight.

"Their battleship works?" Desjani asked, sounding as if she didn't know whether to be happy or worried.

"Not even close. A lot of the work is deceptive, designed to make the ship look fully combat-ready. But as far as Boyens will be able to tell, the authorities at Midway now have their own battleship ready to engage the next Syndic attack."

"And he'll carry that news back to Prime with him," Rione commented. "Very nice, Admiral."

"What if the Syndics try another attack soon anyway?" Charban asked.

"I'm doing what I can," Geary said, glancing at Desjani, "with what I have."

"Dealing with reality?" Charban commented. "How did you make high rank with that kind of attitude?"

"Damned if I know." On his display, the entire Syndic flotilla was together again, every ship headed for the hypernet gate, less than a minute from the point at which Geary could order his weapons to fire.

Desjani gave him a look, her hand hovering near her weapons controls. Everyone on the bridge was looking at him, everyone in the fleet waiting for his next words.

The Syndic flotilla vanished as it entered the gate.

He let out a long breath. "All units in Formation Alpha, reduce velocity to point zero two light speed, come port one nine zero degrees at time three zero. All units return to normal readiness condition."

Desjani seemed to be out of sorts as she passed on the commands, so Geary smiled at her. "Are you unhappy that it worked?"

She didn't return the smile. "We should have blown him away. We're going to have to deal with him and that battleship again."

"You may be right," Geary conceded. "But I didn't want to restart the war here and now."

"Which sort of implies you expect to restart the war at some other place and time?"

He had a denial ready to go but felt a great uncertainty inside that stopped the words before they were spoken.

Now the only things holding the First Fleet at Midway were some final repair work and a personnel transfer. The personnel transfer was no afterthought, of course. Some of the humans once held prisoner by the enigmas would be handed over to the authorities at Midway. Those people had come from Midway and nearby star systems, and now dreamed of going home. Dr. Nasr, and Geary himself, didn't believe that dream could come true, not as the former prisoners hoped and wished, but those individuals had the right to choose their own fates.

The repair work was only final in the sense of being the last to be done here. Only a few of Geary's ships didn't need additional work, and overage systems continued to fail on ships at random intervals that somehow seemed to occur in clusters whenever he was starting to feel better about the material condition of the ships in his fleet.

"We could spend the next six months here," Captain Smythe explained, his image standing in Geary's stateroom aboard *Dauntless* while Smythe remained physically aboard *Tanuki*, "and I couldn't really get ahead of the game. Not with only eight auxiliaries and so many old ships to deal with."

Old ships. Meaning more than two or three years since they were commissioned and sent off to battle in the expectation that they would be destroyed within a couple of years or less. "You and your engineers have done wonders," Geary said. "I didn't think some of the battleships would hold together this long."

"It takes a lot to kill a *Guardian*-class battleship, Admiral," Smythe reminded him. "All of that armor holds them together when by all rights they ought to be coming apart, and it's not like warships in space can sink when they get too many holes in them."

"Sink?"

"You know," Smythe explained, "when a ship or a boat on a planetary ocean or sea loses buoyancy, when it takes on too much water, it sinks. It goes beneath the water. Some are designed to do that. Sub... somethings. But those can come up again. A ship designed to ride on the surface of the water is a write-off if it sinks. That's how battleships and battle cruisers on planets, on oceans, used to be destroyed. They'd get enough holes in them to sink. I suppose at least a few must have blown up, but usually it was a matter of getting them under the water."

Geary frowned at Smythe in puzzlement. "Why couldn't the crews keep operating the battleships? Why did being under the water matter so much?"

"They didn't have survival suits, Admiral. They couldn't breathe! And the equipment didn't work under the water. The engines used... internal combustion and... steam and... other methods that required oxygen and flame and… things."

"Things?" Geary asked, smiling. "Is that the technical term?"

Smythe grinned. "Things. Junk. Stuff. All perfectly good engineering terms. But in all seriousness, if a ship designed to ride on the surface of the water were to sink, it was in some ways like a ship designed to operate in space making a destructive atmospheric entry. It's not something they're designed to survive."

"All right, that comparison I understand. Have you had time to look at any of the data on *Invincible?* This conversation is making me wonder if the Kicks might not have designed it to handle things we don't design our ships for."

"It's possible." Smythe threw his hands upward helplessly. "There's so much about that ship that is almost familiar, but not. As an engineer, it's a fascinating and frustrating puzzle. Of course, it would help a great deal if we were able to power up any of the components aboard that ship."

"No."

"Something small? Something harmless?"

"How can you be sure it's harmless?" Geary asked.

"Ah…" Smythe made the same gesture of confusion and bewilderment. "You have me there, Admiral. But maybe if we found out how at least one piece of equipment worked, we could put a dent in the superstitions developing about that Kick ship."

"Superstitions?"

"The ghosts," Smythe said apologetically.

"Captain, have you actually been aboard *Invincible?*"

"You mean physically? In person? No." Smythe eyed Geary. "You have?"

"Yes." Geary felt a sudden urge to shudder come over him and swallowed before he could speak. "I don't know what the ghosts are, but the sensation is real and powerful. Is there some device that could create a sensation of immaterial dead crowding around you?"

"If they're *immaterial*, they can't *crowd*," Smythe pointed out with an engineer's precision. He pursed his lips in thought. "I'd have to discuss it with medical professionals. Maybe some sort of subsonic vibrations, but we haven't picked any up on our equipment."

"It might be something totally new to us," Geary pointed out.

"Which is another reason for investigating the ship's equipment!" Smythe pointed out triumphantly.

"But all power has been shut down on that ship, and all stored energy sources disconnected. How could something still be operating to unnerve anyone on that ship?"

Smythe leaned back, put a hand to his mouth, and thought. "Maybe... no... or, hmmm. If it was some sort of vibration or harmonic, operating at a level so low we couldn't detect it even though humans could somehow sense it, you could in theory at least construct a structure like a ship so that it generated such harmonics naturally." He nodded and smiled. "That could explain it. Purely guesswork at this point, but if the ship's structure was designed to generate such harmonics, and the ship was equipped with some device that generated counterharmonics to damp out the effect, then shutting down everything would have shut down the counterharmonic equipment."

"Seriously?" Geary asked, amazed.

"In *theory*," Smythe emphasized. "I have no idea if that's even remotely true, or how you would do it in practice. But then, I'm not a Kick."

"Well, it may be just a wild-assed guess, but it's still the only rational explanation I've heard for what *Invincible* feels like inside."

"Admiral," Captain Smythe said with exaggerated dignity, "I am a trained engineer. I don't make wild-assed guesses. I make *scientific* wild-assed guesses."

"I see." Geary laughed, grateful for the diversion from too many problems and too few solutions. "Has Lieutenant Jamenson come up with any new scientific wild-assed guesses?"

"No, sir. She's mined what we have for all that can be found. Once we get home and acquire more resources, I am confident she will be able to produce the sort of material we're looking for."

"Thank you, Captain," Geary said, as an alert blinked for his attention. He ended the call to Smythe and tapped to accept the new call from the bridge of *Dauntless*.

Tanya Desjani gave him one of her I'm-tolerating-this-but-not-liking-it looks. "The freighter the locals sent to pick up former enigma prisoners is matching movement to *Haboob*."

The former enigma prisoners. Humans captured over at least decades, some from Syndic ships that had mysteriously vanished, some from planets in star systems that the enigmas had taken over. There were more than three hundred of them aboard *Haboob*. Three hundred thirty-three, to be exact, a number that the prisoners said had been kept constant and so must have meant something to the enigmas. Figuring out what to do with those people was an ongoing headache, but eighteen of them had asked to be left off at Midway because they had either lived here or at the nearby star Taroa.

Agreeing to that hadn't been an easy decision, either. The rulers of Midway claimed to be no longer despotic Syndics but could easily just be stringing Geary along for their own purposes. "Where is Dr. Nasr?"

"Physically on-scene aboard *Haboob*," she replied.

"Good. Can you join me in the conference room to watch this go down? I want to link in with Dr. Nasr."

"We could do that on the bridge," Desjani complained. "Oh, you want a less public location in case something unpleasant happens when we try to hand over some of those head cases the enigmas kept locked up?"

"Yes, Captain," Geary said patiently. "They're head cases *because* the enigmas kept them locked up. Let's not forget that."

"Aye, Admiral. See you in the conference room in ten."

He made it to the conference compartment well short of ten minutes later and found Tanya already there. "Have the Syndic—I mean, have the Midway shuttles docked yet?"

She shrugged. "I'd know if I were on the bridge…"

"You know anyway."

"Damn. You know me too well." Desjani waved the way inside. "The first Midway shuttle docks in two minutes." She sat down, tapping out the commands that brought the display above the table to life. Virtual windows popped up, one showing a wide-angle view of the hangar deck on the assault transport *Haboob*.

The main display zoomed in on *Haboob*, the exterior shot automatically compiled by the fleet's sensors from every warship with a view of that transport. The Midway freighter hung near *Haboob*, the two ships apparently unmoving against the background of infinite stars and infinite space. Even after so many years in space driving ships, Geary always had to remind himself that the ships, which looked motionless, were actually traveling at great speed as they orbited the star Midway. It was only because of the huge distances involved and the lack of anything nearby to scale their movement against that they appeared still.

Four shuttles were on their way to *Haboob*, making the short crossing from the freighter to the Alliance transport.

"I thought we were only dropping off eighteen of the former enigma prisoners," Desjani remarked. "That's a lot of shuttles for eighteen human passengers."

"They're unusual passengers," Geary replied. He checked the manifest for each shuttle, seeing a long list of medical and technical personnel as well as a couple of security officers on each craft. "Only two cops per shuttle. I expected more."

"From Syndics, yeah," she agreed, peering at the manifests. "Maybe some of those docs and techs are security muscle, too."

"Maybe." Desjani didn't trust the people here. He didn't entirely trust them, either. He could only hope that the home the former prisoners sought to return to would treat them better than the enigmas had.

Dr. Nasr's image appeared in a separate window. "Admiral." He acknowledged Geary. "Captain," he said to Desjani.

"How are you feeling about this?" Geary asked.

"The best option from a lot of less-than-perfect options," Nasr replied. "I still believe that."

Desjani grimaced. "I can't imagine wanting to go back under control of the Syndics."

"But they *are* Syndics," the doctor said. "Their families live here or nearby. And Midway is no longer ruled by the Syndics, so even those who once seemed hesitant are now eager to return to their native stars. I have talked to all eighteen within the last hour, and I am convinced all sincerely wish to leave us here."

"Then we will respect their wishes," Geary said. That would only leave three hundred fifteen more former enigma prisoners to deal with somehow. "I wish we had been able to find out why the enigmas had kept the number of prisoners at exactly three hundred thirty-three," he commented to Tanya Desjani.

She snorted. "Add that to the list. We found out damned little about the enigmas except that they're insanely protective of any information about them. We're breaking up the enigmas' little number game, though. It would probably drive them crazy if they knew," Tanya added in a way that made it clear the prospect of inflicting mental anguish on enigmas didn't bother her at all. "Are you sure the people here will treat well the former prisoners we're dropping off and won't treat them all like lab rats?"

"No."

The single word might have inspired another comment from Desjani, but the way he said it made her glance at him and remain silent. She had come to know him pretty well, too.

The video feed from the assault transport *Haboob* provided crystal-clear images of what must be the entire group of former prisoners clustered together in the transport's starboard loading area. Having spent so long confined in their small world and knowing only themselves, the people freed from the enigmas tended to bunch together at all times since their liberation. Now they formed a tight group in which the eighteen who were to leave the others could be marked by the small Alliance fleet duffel bags they carried, which held the tiny amount of personal possessions they had brought from their asteroid prison or acquired on the voyage back here.

The Marines standing guard around the edges of the loading area were relaxed, talking among themselves. The former prisoners of the enigmas had caused no trouble since arriving on *Haboob*, acting as if they feared the slightest misstep would result in their being sent back to their confinement. That anxiety had caused the fleet medical personnel no end of anguish as they tried to reassure their patients, but as far as the Marines responsible for good order and discipline aboard *Haboob* were concerned, it had made their job a lot easier.

Lights glowed above four main hatches into the loading area as the Midway shuttles finished docking and sealed their own accesses to the transport's. The Alliance Marines stiffened into alert postures as the lights came on, fingering the weapons they held. The Midway shuttles had been built by the Syndicate Worlds and were piloted and crewed by men and women who had fought for the Syndicate Worlds. No one on *Haboob* was going to relax while those shuttles and those men and women were aboard.

The civilian specialists from Midway came out first. Someone had been smart enough not to lead with military personnel. A group led by Dr. Nasr went forward to meet them. Geary didn't bother zooming in on the meeting or activating audio from Dr. Nasr's feed. Even from a distance the routine nature of introductions and the sizing up of each other that occurred whenever two groups of experts met could be easily made out.

Geary studied the civilians from Midway, seeing no signs of the various standard Syndic garments that had been required wear in different levels of the Syndicate Worlds organizational hierarchies. "At least somebody had the sense not to send people wearing Syndic suits."

After the last doctors and technicians boarded *Haboob*, they were followed by the four pilots from the shuttles. The pilots gathered in their own small group near the hatches as the civilians from Midway met with the Alliance medical personnel.

Desjani nodded. "And the pilots have uniforms different from Syndic ones. The outfits the officers on the warships are wearing look like modified Syndic gear, but those shuttle pilots have on entirely new outfits." It was hard to tell from her voice whether she approved of that or thought it just one more Syndic trick.

The anxious former prisoners of the enigmas watched the people from Midway as if searching for anyone they knew. The Marines watched the specialists from Midway and the prisoners. A group of Alliance fleet officers and Marine officers came into the loading area as well, stopping almost immediately to look curiously at everyone else. Sightseers. Anytime anything out of the ordinary took place, anyone without other duties would come to have a look around.

"Admiral?" Dr. Nasr spoke with unusual abruptness. "The officer in charge here wants to know if it is all right for these nonassigned people to be present."

"The looky-loos?" Geary asked. "Why not?"

"That was my opinion as well, but the operational officers here required another opinion."

"I see. Tell them the admiral authorizes and approves the presence of nonassigned personnel to witness the event."

As unusual as this event was, the officious attempt to chase away unauthorized personnel felt reassuringly routine to Geary. But when he looked at Desjani, he saw worry riding her brow. "What's the matter?"

"What are they doing?"

"The specialists from Midway? They're getting all the information they can about the people they're taking. Dr. Nasr told me the data handover was coordinated well in advance of this meeting. Medical records, any treatments since we picked them up, records of the tests we ran on them to ensure they didn't have enigma poisons or plagues implanted in them. That sort of thing."

"It looks," Desjani said in a wondering voice, "like any other handoff of people."

"Of course it—" Geary stopped speaking as he realized that Desjani had never seen this sort of thing happen. No one living had, except for him. Before the war, there had been peaceful encounters between the Alliance and the Syndicate Worlds. He had viewed some of them firsthand when official delegations had met. But there had been no such meetings for a long time. As part of the degeneration of the conduct of the century-long war, the two sides had stopped talking to each other at all. If they met, it was in combat, or as prisoner and captor. "That's how it's supposed to work," he finished.

Desjani didn't answer, pointing to draw his attention as one of the Midway shuttle pilots abruptly turned toward the Alliance fleet officers and Marines watching the process and walked toward them, her face determined. Even from a wide-angle image, Geary had no trouble spotting the way tension ramped up inside the loading area at the pilot's movement, the Alliance Marines visibly clicking off safeties on their weapons though still holding them at port arms.

But the shuttle pilot stopped a few meters short of the Alliance officers and looked at them as if baffled. "I— My pardon. How do I say? Can you... will you... tell me something?"

"Maybe," one of the fleet officers replied in noncommittal tones. "What is it?"

"Were you," the shuttle pilot continued, her words halting, "were any of you at Lakota? When this fleet fought there?"

After a pause, one of the Alliance fleet officers nodded. "Not on this ship. *Haboob* wasn't with the fleet then. But I was there."

"My brother died at Lakota," the shuttle pilot said, each word now blunt and abrupt. "I don't know anything about it. I was hoping... you might know how he died."

The stiff postures and expressions of the Alliance officers relaxed slightly. "There were several different engagements," the one who admitted being at Lakota said.

"He was on a light cruiser. CL-901."

"I'm sorry." The officer sounded as if he meant it, and he probably did. This was the sort of thing anyone who had served in the war could empathize with. "We didn't know the designations of the ships we fought."

The pilot bit her lip, looking downward, then back at the Alliance officers. "I heard you took prisoners. Under Black Jack's command. There were rumors."

"We did. We *do*. But not at Lakota. We didn't get a chance." The Alliance officer hesitated, then asked his own question. "Do you know anything about what happened there?"

"No. Security. We never heard anything official except the usual lies. Even the news that my brother had died there came to me by back channels."

"The hypernet gate at Lakota collapsed. There was a Syndic flotilla guarding it, and I guess they had orders to destroy it if we beat the rest of the Syndic forces at Lakota. They fired on the tethers."

The shuttle pilot twitched, her eyes shutting tightly, before she regained control and opened them again. "They didn't know. We didn't hear until after we killed the snakes. Then we found out what happens when gates collapse. They didn't know," she repeated.

"We already guessed they couldn't have known. It was suicide. Those ships probably never knew what hit them. The shock wave spread through Lakota and wiped out escape pods, merchant ships, anything that didn't have decent shields. We were lucky. We were far enough from the gate that the shock wave that hit us had spread out and couldn't do much damage to us. It tore up that star system, though. I'm sorry, but I can't tell you what happened to your brother."

The shuttle pilot nodded, her face working as emotions came and went. "That's all right. I know how it is."

"You a warship shuttle driver?"

"No." She jerked a thumb at the shoulder patch on her uniform. "Ground forces. Aerospace."

"Regular flights in atmosphere? Storms and wind and fog? Better you than me."

The shuttle pilot smiled very briefly. "It gets hairy sometimes, but nothing we can't handle. I work for General Drakon. He doesn't send workers anywhere he wouldn't go himself."

"What do you do for General Drakon?" a Marine officer asked.

"Planetary defense actions and ground forces support, usually. I was at Taroa for that op, where we helped kick the Syndicate out of that star system, too. General Drakon tapped us for this run because the Midway mobile forces—I mean, the Midway warship flotilla—doesn't have many shuttles."

The Alliance officers exchanged glances. "What was that about snakes?" another fleet officer asked. "You said you killed snakes?"

"Snakes. Internal Security Service agents. Syndicate secret police." The shuttle pilot looked like she wanted to spit but refrained from the action. "They used to run everything. Always watching, looking over your shoulder, hauling people away to labor camps if you did anything wrong, or if they suspected you, or if they just wanted to. We killed them. Wiped them out in this star system." She straightened, her gaze fierce now. "We're free of them. We'll die before we let them back in control here. Nobody owns us. Not any corporation. Not any CEO. Not anymore."

"You're not Syndics?" another of the fleet officers asked with obvious skepticism.

"Syndicate? No! Never again. We are free. We'll die free before we become slaves of the Syndicate again." She turned to go, then looked back at the Alliance officers, uncertain once more. "You… have my thanks."

"Sorry we couldn't tell you what happened to your brother."

"You told me what you knew, and that's a lot more than I

knew." She paused, then came to attention and saluted in the Syndic fashion, right arm coming across so her fist rapped her left breast. Turning again before the Alliance officers could decide whether or not to return the salute, she walked back toward the other shuttle pilots.

"Hey," one of the Alliance officers called sharply.

The shuttle pilot jerked as if she had expected a bullet instead of a shout, then turned back to face them.

"Tell me one thing." The voice of the Alliance officer was openly hostile, angry but also puzzled. "One thing I never understood. Why? Why the hell did you attack the Alliance?"

"Us? Attack? We did not—"

"Not now. A century ago. Why did the Syndicate Worlds start that damned war in the first place?"

This time the shuttle pilot just stared for a long moment, her face working. When her voice finally came out, it was half-strangled by emotion. "They told us you started it. The Syndicate. They taught us that *we'd* been attacked."

"We didn't—" the Alliance officer began hotly.

"No! *I believe you!* Our government lied to us about everything! Why the hell wouldn't they have lied about that as well?"

She spun on her heel and stumbled back to the other shuttle pilots.

Geary glanced at Desjani, trying to judge her reaction, but Tanya wasn't revealing anything this time. "What's your impression?" he asked.

Desjani shrugged. "If she's faking her feelings about the Syndicate Worlds, she's a great actor."

"I noticed that. When she talked about the, uh, snakes, it sounded like she had personally slit a few of their throats."

"Why did they fight?" Desjani said in a low, angry voice. "They hated the Syndicate Worlds, they hated those snakes. What the hell were they fighting for? Why the hell did they kill so many people when they hated their own government?"

"I don't know." Or did he? "We know they thought they were defending their own people from us."

"By attacking us?" Desjani asked, her tone now savage.

"They'd been told we were the aggressors. I'm not saying they were right, Tanya. I'm not saying they should have fought. Their own efforts kept alive the Syndicate Worlds that they hated. It was stupid. But they must have thought they were doing the only thing they could."

"As long as you're not excusing them," she muttered.

"I lost a lot, too, Tanya."

She sat silent for a minute, then nodded. "You did. Well, if I have to choose between former Syndics who now hate the Syndicate Worlds, or others like the Syndicate Worlds, the enigmas, and the Kicks, I guess I can give the ex-Syndics a chance."

On *Haboob's* loading dock, the turnover process must have been completed. The eighteen former prisoners who were leaving walked slowly in their own tight group toward the hatches leading to the shuttles.

And then the other three hundred fifteen former prisoners surged after them en masse, crying out a babble of pleas and shouts. The Marine guards, taken totally by surprise, jolted into motion, trying to stop the sudden mob with yells and threats. The doctors and technicians from both sides, as startled as the

Marines, milled about, their own movements and cries adding to the confusion.

"What the hell is going on?" Geary demanded.

4

It took a couple of long minutes before the Marines, assisted by extra personnel who had been standing by in case they were needed, corralled the agitated former prisoners and shouted them into a tight group, shivering and whimpering but otherwise quiet. With the situation calmed enough, Dr. Nasr spoke to Geary over the bevy of voices in the loading area. "Admiral, we have a situation."

"I noticed," Geary snapped, trying not to sound too angry. "What's the problem? Did the eighteen who were going to leave decide not to stay at Midway?"

"No, Admiral. We're still trying to sort things out, but as far as I can determine, now they *all* want to get off and stay at Midway."

"All?" Geary repeated.

"Yes. All three hundred thirty-three of them."

Geary heard a thudding sound and glanced over the see that Tanya, looking pained, had slapped her palm against her forehead.

He felt the same way. "How many times did we already ask them if they wanted to stay here?"

Dr. Nasr came as close to rolling his eyes as a senior medical officer could. "On the record, with official refusals? Twenty times, Admiral. But they changed their minds when they saw the others going. They want to stay together. They want to go home. This isn't home for the other three-hundred-odd former prisoners, but it's a lot closer to their previous homes than Varandal or any other point in Alliance space. And we are Alliance. We frighten them."

"We frighten them?" Desjani asked, incredulous. "Do they think Syndic CEOs are warm and cuddly? Did they hear that shuttle pilot talking about snakes?"

"Syndic CEOs, the entire Syndic system, is the devil they know. And they know from hearing that pilot that the snakes are gone from Midway. The pilot is one of them. They believed her where they would not believe us. Faced with separation from those who have been part of their group for decades, they decided to stay together rather than risk the unknowns of the Alliance."

"Doctor," Geary growled, "Midway only agreed to take eighteen."

"We're talking to the representatives from Midway, Admiral." In the wide-view image, Geary could see the civilian specialists and fleet physicians on *Haboob* speaking, arguing, debating, and, in general, looking as frustrated as he himself felt, while the panicky former prisoners of the enigmas wailed and clamored in the background. "They seem willing to take the others, and their freighter has the capacity though it will be crowded, but they need high-level approval."

Which would take nearly five hours since the planet where

President Iceni and General Drakon were located was currently about two and a half light-hours from where the Alliance fleet was orbiting. "Damn."

Tanya was wisely saying nothing, letting him burn off steam before he spoke again.

"All right," Geary finally said. "Should we send the former prisoners back to their rooms while we wait to hear from the authorities on Midway?"

"No!" Dr. Nasr protested. "If they're panicky now, sending them to their rooms as if we're keeping all of them would just add fuel to the fire."

"All right," Geary repeated, trying to sound much calmer than he felt. "Hold them all there on the loading dock. Tell the Midway people to get off a message immediately asking their superiors if they can take all of the liberated prisoners. Have the officer in charge of the loading dock arrange for food and water for everyone who needs it and keep the guards in place."

"Yes, Admiral. I will pass on those instructions."

As Dr. Nasr went to work on his end, Geary shook his head in frustration at the images from *Haboob*, where the assembled former prisoners were now crying and holding on to each other. "I know they're emotional wrecks because of their long confinement by the enigmas, but did they have to make this difficult by changing their minds at the last moment?"

"Like you told me," Tanya said. "They're wrecks. You have spotted the bright side here, right?"

"There's a bright side?" Geary asked, glumly surveying the slowly subsiding mess aboard *Haboob*.

"Hell, yes, there's a bright side. If we dump them all here, they'll be Midway's problem from now on. We'll be free of worrying about them."

He paused, then felt a smile appear on his face. "That's true. I wasn't looking forward to trying to protect them from Alliance researchers and media vultures once we got back. We'll have freed them and taken them home. The honorable and the right thing to do. Hooray for us. What are you doing?"

"Research." Tanya continued tapping some of her controls, zooming a virtual sound pickup in on the Alliance officers who had spoken with the shuttle pilot. "This is a recording from just before our many freed prisoners decided to freak out on us. I want to know what these officers thought of their conversation with that former Syndic."

"Why?"

"Because I don't know the answer, and I want to find out, Admiral, sir." She finished entering her commands. The officers had all been muttering or speaking in low voices, which would normally have made it hard to sort out the conversations they were having with each other. However, the sound systems automatically analyzed everything and broke out each voice digitally, producing a series of phrases that could be heard clearly by Geary and Desjani.

"Lakota was that bad?" "Worse." "Like Kalixa?" "Worse." "What was that about Taroa? We ought to report that." "They called their own cops snakes?" "Not cops. She said secret police or something." "Maybe she was lying." "Hell of a good liar if she was." "How could they believe we started it?" "Bitch." "She lost her brother." "*So did I!*" "We don't trust our own politicians, do we?" "Hell, no." "Syndics are worse. Everybody knows that." "Maybe our government isn't so bad after all." "Not if you compare it to the Syndics."

"The one great virtue of the Syndics," Desjani said, as the recording ended with the beginning of the former prisoners' panic session that swamped the sound pickups with a cacophony of noise. "Everything about the Syndics makes everything else look so much better when weighed against the Syndics."

"That's something I hadn't thought about," Geary admitted. "We've gone through Syndic space once on this mission, and we'll be doing the same on the way back. The personnel in this fleet are seeing firsthand what happens as the Syndicate Worlds falls apart. They're seeing how bad Syndic rule was. No matter what they think of the Alliance government, no matter how unhappy they are with how our government does things or with Alliance policy or with Alliance politicians, they're seeing firsthand how much worse things could be."

Desjani rolled her eyes. "Saying our government is better than the Syndics' isn't exactly high praise. Anything is better than the Syndics. And claiming our politicians are better than Syndic CEOs might generate some debate."

"Not all politicians are the same. Take a look at some of the star systems where Syndic authority has collapsed," Geary suggested. "The people of Midway were lucky."

"Maybe they were lucky. So far, this place hasn't fallen apart. Doesn't mean it won't. You heard that woman, the shuttle pilot. We're free, she said. How long do you think she and others like her are going to keep taking orders from a couple of former CEOs?"

"It depends upon what those former CEOs do," Geary said. "President Iceni has been asking Rione a lot of questions about the different governments in the Alliance. How they maintain order, how stable they are, how they retain popular support."

"She's asking that witch for advice on how to be a good politician? Or maybe Iceni figures that woman has good advice for dictators."

"Tanya, for all of Victoria Rione's faults, she does believe in the Alliance."

"You may think that counterbalances the faults. I don't."

He sighed and stood up. "All right. There's nothing to do now but wait about five hours, at least five hours, to hear what Iceni says about taking all of them."

"Nothing to do?" Desjani asked, getting up as well. "What world are you living in?"

"Dreamworld," Geary admitted. "There are plenty of other things to do."

"That's my admiral." She raised one hand to gently brush a nonexistent speck from Geary's shoulder. "I miss my husband."

"He misses you."

"Hopefully, the admiral will get us home so we can spend a little while off my ship and his flagship. A little off-duty, private time." She stepped back and smiled briefly. "I'll be on the bridge, Admiral."

"I'll be in my stateroom, Captain."

Five hours and ten minutes later a message came in from *Haboob*. "Midway says they will take them all," Dr. Nasr said, looking happier than he had in months.

That had been quick. Iceni must not have spent much time

thinking about it at all. *Does she really care about them and their fates? Or does she see them as something to exploit, a source of information about the enigmas and leverage with the Syndic government and other star systems? The more, the better.*

But those people aren't prisoners. We freed them from imprisonment. They have expressed the desire to leave this fleet here at Midway, and Midway has agreed to take them. Do I have any choice but to hope Iceni does the decent thing?

No, I don't. "Do you recommend that we turn them all over to Midway?" Geary asked, wanting that to be part of the official record.

"That is my recommendation, Admiral. I think the authorities here will treat in a civilized fashion those we liberated from the enigmas."

"Then get them all on those shuttles. It'll take a few extra runs, but get it done."

One headache disposed of. Too bad there were a lot more left.

But now he could set a departure time. He had no trouble imagining how well received the news would be that the fleet was finally continuing its voyage home.

Humanity had built many large objects since the first hand grasped the first tool. Some of those objects had seemed awesomely large to those who constructed them, only to eventually be eclipsed by some new work that dwarfed what came before.

But the hypernet gates were in a class of their own. The many "tethers" that held together a matrix of energy formed a circle so large that even a human battleship appeared small as it approached a gate. Geary's entire fleet, hundreds of warships, could enter a gate simultaneously. And the net created by the gates was unimaginably huge, spanning a volume hundreds of light-years across and granting direct access to scores of star systems.

The hypernet gate at Midway was close now, looming in space before the Alliance warships, looking like exactly what it was—a gateway to somewhere else.

Geary had his fleet together again, all of the warships in one titanic, egg-shaped formation that would serve well for defense but convey no offensive intent. In the most protected part of the oval were the assault transports, the auxiliaries, and the captured Kick superbattleship, the *Invincible*. Near those ships were most of the battleships in the fleet, forming an armored shell close to the weakest, most valuable units. Ranged outward from them were the battle cruisers, the heavy cruisers, the light cruisers, and the destroyers.

Battered and tired as they were—the crews as well as the ships— they still looked magnificent.

Geary took his eyes away from the reassuring image of strength on his display, carefully touching his comm control. "Captain Bradamont, we're about to depart. I have every confidence in you. Use your best judgment. To the honor of our ancestors, Admiral Geary, out."

He sighed, hoping that he had made the right decision about leaving Bradamont here as a liaison officer. At times it had felt far too much as if he were abandoning a fellow officer to the clutches of an enemy. But Bradamont had volunteered when given the opportunity. Her presence at Midway might make a big difference in the survival of Midway's independence and provide a means to learn how sincere President Iceni was about her claims to be seeking a freer form of government to replace the Syndic tyranny. "Let's go, Tanya."

"Indras?" Desjani asked, her hand poised over the input for the hypernet key.

"Yes. That's the quickest way back to the Alliance." Geary watched her selecting the name of the star. Not every star had a hypernet gate. Not even close, given how expensive the gates were to construct. And the only thing allowing this Alliance fleet to use the Syndic hypernet was a Syndic hypernet key acquired as part of a complex Syndic plot to destroy the Alliance, a plot that had very badly backfired on the Syndicate Worlds.

He waited for the simple procedure to be complete, but instead of indicating that all was ready, Desjani gave him a concerned look. "The Syndic hypernet says it can't access a gate at Indras."

"Something happened to the gate at Indras?"

"Must have." She bit her lip, eyeing her display. "Kalixa would have been the next best alternative, but we know Kalixa's gate is gone. How about Praja?"

He studied his own display, then nodded. "Go for Praja."

Several seconds passed, then Desjani blew out a long breath. "No access to a gate at Praja."

"Try Kachin."

Another pause, then she shook her head. "No access."

"Could there be something wrong with our key? Could the Syndics have somehow reprogrammed their hypernet so our key won't work in it anymore?"

"Admiral, I have no idea. I'm just a ship driver."

Already thrown off-balance by this totally unexpected hurdle,

Geary felt an irrational stab of annoyance at her reply but recognized it as being candid and accurate. "Let's ask someone who might know." He tapped in some commands. "Captain Hiyen, Commander Neeson," he said, as his message went out to the commanders of *Reprisal* and *Implacable*. "We have a problem." He explained what had happened, then sat back to wait for replies that would take a few seconds at least. Hiyen and Neeson were the nearest things to experts on the hypernet that he had left. Having to depend on their limited expertise was not reassuring when something unusual happened, especially given how little humanity really understood about the hypernet.

"We're getting close to the gate," Desjani murmured, as if to herself.

Geary jerked, annoyed with himself this time at not staying on top of the entire situation. "All units in First Fleet, immediate execute, alter course starboard one eight zero, reduce velocity to point zero two light." The entire formation would turn around, each individual ship pivoting in place, then using her main drives to first brake velocity in the fleet's original direction, then accelerate back along the track they had come, though at a much slower pace. "Thank you, Captain Desjani," he muttered.

She just nodded slightly in reply, eyes still on her display.

Yet another reason why I love that woman, Geary thought, trying not to get angry at this unexpected delay or too worried yet about the consequences if this fleet had to jump star by star back to Alliance space.

"Admiral," Captain Hiyen said as his image appeared in a virtual window before Geary, "a hypernet cannot be reprogrammed. Not unless everything we know is wrong."

"You're saying the problem cannot be with our key, or with the Syndic hypernet having been set to not accept our key?"

"Yes, Admiral. Not unless the key has failed, and we would know if that had happened because a broken key wouldn't even link to the gate here."

Commander Neeson's face had appeared next to Captain Hiyen's. "I agree, Admiral. I suggest a test, though. Try a gate near here, somewhere not too far from Midway."

Geary frowned, turning to Desjani. "What's the closest hypernet gate?"

"Taniwah." She tapped in the commands. "Nope. No access."

"Admiral," Neeson said, "try the 'gate listing' command."

"There's a gate listing command?" Desjani asked. "What do you know. There is. Admiral, when the Syndics told you they had a device to keep anyone like the enigmas from collapsing their entire hypernet by remote signal, did they say they had actually installed that device?"

"Yes," Geary said. "Aren't there any gates showing up?"

"One. Sobek."

"Only *one?* Sobek?" Not remembering from the name where it was, he had to enter that one into his display, seeing a star illuminate in response. "That's not too far from the border. Not as close as Indras, but only... three or four jumps from Varandal." His relief rapidly sank beneath a wave of anxiety. "How could the Syndics only have one gate left in their hypernet? Two, counting this one."

"I don't know, sir," Captain Hiyen said. "If the Syndics have lost the rest of their hypernet, it will have catastrophic impacts on their economy as well as on their ability to move military forces. They could not have deliberately done that just to limit our options to only Sobek."

Neeson shook his head. "When that Syndic flotilla used the gate to leave here, they didn't seem to run into any difficulties."

"Then what is going on?" Geary demanded.

"I don't know, Admiral."

Wishing for the thousandth time that the brilliant theorist Captain Cresida had not died during the battle at Varandal, Geary hit a different comm control. "President Iceni, we have encountered an unusual situation."

Hypernet gates were always positioned near the outer edges of a star system, and Midway's was no exception. It took several hours for Geary's message to reach the primary inhabited world and an answer to be received.

With a restive fleet at Geary's back, eager to head home and abruptly stymied in its departure, it was amazing how long that period of time could feel.

When her reply eventually showed up, President Iceni did not look any happier than Geary felt. "A freighter arrived two days ago from the gate with Nanggal and did not report any problems. I assure you that we are extremely concerned by the news you have given us. We cannot explain the problems you are having accessing gates elsewhere in the Syndicate hypernet. My information prior to our break with the Syndicate was that every standing gate had already been equipped to prevent collapse by remote means. I cannot believe that the new government on Prime would have deliberately destroyed almost all of their hypernet. The impact on corporate activity and profits would be incalculable.

"That said, we have no idea what has happened. There are no indications that our own gate is suffering any problems or malfunctions. We have closely monitored it for any signs of software or hardware sabotage, especially during the period when CEO Boyens's flotilla was in this star system.

"If you discover anything, or find any anomalies in the operation of the gate, we would be grateful if you would provide us with that information. For the people. Iceni, out."

Geary rubbed his mouth and chin with one hand, trying to think. "Emissary Rione, I would appreciate your assessment of President Iceni's latest message."

"She could be lying," Rione began, "but I don't think she is. Iceni does appear to be genuinely worried."

"They want us to stay here," Geary said. "This problem with the gate could offer them the means to keep us here."

"She asked us to tell her what was wrong," Rione reminded him. "She did not say they were working on it, did not claim any malfunction here, did not do any of the things someone would do if they were trying to string us along. Moreover, one other gate has been left accessible. Why would they allow access to any gate, especially one in the region we wish to go to, if they wished to keep us here?"

"Admiral," Emissary Charban began diffidently, "if this is the work of the Syndic government, and if it were a ground forces situation, and if all paths in the direction I wanted to go but one were blocked, I would wonder why that one path had been left open."

Geary lowered his hand and gazed at Charban. "A trap? An ambush?"

"I would expect such, yes."

"He's right," Desjani said. Her once-low opinion of Charban had improved a great deal lately. "As much as I don't trust the used-to-be Syndics here at Midway, I can't think of any reason they would leave us a path out if they wanted us to stay."

"And we know," Charban continued, "who controls the gates to which we no longer have access."

"The Syndics," Geary said. "But that comes back to the initial problem. How could slowing us down, or luring us into an ambush, possibly be worth the cost to the Syndic government of destroying almost their entire hypernet?"

"We can't know the answer to that," Rione said. "Even the presence of the captured Kick warship and the Dancer emissaries with us could not explain it. I agree that whatever led to this, it appears designed to force us to go to Sobek. We have to assume that something awaits us there."

"But what?" Geary demanded. "The Syndics couldn't possibly have enough warships to threaten this fleet."

"They still have the gate at Sobek," Desjani pointed out. "They could collapse it and wipe us out, along with the Dancer ships and *Invincible*."

"Which would also render the hypernet gate here at Midway useless," Rione said. "Since it would no longer be connected to any other gates. Yet such a strategy would be like committing suicide to prevent your enemy from killing you. Without the Syndic hypernet, the Syndicate Worlds' government would have no hope of holding together what is left of their empire."

"The Syndics have done stupid things before," Geary said.

"Such as starting the war that only recently ended?" Rione replied. "That is true. But the CEOs ruling the Syndicate Worlds a century ago could have deluded themselves into believing they could win that war. There is no possible scenario in which the Syndicate Worlds today could survive the loss of its entire hypernet."

He glowered at his display. The commanding officers of his ships were reporting that their crews were restless, agitated over the abrupt halt to their voyage home. Even if that weren't a consideration, even if morale were excellent, it would leave the same dilemma. The only Syndic gate they could access was at Sobek. If they didn't use Sobek, they would have to spend several months jumping from star to star to reach Alliance space again, opening themselves up to additional obstacles and dangers at every star. "What is your recommendation, Captain Desjani?"

Tanya made a face. "We have to go to Sobek. But we need to be ready for a fight there."

"I agree," Charban said.

"Emissary Rione?" Geary asked.

She took a moment to answer, gazing fixedly outward, then nodded. "I cannot see any alternative that is realistic. I agree we must go to Sobek."

"We could wait here," Geary pointed out.

"For how long, Admiral?"

"That's my concern. If the gates except for Sobek are gone, sitting here won't buy us anything. It will just delay our getting home. But I wanted to hear someone else say it so I'd know it wasn't just my impatience talking to me." He gestured to Tanya. "Captain Desjani, enter Sobek as our destination. I'm going to arrange the fleet in a combat formation."

"Sobek entered," she replied. "What do you think might be waiting at Sobek?"

"I have no idea. Maybe nothing is waiting there for us. There's always a chance the enigmas figured out a way around the Syndic anticollapse gear, and Sobek somehow didn't get the message."

"If that were the case, Midway didn't, either," Desjani pointed out. "And Midway is the closest to enigma space."

"Yeah. Sort of weakens that theory, doesn't it?" *How do I arrange the fleet to deal with an indeterminate threat?* "Maybe we'd be best off staying in this formation and doing an evasive maneuver as we leave the gate at Sobek."

"Maybe. Which way do you want to evade? You can be sure the Syndics are trying to spot patterns in which way you go."

Geary hesitated, then looked at Charban. "Pick a number between one and three hundred fifty-nine."

Charban raised his eyebrows in question, but after a moment spoke up. "Two hundred six."

"Down and to the right," Geary said to Desjani as he input the maneuver. "Is that random enough?"

"Asking a politician who's a retired grand-forces officer? Yeah, that's random."

He got the fleet turned around again, accelerating toward the hypernet gate once more. "We'll be just under point one light speed when we enter the gate. I guess I should tell Iceni what we're doing."

"Or you could let them guess," Desjani suggested.

"Not this time." Geary sent off a brief message to Iceni, then sat back to wait.

He felt a growing tension as the fleet approached the gate, wondering if Sobek, too, would suddenly show up as unable to access. That would leave two alternatives, neither of which would be good. *Funny. I never wanted to go to Sobek. But now I want to get there very badly.* "All units be ready for combat when we exit at Sobek. Any ship facing danger upon exit is authorized to fire immediately."

Charban sounded worried. "What if the Syndics at Sobek have a picket ship at the gate? A HuK or light cruiser?"

"Then I'll apologize for my fleet having destroyed that picket ship," Geary answered with a glare at Charban. "I didn't create this situation. They did."

"They may *want* you to do that, Admiral."

"I'm sorry, but you were right earlier. This smells like an ambush. I won't tie the hands of my ships when we're heading into something that stinks as bad as this does. Have the Dancers been warned?"

Charban shrugged. "As best as we can communicate such a warning, Admiral. Their ships are ready to enter the gate along with ours. I do want to talk to you about the Dancers when you have the time."

"Here we go," Desjani announced. She sounded cheerful, as she usually did when Geary decided to go weapons free on anything that looked Syndic. "Request permission to enter the gate, Admiral."

"Permission granted."

There was no disorientation like that felt going into jump space.

The stars vanished, replaced not with the gray nothingness of jump space but by literally nothing at all.

Geary slumped back, wondering if he would see Midway again. "How long to Sobek?"

"Twenty days," Desjani said.

They were going an immense distance even by interstellar standards. Long ago, it seemed, when he had assumed command of a trapped fleet in the Syndic home star system, she had told him that with hypernet travel, the farther you went, the less time it could take. It was still jarring to be reminded of that, and disturbing not to see the familiar if uncanny gray of jump space or see the unexplained lights of jump space growing and fading randomly around them. *It's strange how Nothing can be more upsetting to me than the weirdness of jump space.*

Charban shook his head. "It's hard enough for me to grasp the velocities that spacecraft travel within star systems. Tens of thousands of kilometers a second is just too fast for my planetary-surface instincts to visualize. What sort of velocity are we traveling now, to go such a distance in such a span of time?"

"We're not actually going any speed at all," Desjani said with a smile. "That's what an expert told me." Her smile slipped, and Geary knew why. Cresida had been that expert, and a good friend of Desjani's. "We're at one gate, then a bit later we're at another gate, but, technically, we didn't travel the distance between them. We just went from being in one place to being at another."

"Does anyone actually understand things like that?" Charban wondered. "Or are we still children, surrounded by things we don't really grasp and poking at a few of them to see what happens?"

"I don't know," Desjani said, turning back to her display, which now showed nothing but the situation aboard *Dauntless*. "I just drive a battle cruiser."

The enforced isolation of hypernet travel, or that in jump space, left a lot of time to get backed-up work accomplished. Geary, sitting at his stateroom table and sourly eyeing the long list of backed-up items he still had to go through, was trying to decide whether that was a good or a bad thing. *Why did I want to be an admiral? Oh, yeah, I didn't ever want to be an admiral. I just wanted to do my job and do it well. Rise to command of a ship. But command of a fleet? A fleet far larger than the Alliance fleet that existed before the war? And be responsible for every man and woman, and now Dancer as well, who is part of that fleet? Nope, I never wanted that. But I've got it.*

His hatch alert chimed.

Trying to not look too relieved at the diversion from administrative tasks, Geary spun in his seat to face the hatch and tapped an entry authorization.

He had half hoped it might be Tanya, visiting to snatch a few moments of being together without being under the eyes of the entire crew, or maybe Rione, ready to spill a few more clues about her mysterious secret orders. Instead, the hatch opened to reveal the earnest and melancholy face of Emissary Charban. "Have you a few moments, Admiral?"

"Certainly. Come on in." He didn't hesitate to offer his time, as he would have much earlier in the mission. Charban had come aboard *Dauntless* tagged as an aspiring politician, a retired general who had been sorely disillusioned about the usefulness of violence in accomplishing anything as he watched men and women die and little change. But Geary had come to see that Charban was not a fool or a phony. He was a tired man who had seen too much death but could still think and reason well enough to spot things that others could not.

Increasingly, Charban had emerged as the primary point of contact with the Dancers, even Rione giving way to him. Dr. Setin had complained about that before the fleet entered the gate at Midway. *"Why is an amateur being given preference in dealing with this alien species?"*

"Because the alien species keeps asking specifically to deal with him," Geary had pointed out. He knew that thanks to reports from Setin's associate Dr. Shwartz.

"He is an amateur. We have spent our entire academic careers preparing for communication and contact with a nonhuman intelligence!"

"Yes, Dr. Setin, I understand. I will look into the matter and see what should be done." Dr. Setin had spent an academic career preparing to communicate with a nonhuman intelligence but, ironically, wasn't able to identify a classic human bureaucratic brush-off when he received one.

"May I speak with you about the Dancers?" Charban asked Geary as the emissary entered the stateroom.

"Have a seat. I hope this is good news."

Charban grimaced as he sat down opposite Geary. "The experts tell me I am wrong."

"Then you've got good grounds for thinking you may be right," Geary said. "Dr. Shwartz told me those academic experts, herself included, spent their entire careers up until now theorizing about intelligent aliens, and now that they've finally encountered the real things, they're having trouble adjusting to the fact that the realities aren't matching a lot of their theories. What in particular is this about?"

"Our attempts to communicate better with the Dancers." Charban's expression shifted into exasperation, then worry. "I am not certain they are being cooperative."

Having had the same suspicion growing in him for a few weeks now, and not happy at all with the idea that the Dancers might not be playing straight with their human contacts, Geary was less than thrilled to hear that someone else shared his worries. He took a deep breath. "Explain, please."

"It's hard to explain an impression," Charban complained. "Not scientific at all, I am told. You know we have been making slow progress in communicating with the Dancers. *Very* slow progress."

Geary nodded. "They're so very different from us that the slow progress isn't surprising anyone. We have such a huge gap to cross between our species in order to establish the meaning of words and concepts. But I have been wondering why even the basic concepts are coming so slowly."

Charban smiled crookedly. "You've been reading the reports from our experts," he noted. "That is all true. But…" He paused, frowning in thought. "I have the impression that the Dancers are deliberately slow-pedaling the process, that it is taking far longer than it could if they went at the pace of which they are capable."

"Do you have any impression why?"

"You're taking me seriously? Thank you."

"Emissary Charban," Geary said, "you've proven remarkably

good at grasping the way the Dancers think. You figured out why the enigmas fear us so. You explained Kick behavior before any of the rest of us figured it out. You have a talent for this. Of course I am taking you seriously."

This time Charban's smile was genuine. "I thank you again. It has been a humbling and frustrating experience for me since leaving the military, Admiral. Diplomats and politicians know much I do not and yet seem to miss things obvious to me. Our experts in nonhuman intelligent species have a vast formation of advanced degrees following them around, yet often circle around answers instead of seeing them."

"Our experts in nonhuman intelligent species," Geary said dryly, "had never actually known anything about any real nonhuman intelligent species until they joined us on this mission. When it comes to real aliens, you seem to have a feel for the right answers."

"Would you recommend me for a position working with such aliens?" Charban asked. "I should tell you that our experts would be very put out by an amateur like me getting such a job over them."

"All of our experts?"

"Not Dr. Shwartz."

"That doesn't surprise me. Dr. Shwartz seems to be unique among them in recognizing that real-life experience can sometimes be more valuable than academic degrees. But understanding the Dancers is a unique challenge."

Charban frowned. "I don't know why the Dancers would be delaying more open communications with us. I don't have a sense of ill intent. I don't have any sense of any reason. What I do have is a feeling that they are choosing to go slow on this."

Geary looked toward the star display, thinking. "If they can understand us better than they are letting on…"

"It is my feeling that is the case."

"But are keeping their own speech with us at basic levels…" Geary shook his head. "That would mean they can understand what we're saying but would be pretending not to be able to tell us things."

"Yes." Charban nodded toward the star display. "And what would they not want to tell us?"

The potential answers to that question were almost infinite. Geary shook his head once more. "If they think in patterns, as you and Dr. Shwartz suggested, they might be seeing a pattern they don't want to tell us about. What kind of questions are they being asked?"

"All sorts of things. Basic information about themselves, about other alien species, scientific and technical questions, what they know of us, and how long they've known of us." Charban shrugged. "Pick your possible secret."

"But the experts disagree with you?"

"Yes. Except Dr. Shwartz. She listens. I don't know if she agrees, but she's reserving judgment."

Geary caught Charban's eyes. "Tell me your gut feeling. When we take the Dancers back with us to Alliance territory, should we regard them as a potential danger?"

"My gut feeling, Admiral, is that they've already been to Alliance space, that they've been watching us for a long time. If they meant to harm us, as the enigmas did, I believe they have had opportunity. Instead, I *think* they have been studying us. They——" Charban broke off speaking, showing dawning realization. "That could be it. If they've been watching us, they may have seen a pattern. Something involving us. A pattern or patterns that are still playing out."

An odd sense of cold ran down Geary's back. "Something they see coming. Something they don't want to tell us."

"It could be." Charban spread his hands. "Telling us might change the pattern. Change what we do and how we do it."

Geary leaned forward and adjusted the view of the star field, expanding it to include all of human space. "We know what's happening to the Syndicate Worlds right now. We know some of the strains the Alliance is under."

Charban nodded slowly. "And we know that pattern from human history. Great empires, powerful alliances, grow and flourish, then weaken and fall. And afterwards, cultural and political fragmentation, wars, declines in population, standards of living, scientific progress, and much else." His smile now seemed wan and tentative. "I would not wish to tell any friend of mine that sort of prophecy for their future."

"They don't know us, General. Not that well," Geary said, scarcely noting that he had referred to Charban's old rank rather than his current position as emissary. "Patterns can change. They can be altered."

"They can." Charban laughed. "Is that the Dancers' secret? They believe they know what we should do, but if they tell us, it will change what we do? Or they do not know what we will do but do not wish to influence our actions? The Observer Effect, applied to relations to alien species."

"The Observer Effect?"

"Sort of an offshoot of Heisenberg's Uncertainty Principle and Schrödinger's cat."

"I see," Geary said in the way that conveyed that he didn't, in fact, see at all.

This time Charban smiled. "A dissolute youth spent partly in the realms of physics left me with bits of knowledge. Basically, the Observer Effect says that the act of observing something alters the outcome. It's been proven in physics. Even with particles like photons. If you're watching them, they act differently. It's very strange, but it's true. Social scientists still debate whether that concept also applies to their work. But if the Dancers believe that what they tell us can change what we do, they might be slow-pedaling communication for just that reason."

"That could be." Geary gave Charban a questioning look. "The Dancers might have been watching us for a long time, watching us fight that war for the last century. But they only intervened very recently, during the battle with the enigmas at Midway Star System."

"The difference is that now we know we're being observed," Charban said. "However long they have been watching us, we weren't aware of it before. Once we came to them, arriving in a star system where their ships were, that fundamental fact changed."

"That could be it," Geary agreed. "Or is that too simple an answer? Keep doing your best to find out."

"I always do my best, Admiral."

As Charban got up and turned to go, Geary stopped him. "Emissary Charban, if you had received secret orders from the government, would you tell me?"

Charban looked Geary in the eyes and nodded. "I wasn't sent

to do anything to mess you up, Admiral. I think I was sent in the expectation that I would mess things up thanks to my lack of political experience and my disillusionment with the ability of weaponry to resolve issues short of genocide."

"If they expected you to just cause trouble for me, you've exceeded expectations in the right way as far as I'm concerned."

The emissary grinned. "It's not so hard to do when the bar is set so low."

"In this fleet, it's harder to set the bar lower than *politician*," Geary said. "I wish more people would realize how much someone like Victoria Rione has contributed to what we've achieved. And how much someone like you has contributed."

"Thank you, Admiral." Charban shook his head. "But I don't think I'll ever be a politician. I thought I wanted to do that, but after working with the Dancers, I want to continue doing that a lot more."

"I'll do my best to see that you are allowed to continue doing that. Who would have guessed that a career leading ground forces troops would have suited you so well for dealing with different sorts of minds?"

Charban, halfway out the hatch, turned and smiled again. "My career involved a lot of interaction with the aerospace forces, and the fleet, and Marines. If you want to talk about different sorts of minds, all of those were good practice for trying to understand alien ways of thinking."

The hatch closed behind Charban, and Geary turned back to his work. *Results of fleet mess facility cleanliness inspections. Ancestors help me.* Even at the best of times, concentrating on that kind of important but tedious matter was difficult. Right now… "Emissary Rione, are you free to talk?"

"Your place or mine?" her image asked as it appeared near his desk.

"This is fine." For once he didn't have to be too worried about someone's intercepting a conversation. "How is Commander Benan?"

"Sedated."

"Uh…"

"And you're wondering why I'm not in tears of despair because my husband is under sedation?" she asked. "Because being sedated is the best condition he can be in right now. It keeps him out of trouble, and to be honest, which I know is unusual for me, he's a lot easier to handle that way these days. And we are on our way back, where, one way or another, we will be able to deal with his condition."

He regarded Rione's image, wondering exactly what she meant by "deal with his condition." To say that she wanted both Benan cured of his mental block and vengeance against whoever had ordered that mental block was to put it mildly. Even after the months he had known her, Geary was still not certain just how far Rione would go to accomplish something she had resolved on. He did know he wouldn't want to be someone she had resolved to go after. "I promised to get that block lifted, and I will."

"You'll threaten the Alliance grand council if necessary? No, you don't have to promise to do that. I'll threaten the grand council, and they'll know I mean it. Were you just calling to see how I was feeling?"

"Partly," he said. "But I wanted your opinion of the leaders of

Midway now that we've had a week away from them."

"You mean Iceni and Drakon, or others as well?" Rione asked.

"Just those two," Geary said. "The self-styled president and the newly minted general. I think they're the only ones in that star system who count."

"I strongly suspect you're wrong about that. There are hidden currents moving in the star system. I could only observe things from afar, but I am certain of it."

Geary looked at her dubiously. "Lieutenant Iger's intelligence team didn't report anything like that in their analysis of the situation at Midway."

Her smile was scornful. "Lieutenant Iger is not bad at all when it comes to collecting intelligence, but political analysis? I think you'd be well advised to listen to someone who knows politics from the inside. I also think you already know that since you asked me for my opinion despite Iger's report."

"Are you saying that there's some counterrevolution being planned to regain Syndic control of the star system from within? Or a revolution against the revolution of Iceni and Drakon to maintain an independent star system but with different leaders?"

"I don't know. There are monsters in the deep, Admiral. Have you ever heard that saying?" Rione leaned back in her chair, closing her eyes. "Neither Iceni nor Drakon are fools. But neither are they all-wise and all-seeing."

Rione opened her eyes and looked over to one side, her expression darkly thoughtful. "I have the distinct impression that President Iceni is making this up as she goes along. There are strong remnants of the Syndicate CEO attitude in her, leading me to think that Iceni planned on a change in title but not a change in function."

"Just what you'd expect from a Syndicate CEO," Geary said. "She wants to stay an absolute ruler."

"Yes, I think she *wanted* to. But. She's already permitted things no Syndicate CEO would have allowed. There seem to be real reforms under way. Iceni may be faking it all, but my gut feeling is that she is pursuing some real changes despite whatever her initial plans were."

He considered that, measuring it against his own impressions of Iceni. "An interesting assessment. What about General Drakon?"

"Ah. General Drakon." Rione smiled with amusement. "No guesses are needed there. He's military, and that's all he wants to be. The Syndics made him play the CEO game."

"That's all? He just wants to be a soldier?"

"Do you find that so hard to understand, Admiral?"

"Those two aides of his. Morgan and... Malin." Geary spoke slowly, trying to put his impressions into words. "They were... not like the sort of aides I would have expected from someone who just wants to be a soldier."

Rione smiled thinly this time. "The assassins? The bodyguards? The trusted agents in tasks above and below the board? I am certain they are all of those things. Remember the environment in which Drakon operated. Such assistants may be as much a matter of survival for him as armor is for one of your battleships."

She paused, then spoke in more serious tones. "We received a lot of reporting from the planet when the bombardment the enigmas launched was on its way. Free-press reports, but also a lot of chatter in personal conversations that your intelligence people have been busy vacuuming up. I assume you have seen the analysis of all that."

"And I assume you have as well."

"Of course. The bombardment would have inflicted massive damage on that world if the Dancers hadn't stopped it, but every report agrees that neither Iceni nor Drakon made any moves to flee the surface. If what we've learned about Drakon so far is right, he has demonstrated loyalty to those who work for him before this, so that action would have been consistent with a man who never bought into the CEO-first-last-and-always attitude of the Syndicate Worlds."

"That's how I felt about him from the messages I've received from him," Geary said. "I felt... well, I felt like he was somebody not all that different from me."

"Be careful who you say that to," Rione advised dryly. "A former Syndic CEO who is a decent commander and cares about those under him? 'Heresy' is too kind a word."

Geary shook his head. "The Syndicate Worlds couldn't have held together as long as it did, couldn't have sustained the war as long at it did, unless there were *some* capable people in positions of authority. Some people who could inspire those under them or make the right decisions regardless of what it meant to them personally. Why people like that worked for a system like that I have no idea, but they must have been there."

"Maybe you should have asked General Drakon," Rione said with every appearance of meaning it.

"Maybe someday I will. But you said Iceni didn't try to run to safety, either. She didn't before, the first time we were here, when it looked like the enigmas were certain to take over this star system."

"It is a pattern," Rione agreed. "At the least, it implies a sense of responsibility consistent with her position of authority. I think both of them can be worked with in the long run, Admiral. More than that, I think if they avoid giving in to Syndic ways of doing things, they might be able to build something at Midway that the Alliance would be happy to do business with."

"Assuming those monsters in the deep don't devour them."

"Assuming that, yes." She looked over to the side again, a flicker of concern appearing before she could suppress it, and he realized that Commander Benan must be lying in his bunk over there in her stateroom. "Is that all, Admiral?"

"Yes. Thank you, Victoria."

The alerts sounding as the fleet exited the hypernet gate at Sobek were cautionary, not full-scale alarms, but Geary still focused as quickly as possible on the objects highlighted on his display. "What are they?"

"Syndic courier ships," Lieutenant Yuon replied. "Unarmed."

That should have been reassuring information, but not in this case. You might occasionally see a couple of courier ships in a star system, especially if it was an important star system, but never a large group of them. Even stranger, these courier ships were not spread throughout Sobek Star System as if en route various missions, but were clustered together in a narrow swath of space facing the hypernet gate. "Why are there over twenty Syndic courier ships five light-minutes from this gate?"

"They're broadcasting merchant identity codes," Lieutenant

Castries reported. "Not Syndic military and government codes. All twenty-three courier ships are claiming to be private shipping."

"This stinks," Desjani growled. "We've never encountered a Syndic courier model that wasn't government or military. What are they doing here?"

Geary already had Lieutenant Iger on the line. "Can you confirm that, Lieutenant? These courier ships should actually be military or otherwise under the control of the Syndic government?"

"Yes, sir," Iger replied after a two-second pause that felt far longer. "Proving that might be difficult. Very difficult. But all of our experience is that courier ships have always been reserved by the Syndics for official use only. The fact that these are pretending to be something else is highly suspicious."

"What threat can those courier ships pose to us?"

"I don't know, Admiral. Fleet sensors aren't spotting any indications of weapons add-ons."

"They're not here for a party," Desjani said.

He stared at his display, feeling the same sense of threat and wrongness that Tanya obviously was. His fleet had automatically slewed about after exiting the gate, carrying out the preplanned maneuver to avoid a possible minefield. But there were no mines, just that very odd grouping of courier ships. "All units in First Fleet, come starboard three zero degrees, up four five degrees at time two four. Maintain all systems at full readiness."

The ships of the fleet were coming around to face the courier ships when the supposed merchant craft pivoted and began accelerating to meet the Alliance ships. "They're approaching at maximum acceleration," Lieutenant Castries said as alarms pulsed from the fleet's combat systems. "Projected tracks are for an intercept with the center of our formation."

Desjani took in a deep breath, then spoke calmly. "They're coming straight at us at max acceleration, and they have no weapons."

"Reconnaissance?" Geary asked, knowing that wasn't the real answer.

"You know better than that. Those things accelerate like bats out of hell. By the time they reach us, they'll have achieved a closing speed of at least point two light and probably faster. They'd want to be able to see details if they were on a recce mission, and at those kinds of velocities details tend to smear. No. There's only one possible reason why those ships would be coming directly at us that way."

He knew what she meant. "The Syndics haven't done that before," Geary said. "They haven't sent ships on deliberate suicide runs."

"The Syndic warships at Lakota were ordered to destroy the hypernet gate there—"

"Those warships didn't know that was a suicide mission!"

She pointed to her display. "How large a crew does a courier ship need for a one-way mission?"

He took a second to reply. "One."

"Do you think the Syndics could find twenty maniacs willing to die for their CEOs?" Desjani asked. "Or some poor saps given a chance to wipe out their family's debt or get a relative out of a death sentence at one of the Syndic labor camps? I don't know. I do know the Syndics have often shown the willingness to sacrifice their 'workers' at the drop of a hat. It's a suicide attack. That's how the Syndics are balancing the odds since you beat the hell out of them using conventional tactics. Is there any other possible mission those ships coming at us could be carrying out?"

"No." And at the rate they were coming, those ships would be plunging into his formation in about twenty minutes.

5

According to the terms of the peace treaty with the Syndicate Worlds, he couldn't simply fire on unarmed ships broadcasting merchant identification. Geary didn't bother saying that. Tanya knew it, and so did everybody else. Including the Syndic leaders who had ordered this operation. If those leaders had expected him to hesitate, to question what to do under these circumstances, they had made a mistake. "Those ships are operating in an aggressive and dangerous manner," Geary announced for the benefit of the official record. "We have a right to act in self-defense. Broadcast a warning that any ship entering the weapons engagement zone for any of our ships will be fired upon. Repeat the broadcast eight times, on all standard safety and coordination circuits."

As Desjani's comm watch-stander scrambled to get that sent, Geary tapped his fleetwide comm control again. "All units in the First Fleet. The twenty-three courier ships accelerating toward an intercept with our formation have been warned to stay clear of us. If they continue on tracks toward us, they are to be regarded as hostile. Any of them that enter your weapons engagement envelopes are to be engaged with all weapons until disabled or destroyed."

Another call, this time internal. "Emissary Rione and Emissary Charban, tell the Dancers that these ships are dangerous. Say they're out of control, say they're hostile, say whatever works to convince the Dancers that those courier ships might collide with them unless the Dancers evade for all they are worth."

Rione answered, her voice tinged with resignation. "We will try. Even at the best of times, with all the time in the world, the Dancers don't always listen to us. But we will try."

"Thank you," Geary said, putting feeling into the words.

"Lock weapons on those ships and prepare to engage," Desjani told her crew, then gave Geary a measured look. "Just like old times. Kill the Syndics before they kill us. But. The Syndics know the odds of those ships getting through our defensive fire if they're not moving fast enough. They'll accelerate to the maximum velocity they can in the time and distance available in order to screw with our firing solutions."

He grunted a vague reply as he frowned at his display. The courier ships were simply small crew, storage, and command compartments fastened to the front of outsized main propulsion units and a power core suitable for a ship twice their size. Built to move fast, they were already up to point one light speed and still accelerating.

In jump space, human ships did not actually travel faster than light. They went around that speed limit by going somewhere else, a different dimension or different universe. The experts still didn't know which of those jump space represented, but they did know that jump space was a place where distances were much smaller than in our own universe. A week in jump space would take a ship the same distance as years of travel in normal space. Oddly enough, it didn't matter how fast a ship was going when it entered and exited jump space. The length of the journey depended solely on the distance to be covered.

. A hypernet avoided light-speed problems by another method, using quantum physics, which literally tossed human craft into a bubble of nothing that was nowhere, created at one gate and eventually reappearing at another linked gate without technically moving.

Both of those things were weird.

But what happened when human spacecraft pushed their velocities higher and higher in normal space was even weirder. Relativity had predicted the strange physical results long before humans could experience them. Objects accelerating toward light speed gained mass while time slowed inside them, all relative to the outside world. To an outside observer, the objects also got shorter as they moved faster. In theory, at the speed of light, the outside universe would see a ship with infinite mass, zero length, and no time passing inside it.

To those inside the ship, length and mass and time all seemed the same as always, but their vision of the outside would alter. The universe outside their ship grew more distorted to them the faster they went. This relativistic distortion became a significant problem at point one light speed, though human-designed sensors and combat systems could compensate accurately for relativistic errors up to point two light speed. Beyond that, the errors grew too large for existing human technology to compensate for, and the already incredibly difficult problem of hitting an object flying past at tens of thousands of kilometers a second became what fleet engineers described using the technical term TDH, which stood for Too Damned Hard.

Based on the projections of the fleet combat systems, those courier ships would have accelerated up past point two light speed by the time they got close enough for the weapons of Geary's warships to fire at. Since Geary's own ships were still moving at nearly point one light speed, that would produce a closing rate exceeding point three light speed, drastically impacting the accuracy of weapons fire.

Desjani bit her lip and shook her head. "We could slow down to reduce the relative velocity, but that would make it harder for our ships to evade any attempts at ramming."

He nodded. "We'd have to go to a dead stop to get the relative speed of engagement down to point two light, and there's not enough time to slow the fleet that much even if we wanted to do that. If we keep our velocity up, it will make scoring hits a lot harder, but make dodging attacks easier, and the courier ships will have more difficulty hitting their own targets. I'm going to accelerate at the last minute. The extra velocity won't cause more accuracy problems than we're already going to face, and might throw off the ramming courses of the courier ships."

Those small courier ships were still coming, still accelerating, and the projected paths for the Syndic "merchant" craft were now, without doubt, aimed straight into the heart of the Alliance formation, where *Invincible* made perhaps the largest sitting duck in history. *Are they aiming for* Invincible? *Or for the Dancers who, for their own reasons, have been clustered near* Invincible *lately? Or for the assault transports and auxiliaries, which are also in that part of the formation? There are enough of those couriers to target almost all of them.* "All units in First Fleet, the ships heading for us are assessed to be on suicide runs. Vary vectors at random intervals to confuse their attack runs, and make wider individual vector changes when it's too late for the attacker to compensate. All units, screen the assault transports, auxiliaries, and *Invincible*."

"You've done all you can," Desjani murmured, her gaze riveted on her display.

"It's not enough."

"That depends how you define 'enough.'" Her eyes moved to meet his. "We used to lose half of our ships when we *won*. We may lose some now. That's up to the living stars and the skill of each ship's commanding officer."

Geary didn't answer, wanting to deny that reality but unable to muster any arguments. Something nagged at him, though, one more thing that might help but remained stubbornly just out of his mental grasp.

Then he got it, barely in time to do anything about it. Geary's eyes fixed on the estimated time to intercept with the courier ships, a number that was sweeping downward so fast the digital readout seemed to blur. "All units in First Fleet, execute Modified Formation Foxtrot Three at time four one."

"Mod Foxtrot Three?" Desjani asked, her own eyes not leaving her display. "Oh. That might help."

"It can't hurt." Geary paused, trying to time his next command, then tapped his comm controls. "All units in First Fleet, immediate execute accelerate to point one five light speed."

They wouldn't make it. Even the ships capable of the fastest acceleration, Geary's battle cruisers, light cruisers, and destroyers, would barely have begun leaping forward at increasing velocities. But space was very wide, even the largest human ship was very small in that vast emptiness, and at the speeds the Alliance ships and Syndic courier craft were rushing together, even the tiniest difference in a projected track could mean the difference between a near miss and a collision.

Dauntless shuddered slightly as her thrusters fired at time four one, kicking her onto a new vector, while her main propulsion units kept shoving her ahead faster. The entire Alliance formation was splitting into three parts, each group heading outward from the other two, the mass of ships spreading off from their original vectors like water spraying outward in a cone. With vectors for each ship changing by the moment, the oncoming attackers would have to guess where the ship they were aiming for was going, further complicating their deadly task.

The Dancers were staying with *Invincible*, a threat magnet near a threat magnet, and in the last seconds before intercept, Geary could see the twenty-three courier ships bending their own tracks over and down to head where the Dancers and the lumbering mass of *Invincible* were moving. Even with four human battleships towing the mass of *Invincible*, the captured Kick superbattleship seemed to be changing its velocity and course at a snail's pace.

He had eight battleships there, too, moving along with *Invincible*, four actually tethered to *Invincible* and four more escorting her. A fraction of a second before the forces tore into contact, something in Geary's mind noted something about the movement of one of the battleships that seemed slightly off. *Orion's* vector had altered in an unexpected way.

There was no time to ask Commander Shen what he was doing, no time to even understand what about *Orion's* movement felt odd.

Even when warships limited their engagement speeds to point two light, the meetings were far too fast for human senses to register. Geary saw the twenty-three courier ships almost upon the portion of the Alliance formation holding *Invincible*, the assault transports, the auxiliaries, and the Dancer ships, then he saw four courier ships that had missed their targets and been missed by the avalanche of fire which the Alliance warships had pumped out under the control of automated systems able to react much faster than any living creature.

"What the hell happened?" Geary demanded. Something looked very wrong now. Something was missing in the Alliance formation.

The answer appeared on his display.

Orion.

Geary barely noticed as the last four courier ships tried to claw around for another run at the Alliance formation, did not feel any elation as specter missiles pursuing those four ships caught them in their turns and blew them apart.

His display replayed a slow-motion re-creation of the instant of contact. Some courier ships vanishing into irregular blots of dust and energy as lucky shots scored hits, others coming onward, aiming now clearly for the Dancers, who, damn them, seemed to be almost motionless as they hung near *Invincible*, and the rest targeting the assault transports and auxiliaries, the Dancers darting aside at the last moments to frustrate the attackers trying to hit them, *Titan*, *Typhoon*, and *Mistral* almost lined up relative to the attackers and twisting too slowly to evade the courier ships whose vectors aimed at them, hell-lance and grapeshot fire pouring from every Alliance ship in a last-ditch defensive effort, *Orion* rolling slightly in her track, coming over just a small amount, just enough that five surviving courier ships heading for *Titan* and the two assault transports instead struck *Orion* either glancing blows or direct hits.

Even a battleship couldn't withstand that number of impacts by that much mass at those kinds of velocities. The energy liberated by the collisions was vast enough to reduce Orion and all five courier ships to gas and dust.

Orion was gone, along with Commander Shen and his entire crew.

"All attackers destroyed," Lieutenant Castries reported, her tone not jubilant but rather stunned. "Orion has been destroyed. No other damage to fleet ships."

"Damn them," Geary whispered. He could understand the hate Desjani still felt for the Syndics, understand why the Alliance fleet had retaliated and retaliated for such acts, losing track of its own honor and morality along the way, understand why the need to do the right thing had been forgotten in the desire for revenge.

"They're going to claim they didn't know anything about this," Desjani said in a low, savage voice. "The Syndics in charge here. They'll say they had no idea whose ships those were. You know they will."

"Yes." And there was no proof to the contrary. He was certain of that. The courier ships and their one-man crews had been blown to pieces. Dead men and women tell no tales.

He wanted to hurt the Syndics in this star system, hurt all of them, not just those who gave the orders but also those who stood by and let such things happen, whose own actions and passivity supported their leaders.

Don't. Don't do anything that will make this worse.

But *Orion* was gone, victim of an attack that could not possibly have accomplished anything but destruction.

"Admiral." Rione's voice broke through his rage. She sounded odd, too, as if emotions were boiling just beneath the rigid mask of her face. "I wanted to ask, Admiral, if the hypernet gate had been damaged during the fight so close to it. It would be a great loss to this star system if their hypernet gate was damaged so badly during this unnecessary and brutal attack that the gate collapsed."

It took him several seconds to get it, then Geary felt a cold resolve warring with the heat of his anger. He touched a control. "Captain Smythe."

Tanuki was only a few light-seconds distant, so the reply came quickly. "Yes, Admiral?" Smythe asked in a subdued voice.

"I am worried that the hypernet gate may have sustained damage from stray shots or from debris from some of those courier ships. I want it inspected at close range to make sure it has not sustained the level of damage that would cause it to collapse. Even though the safe collapse mechanism will prevent a devastating pulse of energy from being emitted by the collapse, such an event would still cripple commerce through this star system for the foreseeable future."

Smythe pursed his lips. "Admiral, the fight wasn't that close—"

He hesitated, a light of understanding dawning in his eyes, then nodded. "But the gate still might have sustained damage. Damage we can't see, except up close. Catastrophic damage. It would be… so unfortunate for this star system if the gate were to collapse."

"Yes, Captain Smythe, it would be. Will you see to it?"

"I will, Admiral. Perhaps some of the debris from *Orion* will prove to have impacted on some of the gate tethers. That would be ironic, wouldn't it?"

"Yes, Captain Smythe. Ironic. I'm going to slow the fleet to give your engineers time to do a thorough job."

"Oh, we will do a thorough job, Admiral. Have no fear of that." Smythe's grin as he saluted bared his teeth but held no humor.

Rione's image was still visible, showing no reaction to Geary's orders. "Admiral," she said when he closed the call to Smythe, "we should contact the Syndic authorities in this star system, both to formally report our presence and to register a formal protest over the attack on us."

He kept his gaze focused on nothing as he pondered a reply. "I take it accusing them of complicity in murder wouldn't accomplish anything."

"No. If you don't think you can speak to them without spitting blood in their faces, and believe me I would sympathize if that is the case, I can send the message on behalf of the Alliance government."

Geary looked over at Rione's image. "I would be grateful if you would. I don't know what I might say to those… individuals, given the way I feel right now."

"I understand, Admiral." Rione closed her eyes briefly before opening them to gaze at him. "Part of being a politician is being able to speak in a civil fashion to people whom you really want to strangle with their own intestines."

"Thank you, Madam Emissary."

"And may I also extend my official condolences at the loss the fleet suffered this day." Rione's voice almost cracked on the last few words. She hurriedly broke the connection before he could comment on it.

Geary touched his comm controls with a carefully gentle gesture, fearing that if he lost control, he would pound the controls into uselessness. "All units in the First Fleet. Immediate execute, re-form in Formation Delta and reduce velocity to point zero two light." Smythe's engineers would need time to do their work.

The bridge of *Dauntless* was very quiet.

"Commander Shen," Desjani said in a dull voice, "has a daughter in the fleet. I'll let her know what happened."

"I'm… sorry, Tanya. I know Shen was your friend."

"I've lost a lot of friends, Admiral." Desjani bent her head, breathing deeply. "You saw what he did, right?"

"Yes. That last-moment maneuver. I don't know how, but he figured out what he needed to do to swing *Orion* into the path of the suicide attackers aiming at *Titan*, *Typhoon*, and *Mistral*."

"Instinct, Admiral. He was one hell of a good ship driver." Desjani took another deep breath. "Better than me. So, the hypernet gate here was damaged?"

"I think there's a very high probability that it was too badly damaged to save."

"What a shame." One more slow breath, then Tanya straightened, her expression smoothing out. "Lieutenant Yuon."

"Yes, Captain."

"*Dauntless* took out one of those couriers. Well done. Notify the weapons crews that I will be coming to personally congratulate them."

"Yes, Captain."

As Desjani began to rise from her seat, Geary gestured for her attention. "Is there anything I can do?"

"There are lots of things you need to do, Admiral," she said. "You've got a fleet to take care of. And I've got a ship to look after."

"True. I'll talk to you later, Tanya."

She sketched a salute, then headed off the bridge.

Geary turned back to his display, watching his ships re-form into one large grouping, while shuttles winged their ways from two of the auxiliaries toward the hypernet gate.

The one thing he wished he could do right now was order ships to search for survivors from *Orion*. But that would be a meaningless order and a hopeless task. The dead could not be forgotten, but he had to focus his attention on the living.

As Geary's hand moved to send further orders, he paused, looking at his display. *Invincible* was still struggling to get into position, huge and unwieldy.

Invincible. None of the attacking ships had gone after *Invincible*.

Had the ships ordered to strike at *Invincible* been destroyed far enough short of their target that their tracks didn't point to that target?

Or had the attackers been ordered not to strike *Invincible*?

Because the Syndics wanted that ship. He knew they did.

Which could mean—

"Tanya! Captain Desjani!"

She heard him just before the bridge hatch closed. It reopened almost instantly, and she was back beside him almost as fast. "What?"

"I think you'd better stay up here." He hit a comm control. "Admiral Lagemann, do not relax alert status on *Invincible*." Another control. "All units in First Fleet, remain at full combat alert."

Desjani was in her seat, staring at her display. "What do you see?"

"It's what I didn't see."

"You think they have other things planned? Another attack about to go down?"

"I think it's a certainty. They made us come to this star system so those courier ships could hit us, but even under the most optimistic scenario for the Syndics, those suicide attacks couldn't have stopped us."

"But what can they be planning to do when there's nothing else—?"

"Admiral Geary!" the comm watch yelled at the same moment alarms burst from the combat systems. "*Invincible* reports she is under attack!"

"The other shoe just dropped," Geary snapped, as a virtual window appeared next to him.

"We have intruders aboard," Admiral Lagemann said quickly yet calmly. Lagemann's face was in shadow. The entire area of *Invincible* that he was in was darkened, with only stray lights from displays providing light. "They cut what looked like the main comm line out, but that was a decoy."

"You had a decoy comm line, too?" Geary asked, tapping controls to bring up a display showing the Marines aboard

Invincible as well as a direct line to General Carabali.

"Of course." Despite his light words, Lagemann sounded worried. "The indications of the boarding party are still scattered and weak. They must all be in stealth armor, which means Syndic special forces. We know they're on board, but not how many and not exactly where. We're trying to find out more without revealing the real location of the area we occupy inside *Invincible*."

"You and Major Dietz certainly called things right. What about your sentries at the air lock? Did you lose them?"

"No," Lagemann said with a half smile. "They weren't there. We pulled them back inside with the rest of us when those suicide attackers came at us. Maybe that was part of the Syndic boarding plan, but as far as I'm concerned, it's just as well. We might have lost a squad of Marines before we knew we were facing a boarding party in stealth gear. As it is, the Marines with me are fully alert and armoring up."

Geary paused in his reply, glancing at Desjani.

Desjani had uttered an obscene term that he hadn't realized she knew, and now continued speaking with white-hot rage. "A diversion! Those damned suicide ships were a diversion! While we were dealing with them, stealthed shuttles were able to intercept *Invincible* and put their assault force aboard!"

"Yes, *Orion* died because of a diversion." That should have made Geary's own anger flare hotter, but instead he had gone bitter cold inside. "The shuttles the Syndic boarding party used must still be near *Invincible*." There was a maneuver to deal with that, a preplanned operation he only had to order into action. "Search and Destroy Pattern Sigma." He hit his comm control.

"All light cruisers and destroyers in First Fleet, immediate execute Search and Destroy Pattern Sigma. Reference point for search is *Invincible*. Search targets are Syndic stealth shuttles. Engage and destroy any detected."

"Search and Destroy Pattern Sigma?" Desjani checked her database. "I've never actually done one of those. How old is that pattern?"

"More than a century," Geary said. "But it's in the maneuvering systems of every ship in this fleet. All they have to do is punch it in, and the fleet's automated maneuvering systems will get the right ships moving to the right places based on how many ships the formation has for the mission."

"That's a lot," Desjani said, smiling unpleasantly as she watched her display.

Every destroyer and every light cruiser in the First Fleet, roughly two hundred warships, was swinging into a tight, overlapping search pattern focused on the region of space near *Invincible* and the track she had taken through space. Stealthed shuttles, especially if they were not maneuvering at all, could be incredibly hard to spot. But with hundreds of ships searching, all of their sensor readings being combined and compared automatically by fleet combat systems, even the best stealth technology would find it hard to avoid revealing the sort of anomalies that combat systems would pounce on.

If only I'd had time to implement that search pattern as a defensive measure before the Syndics got aboard Invincible, Geary thought bitterly. *But that was the whole point of the suicide attack, to keep us too busy and too distracted to even think about other threats.*

"They're at the decoy main engineering control," Admiral Lagemann announced. "Lamarr sensors on the main hatch report they are being spoofed. And… the Persian Donkey there has ceased emitting."

One decoy dead. Geary fought down an absurd sense of sorrow at the "death" of the faithful and deceitful little Marine Donkey. "What about the decoy bridge?"

Major Dietz's image had also appeared near Geary. Dietz was in full combat armor. "The Syndic boarding party should have coordinated to hit both targets at the same time, but probably ran into delays because of the unknown deck plans of this ship. There go the Lamarr sensors at the decoy bridge. Decoy bridge has been hit. That Donkey is dead, too."

"We've got everything running on minimum power in this area," Lagemann said. "We're all in our suits, so we shut down life support and everything not necessary to communicate and keep track of the action. The boarders will have a hard time finding us, and if they do, they'll find Marines here ready for them."

"Admiral Lagemann," Geary said, "those Syndic soldiers can't be given the run of *Invincible*."

"They won't be," Major Dietz said. "I'm leaving one company to guard this area, reinforced by the sailors." He managed not to sound sarcastic at the idea of armed sailors being effective reinforcement for Marines. "I'm taking the other company out in squads to go after the decoy compartments the Syndics captured. If they brought nukes on board, it's a near certainty they would have left those nukes under guard in the two decoy compartments. We can't hunt people in stealth suits, not with this amount of space to cover and so few Marines, but we can make life difficult for whatever guard force they left in those compartments and hopefully gain possession of the nukes."

"Have you confirmed the presence of Syndic nukes?" Geary asked.

"No, Admiral. That remains an estimate of what the enemy probably intends. I strongly recommend that we operate upon the assumption that the Syndic boarding party does have at least one nuke with them."

"Your estimates have proven to be extremely good, Major Dietz. I approve your recommendation. Admiral Lagemann, General Carabali, we will operate on the basis of the Syndics' having nukes inside *Invincible*."

General Carabali's circuit had come to life and now she nodded in response to Geary's words. "We'll operate on that basis, Admiral. Request permission to land reinforcements aboard *Invincible*."

"How many are you planning on and how quickly?" Geary asked.

"Everybody on *Tsunami*," she replied. "Almost eight hundred Marines. As soon as *Tsunami* can come close alongside *Invincible*. I want to bring *Typhoon* close to *Invincible* in case the Marines aboard her are needed, too."

"Permission granted. Get those Marines onto *Invincible* fast."

"Understood, Admiral. We're going in."

Geary turned back to Major Dietz. "Did you copy that? You have a lot of friends on the way."

"Yes, sir." Dietz studied some of the dim displays near him. "Another Lamarr sensor in one of the passageways just went off. They're looking for us. I'll take my grunts out and make the finding a little easier for them. Two squads will head for the decoy engineering control and two more for the decoy bridge compartment. As our counterattack goes in, it will also distract the Syndics from realizing we have a lot more Marines boarding this ship." He began to move away, then halted with a puzzled expression. "Firing? Admiral, we've got sensors reporting weapons being fired in an area where there's nothing of ours."

"Shooting at shadows?" Admiral Lagemann suggested.

"Shadows? These have to be Syndic special forces. Maybe even those security-force fanatics I fought once. Vipers. They're very tough and very well trained. They wouldn't shoot at shadows..." Dietz's expression changed. "Standard tactics in stealth suits is to operate singly, or in groups of two or three at the most. Even if they've got a battalion aboard us, they would only converge into larger groups at an objective. More likely they're at company strength at the most."

"So?"

"The ghosts, Admiral! Those Syndics are wandering around in the dark alone or in pairs in areas of this ship we only go into at squad strength! One of them just snapped and started shooting at nothing!"

"Isn't them panicking a good thing?" Geary asked.

"It would be, Admiral," Major Dietz said with an obvious attempt at patiently explaining something his superiors should already have realized. "It would be if they didn't have nuclear weapons."

Geary drew in a sudden breath. Isolated soldiers with nuclear weapons, assailed by mobs of unseen, ghostly presences. "Stop them before they go crazy and blow the ship apart from the inside!" he ordered both Major Dietz and General Carabali.

"That's the idea, Admiral," Carabali said. "Move out the instant you're ready," she ordered Major Dietz.

"Got one!" Desjani and Lieutenant Castries both cried out, surprising Geary.

Refocusing on his display, Geary saw a Syndic shuttle symbol sputtering into and out of existence as the fleet's sensors localized the tiny indications of its presence. One of the nearest light cruisers got a fire control solution, and a single hell lance shot speared down and into the shuttle.

The hell lance scored a hit, and a moment later the shuttle blinked fully into view as its power and active stealth systems failed. A half dozen more hell lances tore into it, tearing the shuttle apart.

"There's another," Desjani said, as indications of a second shuttle flickered on the display. "We've got them boxed in with that search formation. If they don't move, it's only a matter of time until we locate them. If they do move, we'll find them a lot faster."

It took a real effort of will for Geary to pull his attention back from the shuttle search, not to turn immediately to the situation on *Invincible*, and instead to concentrate on the entire situation, the entire region near the fleet. "The suicide attacks were at least partly a diversion," he told Desjani. "Maybe the boarding operation is, too."

She bit back an angry reply, thinking. "Maybe. I don't see anything, though, and nobody can stealth a ship bigger than a shuttle effectively enough to keep it undetected by the sensors we've got. Nobody human, anyway, and I doubt the Dancers have shared their stealth tech with the Syndics."

The nearest visible ships were all Syndic freighters, and none of them were within half a light-hour of the Alliance warships. Geary took his time examining his display but saw nothing. "Captain Desjani, I want to watch what's happening on *Invincible*."

"Sure you do. Lieutenant Castries," Desjani called. "Keep track of how many hidden shuttles get blown away. I'm going to be watching everything else while the Admiral keeps an eye on that Syndic attack on *Invincible*." She lowered her voice. "Go ahead. We've got it covered."

"Get my attention if you think you see anything—"

"I've been fighting Syndics for more years than you have, Black Jack! I know my job!"

"Yes, Captain," Geary said. "I'm still learning mine." He focused back on the situation aboard *Invincible* as Lieutenant Castries announced the detection and destruction of two more stealth shuttles.

Invincible was by far the most important issue at the moment. Only there could another devastating blow be inflicted on this fleet if the Syndic boarding party could establish secure positions and threaten to destroy the ship from within.

With only two companies aboard *Invincible*, the number of images of Marines he could monitor was relatively small. Half of those images were unmoving, as the units to which they belonged stayed hunkered down in defensive positions.

But the others were moving. Geary picked one, tapping the image to get a view through the helmet of the Marine squad leader he had chosen.

The window that popped open before him offered the same vision as the Marine had, complete with the symbology on the

Marine's heads-up display overlaid on the view of the dark, empty passageways on the *Invincible*. Geary felt an involuntary shudder as the memory of the Kick ghosts crowding those passageways came back to him.

The Marine he was monitoring was nervous, too, her vision shifting rapidly around as she sought to see the invisible presences. But her voice stayed steady as she led her squad through the maze of *Invincible's* passageways, the Marines pulling themselves along in the zero gravity aboard the ship. "Not too fast. They're in full stealth. Watch for the indications. 'Ski, wake up and watch our six, dammit."

"I'm watching it, Sarge!"

"Like hell."

The Marines pulled, kicked, and glided down one dark passageway to a junction, turned left there, floated up a ladder sized for feet and legs much smaller than humans', then down another passageway. Familiar with the layout of the alien ship from their constant patrolling, the Marines could move with only occasional glances at the deck plans displayed on their helmet shields. "Watch it," the squad leader warned. "The major says they're in this area."

"Sarge! There's something coming!"

"I don't have movement, Tecla."

"There. Look. Like somebody in stealth moving a lot faster than they should, bouncing off stuff."

"Got it. They're coming our way. Watch for when they come around the corner."

But the unseen Syndic special-forces soldier didn't come around the corner. Instead, the soldier must have been staring backwards while moving fast, because the corridor resounded with the sound of the Syndic impacting on the bulkhead when he or she failed to make the turn.

"Got 'em!" one of the Marines yelled, firing.

Shots glanced off something unseen, then the image of a human in battle armor appeared, and moments later a dozen shots riddled it before the Syndic could react.

Geary rubbed his eyes, imagining what the Syndic had been running from. Kicks crowding around on all sides. Real ghosts or something generated by a last-ditch Kick defensive system or the structure of the ship as Captain Smythe had speculated? Whatever it was, it felt real enough to rattle anyone.

He switched to another Marine squad leader who was approaching the decoy main engineering control compartment. The Marines were moving in rushes, several covering their companions as they pulled themselves forward, then those Marines in turn kicking off to fly ahead while the others covered them. It wasn't the fastest form of movement, but when faced with invisible enemies, Geary could understand the need for it despite the urgency of the Marines' reaching that compartment.

The squad halted around the corner from the passageway holding the main air lock into the decoy compartment. The squad leader stuck the tip of one finger around the edge of the turn, the tiny camera in that finger providing a clear image of what was around the corner.

Nothing, apparently. The air lock stood open. No one was visible.

"Why'd they leave the hatch open, Sarge?" one of the Marines asked.

"So we'd go in that way," the sergeant answered. "Old trick. Leave an easy access to where someone wants to go and hope they'll use it without wondering why it was left open. You'd be surprised how often people fall for it."

"What do we do, Sarge?"

"Major?"

Major Dietz answered the sergeant. "We need to get in there as quickly as possible, Sergeant Cortez. If the Syndics have nukes with them, one of those nukes is probably in there. They need to get overwhelmed fast."

"Got it, sir. Squad, we'll use bounce grenades to flush them out and neutralize their stealth. Fire teams one and two, ready grenades. Set them on dust."

"Dust, Sarge? Not shrapnel?"

"You heard me. You guys need another look?"

"Yeah, Sarge."

The sergeant poked out his finger again, letting the image linger on the helmet displays of his squad.

What's a bounce grenade? Geary looked to one side of the Marine display and spotted a list of weaponry. He highlighted the bounce-grenade icon and got a description and an image. A grenade inside some sort of extremely bouncy coating, thick enough to let the explosive act like a superball toy.

"Got it?" the Sergeant said as he pulled back his finger camera.

"Yeah, Sarge. Looks easy. I done harder bounces in my sleep."

"Don't screw it up. When I give the word, fire in sequence in the following order. Denny, Lesperance, Gurganus, Taitano, Caya, Kilcullen. Got it?"

Six Marines answered up.

"The rest of you apes get ready to go. Stand by," Sergeant Cortez said. "Ready. Fire, fire, fire, fire, fire, fire."

Each designated Marine fired a grenade as the command reached their place in the firing sequence. Geary watched as the grenades bounced off the opposite bulkhead at a high angle, bounced again against the bulkhead opposite that as they went down the other passageway, then rebounded yet again through the open hatch to the decoy main engineering control compartment. He realized now why the shots had been slightly spaced, to prevent two or more grenades from glancing off each other and spoiling their bounces. As it was, there were six perfect double-bank shots, each grenade detonating after it entered the compartment.

"Go!" Sergeant Cortez yelled to his squad.

Geary watched the Marines hurling themselves around the corner and toward the open hatch, from which clouds of dust were now billowing.

Vague outlines appeared in the dust gushing from the compartment, the wavering shapes of humans in combat armor, the dust revealing the figures despite the stealth features in the armor. Realizing they were partially visible, the sentries opened fire, hitting one Marine, before a dozen answering shots tore into them.

The Marines kicked off hard on every possible projection, changing direction and bursting into the compartment, which was unrecognizable to Geary despite his previous visit because of the dust filling it. He realized why the grenades had been set to turn their coating into fine powder: that nullified the advantages of the Syndic stealth gear. Figures appeared in the swirling clouds as shots tore through it. The image from the Sergeant's armor jerked wildly as the Marine took a hit, ending up tilted and drifting along one side of the compartment.

Geary hastily switched Marines, picking up the corporal who was now the squad leader. Two more shots resounded in the compartment, then it was silent as the Marines combed it for any remaining foes.

"Sarge is down! Looks bad."

"See what you can do," Corporal Maksomovic ordered. "What about Tsing?"

"Dead."

"Damn. Any Syndics left alive?"

"If they are, not for much longer—"

"Dammit, Caya, if you and the others find a Syndic still breathing, you keep them breathing! We got orders to get prisoners for interrogation, and you will damn well obey those orders!"

"All right, all right, Mack. Hey, this one's still— Never mind."

Geary could see Corporal Maksomovic floating beside a figure in Syndic armor on which all stealth features had failed. "Can we do a revive and recover?"

"Not with a hole that big in her. I don't know how she lasted as long as she did."

"Hey, Mack, I found that nuke we was looking for!"

"Don't touch it, Uulina!" The image moved hastily, focusing on a squat cylinder anchored in one corner of the compartment. On the corporal's helmet display, his combat system automatically identified the enemy weapon and popped up critical information. "Major, we got a confirmed nuke munition. Fusion pack."

Major Dietz sounded both relieved and worried. "Is it armed?"

"Uh. Arming switch." Corporal Maksomovic's helmet display highlighted part of the weapon he was gazing at, providing a schematic with on and off positions for the arming switch helpfully shown. "No, sir. Arming switch has not been thrown."

"What about the timer?"

"No, sir. Timer is not running."

"Good job. Guard that thing yourself while we get a weapons engineer on the line to tell you how to deactivate it. And watch out for any Syndics trying to regain possession."

"Yes, sir. Major, we got a casualty—"

"We saw. There's another squad on the way with two fleet medics. *Don't* let the Syndics regain possession of that nuke."

"Thank you, sir. Understand; we guard the nuke at all costs. All right, you apes," the corporal said. "Even-numbered fire teams guard the open hatch, odd-numbered fire teams guard the closed one. Don't bunch up and make killing you all easy for them! Spread out! Kilcullen, see what you can do for the sergeant until those medics get here."

"Where you going, Mack?"

"I gotta stay next to madam-nuke-your-butt. You watch for more Syndics, and I'll watch it."

Another voice came on, Geary realizing that he was hearing the Marine senior-command circuit. "How's it going, Vili?" General Carabali asked.

"I've got it in hand," Major Dietz replied. "Command area secure and counterattack under way. We have decoy main engineering control and are preparing to retake the decoy bridge."

"I saw. All right, everybody. Major Dietz remains the on-scene commander. Take your orders from him as you board *Invincible*."

A chorus of replies came from the captains and lieutenants commanding the companies and platoons being fed into *Invincible* from *Typhoon*. Major Dietz began calling out orders, sending units to different decks and passageways to form a cordon that would sweep through *Invincible*. "Unit of maneuver is squads," Dietz said. "Nothing smaller is to operate independently."

"Squads?" a captain questioned in a startled voice.

"You'll understand why as you get deeper into the ship," Major Dietz said. "Maintain a full platoon at the air lock the Syndics used to enter the ship and be ready for some of them to come out."

"Come out? To what? There were some shuttles hanging around, but the space squids are blowing them away."

"You'll understand when you get inside the ship," Major Dietz repeated. "The Syndics are going to be wanting to get out. Be prepared for them to hit you and be prepared for them to attack all out as they try to reach the air lock."

"Major, we got the decoy bridge!" a lieutenant reported in. "There's another nuke here, but no Syndics."

"Say again? No Syndics?"

"No, sir. I formed my people into a deck-to-overhead wall and moved them from one side of the compartment to the other. There are no Syndics hiding here."

"They abandoned a nuke?" a captain asked, astonished. "They, um, what the hell? What's that? What's there?"

Geary checked the captain's position, seeing that he was well within *Invincible's* hull.

"Major, what else is in here with us?" a very worried voice demanded.

"Nothing that can hurt you," Dietz replied. "Stay in squad-strength formations. General, the new troops aren't acclimated to the environment inside *Invincible*. That may be a bigger problem than we anticipated."

"Merge them," Carabali commanded. "Make your smallest unit of maneuver platoons and keep the Marines in each platoon in physical contact with each other."

Admiral Lagemann spoke to Geary. "War in a haunted house. I didn't think war could be any worse, but we found a way. The first nuke, in decoy engineering control, had a force of six Syndics with it. If the other group had that same number, it would have been too small to handle the mental pressure of the Kick ghosts, or whatever the phenomenon is."

"You think they just bolted?"

"I think it's likely. Look what's happening to the new Marines coming aboard, and they were in squad strength everywhere, about twice as large a group as the one the Syndics probably left with that second bomb."

Alerts popped to life in several places. In some, Marines were battling Syndic infiltrators. In others, the Syndics must have been firing at ghosts and giving away their locations to the Marines hunting for them.

The Marines who had charged aboard *Invincible* from *Typhoon* moved much more cautiously now, pivoting often to check all about them as they pulled themselves through the deserted, dark passageways of the captured alien warship, and occasionally letting off their own bursts of fire at possible enemies who turned out to be nonexistent.

"We got alerts!" someone was calling.

Geary shifted views again, seeing through the helmet of the Marine lieutenant whose platoon was guarding the air lock. One of the lieutenant's Marines was gesturing frantically. "Three or four of them from the movement! They're coming so fast the gear can pick them up kicking off the walls."

"Smoke that passageway," the lieutenant ordered.

Smoke in this case meant more dust, the grenades going off in a series of bangs that briefly illuminated the dark passageway leading to the air lock before the dust blocked any light from penetrating it. Seconds later, the dust swirled as figures came flying through it.

The Marines opened fire, killing three Syndics, whose bodies were knocked aside to drift lifelessly.

"What the hell?" the platoon sergeant asked the lieutenant. "They didn't even try to shoot. Just flew at us."

"Got more coming! Same passageway!"

"They're retracing their route in," Major Dietz cautioned.

Shots tore through the dust, a wild volley, followed by several more Syndics, who fired in all directions as they erupted into view. The Marines fired back, hitting all of them and killing all but one. The last Syndic special-forces soldier, wounded but still alive, reached the edge of the air lock and locked armored hands on it, facing outward as if fearing he would be pulled back inside *Invincible*.

A Marine slapped a tap onto the Syndic, allowing comms with him. "Stand down now, man! Deactivate your systems!"

"No!" Geary could hear the Syndic's answering howl. "They'll get me! Just let me go! Out there, where it's safe!"

"There's nothing out there! We already blew away your shuttles!"

The Syndic continued to grip the air lock edge, ignoring other attempts to get him to surrender.

"Crash his armor's systems and sedate him," the platoon sergeant ordered.

"If we hard crash his armor's systems, we might kill him," the lieutenant objected. "Our orders are to try to get some prisoners."

"Sir, if we don't crash his armor and knock him out, he'll kill himself. You can see the hits he took. We treat him, or he dies."

"We've got an exploitation team on the way," General Carabali broke in. "Wait until they get there and can question the Syndic. They'll have a medical team with them."

"Who cares whether another Syndic dies?" someone muttered.

Carabali answered, her voice cold. "We care, Private Lud, because we need to know how many Syndics came aboard that ship and how many nukes they brought with them. Understand?"

"Y-yes, General," the unfortunate Private Lud stammered, doubtless anticipating further pointed conversations with his sergeant and lieutenant once the general had finished.

Marines were flooding into *Invincible*. Given the ship's size, and the need to keep the new arrivals into platoon-sized units, they couldn't cover anything like most of the ship, but they could cordon off and begin sweeping the decks near the air lock and the areas around the decoy engineering control and bridge compartments. "I think we've just about got *Invincible* secured," Geary said to Desjani.

As if the living stars had been waiting for his statement to punish his pride, Admiral Lagemann's urgent voice came on the heels of Geary's words.

"Admiral Geary, we just received a communication from a woman claiming to be the commander of the boarding force. She says she has a nuke and demands we halt operations and evacuate *Invincible*, or she'll detonate the munition."

6

"What did you say?" Desjani asked. "Something about *Invincible*?"

"Never mind." Geary had to pause to control his voice before he replied to Lagemann. "Where is she? Do we know where this commander and her nuke are?"

Major Dietz answered, sounding grim. "Our best guess is in this area," he said, indicating a spot aft of amidships and near the centerline of *Invincible*. "You can see the blocking forces we have stopping any movement along these lines, and as our patrols confirm areas are clear, the blocking forces establish new positions. We're not encountering any more Syndics moving alone or in small groups, so it's a reasonable guess that their commander figured out that the only way to prevent them from panicking was to pull her force together."

Dietz highlighted a grouping of compartments. "We think they're here. That's about where the transmission originated, and this block of five compartments offers a compact defensive position with limited access from above and below."

"How long until we *know*?" Geary asked.

"I've instructed the patrols to move faster and converge toward the suspected Syndic location. Once we have them localized, I can send in some look-sees to get a better idea of how many and whether there's actually a nuke in there with them."

"Ten minutes?" Geary pressed.

"Half an hour," Major Dietz said, visibly bracing himself as he delivered the information.

Geary took a long, slow breath as he considered his options. "Get Emissary Rione and Emissary Charban on the line with that Syndic commander. Their instructions are to spin out negotiations and discussions as long as possible." Technically, he didn't have the right to order around either Rione or Charban since as representatives of the Alliance government, they were outside his command authority, but neither of them had made an issue of that lately. He doubted they would in this situation, either. "Let that Syndic commander think we're right on the verge of agreeing to her demands while you figure out exactly where she is, get forces into position around her, and try to determine whether she's bluffing about having a third nuke."

He mentally pulled back from the situation aboard *Invincible*, rubbing his eyes tiredly. "Tanya? What's the big picture look like?"

"Nothing new happening that we can tell," she replied. "Eleven stealth shuttles have been spotted and destroyed. There hasn't been a new detection for some time, so we might have gotten them all. What happened on *Invincible*?"

"We've got two nukes, but there might be a third, and the Syndic commander is threatening to use it." He shifted back to General

Carabali. "Eleven Syndic shuttles have been confirmed and destroyed so far. Does that help estimate how many Syndics came aboard?"

"It gives us an upper limit," Carabali said. "The shuttles might not have been full. An operation like this usually has some excess lift capability in case some of the shuttles develop problems. Unfortunately, it tells us nothing about how many nukes they might have brought aboard."

"Do you think they would really detonate a nuke, if they still have one, when they're also in the blast zone?"

General Carabali frowned. "Admiral, these are Syndic special forces. Not fanatics from the Syndic security service."

"Major Dietz thought they might be fanatics."

"It was a reasonable guess, but from what I've seen of their equipment and tactics, they're soldiers. Syndic special forces are highly trained and reliable, but I can't think of any cases where they conducted deliberate suicide attacks during the war."

"You don't think their commander will carry through with her threat?"

"I don't know, Admiral. It's not typical of the Syndic special forces, but it's not impossible. The Syndics seem to be falling back on suicide attacks out of desperation. An additional factor is that the, uh, atmosphere aboard *Invincible* is extremely unsettling. What impact that might have on the Syndics' decisions even in a larger group I can't say."

"Make sure we keep offering to let them surrender."

Carabali nodded, but she did not look hopeful. "They can't assume if they do surrender that we'll treat them as prisoners of war, Admiral."

"I have never authorized—"

"That's true, Admiral. But those were prisoners who were unquestionably Syndic military personnel. They had uniforms, they were part of units, they carried all the necessary official identifiers. In this case, the woman we're talking to who claims to be the commander of this group isn't giving a rank for herself. The Syndics we've killed, and in a couple of cases captured, have no military insignia or identification on them. They're equipped with Syndic special-forces gear, but the equipment has had all identifying information scrubbed out and filed off. Even the implanted chips that contain medical and other information have been removed from their bodies. There's nothing tying them to being part of the Syndic military and nothing giving them any official status at all."

Geary stared at Carabali. "Are they trying to claim they're pirates or something?"

"Private individuals," Carabali said in a flat voice, "on a private venture. That's all we've gotten out of the one prisoner who is able to talk."

"Do you think they'll stick with that even if it means they face death for terrorist actions?" Geary demanded.

"It's hard to tell, Admiral. We're in unexplored territory when it comes to that. Before, they'd be Syndics, and we were at war, so we'd treat them all as combatants. For better or worse. Now that we're officially at peace, technically the official Syndics have protections as prisoners that freelancers do not. However, they don't seem to have anything on them that would prove any claim they made to official status, if they tried to make one, and I think it's a reasonable assumption that the Syndic CEOs here will deny any knowledge of them and their actions, which means that no matter what they said, we could legally, officially, and with honor execute them all."

And these Syndics surely knew that. Had they known it going into this operation? Or had they only realized it when trapped aboard *Invincible*, their initial attacks foiled and their numbers rapidly dwindling, while the Kick ghosts gnawed at their minds?

"Offer them a chance to live," Geary said slowly. "Tell them I will give my word of honor, officially and on the record, that any of them who surrender and cooperate will not be harmed."

"I'll make sure that offer gets to them," Carabali said. Her expression hadn't wavered, but her tone of voice was that of someone agreeing to a course of action she had no expectation of working. She paused, frowning to one side as she listened to a report. "Admiral, the prisoner who is being interrogated shows signs of having been subjected to mental conditioning."

Why did news like this continue to surprise him? "What kind of mental conditioning?"

"It's not clear yet. Any discussion of a military background generates responses consistent with mental conditioning. They may be incapable of admitting they are, or were, special-forces personnel." Carabali grimaced. "They may also be incapable of surrendering. If they won't, or can't, surrender, we'll have to take whatever actions are necessary."

"I understand." Having seen the impact of such conditioning on Commander Benan, it was easy to understand that the Syndics subjected to it could not override the blocks implanted within their minds. He also understood why the Marine had raised that issue with him. He was in command, and he had the responsibility to either clearly rule out all necessary actions or to clearly order that they be taken. "Your orders are to take the necessary actions to eliminate the threat those Syndics pose to *Invincible* and our personnel aboard the ship."

"Yes, sir. Preparations are under way. We'll notify you before we go in."

Once he had finished speaking with General Carabali, Geary sat back, trying to ease tense muscles. There wasn't any need for him to lean forward while viewing the Marine action, no need for his body to be ready to leap into action, but instincts were not easily overridden. Besides, it would feel somehow *wrong* to be leaning back in a relaxed posture while watching men and women risk death not in a video production but for real.

"When are the Marines going in?" Desjani asked.

"How did you hear they were going in?"

"It's all over the fleet's back channels. This is ironic, isn't it?"

Geary glanced at her. "How so?"

"The Syndic plans are getting messed up because the Kick ghosts freaked out their boarding party. The Kicks are helping us defend that ship."

"Too bad the Kick ghosts can't disarm nukes. Were there any survivors off the Syndic shuttles?"

Desjani shook her head. "Nah. Not surprising. When a shuttle takes hits from warships, there's usually not a lot left. I told some of the destroyers to recover debris, though. It might help as evidence that the Syndics did this."

"Can't hurt. Thanks. Don't be surprised if there's nothing, though. All of the equipment belonging to the Syndic soldiers on

Invincible had been completely sanitized."

"Word is we got at least one prisoner."

"And initial results indicate the Syndic soldiers themselves were sanitized. Mental blocks."

She stared at him. "Ancestors preserve us. Why the hell haven't the people living in the Syndicate Worlds risen up and torn their damned CEOs into tiny pieces?"

"Damned if I know." He thought about some of the star systems they had seen. "I guess some of them are, in some places. Maybe that's why the Syndic CEOs are doing anything and everything against us. They have to be terrified of what will happen to each of them if they show the slightest sign of weakness."

"Trying to save their hides by making their own citizens even madder at them? Yeah, that'll work."

He shared her opinion of the spreading revolts that the Syndic government's tactics would eventually lead to, but in the short term, that still left him, and this fleet, facing the problem of dealing with the increasingly desperate and increasingly vicious tactics the CEOs were adopting to try to save themselves.

Geary scanned his display. The fleet was moving away from the hypernet gate, the destroyers and light cruisers still arrayed around *Invincible* and down along *Invincible's* track. Nothing lay before the fleet... no, nothing could be seen before them, Geary corrected himself, except some Syndic merchant traffic, the nearest of which was still nearly two dozen light-minutes distant. "Tanya, work up a course to the jump exit for Simur. I want to go wide, using a longer path than required, just in case something else is waiting along our path."

"No problem, Admiral. Do you want that implemented right away?"

"No. Hold off on it. I want to avoid moving *Invincible* around until the Marines have finished their job."

His gaze went back to the display. Sobek only had the one jump point, so anyone arriving through the hypernet gate who didn't also leave that way en route another destination could only go to Simur. From Simur, the fleet could jump to Padronis, and from there to Atalia. The Varandal Star System, in Alliance space, could be reached from Atalia. Not that long a path, but one all too predictable if the Syndics had laid other traps. *It's not just Sobek, it's that our options from Sobek are so limited. Sobek to Simur to Padronis, if we want to get home. Atalia wasn't cooperating with the Syndic government anymore when we last went through there, but every star system until Atalia is going to be a gauntlet to run.*

Another call brought him out of his worried thoughts about their route home. Rione was wearing the icy look that meant she was extremely frustrated, but fortunately the frustration wasn't aimed at him.

"If you were counting on diplomacy or negotiations resolving the matter inside *Invincible*, you might want to consider other options," she said.

"I wasn't counting on it. More like it can't hurt to try," Geary admitted. "You don't see any hope for ending this with words instead of actions?"

Rione shook her head. "It might be the environment in there, or it might be the result of finding themselves cut off in a hopeless situation, but the woman I'm talking to isn't giving any ground even though she seems rattled. It's like talking to people with their backs to the wall. They know they can't run, but they won't give up. I was informed that you were willing to promise that we would treat them as military prisoners if they give up. I'm not so sure that you could make that promise stick once we returned to Alliance space, but that doesn't matter because the offer did not make any difference. They don't seem inclined to believe promises from senior officials."

"Of course not. They're Syndics. Did General Carabali tell you that there are indications they may been mentally conditioned?"

"Yes. I can't say from my conversations whether that is true or not. It's not really possible in cases like this to tell the difference between someone who had a mental block implanted and someone who is so certain she is right that she has blocked her own mind," Rione added.

Geary ran one hand through his hair, considering his options. "Do you think they've really got a nuke, and if they do have one, do you think they'll actually detonate it?"

"Those are good questions," Rione said. "I don't have good answers for them."

What else? "Did you get the impression that they still expect some form of rescue? Do they know we've destroyed all of their shuttles?"

"They know what we've told them, Admiral. I doubt that they believe us."

Geary nodded, feeling exhausted. "Keep talking to them. Please."

"Since you ask so nicely, I will." Rione's mouth moved with distaste. "I will keep talking to them until the Marines kill them. Perhaps it will distract them and make the task of the Marines a little easier. Have you ever been speaking with someone at the moment they died?"

"No," Geary said.

"Neither have I. Until today. I suspect I will soon know how it feels." He closed his eyes tightly, grimacing, after Rione ended her call. After a long moment, he straightened and refocused on the Marine situation map.

Aboard *Invincible,* the Marines had closed and tightened their spherical cordon around the area where Major Dietz had estimated the Syndics would be holed up, sealing off passageways and compartments on all sides and above and below the enemy-held compartments. On Geary's image of *Invincible's* deck plan, those five compartments were now marked as enemy-occupied. "We *know* that's where they are?" Geary asked Major Dietz.

"Yes, sir," Dietz reported. "We managed some recon, but with the Syndics still in stealth mode, it's hard to get a good count. Our best guess is about twenty of them are in there, Admiral."

"Good call on where they would hole up, Major. Do we know if they've really got a third nuke?"

Major Dietz flushed slightly at the praise from Geary, then hesitated. "Admiral, we've sent in gnat sensors, which were all we could get in through the bug-netting countermeasures the Syndics have hung across the accesses into there. The gnats aren't picking up any extra radiation that would indicate the presence of a nuke. But gnat sensors are limited because of size and power issues, and if the Syndics have the nuke under extra shielding, it would be very hard to spot even with better gear."

"What would it take to be sure?"

"To be absolutely sure? Fight our way in there and look, Admiral."

Admiral Lagemann was studying the deck plan for the *Invincible*. "I was thinking about something," he said. "We've got a good picture of how *Invincible* looks inside because it's based on our patrolling of the ship and automated mapping drones. We've got a solid picture of the deck plan. Watch this."

On the deck plan, dots began appearing. "Each of these," Lagemann said, "is an indication of Syndic presence. If you look at how the detections develop, they show us where the Syndics went initially."

"What are these detections based on?" Geary asked.

"Lamarr sensor spoofing and fragmentary indications picked up by other sensors," Admiral Lagemann explained. "Not a perfect picture, but the best we can expect when dealing with stealthy opponents in an environment like *Invincible*. Watch the paths the Syndics followed. They converged on the decoy main engineering control and the decoy bridge simultaneously, using a variety of routes that in some cases must indicate backtracking because the Syndics knew nothing about *Invincible's* layout. But, as spread out as they were, everything we spotted was headed for those two compartments. After they occupied the two decoy spaces, they spread out again and moved along this axis."

Major Dietz nodded. "Roughly toward the living and operations spaces we actually occupy. The emissions from the Donkeys helped mask our own actual presence. The Syndics must have picked up some trace indications of our real location on board once the Donkeys were shut down."

"The point being," Lagemann continued, "they only went for *two* locations initially instead of a third grouping trying to also seize the weapons control compartment they would have expected to find."

"Which would argue in favor of their only having two nukes?" General Carabali asked. "That analysis makes sense, but do we want to bet the farm on it?"

Lagemann smiled crookedly. "If we're wrong, and they do have a nuke, I'll be buying the farm."

"We wouldn't be in this position if they hadn't tried to farm our ship," Dietz pointed out.

"Are you all done?" Geary asked, exasperated.

"Sorry," Admiral Lagemann said. "Those jokes weren't exactly breaking new ground. Sorry, sorry. But I think I can be forgiven for a little levity to distract me from the possible consequences for me and the rest of my crew of urging you to order the Marines to go in."

Geary let his eyes rest on the deck plan of *Invincible*. "Does anyone think time is on our side?"

Only Carabali answered, and that was in the negative. "No, sir. If they're ready to die carrying out their mission, and if they've got a nuke, we need to hit them as soon as possible before the nature of *Invincible* drives them crazy enough to just set it off."

"They can certainly feel the ghosts in those compartments they're in," Major Dietz agreed. "Since we powered down a lot of the gear in here and shut off life support, they've been crowding in with us. Having a bunch of people here helps, but it doesn't stop the spooky sensation."

"Go ahead and power up your gear again," Carabali ordered. "Get your life support going, too. If there are any Syndics who avoided the Marine sweeps and haven't been driven crazy by the ghosts, they might come your way once your emissions get stronger. That will give you a chance to take them out. Admiral, I want to go in after those twenty Syndics forted up in those five compartments as soon as we're ready."

Geary had to pause to think. He couldn't spend too much time dwelling on the consequences if the Syndics did have a third nuke and did detonate it, because visualizing that would be certain to unnerve him. Part of him remained very angry with the Syndics, determined that they not win in any way, shape, or form as a result of their sneak attacks here at Sobek. He knew that was also the wrong grounds for making the decision, though.

Invincible was immensely valuable to humanity, even if the cost to this fleet in the taking of the superbattleship from the Kicks wasn't counted in. Dared he risk the destruction of everything humanity might learn from *Invincible?*

On the other hand, did he dare give that up? Suppose *Invincible* did hold somewhere inside the secret to the Kick planetary-defense system? Suppose the Syndics acquired that? The same Syndic CEOs willing to order suicide attacks and willing to threaten the destruction of *Invincible's* trove of knowledge?

"Go in as soon you're ready," Geary said. "If you can take any more prisoners, it would be nice because I want living bodies who can hang this operation on the Syndicate Worlds, but the primary goal is ensuring a quick takedown, so if they do have a nuke, they don't have time to activate it." He didn't ask what the odds of success were, knowing that any reply would only be guesswork.

Major Dietz saluted. "Five minutes, Admiral. We've already

prepared the assault plan. We'll hit them from every direction at once."

"Good." Geary pulled himself back to awareness of the larger situation again, trying to block out mental images of what might soon happen if he had decided wrong. "Still quiet?" he asked Desjani.

"Yeah. I ordered a saturation bombardment of the primary inhabited world. We launched that ten minutes ago, but it will take another half a day to get there, so there's nothing to see yet."

He glared at her. "That's not funny. Is there a reason why everybody has suddenly decided to start making bad jokes?"

She met his eyes. "Because we're scared."

"Oh." Geary couldn't think of anything else to say.

"They're hitting us in unusual ways," Desjani explained. "We don't know what's coming next. We don't know if all of the sacrifice required to get possession of *Invincible* is about to be negated by a little fusion star blooming inside the ship. We want to get home, and we don't know what else the damned Syndics have thrown in our way. All right?"

"All right." He made an apologetic gesture. "I've been too busy to think about those things."

"Too busy commanding? You've got your nerve." Desjani smiled briefly. "We'd be a lot more scared if you weren't in command."

"The Marines are going to take out the remaining Syndics on *Invincible* in… four minutes."

"Should we move the destroyers away from her? There are still several real close in that search pattern."

He had to think about that, balancing the possible risk to the destroyers against the impact on morale of those aboard *Invincible* if they saw such tangible evidence that Geary suspected the worst.

If people were already scared, it wouldn't do much good for them to see that their commander was worried that *Invincible* would blow up. "No. The Marines will take care of the threat." *Besides, there are four battleships literally tethered to* Invincible. *There's no time to get them loose and away.*

"Go ahead and get back into the Marine situation," Desjani urged. "I've got the bubble for the fleet."

He gave her a startled look. "Wait a minute. Are you acting as second in command of the fleet?"

"Duh. Did you just figure that out, sir?"

"No one is objecting?"

"And why would they object?" After waiting a couple of seconds for Geary to search in vain for a safe reply, Desjani went on. "Badaya, Tulev, Duellos, and Armus are fine with it, and as long as they accept it, no one else will complain." She paused again. "Jane Geary is not objecting, either, so I've got the Gearys backing me. I almost feel like family."

"Uh-huh. Well, uh, keep on doing… what you were doing."

"Yes, sir, Admiral." Desjani glanced at the time. "You've got two minutes before the grunts go in."

"Thanks." He focused back on the Marines, identifying the unit leaders among those ranged near the Syndic stronghold and choosing one at random.

It took a few seconds to orient himself to the position of the Marine lieutenant whose view he could now see. Finally, Geary realized that this platoon was positioned above the Syndic-occupied compartments. A couple of combat engineers were finishing up laying hull-breach tape to frame a large area on the deck in the center of the compartment the Marines were in. The platoon, weapons at ready, were ranged around the top of the compartment, drifting weightlessly above the outlined center section.

A timer was running down, second by second, on the lieutenant's helmet display. "One minute," she warned her platoon. "You know the drill. Prisoners if possible, but priority is keeping anyone from setting off a nuke."

"I don't think they'll have any trouble staying focused on that, Lieutenant," the platoon sergeant remarked. He looked around, the motions a little jerky. "Let's get this done and get off this ship."

"They're not real, Sergeant," the lieutenant said in a voice that sounded as if she was trying to convince herself as well as him. "Remember, all of you," she added, *don't touch any equipment*. It's Kick gear."

"No problem, Lieutenant," a corporal said with his own nervous looks around. "Last thing I want is to make 'em madder."

"Ten seconds, people!"

The combat engineers had pulled themselves back down to the deck and were holding the tape detonators while counting off the last seconds. "Fire in the hole," one announced, then punched a detonator while the other engineer did the same.

Brilliant light flared where the breaching tape lay, almost instantly cutting through the deck. In gravity, the severed section would have dropped down to the next deck, but at zero g, it stayed in place until the entire platoon of Marines pushed off hard from the overhead, their armored boots slamming into the loose deck section so that they and the severed deck piece dropped through fast into the compartment beneath them.

Shots were blazing on all sides as the Marines faced outward and pumped out rounds at any indication of enemies. The deck section they were on was tilted up on one side, where it rested on a Syndic whose armor's stealth features had failed when the mass of deck and a platoon of Marines in combat armor had landed on it.

"Got us a prisoner!" one of the Marines shouted, placing a rifle barrel against the helmet of the helpless Syndic.

Geary stared at the bolts of energy blazing through the compartment, through the hatches and through the compartments next to this one, wondering how anyone could remain standing in the blizzard of fire as Marines came in shooting from all sides. Then he saw the lieutenant's weapon sight blink red as she tried to fire a shot and realized the Marine armor's friendly-fire inhibitors were preventing anyone from shooting where another Marine was or would be.

The action lasted less than a minute as the Marines stormed into the compartments in overwhelming numbers. "Is there a nuke? Find the nuke!" someone ordered.

"Cease fire! Everyone cease fire! They're all down."

"Any left alive?"

"Just one. He's not talking."

Another shot went off. "I said cease fire, dammit!"

"I thought I saw— It's those ghosts, Sarge—"

"Safe your weapons! Does anybody see a nuke?"

"Compartment alpha clear. No nuke."

"Compartment bravo clear. No nuke."

"Compartment cable clear. No nuke."

"Compartment delta clear. No nuke."

"Compartment echo clear. No nuke."

Geary slumped in relief, taking a deep breath. The Syndic commander had been bluffing.

Somewhere inside those five compartments, that Syndic lay dead along with the rest of those who had followed her into *Invincible*. Had Rione still been talking to the Syndic commander when Marine firepower had put an end to the commander and the negotiations? The alien warship had picked up more scars and more internal damage, but in every way that counted, *Invincible* was still intact.

Your attack failed, Geary thought, imagining he was speaking to the Syndic CEOs. *How many times do we have to beat you before you stop trying?*

There were still two captured Syndic nuclear munitions to dispose of. Geary looked at his display of Marine icons, choosing Corporal Maksomovic again.

Someone had vacuumed up a lot of the dust in the air created by the bounce grenades. Without that housecleaning, the dust would have drifted indefinitely like a slow-moving sandstorm through the compartments and passageways without working life support and made *Invincible's* interior even more inhospitable.

Geary couldn't see Maksomovic's face, but he could sense the unhappiness of the corporal as he hung in midair right next to the Syndic nuke. How long had Corporal Maksomovic been babysitting the infernal device?

"Corporal." Captain Smythe had linked in, too, and was speaking to Maksomovic. "Commander Plant is here. She'll walk you through disarming the Syndic nuke. Do you recognize the munition, Commander?"

"Oh, yes," Commander Plant said cheerfully, "I recognize it. A standard Syndic Mark Five Fusion munition. Mod... three. Exactly like the other one that we just disarmed while everyone else was busy wiping out the last Syndics. A really nice piece of weaponeering. The Syndics can do some good work."

"Can we render it safe, Commander?" Admiral Lagemann asked as he joined the conversation.

"Yes. Of course. Mostly safe, anyway."

"Mostly safe?" Corporal Maksomovic asked hesitantly. The corporal had to be intently aware that not only was he floating beside a nuclear weapon but that an entire bevy of senior officers had come to watch and listen to him.

"Absolutely," Commander Plant said. "Do you see an access panel with eight fastenings near the top? There? That one."

"This one?" The Marine corporal's hand reached toward the indicated access.

"Yes. Don't touch that one."

Geary watched the corporal's hand jerk back as if a cobra's head had just emerged from the bomb casing.

"Try to find an oval access with five fittings. It should be about midway up the casing. That's it!"

"Am I supposed to touch this one?" Corporal Maksomovic asked.

"Yes. Pull the fittings. Don't worry. The Syndics hardly ever booby-trap those."

The corporal's armored hand, which seemed to be trembling slightly, pried open the fittings.

"Now," Commander Plant continued, "pry open the access. Not the top! Bottom first!"

Corporal Maksomovic's hand jerked back again. He was mumbling something inaudible as he reached for the bottom of the panel and popped it up. A mass of wires was visible inside, reaching from above the access and leading down to separate locations below its rim.

"All right," Plant said, "reach in, grab as many wires as you can, and pull them out."

The corporal's hand froze in midmotion. "Excuse me, ma'am?"

"Reach in, grab as many as you can, and pull them out. One yank."

"Uh, ma'am, I was sort of expecting some directions that were a little more detailed. You know, like find this one wire labeled this way that's this color and carefully snip it without damaging anything else."

"Oh, no, no, no. That would be way too risky," Commander Plant insisted. "It's much safer to just yank them all out at once. It won't explode if you do that. Well, it might explode. But not very much."

"Ma'am, with all due respect, this conversation is not doing my morale any good at all."

"Trust me! I'm telling you to do exactly what I would do if I were there. The first one we disarmed didn't explode, did it?"

Despite the commander's last statement, the corporal didn't seem eager to follow the instructions.

"Corporal Maksomovic, do as she says," Major Dietz instructed.

"Yes, sir," the corporal replied in the fatalistic tones of a man ordered to jump off a high cliff by someone holding a gun on him. Geary watched the corporal's armored fist reach into the access and gather a thick cord of wires in its grasp.

"I just yank 'em out?" Maksomovic asked.

"Yes," Commander Plant said. "All at once. Give it a good, hard yank and pull as many as you can out of there."

Geary noticed in the periphery of the corporal's view that his companions were edging gingerly away, as if an extra meter of distance would offer some sort of critical defense against a fusion bomb going off this close to them.

"Here goes nothing," Corporal Maksomovic said, then tensed for his pull. The augmented strength of the Marine combat armor allowed the corporal to give a very powerful yank. A rat's nest of wires came completely free in his armored fist, leaving broken ends and connectors inside the bomb.

A single spark flared among the torn components visible inside the access. Geary realized his breathing had stopped the moment that spark snapped. But when nothing else followed, he managed to draw a deep breath.

The Marine corporal sounded as if he hadn't been breathing, either. "Now what, ma'am?"

"Recycle the wires," Plant replied, as if she had been directing the repair of nothing more hazardous than a balky bicycle. "I'd recommend putting the munition on a lifter and tossing it out the nearest air lock. You might still get a little explosion out of it, and there's no sense risking that."

"A little explosion?" Admiral Lagemann asked, clearly wondering what level of violence the munitions engineer would classify as "little." But if he meant to ask, he changed his mind. "Do you need it for any kind of study or exploitation?"

"No, thank you, Admiral. We've captured a few of these. I doubt there's anything we could learn from this one."

"There aren't any technical issues we could glean from it," Captain Smythe corrected, "but we should still examine both nuclear munitions for any serial numbers or other data that might link them to a particular Syndic source. If you don't object, Admiral Geary, I'll have a shuttle sent over from *Tanuki* to collect both disarmed munitions."

"Admiral Lagemann?" Geary asked.

"I think I speak for everyone aboard *Invincible* when I say we can't get rid of those nukes any too soon," Lagemann replied. "Captain Smythe is welcome to them."

"Good work, Corporal," Major Dietz said to Maksomovic.

"Thank you, sir. I've gotta confess, I would have been pretty nervous if the timer had been counting down while I was working on that thing," Maksomovic admitted, as if he hadn't actually been nervous as it was.

"The timer?" Commander Plant asked, surprised. "Oh, you wouldn't have to worry about that. The timers on these Syndic munitions are fakes. As soon as you arm the weapon and activate the timer, the weapon goes off immediately."

A long pause followed her words.

"Really?" Admiral Lagemann finally asked. "I'd heard rumors about that, but…"

"The rumors are true. Think about it, Admiral. You've got a target important enough to smuggle a nuke into it. Are you really going to risk having someone come along and deactivate the weapon while its timer is running?"

"What happens to whoever set the weapon and activated the timer?"

Commander Plant sounded puzzled by the question. "They're standing next to a fusion event, Admiral. They don't even have time to know what hit them before they're gone. And I do mean gone. There's nothing left. Plasma, maybe. Some charged particles. That's it."

"But..." Corporal Maksomovic said slowly, "we've got munitions like this."

This time the pause was even longer and more awkward.

"We're not the Syndics!" Captain Smythe declared with what seemed an excessive amount of jovial nonchalance. "Let's stop all this chatter and get that disarmed weapon out of there, shall we?"

Recalling the old saying about not asking questions that you don't really want to know the answers to, Geary exited the link and looked at Desjani. "All right. The situation is completely secure aboard *Invincible*. Let's get back into a regular formation and head for the jump point for Simur. What kind of route to the jump point did you work up?"

She grinned as she sent his display the planned maneuver.

Geary looked at it, looked again, then nodded appreciatively. "Instead of cutting across the edge of the star system, you want to dive toward the star, then loop back up to the jump exit?"

"It adds about a light-hour to the trip, but there's no way they'll have any surprises along that path," Desjani predicted.

"You're right. I wouldn't have gone that far off the optimal trajectory, which might have given the Syndics here a chance to adjust another attack. We'll go with this. There's one more thing I have to check before we head out, though."

He called Captain Smythe again. "We're getting ready to leave this area. Have your engineers completed their inspection of the hypernet gate?"

Smythe sighed heavily. "Yes, Admiral, and I regret to say that the gate was damaged extensively. Oddly enough, the damage could only be detected by a very close examination, but it is serious enough and extensive enough that the hypernet gate will begin to collapse... thirty-seven minutes and twenty seconds from now."

"That's a remarkably precise estimate," Geary said.

"I'm a remarkably precise engineer, Admiral. I have a report you can pass on to the Syndics here. I made sure to emphasize that debris from *Orion* and from some of the courier ships was responsible for the damage. And don't worry about the Syndics analyzing our report and reaching erroneous conclusions about the cause of the gate's collapse. I had Lieutenant Jamenson prepare the report using her skills to the best of her ability."

"Thank you, Captain Smythe." Lieutenant Jamenson, the officer whose gift was to confuse things so that they were technically accurate yet also effectively indecipherable. The Syndics would never be able to produce any meaningful evidence from a report she had put effort into. "I'll get the fleet moving."

Roughly thirty-seven minutes later, with the fleet's warships still taking up their new positions in the formation and the entire force accelerating back up to point one light speed, Geary watched the hypernet gate collapse behind them. The devices called tethers, which held the linked energy matrix in check, failed one at a time or in groups, the entire process occurring in a complex sequence that would prevent that energy matrix from erupting in a burst that could sweep all life from this star system. The ebb and flow of vast forces inside the collapsing gate as the failure sequence balanced and canceled out the contending waves of energy produced distortions in space itself that could be seen with the naked eye.

He had felt those forces, close up, while trying to keep the hypernet gate at Sancere from annihilating that star system. He had no wish to ever be that close to a collapsing gate again. Even now, from this distance, the vision created a queasy sense of viewing something humans were never meant to see. It was one thing to know the science that said how tenuous "reality" was, how bizarre the shape of what lay behind the physical universe, and another thing to actually see the strangeness and instability behind the curtain.

But for all that, there was still a great satisfaction in watching this gate die. It would not bring back *Orion*, but it would put a price on her loss that the Syndics could ill afford.

The final death throes of the hypernet gate were peaking. The size of the distortion in space shrank rapidly even as the energy levels in it grew frighteningly intense, then the last bursts of energy collided, waves canceling each other, and abruptly nothing remained but a few scattered pieces of equipment drifting through space.

7

"The senior Syndic CEO in this star system expressed his sorrow at our loss," Rione reported in a flat voice. "He also claimed to have no idea of the identity of the courier ships, saying the Syndic government had sold all of the ones which attacked us. If I press him for the identity of who the government sold them to, the answer will surely be a shocked avowal that the corporation which bought the ships has turned out to be a shell controlled by unknown parties."

"No surprises there," Geary said, trying to keep his own voice emotionless. They were in the conference room at her request for a private conversation. "How soon after the attack did that message get sent to us?"

"They transmitted it twenty minutes after they would have seen the attack end," Rione said. "Enough time lag to ensure it wasn't obvious they knew the attack would occur as soon as we arrived. They haven't yet denied any involvement in the attack on *Invincible*."

"Aside from the destruction of the stealth shuttles, there weren't external signs of that attack," Geary pointed out. "If they denied being involved in something that they could not have seen, it would look suspicious."

"What shall we tell them about it?" Rione asked, sitting down opposite him and leaning one elbow on the table.

He looked at the star display floating between them, where the star Sobek occupied the center and the track of the First Fleet formed a graceful arc leading toward that star. Light-hours from the fleet, the primary inhabited world in this star system orbited Sobek. The world where the CEOs were located who had at the very least known of, and possibly assisted in, the attacks that had claimed *Orion* as well as some Alliance Marines aboard *Invincible*.

"Nothing," Geary finally said. "Let them wonder what happened."

She pursed her mouth and shook her head. "We could tell them that we have some prisoners who we are taking back to Alliance space as evidence."

"Evidence of what? Those prisoners won't say a thing to confirm any official Syndic involvement. Our doctors say if we try hard enough to force them, it will kill the prisoners."

"We know that," Rione said. "The Syndics do not. They know what they did to those soldiers. They don't know whether or not we have developed new techniques for dealing with mental conditioning."

"Hmmm." That could make some Syndic CEOs very nervous indeed. And perhaps spare some future soldiers being given the same conditioning if the Syndics believed the conditioning wouldn't stop them from talking. "If you can imply something like that, go ahead. But don't offer any details about the attack on *Invincible*."

"Do you think I'm an amateur, Admiral?" She glanced at the star display. "We should also tell them that we were unable to save their hypernet gate despite our best efforts."

"Did you see the report that Captain Smythe prepared for us to send to the Syndics?"

"Smythe didn't write that. I'd like to know who did."

"Why?"

Rione eyed him. "Because whoever it is has some very useful talents."

Geary bent his lips momentarily in a totally fake smile. "That person's identity is my secret for now."

"Have it your way."

She had given in too easily. He had a feeling that Rione would be bending some efforts to learn Lieutenant Jamenson's identity. "Is there anything else?"

"One other thing, Admiral." She turned an enigmatic look on him. "How do you feel about it?"

"About what?"

"Destroying the hypernet gate. How do you feel about it?"

"What kind of question is that?" Geary said, avoiding an answer.

"You stepped across a line, Admiral. You and I both know that. You ordered the destruction of that gate even though legally you had no right to do so. The collapse of the hypernet gate here will send a clear message to the Syndics about the consequences of messing with this fleet, but you need to keep in mind that the limits on what you can do are only those limits that you place on yourself."

He almost shouted at her, almost told her to go to hell, that good men and women had died, and the Syndics here should be extremely grateful that he hadn't launched an orbital bombardment that would have wrecked every human city, town, and installation in this star system. Instead, he counted to ten inside before once again trying to deflect her. "As I recall, someone gave me the idea for that action."

"Someone did," Rione admitted calmly. "Is that a defense or a rationalization? *I did it, but someone else gave me the idea.* You can do better than that."

"Why did you give me the idea if you're so worried about the precedent it sets for me?" Geary pressed.

"Because I could tell how angry you were. How angry everyone in this fleet was. I can only guess what you *wanted* to do after we lost that battleship. The gate offered a means to strike back in a way that would hurt the Syndics badly but not by the sort of overt retaliation that might have created even more trouble."

He kept his eyes on the star display, trying to come up with another way of avoiding a straight answer. But Geary realized that her warning was justified. *That's why I don't want to answer her, to admit that she's right. I wanted to do worse. Maybe I would have, if she hadn't suggested using the gate's collapse as a means to retaliate. But that kind of mass retaliation is exactly what we're supposed to avoid. It's a Syndic tactic. It's not what our ancestors would approve of.*

I cannot forget that. I have moved my own boundaries for behavior I would accept. I have to hold them where they now are because if they slip any more, Black Jack could get away with doing things I once would never have accepted.

Eventually, he looked back at Rione and nodded. "I understand. I know what you mean, and I understand the potential dangers. I will keep your words in mind."

"Good." It was impossible to tell whether or not Rione was

pleased that he had accepted her warning. "I'll send a message to the senior Syndic CEO in Sobek, officially protesting the attack on our forces and explaining that, alas, we could not save the hypernet gate, which was too badly damaged during the fighting. He'll know that's not what happened, but there's nothing he'll be able to do about it. That report from Captain Smythe will infuriate them because it offers them nothing they can use. This star system is well enough off, but it only has one jump point. It's at a dead end in space. They're going to miss that gate."

"I hope so," Geary said. "I hope every minute of every day they look up and realize their hypernet gate is gone and that what's left of the Syndicate Worlds can't afford to replace it. And I hope a lot of other star systems still loyal to the Syndic government hear about it and reconsider what sorts of orders they're willing to follow."

"Don't hold out hopes for that result." She shook her head at him, looking severe. "Remember what *you* reminded this fleet of. Destroying things and killing does not often bend people to your will. They are far more likely to react in classic human fashion, by resolving not to bend or break despite every rational reason to do so. We may have strengthened the hold of the Syndicate Worlds on this star system by destroying their hypernet gate." She paused to let that sink in, then noticing that Geary wasn't going to argue the point, Rione went on. "On another matter, I will mention to the Syndic authorities that we hold… five… yes, I'll say five individuals."

"We only captured two Syndics on *Invincible*," Geary pointed out.

"Details, details. Two prisoners aren't enough to make them sweat. Five is a large enough number of prisoners to really worry them. Five individuals who lack any identification but are responding positively to treatment and are beginning to provide us with answers to the questions we are asking."

"Thank you," Geary said. "I'm glad you're on my side."

"Don't make that mistake, Admiral," she warned with every appearance of sincerity. "I am not on your side. I am on the side of the Alliance. That has never changed. One thing more. I will tell the senior Syndic CEO that the Alliance government will hold the Syndicate Worlds responsible for any further attacks carried out using Syndic ships or equipment no matter who is employing those weapons."

"Can you do that?" Geary asked. "That's threatening war if we get attacked again."

She spread her hands and smiled. "I am officially a voice of the government until we return to Alliance space. The government may repudiate my threats once we return, but until then, the Syndics have to take them seriously." Rione regarded him with a questioning expression, head tilted to one side as if to study him better. "Something else is bothering you, Admiral."

"Yes, it is." Geary clenched one fist, looking down at it as he spoke. "Quite aside from your reminder to me that I forgot my own rules about the limitations of reprisals in altering human behavior."

"Think of the destruction of that gate as vengeance for *Orion*, nothing more or less, and expect no benefits to flow from the act. You're human, Black Jack. Take the lesson to heart and move on."

"All right. But the other thing that worries me isn't so easily disposed of. Even if the Syndics take your threat seriously, word of that threat will have to filter back to the right people. It will take time, as ships carry the threat to the Syndic government at Prime.

Then word will have to come back from Prime. Just because of that time lag, which will measure in months, anything else they have already planned will take place no matter how seriously the Syndic leaders regard your words when they finally hear them."

"That's true," Rione conceded. "Maybe my threats are my own form of retaliation, something I should know won't really work but make me feel better."

"No, the threat is still a good idea. The impact will take place over the long haul, so it can't help us anytime soon, but it might change the plans of the Syndics in coming months. And there's always the chance that if something else is planned for this star system, the local authorities might call it off, using your threats as justification."

She nodded, as if thinking of something else, then spoke abruptly. "This diversion through Sobek is costing us time, isn't it? How much?"

"Not too much," Geary said, knowing that Rione was asking that question because of her concern for her husband, still sedated and now in sick bay on *Dauntless*. "It's a bit longer a path than if we'd come through Indras as originally planned, but only ten days more unless we run into significant obstacles at Simur or Padronis. Atalia is so close to Alliance territory that I don't think the Syndics could have prestaged any attacks there without them being spotted, even assuming that Atalia would cooperate with the Syndics."

"Ten days can be a long time, Admiral," Rione said, one of the few times she openly admitted to the strains upon her.

Geary nodded in reply, not certain what words would be right, if any, and thinking about the sort of obstacles this fleet might encounter the rest of the way back to Varandal.

* * *

Over the next several hours, Geary was bombarded with messages from the Syndic authorities in Sobek Star System. They demanded to know exactly what had caused the hypernet gate to collapse, they demanded to know why the Alliance warships were taking a path diving through the star system if they were simply headed for the jump point for Simur, they demanded that the fleet release to their custody any Syndicate World citizens in Alliance custody, and, in a breathtaking bit of gall, they demanded payment for the Alliance fleet's use of the hypernet gate.

Geary was on the bridge of *Dauntless* when Rione informed him of the latest demand. Before replying, he made sure the privacy field around him was activated so none of the bridge watch-standers could overhear. "Emissary Rione, please inform the Syndicate authorities that they can go to hell, where they will doubtless receive everything that is due them."

"Do you want me to phrase that diplomatically?" she asked.

"If you want to. I'm not worried about offending them. What's the proper reply on the prisoners issue?"

She spread her hands apologetically. "The individuals in our custody have no proof of Syndic citizenship. We have to assume that they are stateless unless the authorities here want to both claim them as citizens and accept responsibility for their actions."

"That works for me." He paused, looking at his display. "Lieutenant Iger and his people have found no evidence of any Alliance prisoners of war in this star system. It's just as well. If they were here, the local Syndics would probably try to bargain a swap for the prisoners we hold now."

"There's been no hint of that," Rione said.

"What about the stealth shuttles we destroyed? Any comments from the CEOs about that?"

Rione actually rolled her eyes in a rare display of open contempt. "The Syndic authorities here blame that and everything else on *rogue elements* and *unknown actors* who are all *not operating under the authority of the Syndicate Worlds.* They are, in their words, shocked that military equipment ended up in the hands of criminals who, for reasons of their own, attacked us."

"Too bad you can't strangle a virtual image in a transmission," Geary said.

"That is a shame. I'm a bit disappointed they aren't making a better effort at lying about what they're doing." Her expression had turned grim. "It may be that they want us to react, to overreact, in a way that nullifies the peace treaty. Or the opposite could be true, that they think Black Jack won't overreact, that you will keep your responses limited and thus allow the Syndics to keep inflicting minor injuries upon us until they add up to major injury."

"*Orion* wasn't a minor injury," Geary said. "What do you think my options are?"

"Walk a tightrope, Admiral. Hit them back harder than they expect but not so hard that they can cry injustice."

"How am I supposed to figure out what's hard enough but not too hard?"

Rione smiled. "I can help with that. As I did with the unfortunate loss of the hypernet gate here."

"I see." Geary cocked a questioning eye at her. "What exactly have the Syndics said about the gate?"

"You just want to hear how upset they are, so you'll be pleased to hear that they're screaming bloody murder about it. Demanding data that explain the collapse of the gate and prove that our engineers didn't themselves inflict the damage on purpose. Demanding compensation. Expressing great distress at such an act of aggression. Don't look so murderous, Admiral. If you answered them looking like that, you'd be proving their, um, *outrageous* claims."

"I have to admit, the sheer nerve of some of these Syndics is starting to get to me," Geary said when he thought he had his voice under control.

Rione smiled again. "I'm a bit more used to it. I am expressing surprise, shock, and dismay at their charges. I am asking for evidence. I am invoking the arbitration clause of the peace treaty. I am promising to look into the matter. They know I am playing with them, that nothing will be done, that their hypernet gate is gone, and they will never be able to prove we had anything to do with its loss, and all of that, I assure you, is driving them completely up the wall."

He smiled back at her. "You're good at driving people up the wall, aren't you?"

"It's a gift."

"Why are you being so helpful again? Did finding the Kicks and the Dancers really change things that much?"

She looked away, then back at him. "What changed things a lot was your discovering what was wrong with my husband. The thing done to Commander Benan, and the reason why it was done, are so far beyond what the public of the Alliance would accept that I now have a weapon that gives me an immense amount of leverage. Those who tried to use me, who blackmailed me, will know that."

"But if you go public with that, it might literally kill your husband."

Rione nodded calmly. "In my place, they would do such a thing anyway, and so they will believe that I would as well. Beware of people who are certain they are right, Admiral. That certainty allows them to justify almost any act in pursuit of their goals."

"Like the Syndic CEOs in this star system?" Geary asked, hearing the bitterness in his voice. *If only there had been some way to make them personally pay for what happened to* Orion...

She shook her head. "I'd be very surprised if there's any idealism there, Admiral, any sense of right and wrong. Those CEOs were doing what they thought would benefit them personally. There might have been private motives of revenge if they had lost someone to the war, but my conversations with former-CEO Iceni at Midway gave me some more insight into the CEO way of thinking. Their internal-security service produced true believers, but everyone else was motivated by self-interest or fear."

"How does a system like that survive?" Geary asked.

"Self-interest and fear."

"I was asking a serious question."

Rione gave him that superior look. "And I was giving you a serious answer. Self-interest and fear work, for a while. Until self-interest, unconstrained by any higher loyalty, becomes more destructive than the system can endure, and until the people's fear of acting against their system becomes less than their fear of continuing to live with it. Eventually, those things always happen. In the case of the Syndicate Worlds, the war meant that their leaders were able to use fear of us to reinforce fear of going against their system. The Syndicate Worlds is coming apart not just because of the stresses from the war and not just because it lost that war and a great deal of its military in the process, but also because fear of the Alliance can no longer be stoked to bind individuals, and individual star systems, to the Syndicate government."

"I see." Geary sat, thinking. "The Alliance is facing some of the same strains because fear of the Syndics helped hold us together."

"An external enemy is a wonderful thing for politicians to have," Rione said dryly. "They can excuse and justify a great many things by pointing to that enemy. But that doesn't mean external enemies are never real. What is that old saying? Just because you are paranoid doesn't mean someone isn't really out to get you."

"And the Syndics are still doing what they can to get us." Geary nodded as a thought came to him. "I've been wondering what the Syndic goal is. Why are they attacking us in these ways? They must know they can't win. But I think you just led me to the answer."

"I'm wonderful that way, aren't I?" Rione said. "If you are not in further need of my wise counsel, I will now compose my reply to the latest Syndic demands."

Geary returned to the bridge and settled back in his fleet command seat, trying for at least the hundredth time not to notice the absence of *Orion* in the fleet's formation. After spending months watching *Orion* because the battleship had been a poorly commanded albatross hanging about the neck of the fleet, and lately watching *Orion* because Commander Shen had done such a miraculous job of turning around the ship, making her a real asset to the fleet, Geary kept finding himself looking for *Orion* and not finding her.

He gave Desjani a sidelong glance. She was working stoically, not displaying grief, but he knew Shen had been a good friend of hers. Another shipmate whose name would adorn the plaque she kept in her stateroom to list those who had died and whom Desjani was determined never to forget.

"Yes, Admiral?" Desjani suddenly asked. She hadn't looked his way, hadn't shown any sign of noticing his glance, but had somehow known of it.

"I was just… thinking," Geary said.

She met his eyes, and he saw there that she knew what he had been thinking of. It was scary sometimes how well Tanya could read him. "We have to remember, but we can't spend too much time thinking about things that distract us from what we *have* to be thinking about."

"Believe me, I've done almost nothing but think about what else the Syndics might be planning to do. I've been holding off on a fleet conference because I wanted to have some ideas to talk about to distract everyone from… our losses."

She watched silently for a few seconds. "I doubt anyone can be distracted, Admiral. Not from that. But if we can't think of ideas, we ought to call in more thinkers. Have you talked to Roberto Duellos? Or Jane Geary? Anyone besides me and that woman?"

"Yes, I've talked to other people. *That woman* just gave me a good idea of what the big-picture plan might be for the Syndic government." He made an angry gesture. "But as far as the local threat, I have to face the fact that we don't have anyone like… well, like those two colonels that worked for General Drakon. Someone who thinks like a Syndic, someone who could guess what their next devious plot is going to be."

"You just want to see Colonel Morgan again," Desjani said. "Oh, don't get all defensive. It was a joke. One of my coping mechanisms. You should be used to it by now. All right, we don't have any Syndics in this fleet, except the prisoners captured aboard *Invincible* who aren't even admitting that they are Syndics, but that doesn't mean we don't have any conniving thinkers available." Desjani tapped a control. "Master Chief Gioninni, I am in need of someone with a devious mind."

Within a couple of minutes, the master chief's image appeared in a virtual window near her. "Someone with a devious mind? Do you want me to locate someone like that for you, Captain?" Gioninni asked with a remarkably sincere tone of voice.

"I'll settle for you, Master Chief. You've been keeping up on events in this star system so far, haven't you?"

"Yes, Captain. At least, I've been keeping up on everything appropriate to my position within the fleet—"

"Spare me the false piety, Master Chief," Desjani said. "I want you to consider the following question very carefully. If you were going to try to inflict more damage on this fleet while it was in this star system, what would you do?"

"You mean if I were a Syndic, Captain?"

"If it makes you more comfortable, imagine that this is a Syndic fleet, and you're trying to figure out how to mess with it again before it leaves this star system."

Gioninni's answer came without hesitation. "Mines at the jump exit. We can take all kinds of paths through the star system to get there, but we've got to use that exit, Captain. They know that."

"How would you keep us from spotting those mines in time to

avoid them?" Desjani asked. "They know that we'd be alert after the earlier attacks and watching for anything else. Syndic stealth tech on their mines is good, but not good enough to keep them undetectable if we're looking for them in a specific spot, and we're fairly close to it."

"A diversion, Captain," Gioninni replied. "Something to distract us again. Something to help hide those mines a little better from our sensors. It's like sleight of hand. It works not because what you're doing couldn't be seen but because you're doing something else as well that draws the attention of the people watching you."

"Any ideas what form that diversion would take?" Desjani asked.

This time Gioninni did pause before answering. "I'd have to think about that, Captain. It would have to complicate the picture for the fleet sensor automated hazard detection as well as divert the attention of the human operators."

"Please do think about it, Master Chief. Thank you for your valuable input. Are there any other matters to report?"

"Ah, one thing, Captain. It's sort of private."

Desjani tapped her controls. "I've got the privacy field activated around me."

And around him, Geary realized, since he had heard her words clearly, but he didn't comment on that and thereby draw Gioninni's attention to it.

"Yes, Captain. All right, you asked me to keep an eye out for anything out of the ordinary in a certain portion of the fleet?"

"The auxiliaries. Right. What is it?"

"Well, Captain, I have it on pretty solid authority that a lot of premium booze got delivered to one of the auxiliaries—"

"*Tanuki?*"

"That's what I heard, Captain. This is embargoed stuff from Syndic planets, the sorts of things that would be in high demand back home."

"I see. And just how did you become aware of this, Master Chief?"

"I got offered a deal by the same supplier, Captain. Naturally, I didn't agree to anything."

"The supplier wanted too much for the product?" Desjani asked. "And even you couldn't haggle the price down?"

"Now, Captain, paying extortionate prices is no way to make a profit. Not that I would ever engage in such a transaction, which, as you know, would be contrary to fleet regulations. But I did feel required to learn all I could about the deal just in case it constituted some sort of threat to the fleet or its personnel," Gioninni added piously.

"Your dedication to duty is a shining example to us all," Desjani said. "Do you have any idea what *Tanuki* paid for the black-market booze?"

"No, Captain. I couldn't find that out."

"Thank you, Master Chief. Do you have anything else?"

"Just one very minor thing, Captain," Gioninni said, smiling winningly. "A question. Will there be any other major course alterations before we reach the jump point?"

"That's hard to say, Master Chief, and it will be up to Admiral Geary in any event."

"I understand that, Captain, but you see when we went on this roundabout track to the jump point, I had to cancel all the bets in the jump pool and restart the whole thing."

"That must have been a lot of work, Master Chief," Desjani said with false sympathy.

Unseen by Gioninni, Geary grinned. Jump pools had been around as long as jump drives. Crew members would place minor wagers on the exact moment when the ship would enter jump, and whoever came closest to the actual time won the whole pot. For some inexplicable reason, the fleet had never cracked down on the practice, instead recognizing its importance for morale and as a relief valve for gambling cravings that might otherwise show up in worse forms. To Geary's knowledge, the only times the official hammer had come down on jump pools were when the sizes of the individual wagers grew too large.

"Master Chief, I will ensure that the Admiral takes into account the impact on your workload if he orders another significant change in the arrival time at the jump point," Desjani continued.

"Now, Captain," Gioninni protested, "you know I'm the hardest-working sailor on this ship. Excepting for you and the Admiral, of course."

"That depends upon how we define 'work,' Master Chief. Thank you again for your information and your suggestion."

Desjani ended the call and looked pointedly at Geary. "What do you think, Admiral?"

"About the jump pool, the booze, or the Syndic plans?"

"I *told* you that you had to keep an eye on Smythe."

"Which you are doing a good job of," Geary pointed out. "Did you know that the auxiliaries also acquired some important rare-earth materials while we were at Midway? They didn't get those from any asteroid mining, but we needed them, so I didn't ask inconvenient questions. Smythe has probably broken half of the rules in the book, but a lot of the time he's breaking the rules to get the job done."

"And you're willing to look the other way at the other times because of that?"

"Yes. As long as he's not hurting the fleet. I will ask some leading questions about Syndic booze to let him know he's being watched and had better not play any criminal games with it." He could see she was getting ready to argue the point. "It's just like your not asking certain questions of Master Chief Gioninni because his particular skills can be very useful to you and to *Dauntless*."

She paused in the midst of starting to say something, then nodded ruefully. "You've got me there. What about the master chief's guess about what the Syndics will do?"

"I think he's very likely right," Geary said. "You and I should have seen that, but we were too focused on threats along the path to that jump point to realize that the final approach to that jump exit is the only place left in this star system that we have to go." He ran a quick query on his display. "There have been a couple of merchant ships seen leaving via that jump point since we arrived, but those ships could have been sent through on purpose on paths to avoid any mines so we would think there's no threat there."

"But there has to be a diversion to distract us when we're near that jump point. What would work? Stealth shuttles aren't cheap or available in large numbers, and we put a decent dent in how many of them the Syndics must have in this region of space. And that boarding operation only succeeded as much as it did because we were already distracted by another attack."

"Something different," Geary said. "They'll know we're watching for the same things coming at us. They'll want to do something we're not watching for. Whatever that is. All right. I'm calling a fleet conference."

He never looked forward to conferences like this, even when there was nothing but good news or routine events to discuss. So far, Sobek had provided nothing good or routine, so this virtual gathering of the fleet's ship captains promised to be the same.

Geary stood in the fleet conference room, looking across the assembled images of his ships' commanding officers. A rather small compartment in reality, the meeting software made it seem vast enough to hold everyone, the table in front of Geary virtually expanded to seat hundreds of men and women. The most senior officers, the captains and commanders in charge of battleships and battle cruisers, General Carabali of the Marines and the senior fleet engineers, were "seated" closest to Geary, with the others farther way in descending order of seniority and the size of their command. He could look at any one of them, though, and the software would automatically zoom in on that individual, displaying name, rank, and command.

It all made meetings very easy to hold. For the most part, Geary considered that a negative aspect of the software. As a rule, he thought that meetings should be hard to hold and hard to get to, crowded into stuffy, uncomfortable rooms where everyone wanted to leave as soon as possible.

But sometimes even he had to hold meetings like this, and at those times the software was a very nice thing to have.

"You're all familiar with the situation," Geary said. "The loss of *Orion* was a terrible blow, but her crew died with honor, doing their duty, and will surely be welcomed by the living stars."

"A terrible loss," Captain Duellos of the battle cruiser *Inspire* commented with unusual harshness. "We have lost too many comrades in battle. I wish *Orion* had been able to take more of the enemy with her and that we had more means of making pay those who ordered that attack. What a shame that the hypernet gate here was so badly damaged as well in that action."

"Yes," Captain Badaya of *Illustrious* agreed, his face reddened with anger. "But not enough of a shame. It's too bad a few stray bombardment projectiles didn't put craters into a lot of important Syndic facilities here."

A low rumble of concurrence sounded around the huge, virtual table.

"Why not?" Commander Neeson of *Implacable* asked. "Why not make them pay a higher price? They attacked us. They destroyed *Orion*. Why not retaliate?"

Geary waited for another burst of agreement to subside instead of quelling it using the meeting software. *Let them blow off a little steam. We all need to.* "I haven't ordered that kind of retaliation because that's exactly what the leaders of the Syndics want us to do. They want us to break the peace agreement in such a way that they can claim we attacked them first."

That statement brought silence, finally broken by Captain Tulev of *Leviathan*. "Why would the Syndics seek war with the Alliance again when the Syndics do not even have the military means left to force all of their own star systems to remain loyal to them?" Tulev sounded questioning, not challenging.

"Because they want an external enemy again," Geary said. "The Syndic leaders know they can't hold what's left of the Syndicate Worlds together by using the force available to them, but they also know that fear of the Alliance provided a powerful reason for star systems not to revolt during the war. They think if we attack them, if the Alliance can be painted as an aggressive enemy that everyone must fear, it will again give the Syndic leaders a strong tool for keeping star systems loyal to them."

Badaya shook his head. "That genie is out of the bottle. Even if we came rampaging through Syndic space bombarding right and left, the Syndic empire isn't going to reconstitute itself."

"I'm not so sure of that," General Carabali said, her words coming slowly and carefully. "As weak as they are in the wake of the war, the Syndicate Worlds can still offer a greater degree of security to individual star systems than those star systems can muster on their own. That greater security against external threats and the promise of internal stability are the only things the Syndics *can* offer those star systems now."

"It creates a choice of enemies again," Duellos said. "At this time, with the Alliance at peace, the only enemies those star systems see are the rulers of the Syndicate Worlds. Their own rulers. Start the war again, and there are other enemies to worry about. It might work."

"It might," Tulev agreed. "If only a little. But from small advantages, large changes can grow over time. I see your logic, Admiral."

Badaya was still angry, but he was thinking. "They are goading us to attack. Why would they do that unless they *want* us to attack? I see your point as well, Admiral. But it is still a very bitter thing to leave this star system with only the loss of their hypernet gate to avenge the loss of *Orion*."

"I agree," said Geary. "It feels like far too little. Yet the loss of the hypernet gate here will have a serious impact on the local economy, as well as on the ability of the Syndics to move military forces quickly."

"As far as we know, this was their last functioning hypernet gate, except for Midway's, which they no longer control," Neeson pointed out.

"Yes, that's why the Syndics here are so upset about—" Geary stopped speaking as he realized that something major didn't fit.

Captain Hiyen grasped just what that was before anyone else. "Why are the Syndics here so upset about losing their hypernet gate if the only other gate they could access was Midway's? The gate was already effectively almost useless."

Emissary Charban had his eyes on the star display positioned above the conference table. "If they are that upset, it argues that the gate was still useful to them, that there were other places they could access through it."

"We ran the checks," Desjani insisted. "The only gate accessible was Sobek."

Hiyen shook his head. "The only gate accessible from *Midway* when *we* tried to access the Syndic hypernet was Sobek," he said, carefully emphasizing certain words. "We know that is true."

Commander Neeson was staring at Hiyen. "Have the Syndics developed some means of selectively blocking access to gates within their hypernet? Is that even possible?"

"I don't know," Hiyen admitted. "I don't know that anyone has ever looked into it. Why would we?"

"Why would the Syndics have done that? Tried to develop something like that?" Badaya demanded.

"Oh, hell," Desjani said with disgust. "The answer to that is aboard *Dauntless*, and has been ever since we got the Syndic hypernet key from that damned supposed Syndic traitor."

Duellos looked pained. "Of course. As soon as we escaped the trap intended for us at Prime, the Syndics knew the Alliance fleet was loose with a key to their hypernet. We assumed they were trying to counter that by catching and destroying this fleet. But why would they stop at that? Why wouldn't they also start trying to figure out how to limit the usefulness of the key to keep us from going anywhere we wanted within their hypernet?"

"They've been working on it ever since we escaped Prime," Neeson said angrily. "And it never even occurred to us."

"We won," Charban said. "Why should we have looked for new capabilities?"

"We do not know the Syndics have done this," Tulev cautioned. "It is a reasonable guess, I agree. But it is not confirmed."

Geary looked toward Rione. She nodded, so he turned to face the whole table again. "We do know the Syndics conducted some new research into the hypernet. They developed a means to block the collapse of hypernet gates by remote signals, the sort of thing that destroyed Kalixa. I don't know whether or not the Alliance has engaged in similar research."

"We didn't have the same incentive, did we?" Duellos asked. "We didn't have a star system turned into a charnel house like the Syndics did at Kalixa."

"The enigmas tried to do the same thing to Petit Star System in the Alliance," Desjani pointed out.

"But they did not succeed thanks to the anticollapse device created by our late and very lamented colleague Jaylen Cresida. A star system without a hypernet gate is a far cry from a star system destroyed by its hypernet gate."

Geary glanced around, but no one else seemed to have any suggestions. *Is this somehow related to fleet headquarters' attempt to pull anyone with hypernet expertise from this fleet prior to our departure from Varandal? I thought it might be to keep us from learning about the possibility of the entire Syndic hypernet being collapsed by remote signal, but was it about more than that?*

Jane Geary looked up with a stunned expression. "Lakota. Didn't you tell me, Admiral, that Syndic reinforcements showed up at Lakota and were surprised to be there because they had entered a different destination into their controls?"

"Yes," Geary said.

"How much do the Syndics know about that? The Syndics at Lakota had time to report it, didn't they, between the time our fleet left Lakota and returned to fight the second battle there? The Syndics would have learned then that there was some means of altering the destination of ships that had already entered the hypernet. What if they've been trying to learn how to do that as well?"

"This just keeps getting better," Badaya said in disgust. "Our trump card, the ability to use the Syndic hypernet while they can't use ours, is turning into a wild card."

"Maybe the Alliance government is researching the same things," Charban suggested. "Perhaps when we return to Varandal, we will find that countermeasures have already been prepared."

There was a slight pause, then scornful mirth rippled around the vast, virtual table.

"With all due respect to your record as a ground forces officer," Duellos said, "are you proposing that we should trust that our government has anticipated a problem and worked to correct it before it went nova?"

Charban had the good grace to smile slightly. "That does sound like a reach, doesn't it? But don't forget that the Syndic system is plagued by many problems, not the least being its own leaders, and still has apparently managed to produce some results."

"We'll find out some of the answers when we go through other Syndic star systems," Geary said, "and when we get back to Varandal. Whatever state the Syndic hypernet is in, whatever the Syndics can do with it, doesn't matter for us now that we're this close to Alliance space. We'll be using jump the rest of the way home, and it's not that far. We don't know what else the Syndics might try along the way, but they lost a lot of courier ships in the suicide attack, and a lot of elite special forces and stealth equipment in the attack on *Invincible*. They won't be able to replace those easily, and they won't be able to use them against us again or against their own people."

"That's not enough," Captain Vitali of *Dragon* said. "We lost a battleship and her entire crew. To an unprovoked attack conducted without warning. We can't lose sight of that just because of our speculations about the Syndic hypernet."

The murmur around the table this time was more of a growl as the reminder of the circumstances of *Orion's* loss generated renewed rage.

How do I respond to that? Geary looked over toward where Tanya Desjani sat. She was looking back at him with an aggravated expression, as if the reply was obvious, and he was taking far too long to come up with it.

Oh.

"It's not the first time I have dealt with an unprovoked attack, conducted without warning," Geary said. The reminder that he had faced the first attack of the war, a surprise assault that he had led a last-ditch defense against at Grendel a century ago, brought everyone up short. "The question is, do we do what they want us to do or what we want to do? Do we let them win, even though we beat them both times they attacked us here?"

The argument was logical but was warring against emotions. He could tell that his commanders, for the most part, wanted to buy into it but were reluctant to.

While he was trying to come up with points to reinforce his position, Captain Jane Geary spoke up. She had been quieter since the desperate fight at Honor, usually watching and listening instead of commenting, but now she spoke with an intensity that held everyone. "As long as the peace agreement stands, the Syndics are required to return all prisoners of war to us. They are required to allow us to enter their space in order to recover prisoners of war. Consider the cost to those men and women still trapped in Syndic labor camps if we play the Syndics' game now."

It was the emotional counterpoint he had sought, and Geary could tell it had hit home.

Badaya nodded firmly. "Captain Geary is right. We could kill every Syndic in this star system, and it wouldn't free a single

Alliance prisoner held elsewhere. Hell, we tried killing every single Syndic, and all we got for it was a hundred years of war. Let's honor the sacrifice of *Orion's* crew by vowing to recover every Alliance prisoner no matter how the Syndics try to provoke us. We'll kill anyone they send against us *and* get our people back!"

This time, those around the table shouted approval, while Desjani stared at Badaya with the same expression of shock she would have worn if a rock had begun debating philosophy with her.

Geary himself barely managed to hide his own amazement at Badaya's speech. "I could not have said it better. That will be our policy. We'll get this fleet home, we'll get *Invincible* home, we'll get the Dancers to our home, and we won't stop until we get all of those Alliance men and women held by the Syndics home as well."

Tumultuous approval reigned on all sides. He let it go for several seconds, then called for silence. "The Syndics may try something else while we're still here. Everyone stay alert. We're expecting trouble at the jump point for Simur, but that doesn't mean something else might not be out there. As you've seen, our path to the jump point is taking a wide detour from the direct route in order to avoid anything else lying in wait along the shortest-distance course. Thank you."

His officers jumped to their fleet, some at the far reaches of the virtual table leading a cheer, then, with salutes and determined expressions, the images of the commanding officers began vanishing and the apparent size of the room shrinking in size.

He forestalled Badaya and Jane Geary from leaving, though, waiting until they were alone except for the real presence of Desjani. "I wanted to thank you both for having my back during that meeting.

You spoke well, and you made some excellent arguments."

"I owed you a few, Admiral," Jane Geary said. "And my brother Michael is out there somewhere. We need to find him." She saluted and vanished.

Badaya made a diffident gesture. "It just made sense, that's all. The simple answers are appealing because they're simple, but that means you have to look a lot closer at them, doesn't it?"

"That's been my experience," Geary agreed.

"Well, you've taught us a few things." Badaya glanced at Desjani, his suggestive smile a return to the Badaya of old. "And you, Tanya. I guess married life has mellowed you! The old Tanya would have been demanding Syndic heads on stakes every kilometer back to Varandal."

Geary could see Tanya tense, but she just smiled back. "If you think I've mellowed, try and cross me."

"I wouldn't dream of it!" Badaya grinned in his customary oafish manner, saluted, and vanished.

"What the hell?" Geary asked the space where Badaya's image had been.

"That's what I was wondering." Desjani rapped the side of her head with one hand. "When he chimed in eloquently about the need for thinking instead of lashing out, I thought I must have gone crazy or slipped into some alternate reality where Badaya's smarter twin exists. Eloquent! Badaya!"

"He's been a bit different since Honor," Geary said.

"There have been rumors that Badaya tried to resign," Tanya said, eyeing him. "And that you turned him down. That you told him that you still had confidence in him."

"I can't comment on rumors or on private discussions with other officers. Not even to you. You know that."

"Did he try to resign?"

"Tanya—"

"He expected to die at Honor. Expected to die along with every person on every ship in his force," she said. "If anything can make someone change, that will."

"So did Jane," Geary said. "She told me she was scared and certain she was going to die at Honor."

"Yeah, well, you either die, or you don't," Desjani said. "If you're lucky, you live, and try to be worthy of that." One hand had stolen upward, as if of its own volition, and touched the Fleet Cross ribbon on her left breast.

"What happened to you, Tanya? When you earned that award?"

She stood up and looked away. "I didn't die."

"Tanya—"

"Not now, Admiral. I'll tell you someday... maybe." Desjani turned back to him with an enigmatic look. "If we both live that long."

8

They had come up on the jump point from a high angle, curving the track of the fleet when close to bring the Alliance warships onto a vector aimed straight at the jump point.

"We're not seeing anything yet," Lieutenant Castries reported, her voice tense.

Everyone expected to see something. After the attacks at the hypernet gate, everyone thought the Syndics would try again here. "Mines still look like the best bet," Desjani commented. "But we're a little too far out to spot them if they're just in front of the jump point."

Geary watched the track of a single ship ahead of the Alliance fleet, one moving much more slowly as it approached the jump point. "Are we going to overtake that merchant ship?"

"It should jump out ten minutes before we reach the exit, Admiral," Lieutenant Castries reported.

"Interesting timing," Desjani commented.

"Yes." He entered the commands to see the freighter's track to this point. "A suspicious mind might wonder why, after we had swung back on a trajectory heading for the jump point, that freighter left an outer planet facility at just the right time to closely proceed us through the jump point."

"It makes it look safe," Desjani commented, "but that doesn't seem enough of a diversion. Watching that freighter doesn't require any concentration at all."

Geary's attention was drawn by movement within his formation. The Dancers. Their ships had left the vicinity of *Invincible*, darting forward through the formation as if eager to reach the jump point before any of the Alliance ships. "Emissary Charban! Tell the Dancers in the strongest possible terms that we suspect danger at that jump point! They must not move ahead of our ships!"

"Yes, Admiral," Charban replied, concern and resignation warring in his expression. "They don't always listen. I'll tell the Dancers and leave out the suspect part. Maybe if we say we know there is danger there, it will make a difference."

"What do we do," Desjani asked, "if the Dancers race ahead of us into what we suspect is a minefield?"

"Pray," Geary replied.

He watched with increasing dread as the Dancers got closer and closer to the leading ships in the Alliance formation. Whatever Charban was telling them wasn't enough. *I should call Charban. Tell him to put the fear of the living stars in the Dancers and do it now. But what if he is doing that and I interrupt him and that causes a critical delay in getting the message across to the Dancers? Damn, damn, damn...*

The Dancer ships leaped past the forwardmost Alliance warships, weaving around each other as the Dancers aimed for the Syndic transport lumbering steadily toward the jump point.

An urgent alert sounded, jarring Geary and everyone else on the bridge out of their dismayed viewing of the Dancers' movements.

"There's a distress signal," Lieutenant Castries said.

Geary squinted at his own display, where a new symbol had appeared on top of the freighter. "From the merchant ship ahead of us?"

"Yes, Admiral. They're reporting fluctuations in their power core."

"What do our sensors say?" Desjani demanded.

"There are fluctuations being detected, Captain. The fluctuations we're picking up are consistent with a failure of power-core-control mechanisms."

Was it the trick they had been expecting? Or a real problem?

And the Dancers were getting very close to the danger radius the fleet's maneuvering systems had just illuminated around the Syndic freighter.

"For the love of our ancestors, Emissary Charban, tell the Dancers that freighter is about to blow up!"

Charban's image, his face lined with strain, appeared just long enough to nod in reply. "Professor Shwartz and I are screaming at the Dancers! We'll add that warning, too!"

"Maybe it won't blow up," Desjani suggested helpfully.

She winced at the look he turned on her. "Sorry, Admiral. But... there's nothing else we can do."

The Dancers were now well inside the danger radius from the freighter, splitting to swing around it as they continued on toward the jump point.

Geary watched them, glum. "The friendly aliens are causing me as much anxiety as the enemy aliens," he grumbled.

"Fluctuations in the freighter's power core are growing worse," Lieutenant Castries reported, dismay creeping into her own voice.

"Warning shots?" Desjani suggested, sounding despairing herself.

"They're out of range," Geary said, "and if they won't or can't understand a warning to stay away from a dangerous region, how can we expect them to understand having us fire at them?"

Lieutenant Castries spoke up again. "Admiral, the freighter just broadcast an abandon-ship alert. The crew is heading for their survival pod."

Geary looked toward Desjani, seeing the stony expression with which she was now watching her display. "Are you thinking what I am?"

"Probably," Desjani said. "They'll eject in their pod and request a humanitarian pickup. Then their freighter will explode. Then, when we're distracted by both of those things and our sensors are hindered by the aftereffects of the freighter's destruction, we start hitting mines. Assuming we're not also distracted by watching the Dancer ships hitting mines."

"Yeah. Another diversion, just as Master Gioninni predicted. There goes their escape pod."

"And here comes the request for rescue."

"Freighter crew requests emergency assistance," Lieutenant Castries said. "They are reporting seriously injured personnel. Power fluctuations on the freighter are exceeding danger levels. We are well outside the danger radius if the freighter's power core detonates. The Dancers—"

"Are well inside," Desjani finished, "but they're about to—*Oh, hell!*"

Geary felt the same way as he watched the Dancer ships, which had been close to the front edge of the danger zone around the freighter, suddenly alter tracks to come swooping back toward the newly launched escape pod. "They *can't* be that stupid!" he erupted. "Even if Charban and Shwartz hadn't told them anything, the Dancers would still have been able to pick up the power fluctuations on that freighter's power core. They *must* know——" He paused as a thought hit him.

"What?" Desjani demanded.

"Are they just messing with us?" Geary wondered. "Are they deliberately going into danger so that they——"

"They're heading for a minefield at high speed!" Desjani broke in. A sudden realization twisted her own expression. "They've got better stealth capability than us. That probably means they have better stealth *detection* capability than us."

"They see mines that are still invisible to us? Then why are they——?" Geary hit the arm of his seat hard enough to hurt his hand. "They're warning us!"

"Or screwing with us!"

The Dancers, displaying a maneuverability human ships could not hope to match, had nearly joined up with the escape pod from the freighter.

"Hold on!" Geary ordered as Desjani started to say something else. Too many things were happening, and his own thoughts were in a whirl. "I need to focus on all of these elements. Get everything straight. The minefield. We have to assume it is there, but beyond the freighter. The freighter. About to blow. We're well outside the danger radius, though."

"Of course," Desjani said. "They don't want us altering course."

"Wait, Tanya, please. The Dancers. Outside our own formation, within the danger zone about the freighter but intercepting the escape pod. If they stay with it, they'll be outside the danger radius when the freighter's power core overloads."

He paused, looking for anything he might have missed. "Lieutenant, are there Syndic assets in this star system that can recover that escape pod in time to save the crew?"

"Uh, yes, sir," Castries replied. "There are at least two Syndic ships that could do a pickup well within the endurance of the life support on that escape pod."

"So we don't need to worry about that even though the pod is requesting rescue."

"Clumsy of them not to forestall that option," Desjani remarked.

"They had to make things look normal," Geary said. "No other traffic within a light-hour would have looked very abnormal. So, the freighter and its crew, if there was one, is not a problem. We have to assume the Dancers are picking up the danger signs from the freighter's power core and will get themselves clear, and that the Dancers can see any mines the Syndics laid near the jump point better than we can see them."

"Right," Desjani agreed. "That leaves just our own ships to worry about."

"But… Captain… they said they have seriously injured personnel," an increasingly baffled Lieutenant Castries reminded Desjani.

"Lieutenant," Desjani replied, "odds are there are no seriously injured personnel on that escape pod. I would, in fact, be surprised if there are any personnel aboard it at all. Everything we're seeing and hearing was very likely preprogrammed and that freighter sent out here without a human crew."

"Very likely," Geary said. The distraction had come too close to working, though that was because the Dancers had thrown an unexpected variable into the situation. He touched his comm controls. "All units in First Fleet. Immediate execute reduce velocity to point zero zero three light speed." Another control. "Emissary Charban—"

The usually controlled Charban looked about ready himself to explode with frustration. "They just keep echoing back to us!" he said. "We say danger ahead, and they say danger ahead, then we do it again!"

"I think the Dancers are trying to warn us," Geary said. "They're not echoing. They're agreeing with what you're saying."

"They're—?" Charban visibly quivered as he fought to regain control. "That means I can stop trying."

"Yes. But I want you to tell them something else. Please inform the Dancers that we are drastically reducing our speed due to the threats in front of the fleet. Tell them they must not precede us to the jump point."

"Drastically reducing speed?" Charban asked. "What velocity does that mean? Never mind. I can't convey it to the Dancers even if you told me. I'll ask them to match our big reduction in speed. They can do that easily."

Dauntless's thrusters fired, bringing her bow over and around before her main propulsion lit off and began dropping the ship's speed dramatically. The structure of *Dauntless* groaned audibly under the strain, but Desjani, her eyes on the strain meters displaying hull-stress readings, watched them with a reassuring lack of visible concern.

"Nine hundred kilometers a second?" she asked. "I could swim through space faster than that. Why are you slowing down the fleet that much? I thought you'd dodge the minefield."

"Too hard," Geary said. "We have to assume the minefield is right across the entrance to the jump exit. They couldn't keep a minefield that close to a jump point for long, but from the prior attacks on us, they obviously knew we would soon arrive at Sobek. We'll get down real slow, crawling along, which will allow the fleet's sensors to spot every mine in our path and our weapons to take out the mines one by one. Our warships will blow a hole in that Syndic minefield big enough for the entire fleet to waltz through."

"While they watch?" Desjani grinned. "They're going to be real unhappy at us thumbing our noses at them like that."

"And we'll come out the jump exit at Simur still moving very slow," Geary added. "That's important. The Syndics are setting traps based on the paths we have to use and our normal methods of operation. If there's a trap set up at Simur, they might have prepared for us evading immediately upon exit. They might have prepared for other actions we could take. The one thing they won't be prepared for is us going at such a slow velocity because we never do that."

"Not until now," Desjani agreed.

"Power core overload imminent," Lieutenant Castries said.

The Dancers, along with the escape pod, were still within the blast radius, but as Geary watched, the six Dancer ships leaped ahead, tearing past the escape pod and into the clear.

The freighter, now less than a light-minute ahead of the fleet, exploded as its power core overloaded, producing a burst of energy as well as a sphere of fragments ranging from dust specks to large chunks, all fouling the vision of the fleet's sensors. As the globe of the explosion rapidly expanded, the escape pod reached the edge of the danger zone, taking enough impacts for damage to be visible.

"Good work on that," Desjani admitted grudgingly. "They timed it perfectly, so the escape pod got hit but not destroyed, making quick rescue seem all the more critical."

"And it looks like the Dancers did always know what they were doing. We've been breaking our backs worrying about protecting them, but then they went out of their way to protect us from a threat they saw."

Desjani grimaced. "I want to feel like the senior partner when it comes to the Dancers. I've got this feeling that they consider themselves the senior partner, though. Older and wiser than us dumb humans."

"I'll ask Charban about that," Geary said, realizing that the idea bothered him, too. *It's one thing to accept powers beyond human comprehension that know more than we do, but another thing entirely to accept another living creature as superior to us in any way. Has Charban picked up any signs of superior attitudes in the Dancers? Or would we even recognize superior attitudes in something so different from us?*

But now was not the time for that discussion. His attention needed to remain focused on events outside of *Dauntless*. And Charban deserved a bit of a rest after the recent attempted-communication-with-aliens fiasco.

Dauntless didn't feel any different when traveling at point zero zero three light speed. Space didn't offer obvious signs of slower or faster movement, the sort of things you would experience on a planet, like air turbulence and noise or nearby objects whose own motion relative to yours would change as your speed did. The battle cruiser felt exactly the same as she did when moving at a velocity of point zero five, or point one, or point two light speed. Endless space outside of *Dauntless's* hull looked the same. But on Geary's display, the speed vector for the fleet had shrunk to a tiny stub, and that reduction in velocity had thrown off the calculations of those preparing this trap. The fragments of the exploded freighter would keep spreading, their density thinning with every cubic meter the sphere of wreckage expanded. By the time the Alliance warships actually reached the region of the explosion, there should be very little hindrance to their sensors.

"Nice," Desjani approved.

"Thank you, Captain."

"But don't get complacent. There might be a trap within this trap." She hit her comm controls. "Master Chief Gioninni, congratulations."

"Excuse me, Captain?"

"You called it, Master Chief. Now I need to know what sort of fallback you might have created in case the mines failed."

Gioninni sounded dubious. "A fallback to the fallback to the diversion?"

"Something like that, yes."

"Captain, I have no idea. There's no room or time left for them to hit us with something else in this star system. Now, the next star system. I'd keep an eye out there. But you'd need someone with a lot better, um, strategizing mind than mine to come up with another trap here before we jump."

Desjani smiled, though it was hard to tell whether that was because of Gioninni's statement or because the fleet's ships were beginning to spot mines and detonate them using hell-lance shots. "No one's better than you at that particular type of strategizing, Master Chief. You just out-thought some Syndics."

"Well, hell, Captain, that ain't nothing. Syndics are as dumb as dirt. That's why they're Syndics."

"Good point, Master Chief. Stay out of trouble." Desjani ended the call and leaned back in her seat, grimacing even though the destruction of mines was happening with greater frequency as the fleet moved into the minefield at a velocity that in space terms qualified as plodding. "If I never see this star system again, it will still be too soon."

"We'll never have any reason to come back here," Geary said.

"We never expected to have to come here in the first place," she reminded him. "Hey, I just thought of something."

"What?" Geary searched his mind frantically for any possible threat he might have missed, any option be should have considered, any—

"The jump pool," she explained. "You slowed us down so much, it'll throw the jump pool off completely."

"Tanya…"

But even he felt his spirits growing lighter as the First Fleet finally jumped out of Sobek Star System.

Four days to Simur.

Four days to second-guess every step he had taken since leaving Varandal.

Four days to dwell on the losses the fleet had suffered as it went through enigma space, into the Kick star system, then fought the Kicks at Honor Star System, before returning to human space through Dancer territory and fighting the enigmas again at Midway. And now the losses at Sobek.

He had thought it was over. That no one else serving under his command would have to die, that no more ships would be lost. But the enigmas, the Kicks, then the Syndics again had proven him wrong.

The enigmas had been beaten once more, and some little bit learned about them, but there had been no visible progress toward mutual understanding and peaceful coexistence. How many of his decisions in enigma space had been wrong, had led to more problems instead of any solutions?

Had he made the right decisions at Midway, or had he backed a couple of dictators who would rule as badly as the Syndic CEOs they had once been?

The last two surviving Kick prisoners continued to hover on the edge of death as Dr. Nasr tried to keep them sufficiently sedated to remain unconscious so they wouldn't will themselves to death, yet not so heavily sedated that they would die from that. Medical calculations that even now sometimes went wrong with humans were much more difficult when dealing with living creatures with which human medicine had no experience.

And they had been forced to kill so many Kicks. Small wonder that *Invincible* felt like she was packed with angry ghosts. There had to be some material explanation for the ghosts, some Kick device, but he couldn't imagine what could create such sensations, and part of him could not help wondering if the ghosts aboard *Invincible* were exactly what they felt like.

If Charban was right, even the Dancers might be playing some subtle games with humanity.

Getting home would offer little respite. If his guesses were right, powerful factions of the government and within the Alliance military were scheming and maneuvering against each other and against Geary and this fleet.

He didn't really know anyone here, in this future a century removed from when he had once lived. Those he had known well, people who had shared the same life experiences as he in an Alliance at peace for the most part, were long dead. In their place were strangers who had grown up knowing nothing but war more terrible than Geary had once thought possible.

He was sitting slumped at his desk when Tanya stopped by his stateroom. "What's the occasion?" he asked. "You never come by here."

"I don't come by often because I don't want people thinking I'm grabbing a quick one with my Admiral and my husband," she replied, eyeing him. "But my Admiral and my husband has been holed up in his stateroom for long enough that my crew is starting to comment on it. And now I'm looking at him, and he looks like hell. What's the matter?"

His reluctance to talk shattered like a dam under too much pressure, words pouring out to his own surprise. "I'm not good enough for this, Tanya. I keep making mistakes. People keep dying. I screwed up with the enigmas and the Kicks. I shouldn't have accepted the orders for this mission, and I shouldn't have accepted command of this fleet."

"Oh. Is that all?"

He stared at her in disbelief for several seconds before he could find his voice again. "How can you—?"

"Admiral, I'd be dead now if not for you. Because I would have fought *Dauntless* to the last when the Syndics crushed the Alliance fleet at Prime. You do remember that, right? What would have happened if you hadn't been there?"

"Dammit, Tanya, that's not—"

"You have to remain focused on the positives, Admiral. Because, yes, you will make mistakes. People under your command will die. Guess what? Even if you were perfect, even if you were the greatest, luckiest, most brilliant, and most talented commander in the entire history of humanity, people under your command would still die."

She was speaking slowly, her tones hard enough to edge against being harsh. "Do you think you're the only one who ever lost someone? Who ever wished they had done things differently? Who felt like they had let down everyone who had depended upon them? If you keep judging yourself against perfection, you *will* fall short. Feel free to aim for perfection. I like that in a commander and much prefer it to superiors who aim for perfection in their subordinates. But when you inevitably fall short of perfection, don't consider yourself a failure. Look at what might have happened. Look at how many might have died. Look at what you couldn't have done. We need Black Jack in command because he is the worst commanding officer we've ever had with the exception of *every other* commanding officer I have ever served under."

"Is that everything?" he asked.

"No." She leaned in closer, her eyes on his. "You've still got me."

235

He felt the darkness that had been weighing upon him lighten. She was a child of war, but they had connected in a way he had never connected with anyone a hundred years before. He wasn't alone. "So, it could be worse."

"Hell, yes." Desjani raised one eyebrow at him. "What else?"

"There isn't anything else."

"Are you lying to me as my Admiral or as my husband?"

Geary shook his head. "I should have known I couldn't get anything past you. I've been wondering."

After a long moment waiting for him to continue, Tanya smiled with obvious insincerity. "Thank you for filling me in on that."

"Why do you put up with me? You could do a lot better."

She laughed, which was the last reaction he had expected. "You found me out! I'm just keeping you around until something better shows up."

"Tanya, dammit—"

"How could you even ask me that? How could you say that?" Desjani blew out a long breath, regaining her composure. "When was the last time you checked in with the head-menders in sick bay?"

"I haven't… I don't know offhand."

"You're supposed to be providing a good example to every other officer, sailor, and Marine in this fleet, Admiral. That includes getting your head checked when trauma stress gets too hard to deal with. If the men and women of this fleet don't see you going to get taken care of, they'll think they shouldn't, either. They need to see you getting help, so they'll get it when they need it, too."

He nodded again. "Yes, ma'am."

"And don't start with that! You know I'm right! Why did I have to come looking for you to find out what was wrong? Why didn't you call me? And when's the last time you had a good talk with your ancestors? *Our* ancestors, that is, since you and I tied the knot."

"About a week ago. To talk about *Orion*."

She bit her lip, taking a moment to reply. "Good. I've been trying to put together a message for Shen's daughter."

"And I've been too sunk in my own slough of despair to help." Geary extended a hand toward her but didn't touch her. "Thanks, Tanya, for reminding me about my responsibilities. I have to use them to motivate me instead of letting them overwhelm me. I'll go down to sick bay."

"When?"

"Uh… later."

"Fifteen minutes, Admiral. I'll give you that long to straighten up. Then meet me at my stateroom, and we'll both go to sick bay, and when we're done there, we'll go down to the worship spaces and have a talk with our ancestors."

"Yes, ma—" Her eyes narrowed at him intensely enough that Geary halted in midword. "What I meant to say was, all right, Tanya."

"Fifteen minutes," she repeated sternly, then left.

He went to get cleaned up but paused for a moment to thank the living stars for her presence in his life. *Even Black Jack needs a good kick in the rear every once in a while, and I'm lucky enough to have someone around who'll do that when necessary.*

Charban spread his hands, shrugged, and shook his head, all at the same time. "I don't know! I don't know what the Dancers think of us beyond the fact that they seem to see us as allies. It occurred to me as I was analyzing my own attempts to communicate with them that I was thinking of the Dancers as children. Perhaps because they can't speak clearly to us, perhaps because they're unpredictable, perhaps because it's more comfortable for me to think of them that way. Do they think of us as children? It's entirely possible. But is it true? I have no idea."

"Has Dr. Shwartz mentioned any impressions like that?" Geary asked. They were in his stateroom, any evidence of Geary's earlier depression put away and neatened up. Dr. Shwartz herself was on one of the assault transports, out of reach of all but the simplest communication while the ships were in jump space. There were other so-called experts on nonhuman intelligence with the fleet, but over time Geary had learned to trust in the insights of Dr. Shwartz far more than those of any other academic.

"No, she hasn't." Charban leaned back, looking up at the overhead. "Admiral, what do you see up there?"

"On the overhead?" Geary bent his head upward as well, seeing the welter of cable runs, piping, tubes, and vents that were a common feature of overheads throughout *Dauntless* and every other warship. "Equipment. It's like an organ system in a living creature. The lifeblood of the ship flows through that junk up there, as does the air, all of the signals that make up what you could call the nerve system of the ship. We keep it uncovered so it's easy to access if it needs repair."

Charban nodded. "Do you see patterns? Pictures?"

"Sure. Sometimes. Doesn't everybody?"

"Every human," Charban said. "But what do the Dancers see?

We haven't been inside their ships. Do they have exposed 'organs' like those on human ships? Or is everything inside their ships as carefully smooth and clean-lined as the exterior of their ships? How would they describe what we are looking at? Would they see obscene clutter? Would they see pictures in that overhead? If they did, what pictures? Or patterns? We don't know. And yet it is exactly those kinds of things that would help us understand the Dancers. We share those things with other humans, forming a connection, a shared understanding, even with humans we might detest. That allows us to guess at their motivations, their reasons for anything they do. But the Dancers? Why do they do anything?"

Geary stared at him for a while before answering. "What about the patterns? The way they seem to think?"

"I agree with Dr. Shwartz. The Dancers very likely do think in patterns, seeing everything in terms of interlocking components that form some image they can understand on their own terms." Charban spread his hands helplessly again. "But where are we in those patterns? We still can only guess. I would interpret their interactions with me as being... polite. But you can be polite with a partner, or to a superior, or to someone far inferior to you. *Noblesse oblige*, as the very old saying has it. But there's another alternative. That's the possibility that the Dancers themselves are not certain of how to think of us, just as we are uncertain about them. In us, that produces contradictory impulses. We are in awe of the Dancers, yet we also view them in part as if they were irresponsible children who need constant supervision."

"You're saying the Dancers may be making it up as they go along?" Geary asked.

"It's possible. They react to each event not in accordance with some unified image of us but in terms of what seems best to them when each of those events occur." Charban paused, his face working as he thought. "I have an impression… Admiral, when someone has something they have to do, you can tell. There's something about them, no matter who they are, that tells you they are preoccupied, driven, busy. Whatever term you want. I sometimes get that feeling with the Dancers. Before we left Midway, it was becoming stronger, a sense that the Dancers were eager to leave, to reach Alliance space, but refraining from saying so openly."

It was Geary's turn to shake his head. "Why would they be eager to go to Alliance space and yet not say so?"

"I don't know. If you figure out the answer, could you tell me?"

Geary managed a smile. "What does Emissary Rione think?"

"Emissary Rione?" Charban asked. "What does she think? If you figure out the answer, could you tell me?"

Not everyone who was acting in unusual ways was an alien. After speaking with Charban, Geary realized something else had been bothering him, something that had been concealed under the stress that had been clouding his mind.

In this case, the answers might be found in the recent past.

He called up records, letting them scroll past, trying to give his subconscious the clues it would need to figure out what was going on.

When his hatch alert chimed, Geary absentmindedly granted entry, only gradually becoming aware that Desjani was back and glowering at him.

"What?" Geary asked, looking away from the display over his desk.

"I thought you were not going to get bogged down again this quickly in useless regrets about the past."

"What?" he repeated, then understood. "I'm sorry, Tanya. Have I been out of communication for a while again?"

"An unusually long while," she replied, eyeing him suspiciously. "If you're not moping about mistakes, what are you doing? That's a playback of the attack on *Invincible* at Sobek."

Geary rubbed his mouth with one hand, looking at the recorded images once more as stealth shuttles were destroyed, and Marines counterattacked inside *Invincible*. "Something has shifted. I'm trying to figure out what."

She came closer, studying the display. "The attack on *Invincible* was a classic special operation. Stealth approach and stealth suits, board a ship undetected, we've seen that before. We've done that as much as the Syndics have. It requires special circumstances to work, though."

"But the suicide attacks. Those were different."

"Yes," Desjani agreed. "The minefield wasn't different, but the way they tried to get us with it was unusual. You're looking for some common element?"

He nodded, watching as the Marines once again annihilated the Syndics who had boarded *Invincible*. "These aren't major attacks. It's a series of small attacks, minor actions. They're not marshaling as many forces in one place as possible. They're not trying to defeat us in open battle." Geary looked at her. "Do they still use the expression being nibbled to death by ducks?"

"Nibbled to—? Oh. We say cows," Desjani said. "Licked to death by cows."

"That's disgusting."

"How is it more disgusting than being nibbled to death by ducks?"

"I don't know." Geary scowled at the display. "The Syndics can't hope to stop us or beat us. But what they're doing is not just wearing us down ship by ship and encounter by encounter. These sudden attacks, without warning, seemed designed to also throw us mentally off-balance."

Desjani nodded, her eyes thoughtful. "Small jabs at unexpected points. Like martial-arts fighting. Instead of going strength against strength, you try to get your opponent off-balance and get them to make mistakes." She paused, then focused intently on him. "They can't beat you."

"I don't need to hear—"

"I'm not praising you, Admiral." She pointed a finger at the display. "Fact. The Syndics don't have enough warships left at the moment to bring us to battle. Fact. If they did gather that many warships, they know that you would beat the hell out of them. They know you don't have any match as a fleet combat commander. Fact. Even Syndics can figure out what they're doing wrong if they get hit hard enough often enough.

"They've got a new plan, Admiral. They're going to avoid a straight-up fight with you until you've been worn down so badly that Black Jack himself couldn't win. Sorry, that's one of those old sayings. Instead, they're going to fight the sorts of battles you haven't proven you can best them at. An ever-changing set of unconventional, surprise attacks, none of them using too many Syndic resources, but all of them aimed at wearing us down physically, mentally, and emotionally."

He did not like hearing that the future would likely hold only more of what they had seen at Sobek. "How did you come up with that idea?"

"I heard it. A long time ago." Desjani bit her lip, blinking as she looked to one side. "My brother. As a kid, he loved the whole ground forces thing. He would lecture us about different kinds of fighting. Guerrilla warfare. He had this fantasy where the Syndics would take over a planet he was on, and he would organize and lead resistance forces that would eventually triumph over the Syndic occupiers. He had it all worked out."

Geary had looked up Desjani's family history, the official side of it, anyway. He knew that Tanya's younger brother had died the first time he fought the Syndics, one of thousands of Alliance ground forces soldiers dead in a failed offensive against a Syndic planet. Her brother had not lived to be the hero his child-self had spent years dreaming of, had never had the chance to carry out the detailed plans a kid had proudly described to his sister and parents.

What could he say? Tanya had recovered, as she must have a thousand thousand times before this, and was looking at him steadily again, as if nothing special or unusual had been said. He had been around her long enough to know what that steady gaze meant. *Don't go there. Nothing you can say will be the right thing, so let's just drop it and move on.*

"I think," Geary said slowly, trying to ensure he didn't say the wrong thing, "you may well be right. I haven't proven any special ability to deal with that kind of frequent, low-level, unconventional attack. Maybe I'm not very good at it. I'm certainly not experienced at dealing with it. And this fleet is already being worn down by the age of the warships and the hard use they've seen."

She nodded. "The Syndics are still fighting to win. They still think they can win. Part of it probably is an attempt to get us to restart the war so they can use that to hold together what's left of the Syndicate Worlds, but even if the war starts again, don't expect the Syndics to fight it on our terms."

"How long could the Alliance sustain a war of attrition?" Geary wondered.

"You already know the answer to that, and it's not a big number if you measure it in years or in months."

After Tanya had left his stateroom with a firm directive that he needed to get out among the sailors again to see and be seen, Geary spent a while thinking, looking at nothing, his eyes unfocused. Physical wounds that didn't kill outright were usually healed these days, everything made as good as new. But mental wounds, the memories and the events that left a different kind of injury, could only be treated. Removing the memories caused more damage than leaving them intact, so treatment was all about managing the injury, not curing it.

During their all-too-brief honeymoon, Tanya had woken him once with a scream that jolted them both out of sleep. She had claimed not to remember what dream had caused it. He would wake up at times drenched in sweat, having relived or imagined events in which death and failure were a common element.

Technically, the war was over. As far as the Syndics were concerned, the war had apparently just taken a different form. As far as the Alliance men and women who had fought in that war were concerned, the war would always be with them.

Geary sighed and got up. He needed to talk to the officers and crew of *Dauntless*, and he needed to swing by sick bay for another check on his meds. Maybe it was jump space getting on his nerves again. Humans could get used to a lot of things over time, but no one ever got used to jump space. Or maybe his nerves were on edge because of what might happen when they left jump space.

What did the Syndics have waiting at Simur?

9

Simur had never been an exceptional star system, and the twin blows of the war and the creation of a Syndic hypernet had done nothing to improve its prospects. Close enough to the border region with the Alliance to be the target of occasional attacks, and never that wealthy a star system to begin with, Simur had been hit especially hard by the creation of a hypernet gate at Sobek. Most of the traffic to and from the rich Sobek Star System that used to have to jump through Simur on its way had been able to go directly to Sobek thanks to the gate. For the last several decades, Simur had been declining from the not-particularly-well-off state it had once enjoyed.

Intelligence collected during the last Alliance attack to strike Simur, which had been eight years ago, had shown stretches of abandoned facilities, abandoned towns, shrinking cities and still-unrepaired damage from a previous attack six years before that. Simur only had a half dozen planets worthy of the name, and four of those were either hot rocks whirling too close to the star or icy rocks too far from the star. Of the remaining two planets, one orbiting a light-hour from the star was barely large enough to qualify as a gas giant, while the last orbited seven light-minutes from the star but was barely habitable by humans, with an axial tilt high enough to keep the northern hemisphere uncomfortably warm and the southern hemisphere uncomfortably chilly.

"At least the lack of worthwhile targets will help us hold back if we're tempted to retaliate for more attacks by bombarding them," Desjani remarked, as they waited for *Dauntless* to exit jump. "Unless the Syndics pumped a huge amount of money and resources into Simur since the last time the Alliance was here, there's not much even worth a rock dropped on it from orbit. Why hasn't Simur been abandoned?"

"Maybe it was cheaper to let it slowly dwindle than it would have been to evacuate the remaining inhabitants," Geary suggested. "Let's hope there's nothing there waiting for us. It's possible the Syndics concentrated all of their efforts at Sobek."

"Do you really believe that?"

"No."

"One minute to jump exit," Lieutenant Castries said.

"All weapons ready, shields at maximum," Lieutenant Yuon added.

"And," Desjani grumbled, "we'll enter normal space barely moving."

"If anything will throw off a Syndic surprise," Geary said, "that will." *I hope.*

He watched his display, waiting for the moment when *Dauntless* and the rest of the fleet would leave jump space, for the moment when the featureless, endless gray would be replaced by the spangled black of familiar space and its countless stars.

The strange lights of jump space always came and went at unpredictable times, but as Geary watched, several bloomed near *Dauntless*, off to one side.

"A cluster?" Desjani asked in disbelief. "Jump-space lights never appear in groups. Do they?"

"Not that I ever heard," Geary said.

"There have been more of them this time," Lieutenant Castries said hesitantly. "More than usual. That's what the old hands say."

Did the presence of the Dancers with the human ships have any relationship to the unusual behavior of the lights in jump space? Geary almost spoke the question out loud, then saw that there were only a few seconds left before jump exit.

Desjani saw that, too. "Everyone focus on your jobs!"

The moment came, Geary striving to fight off the disorientation that entering and exiting jump always caused. He had been doing it enough lately that his recovery periods were getting shorter and now spanned only a few seconds.

He heard combat systems alarms blaring before his eyes could focus.

But as he struggled to see his display, one other fact penetrated.

None of *Dauntless's* weapons were firing. Whatever the alarms warned of, it was not close enough to engage, meaning the threat also was not close enough to fire upon *Dauntless* or hopefully any of the rest of his fleet.

Not yet, anyway.

Geary finally managed to get a clear look at his display, then had to study it for a few seconds to grasp what he was seeing. "Freighters?"

"Junk freighters," Desjani growled. "And obsolete warships."

Directly in the path of the fleet were several ships ranged close to the jump exit. None of them were going anywhere. "They're almost on top of the jump exit," Lieutenant Castries reported. "They must be using their own maneuvering systems to stay on station. We're getting power core readings from them. They're all live ships."

"They may be live," Desjani said sharply, "but they're limping. They look like they were hauled out of a breaking yard. Six light-seconds distant. If we'd come out of jump doing point one light—"

"We'd already be in the middle of them," Geary finished. "At point one light, we couldn't have turned fast enough to avoid them even if the maneuver had been preprogrammed." He hadn't absorbed all of the information on his display, but he had picked up that there was nothing directly above the Alliance ships. "All units in First Fleet, immediate execute, turn up zero nine zero degrees."

Dauntless pitched upward, thrusters firing to alter her trajectory into a climb straight above the plane of this star system. Geary watched the paths of his other ships doing the same. Not all could alter vectors as quickly as *Dauntless*, so his neat formation was smearing across a wide expanse of space, but thanks to the very low velocity at which they had exited the jump point, none of his ships would come within the danger zones surrounding the old freighters and warships positioned directly outside the exit.

That maneuver would get the fleet clear of the potential threats directly in front of the jump exit, but bring it closer to some of the other threats being highlighted on the displays.

Four groups of ships, none of them particularly large, all three light-minutes from the hypernet gate, evenly spaced as if they occupied the corners of a vast, imaginary square centered on the gate.

Three of the small groupings held a single heavy cruiser, two light cruisers, and five Hunter-Killers. The fourth had two heavy cruisers and six HuKs.

"Our systems are assessing those warships as being brand-new," Lieutenant Castries reported. "Minimal signs of wear, and they're all the latest Syndic models of each kind of warship. But... Captain, they're broadcasting identity codes that are *not* Syndic."

"Another star system that revolted?" Geary wondered. "Maybe this reception committee is here in case a Syndic force aimed at suppressing their rebellion came from Sobek after using the hypernet gate to get there."

"I don't like it," Desjani replied. "Where would a star system that revolted get all of those new-construction Syndic warships? They didn't build them here. And there's no sign of combat damage on any of those ships. Did you read the reports Captain Bradamont sent about the fights at Midway when they revolted?"

"Yes," Geary said. "Some very bitter fighting and some ugly events. You're right. The condition of those warships doesn't match what we should see if Midway was in any way representative of what revolt is like for Syndic-controlled star systems."

An alert beeped, and next to Geary a virtual window appeared in which Lieutenant Iger could be seen. "Admiral, everything coming from the old ships directly in front of the jump exit is totally routine, as if they were conducting normal transits or operations. All of that has to be faked given the poor condition of those ships."

"What about the new ones?" Geary asked, eyeing the two groups closest to the upward-bending path of the fleet.

"Their identity codes claim that they are all units of the Strike Combat Attack Forces of the Simur Star System."

Desjani's snort of derision was loud enough for Iger to hear. He nodded in agreement. "There is a *lot* of interesting message traffic flying around this star system, Admiral," Iger continued. "But nothing that would indicate a revolt against Syndic authority. What we are picking up was transmitted prior to our arrival and consists of speculation about what the Syndic warships were doing here. Those warships showed up a couple of weeks ago and have apparently refused to communicate with anyone in this star system."

"They haven't communicated with anyone?" Geary asked. "Not even the senior Syndic CEO in Simur?"

Iger smiled despite his best efforts to suppress a grin. "Since the Syndic warships were hanging out near this jump point, messages sent to them came right where we could pick them up, too. We've got one of them. It's coded, of course, but we could break enough of it to indicate that the senior CEO here is demanding to know what their mission is. There's a fragment of the message that may indicate that the senior CEO received some sort of instructions from the Syndic warships and is disputing those instructions."

"There's no doubt in your mind," Geary said, "that those ships are still Syndic despite claiming to belong to this star system?"

"Don't answer that, Lieutenant," someone interrupted before Iger could speak.

Desjani clenched her teeth but stayed silent as Geary turned to see that Rione was on the bridge. "Why shouldn't Lieutenant Iger answer that question?" Geary demanded.

"Because, Admiral," Rione said, looking and sounding as if she were explaining the obvious, "the Alliance has a peace agreement with the Syndicate Worlds which limits our possible actions against any ships or star systems of the Syndicate Worlds. The Alliance has *no* peace treaty with the Simur Star System. If those warships claiming to belong to Simur and not to the Syndicate Worlds act in a hostile or just a threatening manner, you can act in whatever way you wish without concerning yourself about the legalities of the peace agreement with the Syndicate Worlds."

That could be useful. Geary kept one eye on the nearest groups of Syndic warships as he spoke again. "Why would the Syndics give us that opportunity?"

"I don't know. Perhaps they simply didn't think of that possibility. There is a great deal that we don't know. All we can be certain of is that the Syndics very likely are trying to lure you into doing something that you don't want to do."

Another alert, this time from the displays, as Lieutenant Castries echoed the information. "Ship groups Alpha and Bravo are accelerating on intercept tracks."

The fleet's automated systems had designated the four groups of new warships as Alpha, Bravo, Cable, and Delta. Alpha and Bravo were the two groups at the top of the imaginary square, and the two groups closest to the Alliance fleet as it climbed away from the threat posed by the suspicious old ships in front of the jump exit.

"More suicide attacks?" Geary asked. With the new warships

fairly close and accelerating toward intercept, they were only about twenty minutes from getting within range of his ships. And his fleet was still crawling along at point zero zero three light speed, putting them at a disadvantage. "All units in First Fleet, immediate execute increase velocity to point one light speed. The warships approaching us are assessed hostile. You are authorized to engage and destroy them if they enter your weapons envelopes."

Another transmission, this one on standard coordination and emergency frequencies. "To the unknown warships approaching the formation of the Alliance First Fleet, you are forbidden to approach within weapons range of any Alliance ship. If you come close enough to engage, we will fire upon you and take all other necessary measures to defend ourselves. There will be no further warnings."

And what were the Dancers up to?

The six Dancer ships were doing loops around *Invincible* while matching the movements of the massive Kick superbattleship as *Invincible* was towed along with the fleet. *Whatever the reasons for their actions, as long as they stay close to* Invincible, *and* Invincible *is kept deep inside the Alliance formation, I don't have to worry too much about the Dancers.*

Desjani shook her head, her expression bleak. "Normally, it would be hard as hell to stop a heavy cruiser on a suicide run. But with us starting out so slow and them accelerating from so close, our engagement velocity will be way under point two light. With the amount of firepower we can bring to bear, we'll massacre them."

"That bothers you?" Geary asked, startled.

"I don't mind killing Syndics. But I don't enjoy the idea of people ordered to kill themselves by bosses who are a long, long ways off and perfectly safe."

Yet another alert, calling attention to a high-priority message. Geary saw who it was from and hit the accept command.

Jane Geary looked out at him. "Admiral, what if this isn't a suicide attack? What if those warships intend to survive?"

That was the entire message. Geary frowned at where Jane Geary's image had been. "Tanya?"

Desjani frowned as well. "If they intend to survive? The only way they could do that— Damn! They'd hit some unit or units that are exposed on the edge of our formation."

Geary's surprised check of his formation revealed that he had plenty of those in the region where the Alpha and Bravo warship groups were headed. Several destroyers and light cruisers were on the outer boundary of the formation, screening higher-value units farther inside the formation. But if those destroyers and light cruisers were themselves the targets, they were dangerously exposed. Even those small groups of Syndic ships could take out a destroyer or two in a single pass if they concentrated their fire on one Alliance ship on the outside of the fleet's formation.

"It looks like you were right, Tanya." Changing tactics aimed at slowly wearing down this fleet, taking it down piece by piece and ship by ship, until it was weak enough for the Syndics to try a conventional attack to finish off the remnants. "The Syndics can't hide in space the way ground forces can on a planet, but they're still trying to keep us off-balance with constantly shifting threats and tactics."

There was no time to call out individual ships or plan maneuvers on the display. "Fourth Destroyer Squadron, Seventeenth Destroyer Squadron, Tenth Light Cruiser Squadron, immediate execute turn port zero... three zero degrees. Eighth Heavy Cruiser Division, immediate execute turn starboard zero one zero degrees."

It would take precious seconds for the command to reach the ships, then more seconds for the orders to be understood and carried out. He could only hope that there would be enough seconds left to make a difference, and that these sudden alterations of position among those ships would not expose the formation as a whole to greater damage if the Syndics really did try suicide runs again.

"She really is a Geary," Desjani murmured in admiring tones as she watched her own display. "The rest of us were thinking about what had happened last time, but she thought about what could happen this time."

"What does that make me?" Geary asked, mentally lashing himself for not seeing what Jane had, for making assumptions about what the enemy would do, for being—

"Not perfect," Desjani replied. "And smart enough to listen when someone reminds you that you might have missed something."

Watching the two groups of new warships racing to meet his formation as it climbed above the plane of the star system, Geary could not find much comfort in her words. The exposed destroyers and light cruisers were moving, their vectors curving in toward the mass of the formation, while the warships of the heavy cruiser division nearest those destroyers and light cruisers were curving out slightly to help cover them. Had he acted in time, had Jane Geary's suggestion been right, what would the Syndics actually do...

Groups Alpha and Bravo shot past the Alliance formation, their tracks changing at the last moment to curve outward, weapons slamming shots toward the Alliance light cruiser that was still most exposed.

"*Pectoral* took a hit through her shields," Lieutenant Yuon announced. "Minor damage. One hell lance off-line."

Groups Alpha and Bravo were still turning, arcing up and over in a maneuver Geary knew very well. "They're going to make another run."

Another alert pulsed on his display.

"Groups Cable and Delta are accelerating onto intercept courses," Lieutenant Castries said.

Geary glowered at his display, knowing his options were limited. *If I send a pursuit force after any of those groups, I expose that pursuit force to attack by the other three groups while the group it targets avoids contact. If my pursuit force is strong enough to handle that threat, it will be too slow to catch the highly maneuverable groups of Syndic warships, and it will weaken my main formation.*

Tanya was watching him, confident he would order some sort of pursuit, but Geary shook his head. "They've got us reacting to them. They want me to send ships out of the formation to chase them. I'm going to do the opposite, to give us time to think."

The necessary formation was the oldest in the book, a sphere. But he needed to designate where his units would go on the surface of that sphere, and how large it would be. "Armadillo," he told Desjani.

"What?"

"Formation Armadillo."

"Is that real?" She entered the request, then started in surprise. "Are you serious? A perfect sphere? That formation is—"

"Lousy. It disperses firepower. Against a strong opponent, it's a disaster because the opponent can concentrate against any point on the sphere. But if your opponent is a lot weaker than you, it offers no vulnerable points to attack. Everything is equally well defended."

"We're going on the defensive?" she asked, her voice growing sharp. "They'll see this and think we're afraid. They'll think we're curling up in a fright ball and too scared to fight them. The fleet won't understand that kind of behavior before the enemy."

He felt a stab of anger at her tone of voice and the pointed questions she was asking. "Yes, Captain Desjani, we are going on the defensive until I have time to think and evaluate what's going on in this star system. We are going to frustrate the Syndic tactics aimed at destroying our escorts, and we're going to frustrate whatever plans the Syndics have to stampede me into making decisions."

She subsided, flushing slightly. He thought Desjani might be angry, but from the way she avoided his eyes, it was more likely embarrassment. "My apologies, Admiral."

"That's all right. If I wasn't having to react to your anger, I'd probably be mad as hell myself. Help me set this up. But I'm going to make our attackers' job a little more difficult while we're doing that." Geary tapped his comm controls. "All units in First Fleet, immediate execute down one eight zero degrees."

That would bring them back toward the threatening derelicts right at the jump exit, but on the other side of them since the fleet had curved upward and now would bend downward, looping high over the old ships. He would still have to watch for any unit getting too close to those old ships, though.

Unless...

"I'm seeing that the old ships near the jump exit are not broadcasting any identification. Is that correct?"

"Yes, sir," Lieutenants Castries and Yuon replied in unison.

"Emissary Rione, does anything in the peace agreement with the Syndics restrict any action by me against hazards to navigation?"

She looked puzzled. "I will have to check, Admiral." Rione began entering queries, studying her display intently.

Desjani paused in her work arranging ships around the sphere of the Armadillo formation. "Hazards to navigation? Does that mean what I think it does?"

"I hope so," Geary said, drawing a slight smile from her. Maybe this particular Tanya storm would pass quickly.

Rione blinked as she refocused on Geary. "Admiral, all the peace agreement says is that standard navigational practices are to be respected. I believe that is only in the agreement because it's part of the boilerplate for treaties."

"Thank you, Madam Emissary. Captain Desjani, have the rules for dealing with navigational hazards changed in the last century?"

She shook her head, smiling wider. "No, sir. Any ship encountering a navigational hazard to the movement of other ships is to either post warn-off beacons or take necessary steps to eliminate the hazard."

"I don't think we need to expend any warn-off beacons," Geary said. "Especially since those derelicts are so close to the jump exit. An arriving ship might not have time to avoid them in response to a warn-off." He studied his display briefly, watching the increasingly shabby formation of the First Fleet as it came over and headed straight down relative to the plane of the star system.

The way the fleet's formation was now arranged, one of the

battle cruiser divisions would be on the side closest to the old ships as they went down past the jump exit.

"Captain Tulev, this is Admiral Geary. The ships I have just designated as derelicts pose a hazard to navigation. You are to alter the course of the Second Battle Cruiser Division sufficiently to target and destroy the derelicts using specter missiles. Do not close within hell-lance range. Return to the formation after firing missiles. Geary, out."

Ten seconds later, Captain Tulev called from *Leviathan*. "I understand. We will destroy the derelicts."

Desjani nodded approvingly. "Those small groups of Syndic warships won't want to tangle with Tulev's division of battle cruisers. Permission to ask a question?"

"Dammit, Tanya—"

"I'll take that as a yes, Admiral. Why are we destroying those things? Not that I object to destroying them."

He gave her an annoyed look. "We're destroying them, Captain Desjani, because I don't want to have to worry about them anymore, and because I can eliminate what are very likely Syndic booby traps without the Syndics being able to object or complain."

Rione broke in. "You are certain those derelicts are dangerous?"

"I am, Madam Emissary. You remember what we did at Lakota, rigging badly damaged ships to explode? You told me while we were at Midway that President Iceni said high-level Syndics had seen detailed reports on the tactics I used after I assumed command of the fleet."

"And you think the Syndics are trying to use your own methods against you?" Rione asked.

"From what we heard at Midway, I think they're going to do their best."

The sudden reversal in the track of the Alliance fleet had forced the four groups of Syndic ships to make dramatic changes to their own vectors. Groups Alpha and Bravo found themselves far out of position, required to alter course to dive in pursuit of the Alliance formation. Groups Cable and Delta, coming up toward the Alliance ships, faced the opposite problem as their intercepts with the Alliance fleet abruptly threatened to occur much sooner and at much higher relative velocity than planned.

Geary watched Cable and Delta closely, wanting to see how they reacted. Would they adjust their tracks on the fly to manage a quicker and riskier encounter or pull off to come around again under more controlled conditions?

"Scared them off," Desjani commented in a neutral voice as Cable and Delta both curved outward, avoiding contact with any Alliance ships. "What do you think of this?"

He looked over the work on the Armadillo she had done to supplement his. The Alliance formation would shrink in, forming a fairly tight ball, the assault transports, *Invincible*, and the auxiliaries in the center, battleships and battle cruisers spaced around the outer shell to reinforce tight lattices of smaller warships. "It looks good to me. Are you buying into this now?"

"Yes, sir." She shrugged. "Whatever they're up to, they won't expect this. I've never seen it used."

"Neither have I. It's one hell of a big target. We'll hold it long enough to figure out what to do next, and not a moment longer." He watched Tulev's battle cruisers, *Leviathan*, *Dragon*, *Steadfast*, and

Valiant, sweep outward from the current formation, altering their track enough to come within missile range of the derelicts. The old ships must still have some maneuvering capability in order to stay directly in front of and that close to the jump exit, but whatever that capability was it wouldn't be enough for those half wrecks to avoid missiles.

"Are there any crews aboard them?" Charban asked. Unnoticed, he had also come onto the bridge.

Desjani waved toward Lieutenant Castries, delegating the answer to her.

"It's doubtful there are any crews on any of them, sir," Castries said. "Automated systems would have easily handled the maneuvering to keep those old ships on station, and we've received no indications of any living crew aboard."

"Thank you," Charban said. "What if there *are* people on board?"

"If there are… Sir, if there is anyone aboard any of those ships, they will see the missiles coming in plenty of time to get into an escape pod."

"Which would not do them much good if the Admiral's estimate is right and those ships are rigged as bombs," Rione pointed out.

Geary turned enough to give her a pointed look. *I know she agreed with my decision to take out those derelicts. Sometimes that woman is contrary just for the sake of being contrary.* "If the ships are rigged as bombs, anyone on board would know that. We can't be responsible if they get caught in a trap they intended for us."

He watched as missiles launched from Tulev's four battle cruisers, two specters for each derelict. Geary's hand twitched toward his comm controls. *The auxiliaries have been manufacturing replacement weapons for all they're worth, but we're still not fully up to strength on missiles. I should have told him to only use one per ship—*

"Admiral," Desjani said, "you can always count on Captain Tulev to do the job right without being told exactly how to do it. By using two missiles per target, he's overkilling some of the derelicts but ensuring that every target is eliminated just as you ordered."

This time he looked at her suspiciously. "How do you know...? Never mind. You're right. We're even."

"I'm not keeping count."

"The hell you aren't." Geary let his hand complete the motion to his comm controls this time. "All units in the First Fleet, this is Admiral Geary. At time two zero, all units come up zero eight zero degrees, come starboard three five degrees, assume Formation Armadillo as attached to this transmission. Geary, out."

The fleet would simultaneously swing back up and slightly to one side, aiming for the next jump point, while also compressing down into the Armadillo. It was the sort of maneuver involving hundreds of ships that humans would have required days to work out, but the fleet's maneuvering systems could come up with a coordinated solution within seconds.

The questions began coming in less than a minute later. Geary squinted at the list of incoming transmissions. Almost every senior officer in the fleet was calling, and it didn't take a genius to know what they were calling about.

Desjani glanced toward his comm inbox, gave him an "I told you so" look, then returned to studying her own display.

I thought I was done with this kind of thing, Geary thought crossly. *Being open to advice and input is one thing. Having my decisions questioned is another.*

His hand hovered over the comm controls, but something made him look over toward Desjani. She was giving him a sidelong look that spoke volumes. *Are you* sure *that you want to do that, Admiral?*

Geary lowered his hand, thinking. *No one is challenging my right to command. Not anymore. At least, no one is doing that openly. They are expressing concern about my proposed course of action. These are good officers for the most part. They've followed me and done their jobs well. I need to respect their concerns instead of telling them to shut up and do what they're told.* Taking a deep breath, he hit the fleet-broadcast command that would send his words to every commanding officer in the First Fleet.

"This is Admiral Geary. I understand that there is some concern regarding our currently ordered movements. Be assured that the purpose of the new formation is to confound any Syndic plans against us here at Simur. After ensuring that the Syndics cannot successfully attack us, we will analyze the situation here and determine just what the Syndic plans are. Then we will change our formation and take any measures required not only to frustrate those plans but also respond as appropriate. Geary, out."

He paused, thinking again. "Madam Emissary, would you contact the senior Syndic CEO in this star system and register a formal complaint about aggression by those warships against an Alliance fleet?"

Rione raised her eyebrows at him. "You know what the answer will be. The senior Syndic CEO will claim those warships are not Syndic."

Geary nodded. "Yes, but those warships are also claiming to be under the control of *this* star system. That would make that senior CEO responsible regardless. I want to see what they say about that."

"An interesting suggestion, Admiral." Rione beckoned to

Charban. "Let's go send that message. We'll talk about how to word it on the way to the conference room."

But she paused as the specter missiles from Tulev's battle cruisers began impacting on the derelicts. Some of the explosions were appropriate to the impact, the warheads of the missiles combining with the kinetic energy of the missile itself to blow apart ships that were already rickety.

Of the seven derelicts hit, however, four blew apart with much greater force than missile warhead and impact could explain. Geary watched the spread of shrapnel and high-velocity particles from the explosions, feeling cold satisfaction at having guessed right. Those derelicts had been weapons, planted across the path of the Alliance fleet, kept on station by maneuvering capabilities that mines could not match.

Rione sketched a brief, half-mocking salute Geary's way, then left the bridge with Charban.

Geary kept his eyes on his display as the fleet coalesced into the tight sphere of the Armadillo formation. The four groups of new Syndic warships, apparently uncertain as to what the Alliance ships were doing, had all swung off from intercepts and were proceeding to positions at different points around the Alliance formation. He had a mental image of frustrated mosquitoes swarming around an impenetrable mesh of netting.

No. That's wrong. That image assumes that those Syndic warships aren't still a danger. I can't be sure of that. I don't know what else the Syndics might pull now that they can't fight me on conventional terms. They used suicide attacks, a boarding operation, and a minefield at Sobek. That's what we know of. What else is here?

"So far they haven't repeated themselves," Desjani mused.

Had he spoken that last aloud or was Tanya reading his mind again? "What else can those warships do?" Geary asked.

"Distract us?" She asked that as alerts sounded.

The vectors of all four groups of warships were changing as they swung around and accelerated toward different parts of the Alliance formation.

"They shouldn't be able to damage the hide of the Alliance Armadillo!" Desjani observed with overstated bravado. Muffled laughter sounded from the back of the bridge as assorted lieutenants and other watch-standers absorbed their captain's joke.

Geary ignored the mockery as he ran a couple of quick simulations. "Even if they go onto suicide vectors, we've got a tight enough formation with enough firepower on the outside to be able to blow them apart before they penetrate our, uh, formation." He had almost said "hide," which would have only reinforced Desjani's joke.

As it was, he had a bad feeling that he would be hearing comments about the Alliance Armadillo for years to come.

Despite his certainty that the defensive arrangement of ships would frustrate the Syndic attackers, Geary still felt tense as the four groups of ships swung in against different parts of the outer shell of the Alliance formation. The Syndics bored in, entering the Alliance missile envelopes, and specters began leaping from the nearest Alliance warships.

But the Syndics pitched around and climbed or dove away almost as soon as they had entered missile range. Geary watched, angry, as dozens of missiles were wasted, their targets zooming out of range.

"I should have guessed they'd do something like that."

"They won't get away with it again," Desjani assured him. "I recommend you tell the ships to hold missile fire until the Syndics are too close to evade out of range."

"Yeah. Good idea." He transmitted the orders, glaring at his display. It wasn't a stalemate. As long as the Alliance ships kept moving, they would reach the next jump point and leave Simur. But it felt like a stalemate as the Syndic warships bent their vectors back toward the Alliance formation again. "They may not be able to hurt us, but they've got the initiative. I don't want to give them time to think up something."

"Hmmm," Desjani murmured. She hesitated as a thought struck her, then leaned toward her display, watching intently as she entered commands. "They're using automated maneuvering. I'm sure of it."

"How can you be sure?" Geary asked.

"The movements are extremely precise. Every ship moves at the exact same moment, and every maneuver is identical for every ship. Do a replay of their tracks when those four groups last came at us, then overlay the tracks of all four groups on each other."

"Identical," Geary said. "Not just each ship, the entire formation. The exact same approach vector and the same avoidance vector."

"They're new," Desjani insisted. "Not just the ships. The crews. They don't have the training to maneuver manually, so they're letting their automated systems handle everything. Maybe they've got orders to do that. But if they're using automated systems, then those systems will have patterns."

"How long will it take us to analyze those patterns?"

She paused, then made an uncertain gesture. "A while. We'll need examples of their attack patterns. I don't know how many. Eventually, our combat systems will be able to predict their movements."

"Eventually." Hanging around Simur waiting an indefinite period while Syndic warships made repeated passes at his formation didn't sound like a worthwhile strategy. His fleet wouldn't be happy with remaining on the defensive while the Syndics nipped at the Alliance formation, but if the fleet kept heading home, that should counteract the unhappiness to a considerable extent. He still had to worry about getting the Dancers, and *Invincible*, safely back to Alliance territory. "Tanya, let's aim for the jump point for Padronis. Circuitous path, just in case there are any more surprises in this star system."

Desjani paused again, but whatever she planned to say was interrupted by a call to Geary from the intelligence compartment on *Dauntless*.

Lieutenant Iger looked almost apologetic. "Admiral, there's a new POW camp here. A really big one, on the habitable planet, and there are Alliance military personnel there."

10

His head beginning to throb in time to a familiar headache, Geary rubbed one hand hard against his forehead. "There wasn't before."

"Not the last time the Alliance attacked this star system, no, sir." Images appeared next to Iger. "This is new. Recent construction on the habitable world."

Geary studied the images, seeing large barracks and warehouses arranged in a pattern that had become familiar. The new camp was located far from any of the cities on the planet, in an especially desolate region of the generally desolate planet. That also matched Syndic practice, which placed their prison and labor camps either close to a city or in the middle of nowhere. "It looks like a Syndic POW camp," he conceded.

"We've also intercepted Syndic communications that indicate the camp was recently constructed as a central location for housing Alliance prisoners of war brought from smaller camps in other star systems," Iger continued.

"They're supposed to be turning those prisoners over to the Alliance as part of the peace agreement," Geary said. "Why build a new camp here?"

"Admiral... perhaps the Syndics don't intend to honor that part of the peace agreement."

If that was so, it would be part and parcel of Syndic behavior as far as every other portion of the peace agreement was concerned. "How many POWs are here?"

"As many as twenty thousand, Admiral."

"Twenty thousand?" Finding room on his ships for that many liberated prisoners would be extremely difficult.

"That's the top end, Admiral, what the camp was designed to hold. The Syndic comms we've intercepted since arriving at Simur indicate thousands of Alliance prisoners are there, but we don't know how many."

Thousands. That was enough. Hundreds would be enough. Maybe even a couple would be enough. *There is so much we can't do, but we can liberate prisoners still being held after the war that justified their imprisonment is over.*

"Thank you, Lieutenant." Geary sat back, rubbing his eyes with both hands, after Iger's image vanished.

Desjani's voice came from beside him. "This really stinks."

"It does, doesn't it?"

"Thousands of Alliance POWs. In a new camp. In a star system we had to come home through."

It stank as badly as any bait could. "What's the trap, though?" Geary asked.

"Do we want to find out?"

"Do we have any choice?" He called Rione. "Madam Emissary, we need to talk to the senior Syndic CEO in this star system about a prison camp."

It took hours for Rione's message to reach the habitable world where the Syndic CEO was probably located, and hours more for a reply to be received. Geary made good use of the time by heading his fleet inward toward the star and the habitable world.

The four Syndic ship groups made repeated passes at the fleet during that time, trying to provoke some response from the Alliance formation, but Geary held his fire, waiting for the Syndics to come in close enough to be attacked. They didn't come near enough, and he didn't let any of his ships leave formation to pursue the Syndics, so the stalemate continued. The fact that the Syndics were also being frustrated provided only a marginal sense of satisfaction.

The fleet had started out near the edges of the Simur Star System, about five light-hours from the star. The habitable world orbited about seven light-minutes from the star, so the curved trajectory that would intercept the habitable world was five point one light-hours long. Geary held the fleet's velocity to point one light speed, which produced a travel time of fifty-one hours. Even at a speed of thirty thousand kilometers per second, the distances inside star systems took a while to cross. If the fleet had been limited to that velocity in journeying to the closest star to Simur, it would have required thirty-eight years of travel to reach Padronis at a distance of three point eight light-years.

"We have a reply," Rione's image said, her voice giving no clue as to the nature of the reply. "Do you want to see it?"

He was on *Dauntless's* bridge, so Geary activated his privacy field, making sure it included Tanya so that she could hear and see the message as well. "Sure. Relay it to me."

Another virtual window appeared next to the one that held Rione's image. Geary found himself looking at a very stern-faced, elderly woman in a Syndic CEO suit. The suit, while immaculately tailored as CEO suits always were, appeared a bit worn, betraying how long it had been since the senior CEO at Simur could afford to replace her outfit.

The female CEO spoke in clipped tones, as if biting off the end of each word. "I must protest the aggressive actions of the Alliance armed forces in this star system. Only the commitment of the Syndicate Worlds to honoring the letter and spirit of the peace agreement between our two peoples restrains me from ordering an appropriate response to your fleet's movements."

He tried not to get angry, which would only make it harder to spot subtle clues in the words and actions of the Syndic CEO. But even through his attempts to stay calm and observant, Geary noticed that this CEO sounded slightly different, her posture not the same. She was speaking, he realized, not just to him but to some other audience.

"The mobile forces whose actions you protest are not under my control," the Syndic CEO continued. Somehow, those words held an uncharacteristic ring of truth. Had there been a tiny extra emphasis on the word "my"?

"I can do nothing to stop them, I have not ordered them to harass you, they are not Syndicate Worlds' mobile forces, and therefore I regard this as a matter between you and whoever commands those mobile forces."

The CEO gestured impatiently, one hand flinging outward in a practiced move that must have terrified her subordinates for decades. "As to the prison camp, I am aware of the obligations incurred by the Syndicate Worlds under the peace agreement. I am nonetheless extremely unhappy to have you demanding the release of those prisoners instead of offering to discuss the issue. You have doubtless seen that we have inadequate defenses in this star system, so I cannot resist your demand to yield the prisoners of war to you. However, neither will I cooperate. Bring your fleet here, use your own means to lift the prisoners to it, then depart, the sooner the better. I will be just as glad not to have six thousand additional mouths to worry about feeding.

"For the people, Gawzi, out."

As was usually the case with senior Syndics, the phrase "for the people" was uttered like a single, rushed word, lacking any meaning or feeling. Geary had almost stopped noticing that, until hearing the phrase recited with enthusiasm at Midway had reminded him that it could mean something.

Rione was waiting for his comments, looking mildly impatient. "What do you think of that message?" Geary asked. "That CEO sounded a little different to me."

"That's because someone is holding a gun to her head," Rione replied.

"In what sense?"

"In a literal sense. There's someone near her, but outside the transmission image, who is threatening her. It's obvious."

There were times when Rione's ability to recognize situations could be disturbing. He couldn't help wondering where she had gained experience in this particular situation. "Those internal-security people?"

She nodded judiciously. "Most likely. The ones the Syndic citizens call snakes. We can safely assume that they are running this star system right now. Not simply pulling strings from behind a curtain but overtly forcing actions."

"If that's so," Geary said, "the internal security here is forcing the CEO to invite us to come get prisoners out of that camp."

Rione nodded again. "It wasn't a very nice invitation, but the way she formed it as a challenge to us was interesting. And she sent confirmation that Alliance prisoners are indeed there. Six thousand of them."

"They want us there."

"Indeed. But from what I understand, her statement that she lacks the means to resist us is accurate. The prisoners had better be very carefully screened for pathogens, nanoparticles, or any other form of human-transported sabotage."

"Thank you." Geary drummed his fingers on the arm of his seat for a few seconds, frowning, then glanced at Desjani.

She shrugged. "That's as good a guess as any. They can't do anything else, so they'll try to sneak some kind of plague aboard our ships."

"Isn't that too obvious?"

"They've got four groups of obviously Syndic warships attacking us. and they're claiming they can't control them because they're not really Syndic warships," Desjani pointed out. "Obviousness doesn't seem to worry them."

"Yeah." He hit another control. "Lieutenant Iger. Do we have anything new?"

"No new threats identified, Admiral." Iger smiled slightly. "There are a few messages we've intercepted that indicate the locals are not happy about what the Syndic authorities are doing. This one from an orbiting mining facility near the gas giant is typical."

Another image, this of a middle-aged man in a shabby executive suit. "They're leaving us wide open for retaliatory bombardments! We received no warning, no opportunity to evacuate, and we don't have enough lift capacity here to get everyone out! Am I just supposed to abandon half of my workers and their families? We don't even have any defenses since they were never rebuilt after the last Alliance attack! Can't someone stop those Syndicate mobile forces from provoking the Alliance?"

Geary didn't feel like smiling. He knew why Iger did, and why Desjani probably would have grinned at the Syndic manager's distress. *Serves them right,* those who had endured a lifetime of war would think. *They started it, they bombarded us countless times, they killed countless numbers of our people, and now they deserve to sweat as they wonder when our rocks will come down like vengeful hammers from the sky.*

But he didn't feel that way. *As much as I wanted to get back at the Syndics at Sobek, they had been cooperating with the attacks on us. Or their leaders had been doing that, anyway. But these people are helpless. That Syndic manager is worried about the people who work for him. He and they are just pawns in whatever the Syndic government is doing. Even the Syndic CEO here is being coerced into something.*

"All right," Geary said. "Is that all?"

"There are other messages like that," Iger offered. "Otherwise, just the usual welter of fragmentary information. We can break out portions of coded messages and pick up open conversations where individuals talk about classified matters, but none of that adds up to any threat that we can identify."

"Master Chief Gioninni hasn't come up with anything else," Desjani noted. "I was going to give him access to the intel summaries, but it turned out he'd already read them."

"What was that?" Lieutenant Iger asked, alarmed. "The access list for *Dauntless* doesn't include Master Chief Gioninni."

"Isn't *that* odd? Don't worry about it, Lieutenant."

"Maybe what we need isn't just a scheming mind," Geary said, before an aghast Iger could ask more questions about Gioninni. "Maybe what we need is someone who can spot—" *Someone who can spot patterns in a mess of data. Someone who can see things concealed in a confusing welter of detail.*

And we've got that someone.

"Lieutenant Iger, you are to transmit to *Tanuki* all intelligence collected within this star system since our arrival. Mark it eyes only for Lieutenant Elysia Jamenson."

Iger, appalled this time, stared back at Geary. "All intelligence? Admiral, who is this Lieutenant Jamenson?"

"An engineer."

"An engine—" Iger caught himself and spoke with forced control. "Sir, the classification on some of this material—"

"I am aware of the classification and security concerns. On my authority as fleet commander, I am authorizing Lieutenant Jamenson access to any necessary level of data effective immediately. Make sure she sees everything you've collected here. Send to *Tanuki* any necessary read-in documents and security agreements she has to sign. Get this done quickly, Lieutenant Iger."

"Quickly. Yes, sir." Despite his words, Iger hesitated. "Admiral, I feel obligated to advise you that this action may result in serious ramifications when we return to Alliance space. Even though you have authority to do this, there may be strong questions raised as to the appropriateness of your decision."

"I'll assume that responsibility," Geary said. "And, for the record, I want it to be clear that you properly advised me regarding your misgivings and that I acknowledged them. This is my decision."

"Yes, sir. We will get the information package together and have it sent to *Tanuki* as soon as possible."

"Make it quick," Geary emphasized again.

Desjani was giving him a fish eye, but he ignored that for the moment as Iger's image disappeared, instead calling *Tanuki*. "Captain Smythe, I need Lieutenant Jamenson. Don't worry. It's a temporary assignment, on my word of honor. There will be a package of intel information coming to *Tanuki* soon, eyes only for Lieutenant Jamenson. I want her to go over it and tell me what she sees."

Smythe's expression had shifted through worry to puzzlement and now surprise. "Intelligence material? Lieutenant Jamenson is very good at what she does, Admiral, but that is not something she has experience with."

"I'm aware of that. But we're dealing with new tactics by the enemy, and I want to see what a new perspective might spot among the information we have."

"Very well, Admiral." Smythe had a calculating look in his eyes. Geary could guess what he was thinking. *Is Jamenson even more valuable than I thought?*

"Thank you, Captain Smythe. I have every confidence that I can count on you," Geary said, emphasizing every word.

Smythe jerked as if the phrase had stung him, then smiled. "Of course, Admiral."

Geary ended the call, then looked at Desjani, who was giving him a flat look. "Lieutenant Jamenson?" she asked. "The one with the green hair?"

"You remember her?"

"She's hard to forget. What's the idea?"

"Exactly what I said," Geary explained. "Maybe she will see something going on in this star system that the Syndics have tried to hide."

Desjani considered that, then nodded judiciously. "If the Syndics can get something past Gioninni *and* Jamenson, we might as well throw in the towel."

Geary took his time preparing for the recovery of the prisoners. He brought the fleet, still in the Armadillo, over the inhabited planet at a slant angle from the prison camp, letting his ship's sensors scan the entire area while the Marines launched surveillance drones to drop down and check out the camp from low level and at ground level.

Carabali briefed him personally, her image standing in his stateroom before a series of close-ups of the prison camp.

General Carabali pointed to the images near her. "We couldn't find anything with the remote-surveillance equipment. Nothing is there that shouldn't be there, as far as we can tell. But remote surveillance can't be exhaustive. There are too many ways to block signals and signatures, ways often configured to match weaknesses or limitations in remote-surveillance equipment. That's especially true in a camp that was newly constructed. One of the things we look for is new features. New concrete slabs, newly turned soil, new patches on walls, new underground cisterns and other storage areas, things like that. But the entire camp is new, so that offers us no clues. We know the camp isn't surface mined because we've seen people walk around freely, and command-detonated or -controlled mines could be spotted by the gear we had to check out the camp. Still, the Syndics are very good at booby traps. To be certain that there wasn't anything hidden, we would need to put a few hundred engineers down there and give them a couple of weeks to probe, dig, and examine with the best gear we've got."

The old headache was back. "But the surveillance confirmed the presence of Alliance prisoners of war," Geary noted. He could see them in the images, some of them clearly enough that expressions could be identified, clearly enough that friends and relatives could easily know them. The expressions of the Alliance prisoners reflected wariness, hopefulness, disbelief, and other emotions. Very likely, the Syndics had not told them that the war was over. They did not know what star system they were in, and they had never expected rescue.

"Yes, sir," Carabali agreed. "Roughly six thousand. We talked to some of them through the surveillance gear. They were hauled out of prison camps in other star systems without any notice and dumped here within the last few weeks."

"What else?"

Carabali gestured to the images again, her expression dissatisfied. "There's been a lot of activity outside the camp-construction area.

The ground shows signs of a lot of activity for a radius of about seventy kilometers around the camp, but, again, our sensor sweeps found nothing of concern. There's a dense web of paved and unpaved access roads crisscrossing that area, most showing heavy use from what must have been construction equipment and loads intended for the prison camp. We'd have to go in and dig extensively to see if there was anything under those roads or elsewhere."

"Seventy kilometers?" Geary asked. "Outside the camp?"

"Yes, sir. It doesn't correlate to any kind of threat I know of, and my engineers say when a project is being rushed, they tear up everything around it instead of being careful with grass and trees and stuff." Carabali sounded as if she herself wasn't too sympathetic regarding the fate of "grass and trees and stuff" if important work needed to be done fast.

How could something seventy kilometers outside the camp threaten a recovery operation? If the Syndics wanted to nuke the recovery force, they just needed bombs within the camp. "What's your gut feeling, General?"

Carabali paused, looking at the images. "I don't know of any reason not to go in," she finally said.

"That's not exactly a strong endorsement of that course of action," Geary observed.

"It's not my call, Admiral." Carabali frowned. "I'm dodging the question. If the decision were mine, I'd go in. I can't offer any reasons not to go in except for a total lack of trust in what the Syndics might do."

Geary snorted a derisive laugh. "Anyone who did trust the Syndics at this point would be crazy. What about buried nukes?"

"If they're there, those nukes are buried deep and heavily shielded."

The plan called for eighty shuttles, almost every one available, which would each have to make two trips to get all of the prisoners up to the fleet. "What's the absolute minimum number of personnel I can send down to do the job?"

Carabali considered the question. "Zero personnel. Send the shuttles on full auto, programmed to land, pick up the prisoners, and return. But that runs the risk of the Syndics subverting the systems on the shuttles since they'll have physical access to them. Worst case, they could load them with nukes instead of prisoners and the shuttles would tell us everything was fine until they docked in our ships and went off. Not so worse but still bad, discipline could break down, the prisoners could stampede for the shuttles, killing any number of their own as they all tried to cram on board, and possibly disabling some of the shuttles. Even in the best case, where the Syndics didn't try anything, any major system failures on any of the shuttles could result in loss of the bird and any prisoners it might have picked up."

"How many Marines are required to avoid that?"

"Enough to operate and conduct emergency repairs on the birds if needed, and enough to provide security if the Syndics try to board a shuttle or if crowd control of the prisoners is needed. Shuttle pilot. Copilot. Flight mechanic. A fire team of three Marines for security. Six per shuttle. That is the minimum I would recommend, Admiral."

Six per shuttle. Eighty shuttles. Four hundred and eighty Marines. Geary studied the images for several seconds, thinking. "All right. I think we have to try this. Those six thousand prisoners are counting on us. Put your plan together. I'll have the fleet in position to provide fire support if needed and to provide cover if any of the Syndic warships pretending not to be Syndic warships try to attack the shuttles."

From orbit, worlds displayed different personalities. The ancient standards were living planets like Old Earth, blue and white, with patches of different colors on the landmasses. Geary had heard of the Red Planet near Old Earth, and had himself seen countless planets that revealed different personalities ranging from the multicolored clouds of gas giants to the bare rock of small, hot worlds.

The habitable world in Simur Star System seemed to have been painted by an artist who had nothing but shades of brown. Even the small seas looked like muddy expanses of rust. The stretch of sand dunes at the hot northern pole were a lighter terra-cotta shade. Near the equator, some patches of green could be seen, where farms clung to the planet's narrow temperate zone. The few cities, barely large enough not to be classified as towns, were also near the temperate zone. The prison camp was located halfway down toward the south pole, the construction scars around it a multishaded tan/khaki/beige patch in the middle of a vast, empty plain. At the cold southern pole, the land was a murky chocolate color, like thick mud, interspersed with streaks of dirty ice that was so dark as to be nearly black.

"What a hole," Desjani muttered, putting into words what nearly everyone in the fleet must have been thinking.

"Let's get this done and get out of here," Geary agreed. "General Carabali, begin the operation. All units in the First Fleet, be prepared to engage any warships that threaten the shuttles or the prison camp." At least with the fleet in this tight a formation, communication delays were too tiny to be noticeable.

The four groups of Syndic ships were all less than a light-minute distant, close enough to be worrisome but not close enough to justify postponing the recovery. The guards at the prison camp had fled in the few available vehicles, leaving the prisoners no longer watched over but still effectively imprisoned by the wasteland surrounding the camp.

The planet scrolled by beneath the fleet as the shuttles launched, coming down toward the camp in waves.

Geary, his nerves keyed up to highest alert, watched his display, waiting for something unexpected to happen, for some threat to materialize. The first wave of shuttles were penetrating the atmosphere of the planet, the site of the prison camp becoming visible on the planet as the orbiting fleet approached it from high above.

The high-priority signal that blared at Geary came from an unexpected source. Why would *Tanuki* be calling—?

Geary hit accept, his worries multiplying rapidly.

Instead of Captain Smythe, he saw Lieutenant Jamenson, her green hair contrasting vividly with a face gone pale. "Admiral! You have to call off this operation! They've got the mother of all traps down there!"

Jamenson didn't wait for a reply, but kept talking, the words spilling out of her so fast that Geary could barely understand them. "I just put it all together. I'm sorry... I... there are two engineering units identified in the Syndic comms. They were in this star system recently, and I know those unit designators. They're both the equivalent of what the Alliance calls planet-breakers, engineers who use large and superlarge munitions for certain specialized tasks. *Two* of those units, Admiral. And the only major new construction in this star system is that camp.

"There was lots of large excavation gear here, and a very large amount of drilling equipment. I recognized the Syndic equipment codes. They dug some big holes and did a lot of drilling very recently.

"And there are some strange materials identified in cargo manifests or off-loading documents or transportation requests or gossip between individuals. Individually, those materials have a few uses, but together they are very reminiscent of an Alliance research project five decades ago. The code name... never mind the code name... the nickname for the project was Continental Shotgun. Bury a lot of very powerful nuclear munitions and use their energy when they explode to pump a huge field of single-use particle beam tubes. The research project aimed to turn a section of a planet about a hundred kilometers square into a one-time-only dense field of particle beams that could annihilate an invasion fleet when it passed above that region of the planet."

Jamenson gasped a deep breath before she could continue speaking. "But it was abandoned because the weapon effectively destroyed the planet it was supposed to defend. The seismic impact of that many explosions that massive, the amount of material hurled into the atmosphere, the huge amount of nuclear contamination, it all combined to inflict massive damage and render a planet almost uninhabitable. That, and the target had to pass over the weapon, which was hard to guarantee.

"And there are several indications that senior security-force commanders have left the planet within the last few days. They and their families. Supposedly some expensive off-site gathering at what passes for a luxury resort on the largest moon of the habitable world, a moon that never orbits near the segment of land centered on that new camp."

Geary wondered just how pale he looked. Iger had passed on the reports of the senior personnel leaving the planet, but that was common enough behavior for high-ranking Syndics when danger threatened and hadn't aroused special alarm. The four small groups of Syndic warships, he now realized, were not positioned anywhere near a line drawn upward from the center of the prison-camp location. The hit-and-run attacks by those Syndic warships and their near presence had kept Geary's ships in a tight defensive formation, and the tight Alliance formation would form a perfect target for a dense, wide field of particle beams as it swung above the prison camp to provide protection and orbital-firepower support as the Marine shuttles landed.

Landed on the center of a region rigged with massive nuclear munitions.

He was barely aware of his hand hitting the emergency comm overrides. "All units, this is Admiral Geary. Immediate execute, abort the landing operation. I say again, abort the landing operation. All shuttles are to return and be recovered as fast as possible."

Can I alter course before the shuttles get back? How long do I have? I can see that damned camp. Will the Syndics trigger that continental shotgun if they see us aborting the landing so they can get as many shuttles as possible, or will they wait and see if we'll come back?

They need to think we'll come back.

"Emissary Rione, immediately contact the Syndic authorities and tell them we have to postpone the landing and recovery operation because of... contamination issues. We think there might be an unknown disease among the prisoners and need to recheck the test results before conducting the landing."

Rione watched him, obviously surprised by Geary's anxiety and frantic words. "Immediately? I'll send the message now and ensure they receive it. How serious is this?"

"About as serious as it gets, but *don't let them see that you're worried.* Make it seem like a bureaucratic holdup."

"I'm a good liar," Rione said. "Consider it done."

"Tanya, how hard would it be to... double the size of this formation? Increase the distances between ships by that factor?"

Desjani had already been focused on him, not having heard what Lieutenant Jamenson said but well aware that something had badly rattled Geary. Now she didn't hesitate. "Not hard at all," she said, her hands already flying across her display. "Done. I can transmit the modified formation whenever you ask for it. Let me know what's going on when you can."

"We underestimated them," Geary said, his eyes on his display. The shuttles were turning around and coming back, some of them having already entered atmosphere and having to climb out. Another urgent message came in, this one from Carabali.

"What's going on, Admiral?" the Marine general asked. "Why did we abort the landing?"

"I'll give you the details when I can. Just get those damned shuttles recovered as fast as you possibly can."

Rione was back. "CEO Gawzi has been informed. She wants to know how soon we will carry out the recovery operation."

He checked the orbital data. If the fleet held its current path, it would swing over the prison camp region again in… "One and a half hours. Tell her one and a half hours, then we'll conduct the recovery. Make sure she feels confident we'll go through with it."

Victoria Rione also knew when not to ask questions but just do as he asked. "Yes, Admiral."

What else could he do? "We have to look like everything is routine except for aborting the landing operation," Geary said out loud. "Until we get the shuttles on board. Are there any orbital changes I can make that won't mess up the shuttle recovery but will alter our track over the planet?"

"What are we trying to avoid?" Desjani asked.

"A region about seventy kilometers across centered on the prison camp."

"Seriously? Swing our orbit a couple of degrees toward the planetary equator. That will actually assist recovery of the shuttles and allow us to skim the edge of that region you're worried about."

Geary gave the order, then sat staring at his display, watching the shuttles approach, the closest wave nearly back among the fleet.

"Admiral?" Desjani prompted.

"Admiral!" Rione said, as her image reappeared. "That Syndic CEO is more nervous than she's been before. Very nervous. But she said they would expect us to conduct the recovery in one and a half standard hours. If I know why I'm lying, I can do a better job for you," she added pointedly.

It would take half an hour, a very long half an hour, to get the shuttles recovered. Geary keyed in Carabali and Rione, then spoke so Desjani could also hear as he described what Lieutenant Jamenson had found.

"The entire landing force would be wiped out," Carabali said grimly, "and every prisoner down there would be blown to atoms as well."

"We'd take a lot of damage," Desjani said. "It's hard to say how many hits they'd score, but with our ships in this tight a formation encountering a dense field of powerful particle beams, we'd very likely lose dozens. Not to mention damage to ships that weren't a total loss."

"And they would blame us," Rione said. "Count on it. The Syndic rulers on Prime would announce that we had bombarded that planet, causing all of that damage. No wonder CEO Gawzi looks so nervous. Her planet is about to be shaked and baked, and most of the remaining population killed."

"An expendable planet in an expendable star system," General Carabali agreed. "It's logical enough if you're cold-blooded enough. When will we be clear of this threat?"

"When we get the shuttles aboard and take a course away from the planet," Geary said.

"What about the prisoners in the camp?" Rione asked.

"If Lieutenant Jamenson is right, the only way to keep those prisoners alive is to stay away from the trap. We either get the Syndics to lift them out to us, or we leave them." The words had no sooner left his mouth than Geary felt bitterness fill him. *Leave them.* Leave Alliance military personnel taken as prisoners, who might have been held by the Syndics for several decades, who knew

Alliance ships were here because of the Marine surveillance drones, who might have seen some of the Alliance shuttles high above them turn about and head back for space. "We'll do everything we can to get them out of there."

It sounded weak. It sounded bureaucratic.

I'm getting too good at saying bureaucratic things.

"Ten minutes to complete recovery of all shuttles," Lieutenant Yuon reported.

"Admiral," Rione said, "CEO Gawzi is on the planet. Do we know where other senior Syndic personnel are?"

"We know the senior internal-security officials have gone off planet."

"Do you remember Lakota? Where a Syndic flotilla was ordered to destroy a hypernet gate at close range?"

"And not warned about what would happen," Geary said. "Yes. I saw a former Syndic officer at Midway saying no one was warned by the Syndic leaders."

Rione nodded, smiling unpleasantly. "You can be certain that the junior Syndic internal-security personnel holding guns on the CEO and other important officials on the planet, and the people who will trigger the weapon because that is too important to risk a malfunction in an automated system, have not been told what use of that weapon will do to the planet they are on. Perhaps we should tell them."

"But the CEO knows?" Carabali asked. "Why wouldn't she tell them?"

"I don't know. Maybe she knows it will be bad but doesn't know how very bad it will be. Maybe she has had a mental block implanted to keep her from talking."

"Barbarians," Carabali spat.

Rione slid her eyes toward Geary, but instead of pursuing that dangerous subject, her next words referred back to her earlier statement. "Shall I work on an announcement to the people of the Simur Star System?"

"Yes," Geary said. "But don't send anything until I clear it."

"What about the expanded formation?" Desjani asked.

"Let's hold off on that. We're about to get far away from where that Syndic continental shotgun is aimed, then our main threat will still be those four groups of ships. The Dancers are staying tucked in close to *Invincible*, thanks be to our ancestors, and if we're lucky, they'll remain there."

Seven minutes later, the last shuttle had been docked. Geary took his fleet out of its close-in orbit, aiming for another orbit out past the moons that kept the Alliance warships far from the region of space above the prison camp. The Dancers maintained their positions near *Invincible*, for once offering no extra complications for Geary to deal with.

"What are we going to do?" Desjani muttered. "The Syndics in this star system can't revolt, not with all of those Syndic warships free to bombard them. We can't go anywhere near that prison camp. The Syndic warships can't hurt us as long as we stay in this formation, but as long as we stay in this formation, we can't hurt them."

"Stalemate," Geary agreed. "Even worse than before. I don't know, Tanya. The Syndic CEOs are playing a game as ugly as it gets. How do we counter that? How do we get those prisoners out of there when they're sitting on top of a huge weapon?"

She started to shake her head, then straightened, eyes intent. "What fires the weapon? If we can break the trigger, we can get the prisoners out."

He felt the first sense of hope in a while. "That's an idea worth checking out." It was time to call Lieutenant Jamenson again.

"But, first," Desjani suggested, "you might tell the rest of the fleet's commanding officers what's going on."

The small conference room didn't require the software to make it appear larger for this meeting. Besides Geary, Desjani, Rione, and Lieutenant Iger, who were physically present, the other attendees were limited to the virtual presences of Captain Smythe, Lieutenant Jamenson, General Carabali, and a Commander Hopper, whom Smythe introduced as "a wizard, or a sorceress, at anything to do with comm linkages, coding, and remote signals." Whether that was true or not, Hopper, lean and middle-aged, radiated a reassuring aura of competence from where she sat.

"Have you found anything else?" Geary asked Lieutenant Jamenson.

Jamenson shook her head, her eyes slightly glazed from tension and work, her green hair still vivid against skin still pale. "No, sir. Was I right, sir?"

"We all think so. Captain Smythe?"

Smythe smiled crookedly. "I wouldn't have seen it. I'd never heard of the Continental Shotgun. But I've reviewed Lieutenant Jamenson's findings, and I agree with them."

Lieutenant Iger nodded unhappily. An engineer had discovered a major threat that Iger's office was supposed to have spotted. But, to his credit, Iger hadn't tried to discredit Jamenson's conclusions.

"Nothing about that program was in the intel files, but from what the engineers have provided us, it all fits, Admiral. Either the Syndics learned about the Alliance's experiments with the concept or they came up with it independently."

"You think the Syndics could have thought of that by themselves?" Rione asked.

"Oh, yes," Smythe said. "In engineering terms, it's a really cool concept. The BFG to beat all BFGs. I'd love to build one and set it off just to see the fireworks. But, uh, you'd need a spare planet. That is, a planet you weren't planning on using for anything else."

Rione raised one eyebrow at Smythe. "My reading of the Syndic CEO also fits our conclusions. From the beginning, she seemed oddly encouraging in our desire to recover the prisoners at the camp, and has been just as oddly nervous when we halted our recovery, repeatedly asking what the delay is and making vague warnings about what might happen if we don't recover the prisoners soon."

"They want us back there," Iger agreed.

"What do we know about the trigger for the weapon?" Geary asked. "There's no way to strike at the weapon itself without killing the prisoners."

Smythe spread his hands, looking to either side at Jamenson and Hopper, then to Iger. "The few records we have available on that concept don't specify design features like that."

Hopper made a face. "The trigger is the weak point," she said. "You cannot afford to have something like that go off by accident. Or not go off when you want it to. The trigger has to be extremely reliable and extremely secure."

"Landline?" Smythe said.

"Armored landlines," Hopper agreed. "Buried. Redundant."

"Wouldn't there be one place from which the fire command was sent?" Jamenson suggested.

This time Hopper nodded. "A single location. Multiple locations would drastically increase the risk of a stray signal or of someone's tapping into the extra cables required. Most of all, a single location can remain firmly under control. That trigger has to be accessible only by the highest authority. It really is a doomsday weapon."

"What are the odds we can locate and cut or subvert the comm cables?" Carabali asked her.

"Astronomical," Hopper replied. "These wouldn't be standard cables. They'd not only be heavily armored and shielded against radiation, but also coated with multiple layers of intrusion-detection material and surrounded by other intrusion-detection sensors. I am certain that you couldn't even get a nanoprobe near one of those cables without setting off alarms."

"That leaves the trigger," Carabali said.

"Yes. If you get to the trigger, you can either set off the weapon prematurely or keep anyone else from setting it off. But you have to find the trigger, then you have to get to it. It's going to be the most securely guarded spot on the planet."

"Can we get an attack force down to the surface undetected?" Geary asked.

"Yes, Admiral," Carabali said. "The Syndics left most of the defenses in this star system unrepaired, so we wouldn't suspect what defensive work they had done. Their orbital and atmospheric sensors are few and obsolete. Normally, I wouldn't want to drop scouts in stealth armor through atmosphere onto a heavily guarded area, but under these circumstances, they should be able to reach the target undetected."

"But where do we land those scouts?" Desjani wondered.

Lieutenant Jamenson looked surprised at the question. "At the most heavily guarded spot on the planet, of course."

Iger grinned at Jamenson, his earlier gloom replaced by enthusiasm and perhaps something else as he looked at the green-haired lieutenant. "And we already know where that spot is." Iger worked his controls rapidly, until sharp images appeared above the table. "Not new construction, but recently modified, and close to the main command and control facility on the planet, which is also close to the main Syndic administrative offices. See where the paving is widely cracked along this route leading toward the site? They brought in heavy materials. And these signal signatures indicate an extensive localized sensor net using state-of-the-art Syndic equipment."

Carabali nodded, her eyes studying the images. "New defensive bunkers, too. Automated, from the looks of them, but there are at least three occupied sentry posts. Layered defenses, heavily camouflaged. How did you get these images?"

Iger swelled with pride but kept his tone of voice matter-of-fact. "We identified the Syndic headquarters and sent down stealthed drones for close-in collection when we first approached the planet. That's standard procedure. We had planned to recover the drones during the prisoner pickup, but when that was stopped, and the drones were stuck down there, we took advantage of the extra time to conduct more in-depth surveillance."

"Well done," Carabali said. "Where are the drones now? Still active?"

"Yes, ma'am." Iger was clearly trying very hard not to smile widely. Praise from operational commanders for fleet intel did not come all that often. "The drones are flying random, low-observable patterns, conserving power."

"The Syndics haven't spotted the uplinks from the drones?" Geary asked.

"No, sir," Iger replied confidently. "If they had a decent satellite net about the planet, they would have a good chance of picking something up even though we're using highly directional burst transmissions. But the sat net is old, with a lot of holes in it."

Desjani tapped one finger on the table, looking dissatisfied. "Isn't it a bit obvious? Why didn't they fix the cracks where the heavy stuff was brought in?"

Smythe smiled indulgently. "Not in the task order, most likely. Someone would have had to anticipate the pavement there would crack and write in that the cracks needed to be repaired in ways that weren't easily detected as new work. Someone probably did spot the need for that *after* the pavement was cracked, but fixing that would require a task order *modification*, which would need approval from all the right authorities up the chain of command, and—"

"They'll probably get approval to fix the cracks in another couple of years or so," Geary said.

"At best," Smythe agreed. "If it gets approved at all. Most of this work we're seeing is pretty good. A few sloppy places, but they must have been terribly rushed. Those sloppy places are what keyed Lieutenant Iger's drones to focus on particular spots. I keep telling you, Admiral, that it is always a good idea to give engineers enough time to do a job right."

"When I have the luxury of having enough time," Geary said dryly, "I'll give you enough time as well. Can we do this with a reasonable chance of success? How many Marines can you send down, General?"

"Same as before," Carabali said. "Thirty. That's how much stealth armor we have. Can thirty do the job? Looking at these images, I think so, but I'll have a talk with my most experienced force-recon officers and senior enlisted and see what they say."

Desjani made a face. "We'll have to coordinate the drops of the Marines and the movements of our ships and shuttles so that everything happens within an extremely precise timeline. I don't like timelines that require that kind of precision, that don't have room for the unexpected, but I guess we don't have any choice. How do we get those Marines out after we've pulled up the prisoners?"

"I think our battleships can handle that," Geary said. "General, consult with your experts, give me a firm go/no-go, then get me a plan. Emissary Rione, please contact the Syndic CEO again, tell her the military bureaucracy and regulations are still holding things up but we're planning on heading back in soon to get the prisoner recovery done. Lieutenant Iger, have your drones keep a close eye on that area and collect any more information they can without compromising their presence. Ensure that Lieutenant Jamenson is kept apprised of new information. Lieutenant Jamenson, keep doing what you've been doing. Commander Hopper, anything you can tell the Marines about the likely configuration of the Syndic trigger will be a great help. Contact General Carabali directly but keep Captain Smythe in the loop."

Commander Hopper sighed, her eyes reflecting fatalistic

acceptance. "I need to go along with the Marines when they drop."

"What?" Geary, Smythe, and Carabali all said the same word at the same time.

"There are too many uncertainties about the trigger, and comms may be interrupted when the Syndics realize what we're doing. You need someone there to look at that trigger and figure out what to do with it."

"My scouts—" Carabali began.

"If they do the wrong thing, we lose six thousand prisoners," Hopper said. "This trigger is going to be unique. It may have been designed to thwart the usual disabling techniques. The training and experience of your scouts won't be sufficient to deal with it."

"Can you do a stealth landing?" Smythe asked. "Keeping up with the Marines?"

"I'll have to."

Carabali eyed Hopper, nodding. "Let's see whether you can. I'll need you on *Mistral* as soon as possible, so we can see how you do in the simulators."

"She's even tougher than she looks," Smythe offered.

"Let me know how it goes," Geary ordered. "Let's get to work."

After the images of the others vanished, Lieutenant Iger lingered. "Admiral, about Lieutenant Jameson…"

"Are you still concerned about her access to intel materiel?" Geary asked.

"No, sir! Absolutely not. She would be—she is—a tremendous asset. If she could be transferred to the intelligence office aboard *Dauntless*, I am certain that we would, uh, work very well together."

"I see." Unseen by Iger but visible to Geary, both Desjani

and Rione grinned, though as soon as each realized the other was smiling both changed their expressions. "Don't you think Lieutenant Jamenson's hair would be distracting?"

"Distracting?" Iger asked. "I, uh, didn't... really... notice... That is, no, sir."

Geary nodded solemnly, grateful that a career of dealing with sailors had taught him how to keep a straight face in situations like this. "I will consider your recommendation, Lieutenant. However, I did make Captain Smythe a firm promise that I wouldn't poach Lieutenant Jamenson from his staff, and she is carrying out some extremely important tasks for me aboard *Tanuki*."

"Oh. I see, Admiral. I wouldn't—"

"But I didn't promise Captain Smythe that *you* wouldn't offer her a different position. Feel free to speak to her about it."

"Yes, sir!" Iger saluted hastily and rushed from the compartment, pausing only to hold the hatch as Rione followed.

Desjani waited until the hatch closed before she laughed. "A tremendous asset?"

"She would be," Geary said.

"And I'm absolutely sure that's all that Lieutenant Iger is thinking about." Her smile faded again. "This op is going to be a bitch to carry off successfully."

"I know."

11

"Tell the Syndics we're going to make two passes above the prison camp area," Geary told Rione, "because we require two shuttle lifts to get all of the prisoners up."

The fleet's orbital track had been very carefully calculated so that the planet's surface would track a bit to one side under it between passes. On the first pass, the fleet would pass just west of the prison-camp area. On Syndic displays in their control centers and command posts, the fleet's orbit would be projected with one hundred percent certainty that the second pass would bring the fleet directly over the camp.

Windows showing Captain Armus of *Colossus* and Captain Jane Geary of *Dreadnaught* were open near the fleet command seat on *Dauntless's* bridge. "You've got your initial maneuvering orders. Captain Armus, once your portion of the battleship force is cut loose, I want you to do everything you can to support the Marines on the ground at the trigger site. I don't care how much of the surrounding landscape you have to tear up."

Armus nodded, stolid and unperturbed. This fire-support mission was right up his alley.

"Captain Geary," Geary continued, "your part of the battleship force is to keep those four groups of Syndic warships off Armus's units and off the shuttles going down to pick up the Marines. Anticipate the movements of the Syndics and be there first. They don't have the muscle to stand up to your ships, and if they try, I want them shot to pieces."

"It will be a pleasure, Admiral," Jane Geary replied. If anyone could use battleships in an active defense role, it would be her.

Desjani, sitting on the other side of the admiral, was trying not to let her displeasure show at the lesser role of the battle cruisers.

Orion had been destroyed. *Relentless*, *Reprisal*, *Superb*, and *Splendid* were tied to *Invincible*, not only towing the superbattleship but also providing point defense for her. That left Geary with eighteen battleships, many of them scarred by fighting against enigmas, Kicks, and Syndics. Those battleships also lacked the maneuverability and speed of other warships, but all were massive, heavily armored, and bristling with weapons. Nothing but superior firepower, and a lot of it, could best them in a fight.

Armus would have *Colossus*, *Encroach*, *Amazon*, *Spartan*, *Gallant*, *Indomitable*, *Glorious*, and *Magnificent*. Jane Geary would have *Dreadnaught*, *Dependable*, *Conqueror*, *Warspite*, *Vengeance*, *Revenge*, *Guardian*, *Fearless*, *Resolution*, and *Redoubtable*.

The images of the two battleship commanders disappeared. Geary called Carabali. "Are your people ready to go, General?"

Carabali saluted formally. "Yes, Admiral. Twenty-nine Marines, and one fleet engineer. Commander Hopper has received a crash course in stealth armor operation and employment, as well as planetary infiltration, and has received emergency certification as qualified for this action."

To say the Marine force-recon scouts had been less than thrilled to have a fleet engineer tapped to join their mission would have been seriously downplaying their reaction. Geary could have sworn he heard their chorus of protests even across the empty space separating ships. But the Marines had been forced to acknowledge that none of their personnel had a fraction of Hopper's expertise and experience with the sort of challenge the trigger would pose, and she had completed the necessary simulator work.

"Launch your people on schedule," Geary ordered.

He sat back, trying to relax, studying his display. The globe of the inhabited world slowly grew closer. The fleet had drastically scaled back its speed again for this operation and to achieve a stable orbit about the planet. That would give the Marines a little less than two hours after launch to reach the surface, reach their objective, infiltrate it, and seize control of the trigger before the fleet made its second orbital pass directly above the Syndic version of a Continental Shotgun.

"Tanya, I want you to be ready."

Desjani perked up and looked at him. "For what?"

"If necessary, or if a good opportunity offers, I'm going to set loose the battle cruisers by divisions to chase off or chase down those Syndic warships that have been hounding us."

"That just leaves escorts and the four battleships tied to *Invincible* to protect the assault transports and auxiliaries," she pointed out.

"It will depend on the situation," Geary said. "And I'll keep *Adroit* within the formation as a last-ditch defense, too. Just be ready to go all out if I give the order."

Desjani grinned like a wolf. "I'm always ready to do that. Haven't you figured that out yet?"

Geary smiled back, then called Captain Tulev on *Leviathan*, Captain Badaya on *Illustrious*, and Captain Duellos on *Inspire* to pass on the same heads-up.

The four Syndic warship groups had come within several light-seconds, teasing the Alliance warships and forcing the Alliance fleet to remain in a tight defensive formation. Geary smiled as he watched them. *It won't be too long before you have to react to us. Then we may finally get a chance to grapple with you.*

A soft alert tone notified Geary that the Marine scouts were launching from some of the assault transports, using special launch tubes that ejected them without using any energy or propellant that would alert watching Syndics that anything had happened.

He gazed at the planet turning below the fleet, the north pole currently behind the fleet to the right, and the south pole ahead to the left. The city holding the Syndic command and control center, and the site of the trigger, was off below and to Geary's right. Just coming into view again on the globe's horizon was the prison-camp location slightly to Geary's left. On the planet's surface, the trigger site and the prison camp were far apart. From this high, they could both be seen at once.

The Marines were dropping toward that surface now, in suits equipped to slow and conceal their descent while preventing detection by any available sensor. The suits weren't foolproof.

Good enough sensors focused on the right spots at the right times would pick up indications that something unusual was going on. But right now every available Syndic sensor and set of eyeballs would be focused on the Alliance fleet as it headed for the vicinity of the prison camp and began launching shuttles.

What would it be like for the Marines? Falling for kilometers toward the planet, the land growing in size beneath them, knowing that hostile eyes, ears, and weapons were on the lookout for intruders. The inside of the armor becoming uncomfortably hot as the suits absorbed heat they could not radiate without betraying the location of the wearer. Heavily armored and armed Marines planning to hit dirt after a kilometers-long fall in such a gentle way that even seismic sensors would not spot anything untoward.

And Commander Hopper among them, doing something she had never trained for except in a few hasty simulator sessions.

He couldn't activate links to see through the eyes of the Marines. Not this time. The scouts would maintain silence except for occasional low-power microburst transmissions among their own force.

"All shuttles launched," Lieutenant Castries said.

Geary nodded. "Very well." He hoped his voice sounded steady, in contrast to the tightness strumming through his nerves.

Eighty shuttles fell toward the planet, their descents graceful and oddly like the birds they were nicknamed for. Unlike the Marine scouts, these shuttles carried only standard detection-avoidance gear, and were visible to a variety of sensors.

Geary's eyes went back to the four groups of Syndic warships. Still close, still not getting closer. "That should have been a hint for us the first time. Why didn't those four groups of ships try to hit the shuttles or at least disrupt their movement? Because they wanted to make sure we didn't halt the recovery or break up the fleet to chase them."

"Uh-huh," Desjani said.

"I can't even imagine going on an operation like those Marine scouts. The trip down, the attempts to avoid detection while walking among alert enemy sentries, everything." Geary knew he was talking too much, but it helped relax his nerves as he waited. "I don't know how they do it."

Desjani glanced at him. "They do it because they're crazy. All Marines are crazy. Force-recon Marines are even crazier than other Marines."

"How do you know so much about different kinds of Marines?"

She looked back at her display. "There are parts of my dating history that you probably don't want to know about."

"You're... probably right."

He was saved from further comment by a call from intelligence. "Admiral," Lieutenant Iger's image reported, "the drones we have on the planet are spotting an unusual level of activity at and around the trigger location."

Trying not to let that news rattle him, Geary looked at the images Iger was forwarding. "Is this some sort of alert? Extra security?" *If the Syndics have picked up the Marines coming in...*

"No, sir. As far as we can tell, it's just extra traffic into and out of the trigger location. They're definitely gearing up for something, but there's not increased security activity. If anything, the sentries are being distracted by checking the visitors in and out."

In a normal operation, that information and those images would be forwarded to the Marines. But not in a stealth op. That kind of comm linkage would all too easily betray the presence of the Marines. "Make sure General Carabali sees these images."

"Yes, sir. The Marines should be on the ground now, so the lack of reaction by the Syndics is a good sign."

Iger's image had no sooner vanished than Rione's image appeared. "I've heard from CEO Gawzi again. An explicit warning that if we do not go through with the pickup this time, there are no guarantees for the safety of the prisoners. That confirms how badly the Syndics want us to go through with this. The fact that it wasn't CEO Gawzi speaking to me, but a digital avatar instead, confirms that the Syndic internal-security forces are calling all the shots now."

"How certain are you that it was an avatar?" Geary asked.

"Completely certain."

He didn't question her assessment any further. Machines could be easily fooled by digital avatars, but people rarely were. No matter how perfect the illusion, people sensed something that couldn't be detected by equipment. He had read speculation once that this skill had developed after the creation of nearly perfect digital-avatar technology, but no one really knew if that was true or if humans had always been able to feel the difference between the fake and the real.

"Gawzi may well be dead," Rione continued. "Her level of nervousness in our last few conversations told me that she was very unhappy with the Syndic plan here. Maybe she attempted something to stop the plan. Maybe she was blocked, and the extreme horror of the information she could not divulge caused her to lose her sanity in fairly short order."

Geary felt an unexpected stab of sympathy for the elderly Syndic CEO. Perhaps she had cared about the people in this star system, cared about them the same way that the manager at the facility near the gas giant cared. But she had been able to do nothing to help them, nothing to prevent tragedy. She had spent her life supporting a system which in the end had repaid her with callously efficient betrayal. Maybe she deserved such a fate for a lifetime of work in support of a system she must have known was capable of such deeds. But perhaps she hadn't had any choice, and had done all she could to protect those under her. *I don't know. It's not my place to judge her. If she's already dead, that judgment is being rendered by those far wiser than I'll ever be. My job is to make sure the Syndic plans fail.* "Thank you for the update. The Marines should be on the surface. Keep your fingers crossed. They are running incredible risks."

She nodded slowly. "They will have my prayers. As does everyone else in this fleet. Is it not amazing, Admiral Geary, what remarkable efforts some will go to in order to save the lives of their fellow humans, and what remarkable efforts others will go to in order to take the lives of their fellow humans?"

He was still fumbling for some kind of reply when Rione's image disappeared. "Tanya, I was wondering at one point how to explain what's going on to the Dancers. Now I'm wondering how to explain it at all."

Desjani lowered a furious brow at him. "I should never let you talk to that woman."

"She's an emissary of the Alliance government!"

"And I'm… the commanding officer of your flagship! The first wave of shuttles is hitting dirt."

The Marines would not need his personal oversight of what was becoming a routine for them, recovering Alliance prisoners under nonpermissive conditions. He could have tapped into the Marine command and control net, seeing events on the ground in the prison camp, but not this time. *General Carabali will notify me if anything goes wrong on the Marine end, and the watch-standers here on* Dauntless *will tell me if anything happens to the shuttles.*

Instead of focusing on that, Geary looked to other parts of his display. The four groups of Syndic warships had not yet moved. They shouldn't move until it became apparent that the Alliance fleet was not playing the game as the Syndics intended, but those warships remained an unpredictable element. If they started moving before any other signs of problems below, it would be a sign that the Alliance plan was in trouble.

The Marine plan allowed half an hour for the scouts to assemble at the trigger location and infiltrate close to the entrance, and another twenty minutes to actually penetrate the installation and gain control of the trigger just before the fleet approached the region above the prison camp on its second orbital pass. If anything went wrong, Lieutenant Iger's drones would spot the uproar before the Marines could report in.

"Loading first wave of shuttles. No problems reported with crowd control," Lieutenant Castries called. "Prisoners report no Syndics in the camp or nearby for the last twenty-four hours."

The fleet had crossed over the nighttime southern portion of the globe and was now climbing back over the sunward side. The shuttles, when loaded, would lift to meet the fleet as it crested the top of the globe and headed back down, on a path aimed to go straight over the prison camp in low orbit.

The Syndics plotting this attack must be watching the fleet's movements like gamblers following each turn of a card. *Just keep on going. Finish the orbit. Get into position. And then…*

"Admiral!" Lieutenant Iger couldn't suppress his excitement. "Look."

Geary peered at the image of one of the Syndic sentry posts near the trigger.

The sentry wasn't there.

"The sentry must have spotted something," Iger explained, "and the Marines took them out before they could sound an alarm."

"Why aren't the sentry alerts sounding? Aren't those set to go off automatically if anything happens to the sentry?"

"Yes, sir. They can be spoofed—"

The feed from the drone blanked for a moment.

"—but not for long," Iger continued, as the drone feed came to life again. "The Syndics just lit off jammers, and our drone had to work around them."

Extra security lights had flared to life near the trigger installation, and nozzles were pumping out a fine mist designed to reveal anyone in a stealth suit. Geary couldn't hear alarms sounding but knew they must be. Syndic ground forces personnel and security guards were running about, weapons at the ready. "Where are the Marines?"

"We don't see any being engaged by the Syndics, sir. That's a good sign. It means they're inside."

Inside an installation of unknown design, with unknown security features, and an unknown number of armed defenders.

Geary's eyes went back to his display. How long until the Syndic warships reacted? The Syndics would be rushing additional ground forces to the trigger site, trying to figure out what had happened, whether there was a real threat, how serious the threat was—

"Shuttles docking," Lieutenant Yuon reported. "The prisoners are being dumped into quarantined loading docks until full medical and security screening can be conducted. Screening on the way up didn't find any threats in or on the prisoners. Estimated time to shuttles heading back down is two minutes."

"Why bother sabotaging the prisoners when the Syndics expected them to be blown to atoms?" Desjani commented.

Geary didn't reply, looking at the globe scrolling by below, the location of the prison camp directly ahead of the tight fleet formation.

For the first time, it occurred to him that they didn't know if the particle beams were rigged to fire straight up, or at a slight angle to catch an orbiting formation just before it reached a point over the camp.

It's time. "Captain Armus, your force is detached to proceed on previously assigned duties. Captain Geary, your force is detached to proceed on previously assigned duties. All units in the First Fleet, immediate execute, come starboard five degrees." Enough to get the fleet out of line with those particle beams but close enough for the shuttles to be able to make the second drop and recovery.

Eighteen battleships swung away from the fleet formation, ponderous and majestic. Armus kept his eight battleships close together in a roughly circular arrangement. Once positioned over the trigger site, they would all be able to fire the majority of their weapons downward. Jane Geary sent two battleships to hover just above Armus's grouping, the other eight arranged in pairs around the ground-support battleships.

"Shuttles launching," Lieutenant Yuon reported. "Second wave on its way."

Alarms chirped as a hell-lance battery lost power on *Revenge*, partial shield failure afflicted *Colossus*, and the forward part of *Fearless* suffered spot power interruptions in a score of places. Geary glowered at his display, knowing the systems had failed as aging components on ships which had exceeded their planned hull lives were brought to full power for the action. *I guess I should be glad there weren't more failures.* "All ships in First Fleet, bring your systems up to full power now." If there were going to be more failures, better to have it happen right away, so there would be time to try to fix or jury-rig the problems.

Something caught Geary's eye. He swung his gaze to see explosions erupting on the drone image of the trigger site.

"Our people are inside and holding the entrance," General Carabali said as her image appeared. "The situation farther inside is uncertain. I don't know if we have control of the trigger. Request all available fleet ground support as close to the trigger building as possible."

"Captain Armus," Geary ordered, "you are cleared to engage any target and lay down a suppression barrage. Don't hit the trigger building. General Carabali is linking to your coordination circuit."

"Understood," Captain Armus said as laconically as if Geary had just ordered the fleet to stand down for the night. "Opening fire."

The image from the drone wavered as dozens of hell-lance

particle beams stabbed down from high above, hitting targets with pinpoint precision. Armored vehicles and bunkers shuddered as the hell lances tore large holes completely through them.

Alerts were popping up all over the fleet as minor and major systems on a few dozen warships suffered failures or partial failures. Not nearly as many as at Honor, and nothing that would render any ship unable to fight at all, but still a concern. Ironically, but understandably, many of the ships suffering system failures now had avoided major damage during earlier fights. Without immediate need to repair and replace battle damage, their older systems had remained in place and were now showing their age.

Geary's attention jerked back to the scene from Iger's drone. The view was momentarily obscured completely as small bombardment projectiles launched from the battleships plummeted to contact with the ground. Nothing but rocket-shaped chunks of solid metal, the bombardment rounds gained their destructive power from the immense energy built up as they dropped from orbit.

Geary shifted his view to an overhead look from Armus's battleships. Dust and debris now filled the air around the trigger site, but multispectrum sensors could partially penetrate the murk to spot moving objects. More hell lances stabbed down, aimed at targets ranging from individual Syndics to more vehicles screeching to halts at the edge of the bombardment area. More rocks headed down from the battleships, aimed not only at Syndics trying to reach the trigger site but also at forcing anyone near the building to keep their heads down. Rubble from collapsed buildings in the area around the trigger site bounced, producing false moving-target alerts on the fleet's sensors, as another bombardment plunged home.

The trigger building itself remained untouched except for scars on its sides where shrapnel from nearby bombardment impacts had exposed the heavy armor beneath the unassuming facade.

Geary yanked his attention away from that scene, checking on the Syndic warships again. How long until they got orders to intervene?

The Syndic leaders would be shocked, trying to grasp what was going on, disoriented by the sudden unraveling of their plan, which had seemed to be going perfectly before the Alliance abruptly altered the game.

The fleet was well clear of the prison-camp region by now, but the shuttles were dropping back down toward it as fast as they could without coming apart, and three thousand prisoners of war still waited for rescue.

If the Syndics still controlled the trigger, an apocalypse centered on that prison camp would very soon erupt, taking with it the shuttles, the Marines on them, and the waiting prisoners.

Alerts sounded as the four Syndic warship groups finally surged into motion, whipping around and accelerating at maximum. Two were coming around toward Armus's battleships, and the other two were angling toward either the fleet or the shuttles that would be rising back to meet it.

"They screwed up," Desjani said with a fierce grin. "They split their effort, and the only way they can make a difference is by coming within range of us."

"Yes, they did," Geary agreed. "Work up an intercept for Group Cable. I'll tell Duellos to go for it as well, and send Tulev and Badaya after Delta."

They would have this, they would totally frustrate the Syndic plans and hit the Syndics hard, if only the Syndic weapon didn't go off...

"I have comms from the force recon on the surface," General Carabali announced. "They're requesting pickup."

"What about the trigger?"

"Commander Hopper says the trigger is Bravo Delta. That's a slang term, Admiral. It stands for—"

"I know what it stands for. The trigger is out of commission. That term has been around a lot longer than I have. Captain Geary! The Marines need a ride."

"On the way," Jane Geary replied.

More alerts on the display. Ground forces on the planet had launched atmospheric combat aircraft, old models that were easy to spot from low orbit. *Guardian*, almost skimming the stratosphere, took out the aircraft with a series of hell-lance shots, then launched four shuttles that spiraled downward, protected by a wall of fire from *Guardian* and the other battleships.

Syndic Group Alpha, already rocketing toward the trigger site, altered vector slightly to skim atmosphere, their hulls glowing with heat as the friction wore down their shields, aiming for *Guardian's* shuttles.

Syndic Group Bravo, higher up, aimed a hopeless firing run at Armus's group of battleships. Jane Geary was vectoring *Conqueror*, *Dependable*, *Vengeance*, and *Revenge* to box in Bravo if that group continued its strike.

The main shuttle force was grounding at the prison-camp site again.

Syndic warship groups Cable and Delta were swinging wide around the Alliance fleet formation, their goal obviously the shuttles when they lifted back toward the fleet loaded with freed prisoners.

"Go, Tanya," Geary said, transmitting similar orders to Duellos, Tulev, and Badaya. "All units in First Fleet, immediate execute formation guide shifts to *Invincible*. Admiral Lagemann, take any necessary action to provide cover for the shuttles as they return." There shouldn't be any action necessary, but if Lagemann did have to order any more ships out of the formation, he had well over two hundred heavy cruisers, light cruisers, and destroyers to play with.

Desjani whooped as she sent *Dauntless*, *Daring*, *Victorious*, and *Intemperate* on an angled climb toward an intercept with Syndic Group Cable. Behind her, the other battle cruisers in the Alliance fleet tore away on their own intercept vectors.

"Shuttles lifting!" Lieutenant Yuon cried.

Geary checked to ensure Yuon meant the shuttles at the prison camp. Those headed to pick up the Marines at the trigger site were still weaving downward through a hail of fire from Syndic ground defenses that were being knocked out by *Guardian* almost as fast as they opened up.

Syndic Group Alpha kept coming, probably still under automated maneuvering control in response to orders from distant superiors, as *Guardian* and *Warspite* opened up on the Syndic warships. Captain Armus, lacking enough decent targets in the heavily cratered wasteland around the trigger site, shifted the fire of four of his battleships to engage Alpha as well.

Their shields already weak from fighting through the upper atmosphere, the ships of Alpha ran head-on into the fire of six battleships.

The heavy cruiser and four of the Hunter-Killers simply exploded under the hammerblows, coming apart as specter missiles, hell lances, and grapeshot hit in quick succession. One of the light cruisers was shredded by hits and knocked even farther into the atmosphere. Without shields, traveling at tremendous velocity, the remains of the light cruiser dissolved in a flash of heat and light, a ball of plasma forming a brief, fiery streak across the planet's sky.

The second light cruiser survived only because it had wrenched onto a new vector seconds before impact, leaping upward and away from the Alliance barrage.

Syndic Group Bravo, bearing down on Armus's force, saw the fate of Alpha and also whipped into turns, the Syndic ships sliding through wide arcs as they tried to avoid the fate of Alpha's warships. The heavy cruiser slid too far, coming deep enough inside the battleships' missile envelopes to catch a dozen specters that broke it into several large fragments that spun away, some heading out into space and some falling to their doom in the planet's atmosphere.

"Marine recovery shuttles are on the ground," Jane Geary reported.

"Shuttles lifting from prison camp," Lieutenant Yuon said. "Half of them are overloaded. They're requesting the fleet brake to assist their recovery."

"Admiral Lagemann," Geary said as he hit his comm controls. "Brake the fleet formation as necessary to help the shuttles catch you."

He felt a sense of liberation despite the chaos of the battle raging from the surface of the planet up into space above it. *I don't have to call all the shots. I have commanders I trust who can manage the details if I give them the job. All I have to do is make sure I keep a handle on the big picture, so everything is coordinated, and every threat is dealt with.*

Syndic Groups Cable and Delta had realized that they were too late to bombard the prison camp, and that the Alliance battle cruisers were going to ensure that none of the Syndic warships made it through to the climbing shuttles. The Syndics bent away, their groups breaking into individual ships as commanders overrode the automated maneuvering controls. One of the inexperienced Syndic commanders overstressed his or her ship's structure on the turn, the light cruiser shattering into pieces that spun toward the planet below.

As the Syndics tried to flee, Desjani cursed, altering *Dauntless's* vector a bit to close on another one of the light cruisers that was the only Syndic warship the Alliance battle cruiser still had a hope of catching. "We're going to get one shot," she warned her crew. "Make sure it counts."

Dauntless tore past the intercept, hell lances stabbing out at the light cruiser, which rocked under the impacts, straining to get away. Before the light cruiser could recover from the hell-lance hits, two specters slammed into its stern, blowing apart the back half of the Syndic warship.

Inspire managed to take out a HuK, as did *Dragon. Daring* and *Victorious* battered a heavy cruiser, but the Syndic ship didn't take any damage to its propulsion and kept going.

The Syndics, their groups broken into individual warships, were fleeing all out on dozens of vectors. "We can't catch any more," Geary said.

Desjani, her face red with frustration, nodded. "Not if they keep running."

"They will. Get your division back into formation." He called

Duellos, Tulev, and Badaya with the same orders, knowing the disappointment they would all feel. But you couldn't beat the physics of time, distance, and available acceleration.

"Shuttles are docking," Lieutenant Yuon said. "Estimate twenty minutes to complete recovery."

Geary checked the status of *Guardian's* shuttles, themselves rising out of the maelstrom of dust raised by the Alliance bombardment.

"Admiral?" General Carabali called. "My Marines and Commander Hopper recommend we flatten the trigger site. Commander Hopper says there is no chance the destruction of the site will set off the Syndic weapon, but destroying the site will seriously complicate attempts to rebuild the trigger."

"Captain Armus," Geary ordered. "Destroy the trigger site."

Another barrage of bombardment projectiles dropped, these rocks bigger, falling from orbit onto the trigger-site building, which sat bizarrely almost undamaged amid the sea of wreckage around it.

As *Guardian* recovered her shuttles, the rocks hit the trigger site, producing a gratifying series of explosions that tossed debris high up toward the battleships and leaving twisted ruins and craters in their wake.

"Admiral, look at this," Desjani urged.

Geary checked his display. The Syndic light cruiser that was the sole survivor of Group Alpha, which had left the group in time to save itself, had launched several bombardment projectiles.

A bombardment aimed at the larger moon of this planet.

Aimed at the luxury resort where the senior Syndic internal-security leaders in this star system had fled. If those leaders weren't already in hidden deep shelters, they would have time to flee the resort in the available ships there before the rocks hit, but the bombardment was still a powerful symbolic act.

"I guess they had a mutiny," Geary commented. "A successful one. I wonder if their ship had that remote power-core-overload device we saw at Midway, and if the Syndic crews are already figuring out how to block it. All units in First Fleet, rejoin formation. General Carabali, please pass on my personal admiration for the skill with which your force-recon team carried out its mission. Emissary Rione, now is the time to let the people of this star system know what fate their Syndic overlords intended for that planet."

Desjani looked around her bridge, smiling. "Good job, everyone. I think we reminded the Syndics who's boss. What now, Admiral?"

"We're heading for Padronis," Geary said, knowing his next words would be repeated around the fleet. "For the sake of the Syndics, I hope they don't try to mess with us there."

As the fleet neared the jump point for Padronis, they watched the mutinous Syndic light cruiser jump through well ahead of them. "Looks like this jump exit is clear," Desjani commented.

"We'll go through carefully anyway," Geary said. He turned at a sound and saw that Rione had come onto the bridge. "Have we heard any more from the Syndics?"

"No," Rione replied. "Aside from two fragmentary messages using the avatar of CEO Gawzi that complained of unprovoked aggression, there's been nothing else. They can't complain about the warships we destroyed since they insisted those weren't under Syndic control, and I suspect the Syndics in Simur are too busy with internal matters to pursue further complaints about events we were involved in."

"Internal matters? Internal revolt, you mean."

"Of course. There's no telling who will win this one. We don't know enough about the Syndic security forces here and what the locals might be able to muster. Did you want me to look into getting supplies from anywhere within this star system? Some of the facilities in the outer reaches of the star system might be willing to deal."

"No," Geary said immediately. "We don't need anything they could provide, and there's no source here we could trust. Even the people fighting the Syndic security police might see us as still just another enemy. In any case, I don't want to linger here. That would just give the Syndics more time to prepare surprises at Padronis. What have you heard from the Dancers? Emissary Charban says the Dancers have been singularly uncurious about everything that happened here."

"Yes. Strangely so," Rione agreed. "Either they understood it all without our having to explain it, or it was so incomprehensible to them that they aren't trying to understand it."

Geary gave his display a glance as it beeped for his attention. "The last shuttle run is complete. I thought we'd never find room for all of those prisoners we liberated. Let's hope we don't have to go into battle with all of those extra people clogging our ships."

That reminded him of something. He called *Tanuki*. "Captain Smythe, how is Commander Hopper? Home safe and sound?"

Smythe grinned. "And happy to be home. We had some trouble prying her away from the Marines. They wanted to keep her. I think the stock of fleet engineers has risen considerably among the Marines. They really did need her. She says that trigger was an impressive mess of misleading circuitry, false mechanisms, and trip wires, all of it designed to fool anyone trying to disable it or override it by standard methods."

"I'd like to see Commander Hopper's postaction report when she completes it," Geary said. "Oh, you can have Lieutenant Jamenson back full-time. Have her destroy all intel files she was sent."

"Of course," Captain Smythe said.

"We'll know if they aren't destroyed," Geary added casually. "Special tags embedded in the files."

"Why would that be a problem?" Smythe asked heartily. "Speaking of Lieutenant Jamenson, she's being harassed by some fellow named Iger."

"Harassed? Is that the term she is using?"

"Possibly not. I can't spare her, Admiral."

"Understood, Captain, but we have to think of her career and wellbeing, too. I won't hijack her. But if she wants to move on, I hope she'll get the assistance in that effort that she has earned from both of us."

Smythe sighed dramatically. "You're right. Keep good people in servitude, and you end up like the Syndics. We've almost completed repairs on *Revenge*, *Colossus*, and *Fearless*, by the way. They'll be fine before we jump. Until something else breaks on them or other ships."

"We'll be home soon and have time to work on everything," Geary said. "Everything except my report on what's been going on from the time we left Varandal, since I have to turn it in as soon as we arrive. That's going to be a book before I get everything into it."

"Too bad we don't have a faster-than-light message system like the enigmas, isn't it? Not having to physically send ships with messages could be useful at times."

Or a pain in the neck if it allowed fleet headquarters to reach across the light-years to try to micromanage us in real time. "If you come up with one, or figure out how the enigmas do it, let me know."

After talking to Smythe, and before he could forget, he called Lieutenant Iger. "Just for the sake of observing all of the formalities, let me know when Lieutenant Jamenson has destroyed all the files she was sent and signed off on all of the debriefing and disclosure paperwork."

Iger nodded quickly. "I don't anticipate problems with that, Admiral. Shamrock is extremely professional in her work."

"Shamrock?"

"Uh… I mean, Lieutenant Jamenson… of course, sir."

Geary made sure that he didn't smile. "Then all of your misgivings regarding her have been put to rest?"

"Absolutely, sir! Lieutenant Jamenson has requested to visit *Dauntless* and tour the intelligence spaces here once we return to Varandal. With your permission and approval, Admiral, and that of Captain Desjani."

Apparently Jamenson wasn't really feeling harassed. No wonder Smythe was worried about losing her. Geary hoped for Lieutenant Iger's sake that her interest wasn't entirely in the intriguing new world of intelligence. "I don't anticipate any problem with that, Lieutenant."

Nor was there any problem at the jump exit. Perhaps the Syndics had temporarily run out of mines in this region.

Geary felt relief as the stars around Simur vanished, and the gray of jump space appeared. Not just relief, but a sense that the last major hurdle had been crossed for now.

They would learn whether that was true when they reached Padronis.

12

There was almost nothing at Padronis.

The fleet came out of jump space prepared for surprises, for threats, and found only two ships in the star system.

Under normal circumstances, even that would be surprising. A white dwarf star, Padronis had no companions in space, no planets or asteroids in orbit. White dwarf stars slowly accumulated helium in their outer shells, causing them to go nova at wide intervals. If anything natural had once orbited Padronis, it had been blown away long before humans reached this part of space.

The formerly Syndic light cruiser that had mutinied was trucking at a good rate toward the jump point for Heradao, already far from where Geary's warships had arrived. The light cruiser's crew clearly wanted nothing more to do with fighting the Alliance.

The abandoned Syndic station they had seen when last passing through Padronis was still here, circling in lonely orbit about the star, which would someday in the distant future blast it apart. That's where the other ship was, a single freighter docked to the emergency rescue station the Syndics had built at Padronis over a century ago, before the hypernet, when ships had to jump from star to star to get anywhere, including stars with nothing at them like Padronis. The station had been decommissioned decades ago, everything shut down and left in place because it would cost more to move it than it was worth.

"What's the freighter doing?" Geary asked. Nothing else was visible in the star system even though the fleet's sensors were looking for anything, even the tiniest anomaly. "Make sure nothing unusual the sensors spot gets stuck in the noise filters. I want even junk that looks like junk to be checked carefully."

"There's nothing," Desjani said, shaking her head. "That freighter at the station is three light-hours from us, so it isn't any possible threat."

"Captain?" Lieutenant Castries said. "We've spotted material being loaded on the freighter."

"Material?"

A call came in from *Tanuki*. It wasn't high-priority, but Geary didn't have much else to do at the moment. "What's up, Captain Smythe?"

Smythe twitched a brief smile. "That freighter. He's looting the station."

"Looting? Are you sure?"

"There's a very minor chance that the Syndic authorities chartered the ship to pick up equipment that they need elsewhere, but it's unlikely. Now that the Syndicate Worlds' government has little authority around here and a lot of other things to worry about, that freighter has come out to this mothballed, off-limits station to haul away everything and anything its owners can sell, even if just for scrap."

Geary stared at the image of the freighter, his instincts urging him to do something. But what? "Even though that station was mothballed, it still must have held a lot of equipment and supplies that could be critical for any ship passing through Padronis that suffered a serious problem."

"Right," Smythe agreed. "Absolutely right. And the looters don't care. They're out to make some money even though it could cause tragedy for someone else. That's how things go when central authority collapses, Admiral. The rich and powerful can still take care of themselves. It's the people who need help who get hurt the worst. As usual."

"Thank you, Captain Smythe. I guess there's nothing we can do about it."

"No. We could chase this looter off, but another one would show up after we left." Smythe ended the call with a resigned shrug.

"Admiral," Desjani said, "look at the Dancers."

He looked. At Sobek, the Dancers had tried to warn the fleet of danger. At Simur, they had stayed close to *Invincible*, apparently because of the threats from the Syndics there.

But here the Dancers had left the confines of the Alliance formation, swooping around in a way that made Geary think of giddy elation. "They look like they feel safe."

"I don't," Desjani admitted. "I can't forget what happened the last time we were here." The dust that had been the heavy cruiser *Lorica* and her crew still circled this star, a fate that had nearly befallen *Dauntless* as well. "Can we head for home?"

"Yeah. Let's go. Head straight for the jump point for Atalia."

* * *

Atalia was a living star system though a badly hurt one because of its front-line position during the long war. The fleet came out of jump cautiously again, but Geary had not really expected trouble here. Atalia was too close to Alliance space and had already declared its independence from the Syndicate Worlds. The Syndics would have had a nearly impossible task setting any traps here.

Which made it all the more surprising when combat systems sounded alerts as they arrived from jump.

"Syndics!" Desjani glared at Geary. "Two heavy cruisers near the jump point for Kalixa and four light cruisers and six HuKs near the jump point for Varandal. The Syndics must have moved to take back this star system. Don't we have grounds for kicking them out again?"

"Maybe." After everything they had been through, the idea of pushing the Syndics out of Atalia had a great deal of appeal despite its questionable legal basis. "That's strange. The courier ship is still here, and near those light cruisers and HuKs."

Inexplicably, the Alliance courier ship still orbited near the jump point for Varandal. That ship represented the Alliance's halfhearted commitment to keep an eye on Atalia but had never offered any real defense of the star system if the Syndicate Worlds came storming in to force Atalia back into their empire. As it seemed the Syndicate Worlds had. But why hadn't the courier ship left when that happened? Even if not threatened by the Syndics, it would need to carry the news of the event back to Varandal.

Before Desjani could reply, hull identifications began popping up on their displays. "We know those Syndic ships?" she asked, mystified.

"They're not Syndic ships?" Geary asked as the colors on the display changed. "They're—They're from Midway? They hadn't sent— *Manticore? Kraken?* Those heavy cruisers were still at Midway when we left!"

Desjani's expression had hardened further. "They could only have gotten here before us by using the Syndic hypernet to go somewhere like Indras. The Syndics did do something to temporarily block use of their hypernet, and the ones at Midway *were* in on that trick."

"Hold on." Geary took a moment to think, aware that the unexpectedness of this had left him off-balance. "If they had been part of a Syndic trick, why let us know by being here when we came through? They couldn't have expected this entire fleet or even the majority of it to be destroyed even if everything we ran into had been one hundred percent effective. Let's head for the jump point for Varandal while we wait to hear their explanation for being here."

When that explanation eventually came, they saw Kommodor Marphissa gazing at them. "If she is faking happiness at seeing us, she is doing a good job," Rione commented.

"Admiral Geary," Marphissa said, "we are pleased to see you again. Two days after your departure from Midway, we regained access to all gates on the Syndicate hypernet. The Syndicate must have learned how to temporarily shut down most or all of their hypernet. We are bending every effort to learn how they do this but so far have no information.

"We came here at the suggestion of Captain Bradamont, who told us of the captured Reserve Flotilla survivors at Varandal. Those survivors could provide the crews we need for our warships, so President Iceni approved a recovery mission. Six freighters have gone on to Varandal, accompanied by Captain Bradamont, who assured us that Admiral Timbale would do as you wished in your absence.

"We are nonetheless concerned for her and our ships and are glad that you will soon reach Varandal as well. If there is anything the warships of the Recovery Flotilla of the independent Midway Star System can do to assist you, please let us know. Marphissa, for the people, out."

For a moment, no one spoke, then Rione shrugged. "I wasn't expecting that. What do you suppose happened when Captain Bradamont and those six freighters got to Varandal?"

"Hopefully, they've been picking up those Syndic prisoners," Geary said. "I hope my orders provided sufficient cover for Captain Bradamont."

"That Kommodor actually seemed sincere when she expressed concern for Captain Bradamont," Rione commented.

"Syndics are good liars," Desjani said. "And she was probably actually concerned about her freighters. I know, I know," she added, when Geary turned a look on her. "These aren't Syndics anymore. Well, they're welcome to those deadweight prisoners at Varandal, right?"

"Right," Geary agreed. "And if these ships from Midway are only here waiting for the freighters to return, we don't have to deal with them. They're no threat to Atalia."

"They are actually a defense for Atalia," Rione pointed out.

Geary shook his head. "Another thing I never expected to see." He tapped his comm control. "Kommodor Marphissa, you should be aware that the Syndicate Worlds launched deniable attacks on us at Sobek and Simur. We would appreciate any more information you have about what happened with the Syndic hypernet. We are proceeding to the Varandal jump point. Once at Varandal, if Captain Bradamont and your ships are still present, we will ensure that they depart safely. It is, uh, good to see you again as well. To the honor of our ancestors, Geary, out."

"Did you have to add that good to see you stuff?" Desjani grumbled.

The authorities at Atalia were more than welcoming, falling over themselves to offer the great Black Jack anything he might need (if they had it), expressing cautious thanks for the protection offered by the flotilla from Midway (and implying how nice it would be if the Alliance made a similar commitment of forces) while also complaining that the Midway ships had, since arriving, blocked anyone from jumping for Kalixa and Indras beyond, and by the way just what were those six mysterious ships that resembled no human construction and where had that superbattleship, also of unfamiliar design, come from? Geary let Rione offer ambiguous thanks-but-no-thanks responses that provided no real information on the fleet or where it had been.

The small crew of the courier ship were also hopping with curiosity. They confirmed that six freighters had arrived with the Midway forces and jumped for Varandal several days ago. Knowing how boring and thankless the courier ship's sentry assignment at Atalia was, Geary offered the crew a sanitized version of the report he had prepared for fleet headquarters and the Alliance government.

As they approached the jump point for Varandal, Rione asked to speak with him privately. Suspecting what she was going to say,

Geary only reluctantly granted her request.

"I hope you don't think the danger is over," she began, standing in his stateroom after declining his offer of a seat.

Unhappy to have guessed right, Geary sat down himself and leaned back, looking at the overhead. He had been doing more of that since talking with Charban about the patterns that humans saw in things, wondering what a Dancer would see in those same shapes. Or what an enigma would see, or a Kick. But only the Dancers might someday provide an answer. "I know we're going to face some challenges in Alliance space…"

"The problems we left remain and have likely gotten worse," Rione cautioned. "Too many people in the Alliance think that you're a gift from the living stars who will save the Alliance, and too many others think you're the greatest threat the Alliance has ever faced."

"And," Geary said in a tired voice, "there are plenty of people in between those extremes who are playing their own games in the full belief that they are in the right. What can I do?"

"Wait, watch, and react." She made a helpless gesture. "There are too many players, all working at their own games. Speaking of different players, I am increasingly worried about what the ships from the Callas Republic and the Rift Federation will do when we get to Varandal."

First Dr. Nasr and now Rione. For both to mention it meant the problem was getting serious. "I have told the crews of those ships that I will do everything I can—"

"I don't think that's good enough, Admiral," Rione insisted. "Captain Hiyen is extremely worried. As he put it, there's nothing big happening, but there are constant, minor tremblings in the crews that put him in mind of how earthquakes are forecast. You may not have time to act. Last time they returned to Varandal, they waited for orders and were rewarded by being ordered to go out again with you instead of being allowed to go home, as they had every right to expect. I don't know what may happen this time. Just be prepared for an earthquake from that direction."

Geary nodded wearily. "As opposed to being prepared for earthquakes from every other direction."

"Yes. I don't like playing defense, but it's all we have in this case. Just parrying problems as they come at us is the best we can hope for. Unless some new factor changes things."

"New factor?" Geary looked at her. "We are bringing the Dancers back."

"There's no predicting the impact of *that*," Rione said. "Especially since I can't predict what the Dancers will do. They have chosen to accompany us. I still don't know why. Maybe once we reach Alliance territory, the Dancers will tell us."

He looked back at the tangle of wires, conduits, and cables overhead. "Someone didn't want me, didn't want this fleet, to come back."

"But you are coming back. With a fleet that is still powerful. Why didn't that statement produce any sign of satisfaction in you? Is there something you're not telling *me*, Black Jack?"

"That would be a change."

"It would. And you're avoiding answering the question."

"Do you know that the Alliance government is building a new fleet?"

She stared at him, showing open surprise for possibly the first time since he had met her. "Where did you hear that?"

Geary smiled, a mere bending of his mouth without feeling behind it. "I have my sources."

"How large a fleet?" If Rione had known of this, she was doing an excellent job of hiding it.

"Twenty battleships, twenty battle cruisers, an appropriate number of escorts."

She eyed him for what felt like almost a minute before speaking again. "I can check on that information when we get back. Were you told officially?"

"Hell, no."

"Damn. That could mean several things, all of them bad." Rione shook her head. "What's that old saying? Against stupidity, the gods themselves contend in vain. I'm not even a god."

"Neither am I. Do we have a chance?"

She paused, then smiled in a very enigmatic way. "Of course we do. Black Jack is on our side."

He was still searching for an answer to that when Rione left.

The next day, having gone much farther through unexplored space than humans were known to have ever gone before, and having fought its way out and back again, the fleet jumped for Alliance space and home.

Varandal.

Geary felt a sense of relaxation fill him. This was home. This was part of the Alliance. His friends and advisors would warn that Varandal was full of plots by enemies both political and military, that he could not relax his guard for an instant in so-called "friendly" space, but for now he kept his emotions firmly fixed on denial and imagined that only rest and support awaited him and his fleet at Varandal.

"I hope they don't shoot at us," Tanya mumbled, making Geary's exercise in self-deception that much harder to sustain.

"Why would they shoot at us?" he asked.

"Because you're Black Jack coming back to do something. Because we've got the former Kick superbattleship with us. Because we've got the six Dancer ships with us. Because Bradamont came here with six Syndic freighters and stirred them up. Because they're idiots."

"Admiral Timbale is not an idiot," Geary said, trying to salvage the last shreds of his tranquillity.

"If he's still in command at Varandal." Desjani gave him a narrow-eyed look. "Be ready for anything when we leave jump."

"You know, I *am* the admiral here."

"Then I respectfully advise that the admiral be prepared for any possible event when we exit jump, *sir*."

Sighing and rubbing his eyes, Geary straightened in the command seat. He knew better than to point out that Tanya was echoing the warnings that Rione had given him a few days before. *I didn't think about this sort of thing when I married the commanding officer of my flagship.*

"What?"

"I didn't say anything," Geary insisted.

"Yes, you— Never mind. We're about to arrive." Desjani gave him one more admonishing glance, then focused on her display.

He did the same, seeing one of the lights of jump space suddenly erupt seemingly directly in their path. There was no telling how far off the light was, no way to tell how distant anything was in jump space, but Geary had the sense that *Dauntless* was plunging right into the light as it dropped out of jump.

Intakes of breath by the others on the bridge told him that they had seen the same thing.

Then the welcome blackness of normal space and the lights of countless stars appeared, including the brighter glare of the dot of light that was the nearby star Varandal.

No alarms sounded as the fleet's sensors looked around, taking in the situation. By the time Geary had shaken off the brain fuzz caused by the transition out of jump space, his display had updated to show a comfortingly routine-appearing picture of human activity at Varandal.

Until the display hiccuped, and the images of more than a dozen Alliance stealth shuttles appeared near Ambaru station. "What the hell are they doing out?"

"Ambaru must see them," Desjani muttered, checking her own data. "They've got their tracking emissions on. That's how we can see them this far out."

He called up the data and saw that she was right. The stealth shuttles were putting out tiny emissions that normally would look like background noise within a star system. Only sensors alerted to look for particular patterns hidden within that noise would spot the tracking signatures. "A drill? Why the hell?"

"Maybe they know," Desjani suggested, pointing to the images of an Alliance light cruiser and two destroyers only half a light-hour from the jump point. "Coupe, *Bandolier*, and *Spearhand*. What are they doing out here?"

"Heading back in toward the star," Geary said, frowning. "And no sign of those six Syndic freighters."

"No debris from them, either," Desjani pointed out.

"Let's head in ourselves. We'll send in the standard arrival reports and nothing else while I wait to hear from Timbale."

"And if Timbale isn't still here?"

"Then I'll hear from whoever took over from him."

It took a few hours, of course. *Coupe* and *Bandolier* were tight-lipped when Geary called them, saying only that they had been carrying out special maneuvers on orders from Admiral Timbale. But there had been enough chatter among other ships and stations at Varandal to provide a partial picture of events as Lieutenant Iger pieced it together.

"The Syndic, er, that is, the Midway freighters were here, Admiral. They showed up and asked for the prisoners from the Syndic Reserve Flotilla that you destroyed. There was some sort of major flap, though. Commandos and Marines on Ambaru station, warships moving around quickly, and a lot of high-priority, highly classified message traffic flying."

"But the freighters got out safely? Along with Captain Bradamont?"

"Sir, I've seen no mention of Captain Bradamont, but otherwise, yes, it looks like they jumped out a few days ago."

When Admiral Timbale's message finally showed up, he confirmed that. "Captain Bradamont was with them, though only I know that. If certain parties had discovered she was with those freighters, it would have caused no end of trouble, and things were bad enough as it was. She said you ran into problems using the hypernet gate at Midway, but after your fleet left, the problems cleared up. According to Bradamont, the Syndics—ah, excuse me, the people of the free and independent Midway Star System, were baffled but were certain that the Syndic government must have figured out how to selectively block access to hypernet gates, and they used that to complicate your journey home."

Timbale, still three light-hours distant on Ambaru station, blew out a long breath. "It's been... interesting here. I assume you've noticed the stealth shuttles and commandos hanging around Ambaru, waiting for me to step outside the protection of the Marines on the station. I've had a full platoon of combat-ready Marines following me everywhere for the last few days because I'm pretty sure at least one senior officer thinks he or she has grounds for arresting me. But now you've shown up, just as Captain Bradamont said you would. She got out fine, though it was nip and tuck for a while. She also gave me a rundown on what you ran into out there, including telling me about that captured superbattleship, but I didn't realize just how big that damned thing was. And the six Dancer ships. I knew all that was coming. No one else did, though, so you've made one hell of a dramatic entrance. But then, you make a habit of that." Timbale smiled to show the comment was meant as a compliment.

"I'm still in charge here for the time being. I'm glad you're here to back me up. I think things will finally calm down really fast now, and fleet headquarters will rethink any ideas about relieving me for treason or bad judgment or just on general principles. Ah, what do you know, the commandos look like they're finally heading home. I guess everything is fine, and we're all friends again.

"I'm really looking forward to seeing your detailed report on what you've been doing. Damn, that is one *big* battleship. To the honor of our ancestors, Timbale, out."

The next several days were busy ones. The fleet had to be brought into the inner star system, many ships put into parking orbits reserved for Alliance warships and others eased into orbiting dry docks for repair work. Liberated Alliance prisoners had to be shuttled to Ambaru station for processing. Reports had to be sent, Alliance courier ships racing to the Alliance hypernet gate at Varandal to bear the news of Black Jack's return to the government at Unity and to fleet headquarters. Other courier ships, private ones leased by news organizations, also tore out of Varandal with reports that Black Jack was alive, he was back, he had rescued thousands of Alliance prisoners from the Syndics, including many senior officers, all of them men and women long thought dead, he had found new allies for humanity, he had been betrayed by the Syndics and defeated the enigmas once more, and other news reports that Geary could have done without. That Black Jack had possession of the largest warship ever constructed and he would use it to either defend humanity or take over the Alliance or wipe out the Syndics once and for all or…

"A fleet?" Desjani blurted. "Some people think you're going to build a fleet of ships like *Invincible*? Do they have any idea what that would require?"

"No," Geary said sourly. "They don't have any idea. That's why they think I'll do it." They were in his stateroom, the hatch open, while Geary wondered for the thousandth time since arriving at Varandal when he and Tanya might have a chance to leave her ship, to spend at least a few hours off official property and off official duty, as husband and wife rather than Admiral and Captain.

Another message came in, and Geary almost shunted it to mail before seeing who it was from. "They are still alive," Dr. Nasr reported with a wan smile. "We have kept the last two captured bear-cows alive until we reached Alliance space and until someone else could take custody of them."

"Congratulations, Doctor," Geary said. He could understand the doctor's subdued attitude. Had they done the right thing? What would happen to those two Kicks now? Nasr cared more than anyone else because to him, they were his patients. Even while the entire rest of the fleet used the nickname Kicks, the doctor continued to employ the more polite and respectful term "bear-cows" when speaking of those two.

"I am in receipt of orders to transfer the two bear-cows to custody of the Shilling Institute." Nasr grimaced. "They are good people. Good doctors. It is a good place for treatments of the most difficult kinds. But I do not like turning the bear-cows over to someone who does not know them. We have learned enough to keep the sedation at the right levels though there were a few rough moments even in the last several days."

"The medical authorities will take your experience into account, won't they?" Geary asked. "You say the physicians at the Shilling Institute are capable."

"They are, but they are among the elite. We are fleet physicians, Admiral," Dr. Nasr said with heavy irony. "A lesser form of surgeon in the eyes of the elite. They will listen to us, some of them will pay heed, but I fear others will discount what we say and make their own mistakes." All trace of humor was gone now. "And the last two bear-cows may die. Not because the people gaining custody of them are evil or wrong but because humans make mistakes, even in cases that do not involve very cute creatures who do not think as we do and did not evolve as we did."

Geary clenched his teeth, fighting down a sense of futility that he knew the doctor must share. "We did the best we could. I don't know what else we could have done."

"Neither do I, Admiral. I wanted you to know. Perhaps I am being unduly pessimistic, the doctor unwilling to hand his patient off to another doctor. Perhaps I am the one suffering from the belief that I know more than anyone else." Nasr seemed wistful for a moment. "It is a great pity. The bear-cows will never know how hard we tried to save them, to keep them alive, to help them. But they think they already know what we intend toward them, and so they would not listen, not even for a few seconds. How do we explain this to others, to those who would blame us? I have already heard it. How could you have fought them? How could you have killed them?"

"They didn't give us any choice."

"Our records should make that clear," the doctor agreed. "Unless people do not want to believe those records."

"Thank you, Doctor. For everything." Geary turned to talk to Tanya, only to hear the high-pitched squeal that warned of an urgent message.

Captain Hiyen had the fixed expression of someone facing a firing squad, that combination of resignation that nothing could be done and determination to face fate's last throw with as much courage as possible. It was not the sort of fatalistic cast any commander wanted to see on a subordinate when they reported in. It seemed particularly out of place here, in supposed safety at

Varandal. "Admiral, I must speak with you, privately and as soon as possible."

The battleship *Reprisal* orbited only a few light-seconds distant, making a real conversation possible without long, awkward pauses as light crawled between ships carrying human messages. "What exactly does this concern?" Geary asked, gesturing urgently to Desjani.

"It... concerns the ships of the Callas Republic. And, I believe, those of the Rift Federation. Please, Admiral. There may be little time."

Rione had warned him that a long-simmering pot might be on the verge of boiling over. Geary paused, thinking, then glanced over at where Tanya sitting, her whole attitude alert as she sensed Geary's concern. "Captain Desjani, please accompany me to the high-security conference room." Private talk, hell. He needed other ears, other minds, working with him if this involved what he feared.

And if this matter involving the ships of the Callas Republic was what he thought it was... Geary hit an internal comm control. "Emissary Rione, I need you in the high-security conference room as soon as possible." Rione had been Co-President of the Callas Republic, and respected by the crews of the ships from that republic and the Rift Federation, before being recently voted out of office in one of the wave of special elections convulsing the Alliance's political order. The republic and the federation had only joined with the Alliance during the war out of fear of the Syndicate Worlds, and with their populations now chafing to sever formal ties, Rione's loyalty to the Alliance had been a serious drawback for her with the voters.

"That call was from *Reprisal*," Tanya noted, as they started toward the conference room, walking briskly but not so fast as to arouse alarm among the crew members who saw them.

"Right. You can guess what this is probably about."

She nodded with a slow deliberation that startled Geary. "They want to go home."

"We all do."

"Not as bad as them. And we are home, in the Alliance. Those ships are from the Callas Republic. They haven't been home in a long time."

"I know."

A few minutes later, the hatch to the room sealed behind Rione as she joined them, the lights above the hatch came on declaring the room and its communications to be as secure as current fleet hardware and software could achieve, and Geary gestured to Tanya to open the link to Captain Hiyen.

Hiyen did not appear happy to see the others present but then sighed heavily in acceptance. "Admiral, I will trust in your judgment on including these others. Madam Co-President, I still call you that, but many of our people no longer trust you."

Rione took that news impassively, but Geary could see the hurt in her eyes. "I did not write the orders that kept you here. I was called on to deliver them, but I never approved of them."

"I believe you," Hiyen said. "Admiral, to put it bluntly, I have the sad duty to report that mutiny is imminent on the ships of this fleet from the Callas Republic and, I believe, on those from the Rift Federation as well. In my professional opinion, at any moment, my officers and crew, and those of the other ships from the republic and the federation, will cease responding to orders and break away from the fleet en route their homes.

"There is nothing," Hiyen added, "that I can do to stop this. It is in some ways a miracle that we came this far without mutiny. But now it is inevitable."

Desjani clenched one fist. "If those ships mutiny and take off on their own, the rest of the fleet is going to go unstable really fast. But if you send Marines to subdue the crews, or order our ships to fire on those ships, the result might be even worse."

And, of course, Geary knew that even though he had not created this situation, the decision on what to do was his, and his alone, just as the blame for any negative consequences would be his.

"You've tried everything to keep a lid on the situation?" Geary asked Hiyen.

"Everything except mass arrests," Captain Hiyen replied heavily. "I fear attempting that would cause the entire situation to go nova."

"He's right," Rione said, her voice quiet but full of certainty. "We can't contain this any longer."

"But Captain Desjani is right," Geary said. "If I just let those ships head for home, every other sailor and Marine in this fleet is going to start wondering about taking decisions like that into their own hands. A lot of them don't want to mutiny, they want to be fleet, but they're feeling badly used. Trying to stop any of them by force would produce even worse results."

"Talk to them," Desjani urged.

"Force is the only remaining option to stop this," Hiyen said. "They will not listen, not even to Black Jack. They are grateful to him, but they have been through too much. I will be removed from command by my crew if I try to stop them, and they will fight back if you try to stop them."

If only Hiyen had been incompetent, a bad leader whose assessments were not to be trusted and whose removal could stabilize the situation. But Captain Hiyen was capable enough. Not the finest officer in the fleet, but a good officer who knew how to lead. Geary looked at Tanya and saw his assessment mirrored in her eyes.

"How is the fleet supposed to handle such situations?" Rione asked.

Geary shrugged. "The traditional response is to shoot the messenger. Blame Captain Hiyen for telling us about the problem, blame him for the problem, and do nothing else until everything blows up."

Desjani nodded and bared her teeth in a humorless smile. "At which point, we blame Captain Hiyen's subordinates, the most junior ones possible, for the entire problem."

"We cannot stop the explosion," Rione said. "What can we do to... minimize its effects? To... what is the right word... redirect it?"

Hiyen shook his head in despair. "You cannot redirect a mutiny, Madam Co-President."

Desjani leaned forward, her eyes intent. "Wait a minute. Redirect. Those ships were told to stay with this fleet by their government, Admiral Geary, but they are under *your* command."

"Isn't that the problem?" Geary snapped.

He saw Desjani flush at his tone and knew he would pay for it later. But for now her voice stayed level. "You are their commander. Send them somewhere. Send them *now*."

"Where could I order them," Geary demanded in frustration, "that wouldn't make them just as unhappy? They want to go home—"

He stopped speaking as he understood. "Victoria, you know those orders you brought. Can I do that?"

"I..." Normally composed, Rione had been badly rattled by this situation, but she got control of herself by an effort so strong it was visible to everyone. "It depends. You can't just send them somewhere. There has to be an official reason related to the defense of the Alliance."

Geary called up a display, entered a quick query, then studied the detailed information about the ships of the Callas Republic and the Rift Federation. Names of ships, names of commanding officers, status of ships... Old ships, tired ships, and tired crews. "They need repair and refit. And new personnel. Replacements for those lost in battle. Right now the Alliance is paying for all of that. Why shouldn't the Callas Republic and the Rift Federation be responsible for repairs?"

"Admiral?" Captain Hiyen asked. "Our orders are to remain with the Alliance fleet."

"Your orders," Rione said, "are to stay attached to the fleet and respond to the orders of Alliance officers in command."

"Which doesn't mean being physically attached to the fleet," Desjani said.

"Exactly," Geary added. "If I tell your ships to leave, if I give them orders to return to their home space, they will be following orders when they do leave. It won't be a mutiny, it will be obedience to orders. Captain Hiyen, all ships of the Callas Republic are going to be formed into a task force, effective immediately, with orders to proceed under your command back to the Callas Republic for refit, repair, and resupply. How soon can you depart?"

Hiyen stared at Geary, then laughed briefly in a disbelieving way. "Probably immediately. We've all got enough provisions and fuel for the hypernet hop back to the Republic. But for how long? What if the government of the Republic simply sends us back here? Or *tries* to send us back here right away?"

Rione shook her head. "Captain Hiyen, the government ordered you to follow the commands of the Alliance. You will be back in the Republic by order of the Alliance. If the Republic wants to counter the orders of the Alliance, it must first revoke the orders placing you under command of the Alliance."

Captain Hiyen nodded, his eyes bright. "Yes. But how long?"

"What is the right wording?" Rione asked Geary.

"Until further notice," he replied. "Proper military phrasing, proper orders, all in keeping with the requirements that placed those ships under Alliance authority." Geary turned to Desjani. "Help me get the orders put together as fast as possible. We'll use the boilerplate wording for detaching part of a force."

"We can get it done in five minutes," Desjani said. "Captain Hiyen, get the word spread of what's happening just in case we don't have five minutes. Admiral, you need to talk to the Rift Federation ships, too."

"Who is the senior officer from the Rift now?" Geary asked, scanning the display.

Hiyen answered. "Commander Kapelka on the *Passguard*."

It took a moment to review Kapelka's record before calling *Passguard*. Kapelka had a decent record, too. She probably never would have risen beyond command of the heavy cruiser *Passguard*, but among the few star systems belonging to the Rift Federation, that was a substantial command.

Geary put in a high-priority call to *Passguard*.

Less than a minute later, the image of Commander Kapelka appeared. She was sitting at a conference table, too, and had a harried look to her. Geary wondered who else was sitting at that table and what they had just been arguing about.

"Your pardon, Admiral, for taking this call here, but it was marked for immediate reply," Kapelka said. The stress in her voice was obvious, and that stress clearly wasn't because the admiral had just called.

"That's fine," Geary said, trying to sound calm and routine. "I wanted to notify you of orders for all ships from the Rift Federation. Effective immediately, you are appointed commander of a task force composed of all of the ships from the Rift Federation. That task force is to detach from the main body of the fleet and proceed as soon as possible back to the Rift Federation for refit, repair, and resupply. Your ships are to remain in the Federation until further notice."

Kapelka's jaw literally dropped, hanging there for several seconds until she managed to recover enough to snap it shut. "Immediately? You are ordering us to go home immediately?"

"As soon as possible," Geary corrected. "Your ships need a lot of work. Ensure all of your ships have the necessary provisions and fuel for the trip home before you depart, but I don't want any unnecessary delays."

"Thank the living stars!" Commander Kapelka looked around, though not at those with Geary. She was plainly looking at the others at her own conference table. "You heard?" she told them. "Get the word to all ships. *Now.*"

"You will be receiving your formal orders within a few minutes," Geary continued, as if this was all routine, and as if he hadn't noticed Kapelka's reaction. "Let me know if there are any difficulties."

Ending that call, Geary looked back at Captain Hiyen's image. "You'll get the detailed orders within a few minutes as well. Notify your crew and the other Callas Republic ships."

An unexpected reprieve had occurred, a pardon had appeared at the last minute, the rifles of the firing squad had jammed. Captain Hiyen smiled in wonderment as he saluted, then his image vanished.

"Not to throw a monkey wrench into the only solution we had, but are you certain this won't make you look weak?" Desjani asked. "Everybody in the fleet knows how the ships from the republic and the federation felt. They might well guess that your hand was forced."

He gave her an irritated look. "What else was I supposed to do?"

"Every other option was worse. A lot worse. But do we know this solution won't still create some problems?"

Why was she—? *Because she can read my attitude. I'm so relieved that we defused this situation that I'm not thinking about possible consequences. Trust Tanya to keep me grounded when I was ready to bask in the glory of disaster averted.* "It might," Geary conceded. "How do I handle that?"

"I'll handle it," Rione said, pretending not to notice Desjani's reflexive frown. "All we have to do is start the right rumors on your Alliance warships. I have people in place who can do that."

"Which rumors?" Geary asked, wishing he knew more about the agents that Rione had scattered through his fleet.

"Rumors that Black Jack is tired of the governments of the Callas Republic and the Rift Federation not pulling their share in supporting their own warships. You'll remember I told you that funding for upkeep and repair would not be forthcoming in the expectation that the ships would wear out and eventually be useless."

"In the hopes of that, you mean."

Rione inclined her head in a small nod of agreement, her expression betraying no feeling. "But you, Admiral, are unhappy with this. You made the decision that you would force the issue when you returned to Alliance space."

"No," Desjani put in, her voice sharp. "Admiral Geary would be primarily motivated by the mistreatment of the crews of those ships who have been allowed very little time at home since the end of the war. The maintenance and funding issue would be secondary."

"That's true," Geary agreed.

After a pause, Rione nodded. "That additional reason will only strengthen your position. You have made up your mind, you have the authority, and the decision is now being implemented by you, without anyone else having a say in the matter. It's just what would be expected of Black Jack, isn't it?"

"I hope so. That legend makes Black Jack a better officer than I'll ever be."

Desjani broke off her work on the orders to glare at him. "You are *better* than that legend."

"Your Captain is right," Rione said, then faced Desjani squarely. "You found the solution. I am deeply in your debt again."

"That's... all right," Desjani mumbled, unsure how to respond. "Don't worry, Captain. I won't start acting like we're sisters."

"Good. I couldn't handle that." Desjani grimaced. "Thank you for the assistance you have given the Admiral."

Rione looked back at Geary. "I'll go do my part."

She left, and both Geary and Desjani bent back to frantically crafting the necessary orders. Fortunately, those orders could be fairly simple and fairly short, with the bulk of them made up of standard phrasing. "I think that's good," Geary said. "Let's read them over slowly one more time." He did, spotting a misplaced word and correcting that, then looked to Tanya. She nodded, and Geary hit the transmit command.

"Four and a half minutes," Desjani said with satisfaction. "Even with the interruption."

"The interruption? When Rione thanked you?"

"Whatever."

Geary slumped back and rubbed his eyes with the palms of both hands. He had a feeling Rione would be similarly dismissive if he brought the matter up with her. "That was close. From the way Kapelka was acting, her crew was about to give her an ultimatum."

"Yup." Desjani leaned back as well, smiling. "And Hiyen was expecting you to shoot the messenger."

"I've seen that done, Tanya. Too many times. Compared to now, they were about pretty minor issues, I guess. Problems being covered up with equipment on a single light cruiser, a destroyer commander whose own officers were reporting him as dangerously incompetent, that sort of thing. Sometimes the messenger is really exaggerating or even making things up, but all the more reason to find out if what you've been told is true or not."

"Are you expecting an argument from me?" She stood up. "The usual response nowadays is to classify everything so everyone can pretend nothing actually happened. Good luck keeping this incident quiet if all of those ships had mutinied within Alliance space, though."

Geary stared at her, the mention of mutiny calling to mind past events. "When Captain Numos participated in the mutiny led by Captain Falco, that was outside Alliance space. Not too many people know about that, or exactly what led to the loss of ships like *Triumph*, *Polaris*, and *Vanguard*. Do you think that's why Numos hasn't been court-martialed yet?"

She paused. "Yes, now that you mention it. Too many details of what happened would make high-ranking people look bad. With Falco dead, Numos stands to take full blame for the mutiny, so he wouldn't hesitate to make as big a public stink as possible. And now that Admiral Bloch is back, he sure as hell wouldn't want word getting out about what a mess he got the fleet into."

That news had come in, too. Admiral Bloch, released as a goodwill gesture by the Syndics along with a hundred other Alliance prisoners. But just where Bloch was at the moment and what he was doing remained a mystery that not even Rione's sources had been able to penetrate. "If they weren't going to arrest Bloch," Geary said, "they should at least have retired him."

"There you go, expecting the government to do the rational thing." Desjani paused, then spoke light words with a spine of steel running through them. "Oh, that reminds me. When we were having that discussion about averting the mutiny, I could have sworn that you spoke to me in a tone of voice more appropriate to a chief chewing out a deckhand who had made a dumb mistake."

"I... would not..." Geary fumbled.

"And I seem to recall that you spoke to me that way while that woman was in here listening."

Ancestors, please save me.

Her eyes were locked on him. "Well?"

"I..."

An urgent alert sounded. Geary lunged for the comm panel as

if it were the last source of air in a spacecraft losing atmosphere.

"Admiral, a delegation from the grand council of the Alliance has arrived at Varandal and wants to meet with you on Ambaru station as soon as possible."

"All right. Thank you." The call ended and he stood up. "There's an important—"

"I'd like an answer, Admiral," Desjani said, her tone polite but unyielding.

He pressed his lips tightly together, then nodded. "My behavior toward you was disrespectful and unprofessional. I apologize for that."

She nodded in return. "Yes. Disrespectful. If you want to chew me out, do it in private. In public, treat me with the respect I have earned and deserve. You already know you should do that with me and with every other subordinate of yours."

"Yes, I do," Geary said. "I shouldn't have to be reminded of it."

"Then we understand each other." Desjani jerked her head toward the hatch.

He reached for it, then paused and looked at her. "You're letting me off rather easy."

"Oh? You think so? We've only addressed your actions in terms of our professional relationship, Admiral. The next time we're alone together, off my ship and in a private status, we'll discuss your actions in terms of our personal relationship."

Maybe I shouldn't look forward to being alone with Tanya off Dauntless.

Oh, hell. You screwed up. Face it like a man. "After you, Captain. We've got work to do."

"Sure do," she agreed, as they left the room. "Are you going to tell the grand council's representatives that a bunch of this fleet's warships are going to be heading real soon for the hypernet gate and their homes?"

Geary thought about that, then shook his head. "They might try to stop it if they know it's going to happen. Let's save it for a surprise."

Once more, the Grand Council had sent a delegation to see him instead of the grand council's summoning him to go to them at Unity. Was that good or bad?

13

"A couple of other people needed a ride to Ambaru, so I arranged for them to be on this one," Desjani remarked, as they waited to board the shuttle that was coming to dock aboard *Dauntless*.

"I wish you had asked me about that first," Geary grumbled. "I am not looking forward to this meeting. I don't even know which senators will be here as representatives of the grand council."

"It scarcely matters," Rione said as she walked up to them. "Some will trust you, some will mistrust you, and all will be scheming and plotting. Do you mind if I tag along? I received a rather urgent invitation."

Whatever Desjani was about to reply went unsaid as a medical team entered the dock with a stretcher on which Commander Benan lay. Rione's husband was unconscious, but the readouts on the stretcher indicated he was physically healthy aside from the sedation keeping him insensible.

"An invitation for me to be at the grand council meeting,"

Rione continued, and an... invitation for my husband to proceed for emergency, specialized medical treatment." Only the uncharacteristic catch in her voice when she spoke of Commander Benan betrayed Rione's emotions.

"It's what we demanded?" Geary asked.

"It is," Rione confirmed. "That ill will be removed." Neither of them would openly refer to the mental block that the Alliance itself had placed on Benan to ensure the secrecy of a forbidden research program. "That won't cure the damage that was done, but it will allow the damage to finally be effectively treated."

One of the corpsmen with the stretcher spoke apologetically. "Ma'am, we're going to have to go straight from the dock at Ambaru to another dock for the shuttle down to the surface. If you want to say anything to him before you're separated for a while, we can rouse him enough."

"I..." Rione glanced at Geary and Desjani. "Yes. I don't want to risk him awakening at the treatment facility and not knowing."

The corpsman worked for several seconds, then both medical personnel stepped away to give her and Benan some privacy. Geary and Desjani started to do the same, but Rione forestalled them.

"Paol," she whispered, kneeling beside the stretcher.

Benan's eyes opened, looking about with a puzzled expression. "Vic?"

"You're on your way to get the block removed. I'll join you there, after I take care of something else. You'll be all right."

Benan smiled at her with a gentleness surprising to those who had seen the rages the mental block had created in him. "Not totally useless yet, huh?" he said in a low, hoarse voice. "Not yet.

Shot to hell and barely operational, but you think I'm still worth fixing." He blinked. "You'll be there?"

"As soon as possible," Rione promised.

Commander Benan twitched, and a low tone sounded from the stretcher's monitor. The corpsmen hurried back. "His brain's ramping up, ma'am. We've got to get him quiet, or he'll lose it."

Within another couple of seconds after the corpsman adjusted a setting, Benan had closed his eyes, out cold again.

The shuttle had landed and extended its ramp. Geary indicated Rione and the corpsmen with the stretcher. "You go on board first."

Desjani stood gazing at them as they headed for the shuttle, her expression tight with anger. "No one should be used that way."

"The block, you mean?"

"Yeah. To one of our own. What do you want to bet that the rules prevented whoever ordered that block put on him from doing to Syndic prisoners what they did to a fleet officer?"

"I won't take that bet."

"Sometimes I feel sorry for that woman," Desjani admitted of Rione. "Sometimes she seems almost human."

"Sometimes she is," Geary said. "But don't let her know you spotted that."

He and Desjani walked up to the shuttle ramp and inside, joining those already there. Geary's misgivings at having other company evaporated as he saw Dr. Shwartz and Admiral Lagemann. "You're both leaving?" Geary asked as he sat down and strapped in.

Lagemann smiled lopsidedly. "I have been relieved of command. The good ship *Invincible* has been officially reclassified as an artifact."

"I thought the government techs were going to take over *Invincible* a week ago."

"They were." Lagemann winked. "We suggested they might want to take a little time to get accustomed to *Invincible*, but they brushed aside our superstitious concerns, came charging on board to take custody and eject us, then went charging back into their shuttles much faster than they had come aboard. After a week spent working out how they would deal with the Kick ghosts, the techs finally took full custody late yesterday. The last fleet sailors, Marines, and I left this morning."

"Maybe the techs will figure out what the ghosts are."

Lagemann looked into the distance. "Would you think it odd if I wanted the ghosts to remain a mystery? To maybe fade away and disappear, their cause and their nature remaining unknown?"

"I wouldn't be surprised," Desjani tossed in, "if that's exactly what happens."

"Are you going home?" Geary asked Lagemann.

"Yes. For a brief visit with those who thought me dead. Then I have to report for extensive debriefing on everything I learned about *Invincible* while serving as her commanding officer."

"That should be fun," Geary remarked. "What about you, Doctor?"

Shwartz gazed longingly around her. "I will miss being here, Admiral. Here with your ships. No luxuries at all, and food worse than even universities provide in their cafeterias, but I finally had the opportunity to really work in my field! And I *enjoyed* working with you, against all expectations about rigid military minds and institutions. Now we must go our separate ways and fight our separate battles."

"You have battles?"

"Vicious and ugly battles," she confirmed. "Battles for academic primacy, battles for credit for discoveries, findings, and interpretations, battles for positions on boards and study groups. There will be ambushes to strike the unwary, no end of verbal and written atrocities inflicted on the combatants and innocent bystanders, and horrible barrages of rhetoric exchanged in unending debate until some bloodied figures manage to surmount the smoking wreckage of truth and declare themselves authorities over the scholarly rubble that remains."

Geary smiled. "You make it sound worse than actual warfare."

"Having seen both academic and real warfare, Admiral, I find the relative honesty of the real thing something of a relief." Shwartz gestured vaguely. "The fight for access to that Kick superbattleship has just begun, and the amount of academic bloodletting over that alone will probably exceed what your Marines encountered. I only hope the entire ship is not declared classified and off-limits to scientific inquiry."

"The military and the government wouldn't do something that stupid—"

Lagemann intervened. "Sad to say, I think the techs may have intended doing that until they got aboard and realized the enormity of what was inside that ship. Before I left, the most common comment among the techs was *we're going to need a lot of help*."

"Good," Desjani said. "Personally, I think the limits of enigma space were a lot easier to find than the limits of official stupidity would be."

"You know," Professor Shwartz said with a wicked smile, "you might *want* anyone working against you to get their hooks into that Kick warship. The superbattleship looks so terribly powerful. And yet it is helpless, a burden to whoever has it."

"Yes," Geary agreed, remembering the long and difficult journey to get *Invincible* back here in one piece. "Having the ship with us was a real headache."

"A white elephant." Her smiled broadened. "I'm going to be an academic and lecture you, Admiral. Do you know where the term 'white elephant' originated? Back on Old Earth. It literally referred to an elephant who was white. In one particular civilization in ancient times, an elephant who was naturally white was regarded as sacred. Such an animal required no end of caring for and rituals and special treatment. It was ruinously expensive. Because of that, when a white elephant was born, the rulers of that land would bestow it as a gift upon their richest, most powerful enemy, who would be forced by law and custom to drain their fortune on the upkeep of the animal. No one could refuse such a gift, and no one could afford to keep it. Do you have any powerful enemies who could benefit from the gift of your white elephant, Admiral?" Shwartz finished in teasing tone. "You might try to lure them into seeking that prize."

Geary laughed. "I might be able to think of some who would benefit from that sort of thing. If the opportunity arises, would you be open to being invited to return to work with the Dancers?"

"Admiral, if you arrange such an invitation I will be here so fast that even the hypernet will look slow by comparison." Shwartz hesitated. "Admiral, I really don't know how to thank you. You found them. You found three intelligent, nonhuman species, and even though only one of those will speak to us, you still found all of them."

"We all found them. I'm just glad we survived the experience."

After the shuttle docked, the corpsmen raced off with the stretcher while Rione watched them go with a blank expression.

Dr. Shwartz ambled away, waving farewell and looking around like a tourist as she went.

Admiral Lagemann saluted Geary, then grabbed his hand. "Thank the living stars, I'm home. And thank you. A rescue, an astounding adventure, and a final command that no one else can match. I hope to see you and your, uh, Captain Desjani again."

"We'll look forward to it, Admiral," Desjani said. As Lagemann left, she looked at Geary. "You're welcome. I figured you could use some more pleasant diversion on the ride than worrying about politics."

"And, as always, you were right. Here comes our escort."

This time there were no armed soldiers threatening to arrest Geary, just some military police handling crowd control to keep a quickly gathering mass of people from swamping the area as they sought to meet and see Black Jack. From the happy buzz of conversation, Black Jack's stock was still pretty high among the residents of Ambaru station.

"Admiral, Captain, Madam Emissary," Admiral Timbale greeted them. "I was delayed seeing to the arrangements for the delegation from the grand council. I'm to bring you to them right away. Ah, that is, I'm to take Admiral Geary."

"I received a late invitation," Rione said. "Someone realized that they might want to have someone else present who has conversed extensively with the Dancers. I recommended Emissary Charban come as well, but that suggestion was vetoed."

"I never get to go to these meetings," Desjani said. "But I'm sure I'm happier as a result."

Timbale grinned and gestured to them to accompany him as he began walking down a passageway cleared of other traffic. "Have you seen the news?" he asked.

"I've been trying to avoid it," Geary admitted.

"Understandable. But you need to know what's going on before you end up in front of the grand council." Timbale exhaled heavily, gazing upward. "Here's what they've been seeing. Cute aliens. *Really* cute aliens. We killed them. A lot of them. Ugly aliens. *Really* ugly aliens. We brought them home with us."

Desjani hissed in exasperation. "Do they know that the really ugly aliens helped us kill the really cute aliens?"

"Thank the living stars, no. Even though the records of your encounters with the Kicks have been highly classified by the government, somehow detailed accounts of how hard you tried to communicate with them and avoid bloodshed have been leaked to the press."

"Somehow?" Geary asked.

Timbale shrugged in reply, doing his best to look innocent. "The upshot is that people all around the Alliance are confused. Did Black Jack do the right thing? Or did his heavy-handed missteps cause another war? Many of the academic experts you had along are hinting broadly that if you had just listened to them in particular, then all would have been well."

"What are they saying about the enigmas?"

"Hurrah! Black Jack rescued humans from the enigmas! Also highly classified by the government, also mysteriously leaked to the press." Timbale scratched his nose thoughtfully. "I'm pretty certain that leak came out at Unity. Someone in the government is either your friend or playing their own games that happened to benefit you that time. Otherwise, the enigmas remain, well, enigmas, but the second attack on human space and the attempt by an alien race to bombard a human-occupied planet from space have aroused vast indignation."

Geary shook his head in wonderment. "It's okay if we bomb human planets but aliens can't do it?"

"You have to keep things like that in the family," Timbale advised mockingly. "Oh, the ugly aliens. Public opinion was very much against them, but—"

"Mysteriously," Desjani guessed, "the information was leaked that they had prevented a bombardment of a human planet?"

"Very mysteriously," Timbale agreed. "The Syndics. Everything you ran into in Syndic space has been classified above and beyond top secret, but…"

"You've got a lot of leaks on this space station."

"No one can prove any of them came from here." Timbale eyed Geary. "You do realize how much of a role good press relations have played for the last few decades in promotions to the highest rank? No? I won't burden you with that information, then. There have also been leaks with no basis in your reporting. A big story claims that you received direct communications from the lights while in jump space. There are all kinds of variations of that story circulating. The lights led you to the Kicks and the Dancers.

The lights told you what to do. The lights told you to save the Alliance again—"

"Save the Alliance again?" Geary demanded. "From what?"

"If you had been reading the news, you could guess some of the possible answers to that question." Timbale grinned crookedly. "The rather large number of VIP former prisoners you brought back have helped keep things confused. And the six thousand other liberated prisoners were a real shot in the arm for the government, an accomplishment it can claim credit for."

His smile slipped. "The bottom line is there's a vast amount of uncertainty. Three alien races, and one wants to talk with us. No one wants to start fighting the Syndics again, but the Syndics are taking advantage of that. Your intentions are still critically important and just as subject to interpretation as ever. Your fleet got shot to hell, but you won some important fights. That reminds me. How are you paying for all of this repair work? I haven't heard a single squawk from the budget bean counters."

"We're effectively utilizing all available resources," Geary said.

"Ha! The less I know about that the better. Oh, one bit of good news. Nothing has leaked so far about those freighters from Midway and the role of Captain Bradamont except the official and acceptable-to-almost-everyone reports that Syndic ships came to take some Syndic prisoners off our hands. I don't think anyone who knows more has figured out how to use the information." They had reached a high-security hatch. Admiral Timbale pointed inside. "Good luck."

"Tanya, will you keep an eye on things out here while I'm in there?" Geary asked.

"Why did you think you needed to ask?" Desjani saluted. "Tell them you want a day off."

"I'll do that."

The delegation of the grand council once again awaited him and Rione from seats behind a long table. Geary recognized some of the faces but not others. He was glad to see Senator Navarro among them and cautiously optimistic at the sight of Senator Sakai. Balanced against them were Senator Suva, who had never made any attempt to hide her distrust of Geary and the fleet, and Senator Costa, who rarely bothered to hide her contempt for Senator Suva or her willingness to do anything she thought necessary. Geary wondered if Costa, who had once pushed for Admiral Bloch to command the fleet despite knowing (or perhaps because she knew) that Bloch was considering a military coup, had been in contact with Bloch since the Syndics had returned him in hopes of further destabilizing the tottering Alliance government.

"Why is she here?" Senator Suva demanded, pointing at Rione, before any greetings could be exchanged.

Navarro gave Suva a sharp look. "Among other reasons, because Victoria Rione was appointed an emissary of the Alliance government during Admiral Geary's mission."

"That was when the Callas Republic was part of the Alliance," Suva said. "Since we heard just before leaving Unity that the Callas Republic has formally requested to leave the Alliance, a request which must be automatically granted under the terms by which the Republic joined the Alliance, this Rione is no longer a citizen of the Alliance."

All eyes went to Rione, whom Geary had spotted flinching

slightly at the news of the Callas Republic's intentions. But Rione maintained a bland expression, raising one hand as if asking for the attention she already had. "In that case, I should like to request that the grand council grant me asylum."

The resulting silence lasted until Navarro, obviously trying not to smile, spoke. "You wish to become a legal resident of the Alliance? That might be classified as refugee status."

"Or defection," Senator Costa remarked. She didn't seem amused at all. "Or treason against the Callas Republic."

"The warships of the Callas Republic," Geary interjected, trying not to get angry so soon into the meeting, "fought loyally and well for the Alliance. Even if the Callas Republic is not formally part of the Alliance any longer, I still consider them friends and hope they think of us in the same way."

"Why then did you send those ships away?" brusquely demanded a short, thin senator whom Geary did not recognize.

"They needed repairs, which the Callas Republic should provide, and they deserved some time at home after so much time away and so many sacrifices," Geary said. Expecting to be asked that question, he had gone over his response quite a bit to try to get it right.

"Senator Wilkes," Sakai said to the small senator before he could speak again, "we must focus on the issue at hand. As to the matter of Emissary Rione, I would point out that she was invited to this meeting as the person who can tell us the most about the aliens known as the Dancers since she is the person who has had the most interaction with them."

"The Alliance," Navarro added pointedly, "needs that person."

Suva, clearly unhappy, turned her attention to Geary. "We've read your report. You were sent on a mission of exploration."

"That is what I did, Senator," Geary replied.

"You started two more wars!" Senator Wilkes said. "You were sent to explore and learn, but you started two more wars." He paused as if waiting for applause.

Senator Navarro grimaced. "The record is pretty clear that the enigmas have been fighting humanity since long before we knew they existed. Admiral Geary didn't start anything with them. From the official reports, he in fact tried to stop further fighting and negotiate with the enigmas."

"Those records are from the *Syndics*, Senator."

"Not the records from *our* ships, Senator. They show us trying to talk, trying to resolve things, and the enigmas persisting in attacking."

"Even *if* the enigmas would not speak with us," Senator Suva said, "and given the probable actions of the Syndics and provocative actions by our own forces—"

"Provocative actions?" Senator Costa asked. Geary had learned enough to know that Costa was not so much defending him as reflexively attacking Suva.

"We entered space occupied by them without permission—" Suva plowed on.

"Didn't *you* push for Admiral Geary's fleet to be given that exact mission?" Costa needled.

Geary wondered whether anyone would notice if he got up and left the room. The senators were all locked in verbal combat now, each shouting over the others.

"I really didn't miss this," Rione commented. She rested her right elbow on the palm of her left hand, lowered her chin into her right hand, and closed her eyes. "Wake me up when they're done."

"You can sleep through this?"

"It beats staying awake through it."

A sudden lack of noise caught Geary's attention. He looked toward the table, where the various senators were all glaring at each other but no longer yelling. Senator Sakai, standing, was looking down at the seated senators with an expression that as usual revealed little but this time somehow conveyed disapproval. "Was there a question for Admiral Geary?" Sakai asked as he sat down again.

Wilkes spoke up first, chastened but still aggressive. "We are now at war with *two* other species. I trust no one will argue that? Why was our first encounter with the bov-ursoids a deadly battle?"

"Bov-ursoids?" Geary asked. "You mean the Kicks?"

"That is an insulting term. I will not tolerate its use here."

Costa laughed harshly. "No one cares whether your feelings are bruised by the nickname given to that maniacal species."

Another verbal riot seemed about to erupt, only to be quelled when Sakai bent cold looks down each side of the table.

Geary glanced at Rione as he began speaking again. "We did everything we could to try to communicate with them. The first thing they did was attack us the instant they saw us. We took the actions necessary to defend ourselves. We kept trying to talk with them as long as we were in their star system. They never responded in any way except with further attacks."

"You all saw the reports," Rione added in a matter-of-fact voice. "They attacked us, they pursued us, they continued the pursuit into another star system; even when facing certain defeat and death, they would not communicate with us, preferring suicide. You cannot talk to those who refuse to reply with anything other than further attempts to kill you."

"Perhaps they were frightened of us!" Wilkes insisted.

"Perhaps they were. They may well have had what were for them excellent reasons for not communicating with us and fighting us to the death," Rione said. "However, I did not feel any obligation to die simply because they thought they had a good reason to kill us."

"If you had not barged into their star system with all weapons blazing—"

"We did not fire first," Geary said.

"Admiral," Senator Navarro said, "did you enter, where was it, Honor Star System, in the same fashion as you did the enigma and uh, other alien species star systems that you visited?"

"Yes, Senator. In a defensive formation."

"And at Honor, the representatives of the Dancers there welcomed you."

"They helped our fleet there!" Senator Costa declared triumphantly.

"But…" another senator began, "these Dancers. They're…"

Costa kept grinning. "What's the matter, Tsen? Would saying they're ugly as sin be politically incorrect?"

"We cannot judge them by appearances!"

"But you are doing just that, aren't you? And it's tearing you apart, isn't it?"

"Senator Costa," a tall, dark woman said wearily, "you might win more converts if you didn't take such obvious joy in ripping your opponents' arms off and beating them with the bloody stumps."

"I have a statement to make!" Senator Suva insisted.

"We've hardly asked any questions, Senator," the dark woman said. "Could we break with long-standing precedent and actually learn something about a subject before we make statements about it?"

"Senator Unruh has a point," Navarro said.

Wilkes erupted again before anyone else could, pointing at Geary. "Why did you turn over every human liberated from the enigmas to the Syndics?" The senator's tone was accusing, making the words sound as if a capital murder charge were being leveled against Geary.

Geary did his best not to sound defensive. "They were all citizens of the Syndicate Worlds."

"They could have provided us with critical information about the enigmas!"

"They knew nothing about the enigmas!" Geary controlled his anger before saying more. "Absolutely nothing. If you read my report—"

"You gave away—"

"I am NOT finished answering you, sir!" Everyone was staring at him. Fine. Let them stare. He had been through too much to put up with this. "Before you question me, read the available information so you know what you're talking about. Then permit me to answer you in full without interruption. Every one of those humans we liberated from the enigma prison asteroid was a citizen of the Syndicate Worlds. I had no *right* to hold them against their will. None of them knew anything about the enigmas. None had ever seen an enigma, or spoken with one, or even seen any of their artifacts. They knew far less than we did even before the First

Fleet entered enigma space. But the most important factor in my decision was that *I had no right to hold them.* They were free to make their own decisions about their fates."

Navarro spoke with an unusual level of sarcasm. "Are we to condemn Admiral Geary for acting in accordance with Alliance law? With Alliance principles?"

"Since you brought up Alliance law," Senator Costa said, "and the subject of leaving people with the Syndics has already been raised, I wonder if the Admiral would care to explain leaving one of his senior officers in the custody of the Syndics?"

"One of my officers?" Geary asked. "We lost far too many officers in combat, and most of those received honorable burials in space. The only living officer who did not accompany the fleet home was Captain Bradamont. She has been assigned as liaison officer for the Alliance to the Midway Star System."

"Who *approved* leaving a liaison officer at Midway, Admiral?" Senator Costa asked, her voice harsh.

"I wrote the orders," Geary said in his blandest voice. "The idea was mine." That was the official story he and Rione had agreed upon, and he was going to stick to it. One or more of the senators he was facing might have been among those planning on blackmailing Bradamont over her work for Alliance intelligence during the war. "Naturally, I first gained approval from the representatives of the government who accompanied the fleet."

"That would be me, and Emissary Charban," Rione said brightly.

"Your instructions as emissaries——" Costa began.

"Granted us full discretion," Rione finished. "Instructions approved by the grand council as a whole, I might add."

"Why was Captain Bradamont chosen to operate with the Syndics?" Senator Wilkes demanded. "There has been information circulating which raises serious questions regarding Bradamont's loyalty to the Alliance."

Geary let his gaze, hard and unyielding, rest on Wilkes for a long moment before replying. "As I said earlier, and as my report states clearly, Captain Bradamont is liaison officer to the newly independent Midway Star System. The authorities and the people at Midway are extremely hostile toward the Syndicate Worlds' government, which I also put in my report. I have no doubts as to the loyalty of Captain Bradamont, and if you indeed have information impugning her honor, you should present it openly. I assure you and everyone else here that I have more than adequate information to rebut any charges against Captain Bradamont, and I will present such information openly if required."

Senator Wilkes glowered at Geary, plainly searching for words, but Navarro spoke first. "You have attacked the honor of one of the Admiral's officers," he chided Wilkes, speaking as if to a small child. "I have no doubt the Admiral will do exactly as he promised to defend that officer. Are we ready to have *all* of that information publicly disclosed?"

"Are there not restrictions on what can be discussed?" Costa asked.

"What restrictions and pertaining to what information?" Senator Suva demanded.

A few silent seconds passed as senators exchanged meaningful looks, then Wilkes waved an irritated hand. "We can discuss it later. I cannot see what possible benefit the Alliance gains from leaving a senior fleet officer deep in enemy territory."

"We've already gained some very important information from her," Rione said. "Thanks to Captain Bradamont, we have confirmed that the Syndics have learned how to selectively block access to individual gates in their hypernet."

"I saw that in your reporting," Navarro said, leaning back and eyeing Rione and Geary keenly. "That is extremely important. How do they do it?"

"We don't know. It's obviously something our hypernet experts should be looking into."

Senator Unruh shook her head. "Government-funded hypernet research has been drastically scaled back in order to save money." She turned a long, slow look at her fellow senators. "How fortunate that Admiral Geary also brought back a Syndic-designed system to prevent gates from being collapsed by remote signals. How fortunate that the Syndics continue to invest in research that we have decided is beyond the proper scope of the Alliance government."

"We've been over this," Suva complained. "We have to set priorities."

"Our fleet was almost trapped *again* deep in enemy territory," Unruh said. "I wonder at the priorities that produce such great benefits and advantages to our enemies."

Suva's face flushed with anger. "Are you implying that I—"

"I'm certain that Senator Unruh is not implying anything about anyone," Senator Navarro said.

"If I were, I certainly wouldn't be limiting the implications to one senator," Unruh said.

"From what we could learn," Geary said to fill the awkward silence that followed Unruh's statement, "our best estimate is that the Syndics can't tell who is trying to use a gate. All they can do is block a gate to access, which will only benefit them if they know where we are and where we need to go. They had that advantage at Midway. Even if we face that situation again, we now know that we can use jumps to reach other gates and zigzag our way through their space without following a path they want us to take."

"A path littered with traps," Costa growled.

"Are we at peace with the Syndicate Worlds or not?" Suva asked, sounding almost plaintive.

"We're at peace," Navarro replied. "I don't think the Syndics are."

"We brought back two prisoners taken aboard *Invincible*," Geary pointed out.

"Who can tell us nothing," Navarro said with obvious distaste. "They've been mentally conditioned so severely that one has gone catatonic on us, and the second is barely functional. We can't prove any official Syndic involvement in that or the other attacks."

"Screw proof! We know the truth! They need to be destroyed. We need to finish them," Costa insisted.

"We can't break the peace agreement!" Senator Suva cried. "The people would not stand for it!"

A babble of voices sounded as senators broke in from all sides.

"What peace?"

"Ask the people of the Alliance!"

"We can't restart the war! The government would collapse!"

"Fellow Senators," Sakai said in a calm voice that somehow carried over that of his colleagues. "As has been noted, we must at a minimum pursue the liberation of those Alliance citizens still held within Syndic and formerly Syndic space before we give the Syndics legal grounds to discard the peace agreement. Perhaps we should move on to another topic."

Geary waited while the senators considered Sakai's advice. He wondered if any of the senators could tell that he was nervous, that he was worried that someone would ask what the rulers of Midway had asked of him in exchange for the Syndic device that would prevent a gate collapse by remote signal.

But the grand council lacked any desire to keep talking about the hypernet.

"Well," Navarro said, "there is some good news. We need to talk about that. We have a vast amount of, um, Kick technology in that captured warship. We should be able to learn a lot about them."

"We would have learned much more if we could talk to *living* individuals of that race," Senator Suva muttered loudly.

Rione forestalled Geary's reflexive response with a hand gesture. "We tried," she told Suva and the others. "We tried in every way we could."

"The specialists you had with you," Suva said pointedly, "are saying you failed to try several methods that might have worked."

"Some of them may be saying that now, but they certainly didn't propose any such methods at the time," Rione said. "I personally asked more than once. If some of our academic experts now claim to have known of other methods to communicate with the Kicks, they must have deliberately withheld their suggestions. You might ask them why they did that."

Navarro grimaced, tapping his hand lightly against the table. "I suspect those experts had no more ideas than you did. I can't think of anything you didn't try. Maybe we'll figure out how to wake up the two living Kicks we do have."

"I strongly advise against that," Geary said. "They'll suicide."

"The decision may not be ours, Admiral. What's this I heard about ghosts on that captured ship?"

"There's something strange on *Invincible*," Geary said. "It manifests as if Kick ghosts were crowding around you. I don't recommend going anywhere on that ship alone. The sensation gets overwhelming very fast."

"They had a device," Unruh said softly, "that would protect planets from space bombardment. Is there anything aboard that ship that will show us how to do the same?"

Geary could feel the wave of hope that radiated from the entire grand council. How many billions had died in orbital bombardments since humanity had learned how to go into space and use that ability to drop rocks on the surface of worlds? He shook his head, hating to crush the hopes of the senators. "I don't know. Their technology, the way they build equipment, is very different from ours in many ways. I do know even the largest Kick ships, like *Invincible*, did not have that defense against kinetic projectiles. The fleet's engineers speculate that the defense may require an immense amount of power, or a very large mass like a planet or minor planet. But the bottom line is that we just don't know. For obvious reasons, we didn't want to fiddle with the Kick equipment on *Invincible* to see what it could do."

"Do we have to use the insulting name 'Kicks'?" asked Senator Suva. "And why do you keep referring to the ship we took from them using a fleet name?"

"I can call them bear-cows if that's more acceptable," Geary said, not wanting to get into useless debate over that issue. "We don't know what they call themselves. As for why I call the ship *Invincible*, it's because it was as *Invincible* that she came through the voyage back here, and more than one Marine died defending her as *Invincible*."

"Learning more about the technology used aboard the ship will surely be a *priority* for the Alliance," Senator Unruh noted in a pleasant voice that still drove her point home. "And for the enigmas, you believe there may be hope for peace?"

"I believe that Emissary Charban is right in his guess that such a privacy-obsessed species regards a curiosity-driven species such as ourselves as a major threat. Promising not to seek any further knowledge of them, or enter space controlled by them again, might serve as a basis for halting hostilities. But," Geary conceded, "so far the enigmas have not responded to our proposals in that direction."

"And lastly," Unruh continued, "the Dancers." She smiled. "I have seen their ships move. It is an apt name."

"They saved a human-occupied planet," Senator Suva said eagerly. "Can they show us how to do that?"

"Again," Geary said, "I don't know. They are talking to us, they seem helpful and friendly, but they also have an instinctive grasp of maneuvering in space that exceeds the capabilities of human senses or human equipment."

"But can we trust something that looks like... that?" Wilkes said distastefully.

Rione smiled as she replied. "We can be certain that we aren't being mesmerized by their beauty."

"Negotiations are going well?" Navarro asked.

"We're still learning to communicate. We're not at a formal

negotiation stage, yet." Rione's smile went away, replaced by an expression that was impossible to read. "They have communicated something to us since we arrived at Varandal that was unexpected. Emissary Charban and I just managed to work all of this out definitively late last night, so this is the first report of it. I wanted the grand council to be the first to hear." Even the senators hostile to Rione puffed up slightly at her implied acknowledgment of their importance. "The Dancers have told us they need to go somewhere. They will not open further negotiations until they go there. That's not being presented as an ultimatum, rather as sort of an if-then set of conditions. If we take them there, then they will talk about other things."

"They told us?" Costa asked skeptically. "How? I thought our communications with the Dancers were still very basic."

"They said there was a place they had to go. They used the pictograms for *must* and *travel*, so there's no other interpretation possible," Rione said. "They did the same, repeatedly, regarding the if-then condition for further negotiations."

She held out her data pad, tapped a control, and an image of angular characters appeared in the air over the table. "And then they showed us this. It's a word formed from letters from one of the ancient common languages of humanity, so our systems were easily able to translate it. Even one of us can almost make out the word from its ancestry of our current language."

"What does it say?" Senator Navarro asked in amazement.

"Kansas."

"What?"

"The ancient word is Kansas," Rione explained. "We asked in

every way we could, and the Dancers insisted in every way that they could that they must go to Kansas."

"Where the hell is that?" Costa demanded. "I've never heard of a star named Kansas."

"We located Kansas," Rione said. "It's not a star, or a planet. It's a place on a planet, an old name for a province or region on that planet."

"What planet and what star?" Senator Navarro said.

"Old Earth," Rione replied. "Sol Star System."

The resulting silence was so deep and complete that a falling pin would have resounded like an explosion.

When Navarro broke the silence, he almost whispered, but his voice still sounded unnaturally loud. "Old Earth? They want to go to Old Earth?"

"They are insistent upon that," Rione replied.

"Why?"

"They cannot, or will not, explain. Not until we take them there."

"Impossible," Senator Costa declared. "Take aliens to Sol Star System? To Old Earth itself, the Home of our ancestors? We can't do that."

Instantly, Senator Suva turned on her ideological foe Costa. "These are representatives of the first nonhuman intelligent species that has ever sought to communicate with us. It is critically important that we do not offend them!"

"It is critically important that we don't let a bunch of alien warships drop a stellar destabilizer into Sol itself!"

"These aliens have helped us. Helped people," Senator Unruh pointed out. "There is no evidence that they are hostile."

"But *look* at them!" Wilkes insisted. "We're supposed to take them to the most sacred spot in the galaxy? Those *things*?"

"Judge them by their actions," Geary urged.

"But you can't tell us why they want to go to Old Earth! How did they even hear of this Kansas place?"

"I don't know," Rione conceded.

"Wait," Senator Sakai said, as another babble of argument began. "Tell me this, Admiral Geary. You have seen the ships of these Dancers. Could they reach Old Earth on their own?"

"Of course," Geary said, wondering as always what angle Sakai was pursuing. "They have the equivalent of our jump drives, which appear to have at least the same range as our equipment."

"They would have been seen and stopped," Costa said derisively.

"The Dancers have excellent stealth capability," Geary replied. "Better than our own for objects as large as their ships. Even if they were detected, they could easily outmaneuver any human attempt at intercept. And we don't know how long they've had spaceflight and jump drives and stealth capabilities for their spacecraft, which means we don't know when they might have first gone to Old Earth."

Sakai nodded slowly. "Then the Dancers could go anywhere in human space? On their own, they might already have explored human space?"

"Yes, Senator," Geary agreed. "In my report, I speculate that they might have already penetrated human space at least as far as the outer edge of Alliance territory. They recognized the symbol of the Alliance."

"Yet they ask our permission. They ask to be taken to Old Earth even though they could go without asking." Sakai looked around, having made his point. "How can we learn what they want there? By taking them there."

"And if they are secretly hostile?" Costa asked grimly. "Then what happens? Sol has no defenses. Our Home has been neutral and demilitarized for centuries."

"We would escort the Dancer ships," Sakai said. "That escort would defend the Dancers, and, if necessary, defend *against* the Dancers."

"We can't send a fleet of warships to Sol," Suva objected. "That's politically impossible. The uproar would toss all of us out of office and turn every human star system not in the Alliance against the Alliance."

"What could we get away with?" Navarro asked, looking up and down the table. "Politically, what would be acceptable?"

Sakai addressed Geary again. "Admiral, did the Alliance ever send warships to Sol Star System before the war?"

Geary nodded. "Yes, Senator." Increasingly, he had been able to put aside the loss of all he had known a century ago, to live in this time, but questions like Sakai's drove home to him how long ago his life had once been, that he had lived in a time that was the distant past for the people around him. "Every ten years, the Alliance would send one warship for anniversary commemorations."

"One warship?" Suva asked, eyeing Geary suspiciously.

"Yes, Senator. One. Of course, the fleet was much smaller then, but it was usually a capital ship to show due respect for Home. A battleship or battle cruiser."

"A battle cruiser?" Navarro nodded, smiling. "*Dauntless* is a battle cruiser, the flagship of your fleet, and a distinguished ship whose crew has acted heroically and with honor."

Everyone seemed to be waiting for him to say something, so Geary nodded back. "I would not dispute that characterization of *Dauntless* or her crew."

"Or, doubtless, her captain," Costa sneered.

"A ship large enough," Sakai added without acknowledging Costa's jibe at Geary's private relationship with Desjani, "to carry selected members of our government along on this journey, to ensure all feel adequately represented, and to conduct whatever negotiations the Dancers wish following their arrival at this place called Kansas."

"A battle cruiser?" Costa asked, her eyes calculating. "And all... interests... would be represented? I might be willing to buy into that."

"If Senator Costa goes," Senator Suva said, "I will go as well. That is nonnegotiable."

"I'm sure we'd all love to have you along," Costa said with a nasty grin.

"We can agree on this?" Navarro said, as if not believing any agreement could be possible.

"Not just those two," Senator Unruh insisted.

"Someone acceptable to all," Navarro agreed. "I know that doesn't include me. What about Senator Sakai? Would anyone object?"

No one did.

"So, we agree that Senators Sakai, Suva, and Costa will travel on the battle cruiser *Dauntless* as that Alliance warship escorts the six Dancer ships to Old Earth. The orders to *Dauntless* will be to escort and protect the Dancer ships, unless the Dancers unexpectedly act in a hostile manner, in which case *Dauntless* will protect Old Earth and the rest of Sol Star System. In addition, Admiral Geary will go along, as will Emissary Rione—"

"Her?" Suva demanded. "Why?"

"To talk to the Dancers," Unruh said, sounding tired again. "What about the other? Charban?"

"The Dancers prefer to communicate with both of us," Rione said.

Geary knew the Dancers actually preferred communicating with Charban, but since he wanted Rione along, he simply nodded as if in agreement.

"It is better to have two intermediaries," Sakai noted. "One could become fatigued by constant demands. Both Rione and Charban should come."

"But not as emissaries!" Suva insisted.

"No. There is no need of that when representatives of the grand council will be present. They will need a title. Ambassador? Speaker?"

"Envoy," Navarro suggested.

"That is acceptable to me."

Suva and Costa gave reluctant agreement as well, followed by the rest of the senators present.

Navarro smiled encouragingly at Geary. "That's decided, then. Make your preparations for this journey. I envy you, I admit. There has been no luxury for journeys to Old Earth in recent decades despite the hypernet gate the Alliance constructed there decades ago. You, *Dauntless*, and her crew, deserve the chance to see the Home of our ancestors, and the chance to rest after your arduous mission outside human space and back through Syndic space. This trip to Old Earth should give you all a well-earned break from the blood and fire you have faced for far too long."

After Geary and Rione had left the room and were facing Timbale and Desjani once more, Rione turned to Geary. "Do you believe in jinxes, Admiral?"

He made an uncertain gesture in reply. "I believe that sometimes they seem real. Why do you ask?"

"Because I wish that Senator Navarro had not made that last statement. It is never good to tempt fate."

14

"I've been officially notified that I and my Marines are to remain attached to your fleet until further notice," General Carabali said.

Geary's smile told her how he felt about that. "I'm glad to hear it. General, I've already authorized every ship in the fleet to grant stand-down liberty and leave, letting as much of their crew as possible take as much leave as possible. You are authorized to apply that same policy to the Marine units attached to the fleet."

"Thank you, Admiral, though I understand that policy will not include the Marine detachment aboard *Dauntless*?"

"Unfortunately, no, it will not," Geary said.

"They'll have a special task to carry out, anyway. Old Earth is also Home for the Marines. The detachment will be responsible for a small ceremony marking that."

After ending the call with Carabali, Geary looked ruefully at his own message queue. The Marines weren't the only ones who wanted some special ceremony or commemoration when *Dauntless* went to Old Earth. The requests for special events were coming in right and left.

His stateroom had felt oddly quiet of late even though *Dauntless* was trembling with anticipation of this journey. The crew's disappointment at not going on leave to Kosatka, where most of them had come from, had been more than offset by the excitement of seeing Home. The crew's stock on Kosatka, already high due to *Dauntless's* being Black Jack's flagship, would be astronomical after they had personally visited Sol Star System.

That train of thought led Geary to wondering why he hadn't heard from Tanya today. He called her stateroom.

"Good afternoon, Admiral." Desjani greeted him with a brief smile.

"I'm sorry we haven't gotten that day off yet."

"Maybe we'll get it on Old Earth. We can visit someplace famous, like Tranquility Base Site."

"That sounds romantic," Geary said.

She didn't rise to the humor, frowning at her desk. "There's a lot to do. *Dauntless* has a lot of battle scars. That's all right. She earned them honorably. But everything else has to be perfect."

"I seem to recall someone lecturing me on not seeking perfection," Geary said. "*Dauntless* got priority on replacement of aging systems, so she's practically as good as new, and even before that she was the best battle cruiser in the fleet."

"She's the best battle cruiser, anywhere, anytime," Desjani corrected him, then frowned again. "Can you afford to leave Smythe in charge of overseeing the fleet's repair work while we're gone?"

"Admiral Timbale will be watching Captain Smythe. Tanya, are you sure there's nothing else besides getting ready for this trip? I know it's not pleasant thinking of having those three senators on board, but you won't have to interact with them much."

"I won't if my prayers are answered." Desjani buried her face in both hands for a moment, then looked up at Geary. "I need to ask a favor."

"What is it?"

She was uncharacteristically hesitant. "There's someone coming aboard to see me, someone who came to Varandal because she hoped the fleet would still be here. She wants to see me… and I can't deny her that. I know she would like to see you as well. Can you make time?"

"Tanya, time is one of the things I have in shortest supply, but if there is anyone who has a priority claim on my time, it's you. Even though there are a million things I have to be doing, and half of them should have been done yesterday." If this was what running a fleet required, what would trying to run the Alliance as a dictator entail? Anyone who really thought about it would never want such a job.

But then, Admiral Bloch hadn't struck Geary as a deep thinker.

"I know there are a lot of demands on you," Desjani said. "This is important to me. Please, Jack."

She rarely called him that, even when they were alone. Geary gave her a startled look. "Tanya, I already promised I would do it. What is this about? Who is this woman?"

"What's it about?" Her hand rose to touch the Fleet Cross ribbon on her breast. "It's about this. Who is she? She's the daughter of a man I sent to his death."

* * *

Greta Milam was tall, thin, with a face that seemed serious even when she was trying to smile. Even though she was probably in her earlier twenties, she appeared older. "I am honored to meet you, Admiral," she said as she took the seat in Desjani's stateroom that Tanya had offered.

"The honor is mine," Geary replied. "I understand your father served with Captain Desjani."

That had obviously been a very clumsy and stupid thing to say. Desjani winced, and Milam looked distressed.

Greta Milam looked at Tanya, her expression flickering with mixed feelings. "Yes. On the *Fleche*. I have always been grateful for the letter you sent after that action, Captain, describing what my father had done. It gave my mother and me as much comfort as anything could have."

Desjani sounded as if she were fighting to keep her own emotions in check. "Master Chief Milam was a true hero. He deserved the Fleet Cross much more than I did."

"I have learned that you insisted he receive that award," Greta Milam said. "I have it. It means so very much to me."

"I'm glad," Desjani said in a low voice.

"I have always wondered… you were the last to speak with him?"

"Yes. While he was alive."

"What were his last words? Your letter didn't specifically say, so I've wondered. It's odd the things people latch onto. As a little girl, I noticed the letter didn't say that, so… I've always wondered."

Tanya gazed at Master Chief Milam's daughter for a long moment before answering. "He told me that I only had about a minute."

"Excuse me?" That was apparently not something that Greta Milam had expected to hear.

"He was at the power core on the Syndic heavy cruiser we had boarded," Tanya said. "He was setting it to suffer a partial collapse. I was at one of the boarding tubes aboard the cruiser, engaging the Syndic boarding parties that were trying to get back to their own ship to stop us. He said... he said there were only six sailors left alive with him, and the Syndics were breaking into the compartment. He asked me to tell you, his family, that he had died with honor. I did. I told you what he had done. I told you he said that."

Tanya looked away, composing herself, then back at Greta Milam. "I wished him an honored reception by the living stars, and then he told me to take any sailors left with me back to *Fleche*, that if we could make it back within the next minute, we might survive even though *Fleche* was a total wreck."

"How many sailors was that?" Geary asked, feeling like an intruder into a place he did not belong.

"With me? Nine. We had started with a hundred. No. We had started with two hundred thirty-five. Only a hundred were left to fight when the Syndics boarded us."

Greta Milam blinked back tears. "I have to confess to you, Captain, that I blamed you for a while. For living while my father died."

"Don't worry about that," Desjani replied. "I did the same."

"But I've already talked to some of the others who survived. They said you all expected to die. It was a miracle some of you made it back off the Syndic heavy cruiser. But they said you did that. If not for you, my father would have died anyway, and the Syndics would have won the whole battle, and no one would have ever known how my father died. Because of you, he got the chance to die doing something that everyone will remember, and we all were allowed to know what he had done. I wanted to thank you and beg your forgiveness for ever blaming you."

Desjani nodded slowly. "Of course. I… often wish I could have saved him as well. He saved me and the rest."

"It's a tangled web, isn't it?" Greta Milam said. "Who owes whom what. But the war is over now. We can be grateful for that."

"Sailors are still dying."

Greta Milam stayed silent for several seconds. "I did not mean to sound as if that didn't matter."

Desjani grimaced and shook her head. "I'm sorry. It's still hard to remember that day. I don't… talk about it."

"I'm sorry."

"Don't be. Your father… I could not have ordered him to do what he did. I would not have. He chose to sacrifice himself so that many others could live, and I am certain his last living thoughts were of you and your mother."

Milam bent her head in an unsuccessful attempt to hide tears, then rose. "I should go. Thank you. This… this is something I wanted badly. Thank you."

But Milam paused as Desjani led the way out of her stateroom, her eyes on the plaque near the hatch. "My father's name is on that. Are… are all of these friends of yours who have died?"

"Yes," Tanya said in a low voice. "I don't forget any of them."

After Milam had left in the care of Master Chief Gioninni, resplendent in his dress uniform to honor the daughter of a deceased Master Chief, Desjani sat down again. "That was hard."

"Now I know something about the fight where you earned the Fleet Cross," Geary said.

"I didn't earn it. Master Chief Milam did. I don't know why I got it, too." She took a deep breath, closing her eyes tightly as if in pain. "Did I ever tell you about my dream after that action?" Desjani asked abruptly.

He shook his head. "No. You've never told me anything about it, or after it."

"Look, I give you permission to call up the official record of the action if you want to. I'm not going to talk about it. But you deserve to know…"

"You had some dream?" Geary prompted.

She was looking steadily at the deck, avoiding his eyes. "I was… stressed. My ship destroyed, the crew almost wiped out, hand-to-hand fighting… I wasn't in very good shape. They gave me some meds to make me sleep. I dreamed. I dreamed I saw you sleeping."

"What?"

Her head came up, eyes catching his, daring him to disbelieve, to question what she said. "I saw you sleeping. I knew it was you. Black Jack."

"Me? You saw *me*?"

"Not exactly." Her voice remained firm, though. "I couldn't make out your face. It was shadowed. But I knew who it was. You were lying there in the dark. I didn't understand that. Black Jack was supposed to be among the living stars, or in the lights in jump space, somewhere bright. But it was dark around you. And cold. I remember that."

Dark and cold. At the time, he had been in survival sleep, frozen, drifting through space in a damaged escape pod. Geary stared at her. "Are you sure this isn't some memory influenced by what you learned after your ship picked me up?"

"No. I never forgot one detail of that dream. I saw you in the dream, and I yelled at you."

"Your reaction on seeing me was to yell at me? That I have no trouble believing."

"Very funny." Desjani ran both hands through her hair, her expression that of someone reliving old trauma. "I was telling you to wake up. To come help us. But then the Master Chief was there. Milam. He gestured to me that it wasn't time yet. Then you and he just faded away. I couldn't remember any other dream when I woke up from that sleep, not even a fragment, but I remembered everything about that." She gazed at him again. "And when we found you years later, and they brought you aboard my ship, I looked at you, and I knew. I didn't need the DNA or the other tests. I knew you were the man I had seen in that dream. Come back to save us at last."

He felt the old discomfort arise, the sense of being totally inadequate to the myths that had grown up around the hero he was supposed to be. Her faith in that hero still burned strong, though somehow Desjani could keep the hero separate in her mind from the man he really was. She worshipped Black Jack. She loved John Geary, but she would never worship him, and thank the living stars for that. "Tanya, by now you know who I really am."

"I knew you then, and I know you now. Do you remember the first time you saw me?"

"Yes. Very clearly." Coming out of the stupor brought on by the very long period of survival sleep, he had seen above him a female captain who inexplicably wore an Alliance Fleet Cross. When he had fought at Grendel, no one in the fleet had earned that award for a generation. The sight of that Fleet Cross had been his first clue that his sleep had been far longer than it should have been. "You looked at me like…"

"Like I knew you. I've never told anyone else of that dream. I didn't know if it had just been born of fever and stress. Or had my ancestors sent me a vision? Would I someday meet that man in my dream? Would I help him end the long and bloody war? And then you showed up, and I knew I did have a role. It would be shown me."

No wonder Tanya had offered any support he needed, had even offered him her honor if that was what he demanded of her. "You did everything because you thought it was some job you'd been given?"

"Oh, please. I wanted to do it. No, I didn't want to end up in love with a superior officer. I fought that. It happened anyway. But, every other thing I did because I chose to. The living stars can lead us to tasks, but only we can decide whether or not to carry them out. Of all the people in the universe, Black Jack should be able to understand that."

"I guess he should." Geary tried to find words that felt right, and failed. "Are you all right?"

"I'm fine." Desjani blinked, straightened in her seat, and looked back at him as if they had just been discussing some routine matter. "My pity party is over. Now, how about you? I haven't been so preoccupied that I hadn't noticed you are worrying about something else."

There wasn't any sense in avoiding the truth when Tanya was watching him. "It's the grand council. I've never gotten the impression the grand council is a smooth-running machine, but they seem a lot worse. Instead of talking over issues, they're just zinging each other with verbal put-downs."

"Haven't they always been that way?"

Of course, that would be Desjani's reaction. Her opinion of the politicians running the Alliance could probably not get a single notch lower. "Not as bad. Not during my first meeting with them. And at the second meeting, the one where I got the orders for our mission into enigma space, I had the feeling the grand council was pretty much united in agreeing on those orders even though different senators had different reasons for wanting us to go on that mission."

She nodded, smiling without any hint of humor. "Including the hope that we'd go out and never come back."

"Including that," Geary said. He didn't know how many had felt that way. He suspected even Rione didn't know the exact number. It wasn't the sort of sentiment anyone would advertise or leave a written record of. "I don't know how to fix the Alliance, Tanya. The people who might know how to do it are on the grand council, but they don't seem to be interested in actually doing it."

"Good thing you're not dictator of the whole mess, huh?" Desjani asked. "Speaking of which, have you noticed who hasn't been around?"

"Who *hasn't* been around? Tanya, I have no idea—"

"Sure you do." She waved grandly. "Captain Badaya, who represents those who think Black Jack can wave his magic wand and cure everything that ails the Alliance."

Geary started to answer her, then stopped. "You're right. Why hasn't he been around?" In order to forestall a coup attempt in Geary's name, Badaya had been led to believe that Geary was secretly running the government already. But then why hadn't Badaya been by since the fleet made it back to Varandal to ask what Black Jack was doing about the damned politicians?

"If you want my honest opinion, and I know you do," Desjani said, leaning forward with both elbows on her desk and gazing at him, "Captain Badaya has slowly figured out that if Black Jack did take over, the Alliance house of cards would collapse even quicker. He's been thinking, which I know is uncharacteristic of him, and he's putting two and two together at last. He probably figures now that you're just nudging the grand council in the right directions and otherwise trying to prop up the Alliance rather than knock the legs out from under it."

She sighed, looking upward. "And after you got us through enigma space, and Kick space, and beat the Kicks and the enigmas and the Syndics again, and didn't throw him to the wolves because he made some mistakes during the battle at Honor, Badaya is one of your closest allies now regardless of what you do. Which makes it a real shame that I can't stand the man, but what are you going to do?"

"I hope you're right. Fleet headquarters has also been oddly silent. We haven't received any rants from them, any demands to yield important ships or personnel to immediate reassignment, nothing except routine acknowledgment of the reports we've forwarded."

"Do you want my opinion again?"

"You know I do."

"Yes." Desjani waved again in the general direction in which fleet headquarters lay numerous light-years distant. "I think they're scared of you and trying to figure out what to do next."

"Tanya—"

"I am serious. They thought they had screwed you. Different parts of fleet headquarters thought they had handed you a rotten job and tripped you up in different ways, and at the best you were going to limp home with your reputation and your fleet in shreds. Instead, you came home having far exceeded the scope of your orders, the fleet mostly intact, and won the day for humanity!" Desjani nodded at him. "You've got them scared. They're wondering if you *can* be beat."

That was not good news, but it would explain the mysterious silence from fleet headquarters, and perhaps the increased disarray on the grand council. "I hope you're wrong because I don't want people trying to think up ever-more-challenging ways to beat me."

Last time they had lost *Orion*, and *Brilliant*, and the-*Invincible*-before-the-latest-*Invincible*, along with a number of smaller warships. He didn't want any more ships and their crews to die because various people were separately trying to figure out how to beat him instead of jointly trying to figure out how to save the Alliance.

Two days before departure, and Geary had to pry more time out of his day in order to grant a request from the senior fleet physician for a meeting. He greeted Dr. Nasr as the physician debarked from a shuttle onto *Dauntless*. Despite their many face-to-face conversations, this was the first time they had had actually met.

Dr. Nasr looked tired and sad. Geary had often seen him tired, especially in the wake of battles when the fleet's medical staff had bent every effort to save every injured man and woman they could. But the sadness was a different thing.

"What brings you to *Dauntless*?" Geary asked.

"May we speak privately?" Dr. Nasr requested.

"My stateroom?"

"I would be honored, Admiral."

They walked through the ship's passageways, Nasr silent and carrying a thermal carafe. Once inside Geary's stateroom, with the hatch sealed, the doctor carefully removed the lid of the carafe and brought out two small, white, porcelain glasses, which he set on Geary's desk. The doctor then poured a dark, steaming liquid into each glass, not spilling a drop, his every move that of someone used to the most careful and precise motions.

Nasr offered one of the glasses to Geary. "Coffee, Admiral. A special blend. Will you drink a toast with me?"

"Certainly," Geary said, taking the small glass gingerly. It was warm from the coffee, but not painfully so. "What are we toasting?"

"Our efforts, our failure, the eternal struggle of humans to do what is right, the eternal disagreement on what right is, and the death of the last two bear-cows."

Geary halted his movement with the glass poised near his lips. "They're dead?"

"Yes. Please drink, Admiral."

He finished raising the glass, tasting a powerful, bitter, yet smooth coffee that he could feel flowing all the way down to his stomach. "What happened?" Even though the news had been expected, even though there had been nothing else he could have done,

Geary still felt a great sorrow at the news. Now he understood Dr. Nasr's sadness.

"The Shilling Institute was keeping them alive, doing a very creditable job," Nasr said, lowering his own now-empty glass. "But the bear-cows were taken from the Shilling Institute."

"The government?"

"No. The courts." Nasr shrugged. "Well-meaning individuals, well-meaning groups, claimed that the bear-cows deserved a chance to speak on their own behalf, to express their own wishes, to not be kept in what they called a living death. I understand. I was not happy with it, either. But I knew it was all we could do. However, the courts did what they felt obligated to do. They appointed lawyers to act as guardians for the bear-cows, to speak for them in court. And the lawyers argued very well that the bear-cows must be given the same rights as humans."

Geary sat down heavily, shaking his head. "But they're not humans. That doesn't mean they are less than us, but it does mean you can't use our standards with them. They think differently than we do."

"So the Shilling Institute argued," Dr. Nasr said, sitting down opposite Geary. "I was called to testify. I spoke of my experiences with treating the bear-cows. I showed them my medical records. Let them awake, and they would die by willed suicide. It was that simple."

"But they didn't believe you."

Nasr frowned at the deck. "It is a difficult argument, Admiral, to claim that the best treatment for a thinking creature is to keep it forever unconscious. The lawyers, the courts, the well-meaning individuals and groups, they did not want to believe me. Custody was given to the court-appointed guardians. The bear-cows were moved to another medical facility. Well-meaning individuals gathered about them, ready to welcome a new species into friendship with humanity, the sedation was reduced until awareness came to the two bear-cows, and, five seconds later, both were dead."

The doctor shook his head. "One of the well-meaning people came from the room, looked at me, and cried why? And I said, because they are who they are, not who you wanted them to be."

"Damn," Geary whispered.

"It was inevitable, Admiral. You and I deluded ourselves. We did what we would do for humans. Keep them alive and try to find a solution. But any solution is far off. You know some blame you for the awful slaughter of the bear-cows when capturing their ship. I have never been comfortable with that battle, yet I also knew we tried everything we could to avoid such a slaughter. Some commentators outside the fleet, though, have assigned us sole blame for the deaths of the bear-cows, for any hostilities with the bear-cows."

"I know," Geary said. "I've heard that. Half of the critics claim we caused it because those critics distrust the government, and the other half claim we caused it because those critics distrust the military. There don't seem to be a lot who are willing to consider the possibility that the Kicks might have had their own reasons for acting."

"There are many," Nasr said. "Many who note our attempts to communicate and avoid fighting. But those are not nearly as loud as the others." The doctor's tone took on an acid edge of bitterness as he continued. "I have never before been accused of malpractice, not until now. In the court, they said I must have caused the deaths of the other bear-cows by somehow radiating an attitude that led the bear-cows who gained consciousness to assume they had to immediately kill themselves."

"You're being blamed?" Geary asked, appalled. "Nobody cared more for the fate of those creatures than you did."

"But there must be a villain, Admiral." Nasr sighed heavily. "I was not permitted in the room, or near the room, where they awakened the bear-cows. I understand from those who were there that the well-meaning individuals were offering wide smiles of welcome to the bear-cows as the sedation was reduced."

"Smiles? Did no one read our reports? Didn't they realize that to a prey animal those smiles looked like predators getting ready to chow down?"

"Data that conflicts with beliefs is often ignored," the doctor said. "It has been a serious problem in every field, including in medicine, even among those who should know better."

Geary closed his eyes, trying to calm himself instead of shouting out in anger. The coffee in his stomach felt heavy now. "So those last two Kicks didn't just die. In a very real sense, they were murdered by willful ignorance."

"That is too harsh, Admiral. They meant well, as did we. The difference is that we formed our intentions based on our ideals and what we saw. They formed their intentions based on their ideals and what they wanted to see. I should mention that we are already being blamed by a few for these last two deaths," Nasr said, "even though news of the deaths is being kept very quiet. Some former critics have been convinced that we spoke the truth, but not all.

The self-generated toxins in the bear-cows that caused their deaths are undeniable proof. Except to those who would accept no proof that conflicts with what they have decided must be true."

Geary nodded. "I wish… Hell, I wish there had been another answer. I do know that you did everything that you possibly could."

"As did you, Admiral." Dr. Nasr stood up. "I have taken enough of your time."

Geary rose to forestall his departure. "Doctor, the Dancers have asked to be escorted to another destination in human space. I'm sure you've heard. Would you be willing to ride *Dauntless* on that trip?"

"I am honored by the offer, Admiral. Is the destination truly what I have heard?"

"Yes. Old Earth."

Nasr took a while to speak again. "I see. Yes, a great honor. I will certainly come along, Admiral. Perhaps Old Earth will hold some answers to the questions that we struggle with."

"That would be nice," Geary agreed.

But he didn't believe it.

The three senators who would represent the grand council and the government of the Alliance had been brought aboard *Dauntless* with all of the pomp and ceremony mandated in protocol regulations. Dr. Nasr had been assigned a stateroom on board as well. Both Rione and Charban had remained in the same staterooms they had previously occupied, though the nameplates had been changed to reflect their new titles as envoys. Every storage compartment on *Dauntless* was filled with every spare part, every material for making other parts, every solid and liquid and soggy form of food and drink, and every weapon that regulations mandated for a battle cruiser of her class.

It felt very odd for *Dauntless* to be breaking orbit on her own. Instead of being the center of a fleet, the battle cruiser moved with solitary dignity toward Varandal's hypernet gate. The Dancer ships would join her at the gate, but for now the alien spacecraft were still performing an intricate series of maneuvers distant from human installations.

The rest of the First Fleet remained in their orbits, a seemingly unshakable armada. Those warships had bested every threat thrown at them while under Geary's command, but Geary had grown to realize that they were in fact highly vulnerable to the same pressures undermining the Alliance. The fleet could not be stronger than the Alliance that it represented. Factionalism, cynicism, uncertainty, and shortsighted political games might destroy a fleet that the Syndics, the enigmas, and the Kicks could not defeat.

The night before, Geary had held a meeting with Captains Badaya, Duellos, Tulev, Armus, and Jane Geary. "I'm going to announce tomorrow that Captain Badaya will be acting commander of the fleet while I'm gone. I hope the other four of you will do everything you can to support him. Hold everything together. No matter what happens, keep this fleet stable and focused on its duty. I know the five of you can do that."

Badaya shook his head. "Not with me in command," he said.

"It would be a mistake," Duellos agreed.

Geary stared at them, disbelieving. "Captain Badaya has the most seniority. There are no grounds for denying him the position of acting fleet commander."

"I do not have enough backing," Badaya insisted. "There are a number of ship commanders who will follow me without hesitation, but many others who don't trust me."

"Not as many as there were," Duellos said, "but if something serious were to happen, there would be doubt in some quarters as to Captain Badaya's standing."

"And loyalty," Badaya added. "Let's have it out there. There have been strong disagreements in the past about the right courses of action. My opinions at those times are well-known. If the fleet faces a strong challenge while I command, a challenge dealing with political matters, it very well could fracture."

Geary looked from one captain to another. One by one, they nodded in agreement with Badaya. "You're putting me in a difficult position," Geary said, frustrated. "If I bypass Captain Badaya, it will be seen as a snub to him. But if I select him, you're saying it could create serious command issues in a crisis."

"It will not be seen as snub," Armus said, each word coming out with careful deliberation, "if it is known you intended Captain Badaya for the assignment but he declined. Hold a fleet meeting tomorrow as you intended, say you want Badaya to take temporary command, and allow him to decline the honor."

Annoyed, but seeing the wisdom of their advice, Geary nodded. "Fine. Then after Captain Badaya declines I will appoint Captain Tulev—"

"No, sir," Tulev said. "I must also decline."

Annoyance was becoming anger. Why did something so simple have to be so difficult? "Why?" Geary demanded.

"Because I am a man with no world," Tulev said, betraying no hint of the feelings that statement must evoke in him. "The Syndics destroyed my home planet during the war. There are portions of the fleet that regard me as only belonging to the Alliance now, without loyalty to a home world to counterbalance that."

Geary tamped down his anger. If Tulev could speak so calmly about something so personally painful to him, upset by others for lesser reasons could only seem petty. "Should I bother naming a third choice, or have you all decided on that for me?"

"This isn't a mutiny," Duellos pointed out. "You chose to gather us now instead of just announcing your decision to everyone in the fleet because you trust our judgment, and we are giving you that judgment. You wanted to see what we would say about selecting Captain Badaya as acting commander, didn't you?"

After a brief hesitation, Geary nodded. "I suppose I did. What's your advice then?"

"It would help," Captain Tulev said, "if the fleet remained under command of a Geary."

To Geary's surprise, the others nodded, while Jane Geary looked uncomfortable. "She's not senior to any of you," he pointed out to the others.

"She has the name," Badaya said. "As well as an impressive record. And we will all back her. Together, those things will keep the fleet safe until you return."

Duellos was examining one hand intently as he spoke with studied casualness. "Tanya agrees, too."

It would have been nice if she had told me about that before this. "This fleet shouldn't be commanded on the basis of some family hierarchy," Geary protested.

"It's not that," Duellos said. "Jane has earned her right to the position, and because for a long time she was not part of this fleet, she has no baggage from earlier political squabbles. But the name is important not just to the fleet. If anyone in the government or at fleet headquarters is planning any surprises after you and Tanya leave on *Dauntless*, they would not reconsider their plans on the basis of going up against a Captain Badaya, or a Captain Tulev or Armus or Duellos. But if the fleet commander is named Geary? Then the political fallout becomes much greater, because a descendant of Black Jack has a standing with the populace that no one else can match except Black Jack himself."

Jane Geary nodded, looking unhappy. "I spent a lifetime running away from the name because I knew how much power it held. I did not suggest this to anyone, and I agreed only reluctantly, but I have to admit the strength of the reasoning behind it."

"I see." *And I don't like it. It gives me, and it gives Jane, too much power. But that's the point. It's the sort of power that might give pause to anyone planning on doing anything stupid.* "All right. Tomorrow morning, I'll hold a meeting, Captain Badaya will decline the role of acting commander in my absence, then—"

"I will nominate Captain Geary in your stead," Armus said. "I belong to no faction. Everyone knows I'm just about getting the job done. It will come best from me."

The others nodded in agreement, and the next morning the deal was done.

As *Dauntless* approached the hypernet gate, the six Dancer ships came zooming in from one side and below to take up station in a ring about the Alliance battle cruiser. Senators Sakai, Suva, and

Costa came crowding onto the bridge to watch the event, Captain Desjani greeting them with respectful but cool formality before turning back to her duties.

Geary nodded to her. "Enter the destination, Captain Desjani." He felt a strange sense of fate hovering about them as Tanya manipulated the simple hypernet key controls.

Tanya gave him a half smile and a sidelong look as *Sol* appeared on the hypernet control. "I never expected to enter this destination," she murmured, then spoke more loudly. "Request permission to enter hypernet, destination Sol Star System."

Geary nodded again. "Permission granted."

She entered the command, and the stars vanished.

They weren't in jump space this time. They were, literally, nowhere. There was nothing outside the bubble in which *Dauntless* and the six Dancer ships existed. They weren't moving. They would instead simply be at their destination after the proper amount of time had elapsed, having gone from Varandal to Sol without (as far as the physics were concerned) having traveled between those two places. It didn't make any sense, but then a lot of things about physics didn't make sense to humans once you went far enough up or down the scale from the narrow band of reality in which humans normally operated.

Because so little else made sense, it seemed perfectly appropriate that the length of the journey meant it would take less time than shorter journeys in the hypernet required. "Sixteen days," Desjani said.

"Just a hop to a demilitarized star system and back home again," Geary said. "For once, we don't have to worry about anything going wr—" He broke off at the ferocious glare that Desjani turned on him. "What?"

"Were you really going to say that?" she demanded.

"Tanya, what could—"

"Stop it! I don't want to find out, and neither do you!"

15

Even sixteen days could seem like a long time.

The regulations and procedures for entering Sol Star System had been dug out of the archives to be reviewed by all officers. Reading them in his stateroom, Geary was struck by two odd sensations. The first was a feeling of dusting off old records even though digital files never actually accumulated dust. The second was a dawning realization that he had read through these procedures once before.

When was it? I was an ensign, I think. At some point, I called up these procedures and read them, daydreaming that someday my ship would be the one chosen at the ten-year point for the visit to Old Earth. That feels so long ago.

How many ensigns have there been in the fleet since then? How many of those ensigns died during the century-long war? I'm sure none of them daydreamed about visiting Old Earth. They just hoped to survive, and maybe to be the heroes that young men and women dream of being before they become old enough and experienced enough to realize that real glory never comes to those who seek it.

They dreamed of being like Black Jack. It wasn't my fault they did that. The government and the fleet needed a hero, and I guess I was plausible enough to be built into one even though I'm nothing like the legend they created. But they died wanting to be like me.

I don't know what Black Jack could do to help the Alliance with the mess it is in. I don't know what I can do. But I have to keep trying because people believed in who they thought I was. This trip isn't going to solve anything, but once we get back, I have to think of something. Maybe something I see at Sol will give me some ideas.

There was a link near the procedures for entering Sol that also tickled Geary's memory. He read it, a smile growing. One more thing that had been forgotten, but there was no reason it could not be revived.

His hatch alert chimed. Instead of Tanya, or Rione or anyone else whom Geary might have expected, Senator Sakai had come to see him. For over a minute, Senator Sakai sat without speaking in the seat that Geary offered, just watching Geary with his usual enigmatic expression. Finally, Sakai spoke in a quiet voice that nonetheless commanded attention. "Admiral, you are a rare specimen. An anachronism."

"You don't need to point that out," Geary said, wondering what Sakai was driving at.

"Someone from a hundred years in the past. It has served you well in command of the fleet," Sakai observed, as if Geary had not spoken. "It has served the Alliance well. At least, so far. But this is not the past. We are not the people you knew. This is not the Alliance you knew." Sakai sounded neither happy nor sad about that. He simply said the words as if discussing a fact distant in time and place. "Admiral, where do you believe my loyalties lie?"

"I think, Senator," Geary said, once more choosing his words with care, "that you are loyal to the Alliance."

"Interesting. Do you believe that makes me unusual, or typical among the politicians who lead the Alliance in this time?"

That was an explosive question, and one he might have had a great deal of trouble answering if not for his long experience with Victoria Rione. "I believe that most, if not all, of the politicians in charge of the government believe that they are loyal to the Alliance."

"Again, an interesting choice of words, Admiral."

"Do you disagree with me?" Geary asked.

"Your answer was incomplete," Sakai replied obliquely. The senator frowned slightly, looking off into the distance. "Not all of us who are loyal, who believe we are loyal, believe in the Alliance anymore. Some of us look at the Alliance and wonder not *if* it will perish, but *when*." He focused on Geary with an intent gaze. "And we wonder whether you, with your antiquated ideals born of another time, will contrive to hold together a little longer that which is coming apart, or if your presence and your ideals will only accelerate the collapse of the Alliance."

Geary took a long moment to reply. "I would not do anything to harm the Alliance. I have made every effort to act as necessary to protect and preserve the Alliance."

"Admiral, you believe you will not do anything to harm the Alliance. You believe your every effort has been for the good of the Alliance." Sakai shook his head. "Perhaps I am too jaded, too bitter from watching destruction become a virtue. Perhaps you are the hero the Alliance needs. But I do not believe it."

"Why would you say that to me?"

"Perhaps because you are one of the few left who would not seek to use my words against me. Perhaps because truth is spoken so rarely these days that I wanted the feel of it in my words at least once more." This time, one corner of Sakai's mouth bent very slightly upward in the barest of smiles. "I am a politician, Admiral. Do you know what happens to politicians who tell the truth? They get voted out of office. We must lie to the voters. Tell them the truth, and they punish us. Lie, and they reward us. Like the dogs in the ancient experiment we learn to do what brings rewards. Somehow the system stumbles onward, the Alliance survives, but the pressure on it builds with every refusal by its leaders and its people to face unpleasant truths."

Sakai again sat without speaking for several seconds, his eyes hooded in thought. "We politicians lie for the best of reasons, for the best of causes," he finally said in a monotone. "For the good of the Alliance. For the good of our people. Only by lying can we serve them. Do you believe me?"

"I do," Geary said, bringing what might have been a glimmer of surprise to life in Sakai's eyes. "Isn't that the problem? Just about everyone thinks they are doing the right thing. Or they've convinced themselves that they're doing the right thing, and that others must be both wrong and self-serving."

Sakai regarded Geary again. "You have been speaking with Victoria Rione, I see. Are you aware of how much effort some politicians put into ensuring she was once more placed upon your flagship for your mission into enigma space?"

"I've guessed."

"I am one of those politicians who backed such an effort." A tiny smile once more bent Sakai's mouth. "Though not, perhaps, for the same reasons as others."

What did that admission mean? "Will you tell me your reasons?"

"In part. Emissary Rione—excuse me, Envoy Rione is, shall we say, not the sort of weapon which merely follows the path set for it by others. She is what you in the military would call a smart weapon, one that thinks for itself. Such a weapon may not act as those who unleash it expect." Sakai shook his head. "Envoy Rione believes in the Alliance, too. She is willing to do any number of things that our ancestors would never have agreed to in order to preserve it."

"But what did *you* expect her to do?" Geary pressed.

"Admiral." Sakai paused again, then looked at Geary with another searching gaze. "The legend that grew around Black Jack said that he would return to save the Alliance. Everyone assumed that meant Black Jack would defeat the Syndics. But saving the Alliance is not simply a matter of ending the war. That has become very, painfully, clear to all of us. And now the people of the Alliance increasingly ask themselves whether Black Jack's ultimate mission is not a military one, not aimed against any external foe, but is instead to save the Alliance from the inner forces that threaten to destroy it."

Geary had to bite back an immediate, instinctive denial. Instead, he shook his head and spoke with care once more. "I wouldn't know how to do that. I have never believed in the legend. I do not believe that I am destined or chosen or whatever term you want to use. I'm just trying to do my job, my duty, the best that I can."

"Does what *you* believe matter?" Sakai asked in a low voice. "Belief is a very powerful force, Admiral, for good or for ill. Belief can destroy that which appears unshakable, and belief can accomplish what knowledge tells us must be impossible. I cannot save the Alliance, Admiral. If I believed that I could, I would be one with the fools who think that they alone know wisdom, that they alone know what must be right. But people look at you, Admiral, and do not see a fallible human. They see Black Jack. Do not deny it. I accompanied your fleet on the final campaign against the Syndics so I could see you and so I could see how others acted toward you. Even those who hate you, who wish to see you fail, see Black Jack. And Black Jack can do those things that those who believe in him think he can do. Perhaps even things I believe to be impossible."

"Or that belief in me could be the last straw that breaks the back of the Alliance," Geary said, not trying to hide his bitterness.

"Yes." Sakai inclined his head slightly toward Geary. "An interesting dilemma."

"Can you tell me whether you will help me hold things together?" Geary demanded. "Not as some mythical Black Jack but just doing what I can. Will you help?"

"Why do you ask me this?" Sakai said, this time smiling more openly. "I have already told you that I lie. It is my profession. It is what my people demand of me. You could not believe whatever answer I gave you."

Geary sat back, watching Sakai. From somewhere, words came to him. "One way to avoid lying is to avoid actually answering the question, isn't it? Give an evasive response, and let the listener read whatever meaning they want into it."

Sakai's smile vanished, replaced by an intrigued expression. "You have spent *much* time around Envoy Rione. I should have guessed how much you would learn from her. And so I will finally answer that question you asked. What did I expect Envoy Rione to do aboard your flagship? I believed that Envoy Rione would find creative ways to forestall any plans aimed at you. That is why I supported placing her on your ship. This in turn gave me access to some other… consultations to which I might otherwise have been barred."

"Senator, that sounds suspiciously like you were trying to help me," Geary said.

"Not you. The Alliance. Because whatever you do, however mistaken or correct your actions based on your prewar sense of right and wrong, you are not a fool. Unlike some of those pursuing other means to *save* the Alliance." Sakai held up a single forefinger to forestall Geary from interrupting. "Admiral, you have been told that construction of new warships has been halted. In fact, a new fleet of sufficient strength to rival your own is being built, and I use the term 'rival your own' because that is a great part of its intended purpose."

Geary did his best to feign surprise followed by outrage. "Why would the government mislead me like that?" He could think of any number of reasons but wanted to see which ones Sakai offered up.

"The government is not misleading you. Certain powerful individuals within the government are misleading you. Others do not ask questions whose answers might prove too difficult. Others delude themselves that destructive means will serve creative ends. Here is what you must know. A decision has been made to give command of this fleet to an officer who will, depending upon whom you ask, safeguard the Alliance, or actively counter the threat posed by a certain hero to whom the existing fleet is extremely loyal, or act as a passive counterbalance to the threat posed to the Alliance by you." Sakai paused again. "The reasons all come down to one broad strategy. A majority of the grand council have been convinced that the way to fight fire is with fire. If they fear an ambitious high-ranking military officer with a fleet firmly at his back, the solution is to create another."

"That's insane. Are they trying to create a civil war?"

"They believe," Sakai said, "that they are saving the Alliance. That saving the Alliance requires creating the means to destroy it and giving that means to a man whose desires will destroy it. You said it is insane? You are right. They see only what they wish to see."

Geary stood up and paced slowly back and forth before Sakai, unable to sit still any longer. "If the government persists in actions that are likely to destroy the Alliance, what the hell can I do to save it?"

"I do not know. Perhaps nothing. Perhaps your best efforts will only precipitate the civil war you spoke of."

"Then why are you even helping me this much by telling me about what the government is doing and why?" Geary demanded.

Sakai let out a slow sigh. "Because, Admiral, your most powerful weapon, the belief of others in you, might enable you to save an Alliance I believe to be doomed. Might, I say. It is something. Something small. Yet preferable to surrendering to despair and watching others oh-so-cleverly and oh-so-cunningly bring about the loss of all we and they hold dear."

"Who is getting the command of that new fleet?"

"Admiral Bloch."

That answer had come directly, with no evasion or delay. Why?

"Even though the grand council must know that Bloch intended to stage a military coup if his attack on the Syndic home star system at Prime had succeeded?"

"Even though." Sakai looked off into the distance again as if he could see something there that was invisible to Geary. "I wonder why I still try. Then I think of my children and their children. What might happen to them if the Alliance falls apart? I think of my ancestors. When the day comes that I face them, what will I say I had done with the life granted me? How will they judge me and my actions?" He shrugged. "My wish is to be able to face them and say I did not quit. Perhaps my efforts are doomed to failure, but that will not be because I ceased trying."

"You don't really believe that it is hopeless," Geary suggested.

Senator Sakai stood up to leave, his expression unreadable once more. "Say rather, Admiral, that I am afraid to admit that it is hopeless."

After Sakai had left, Geary found his gaze returning to the link he had opened about returning to Sol Star System. *Anachronism, am I? Fine. Traditions hold us together, but a lot of those traditions faded under the pressure of the war. Maybe it's time for this anachronistic admiral to introduce a few more anachronisms.*

"We're going to cross the line," Geary said.

Tanya, called to his stateroom, gave him a puzzled look. "What line?"

"*The* line."

"That helps. Not."

"The boundary of Sol Star System," Geary explained patiently.

"Star systems don't have boundaries." She tapped in some

queries, then waited for the results to pop up. "Oh. You mean the heliosphere. *The region around the star that defines the boundaries of a star system.* I never heard of that before."

That news should have been astounding coming from a battle cruiser commander whose career had taken her across hundreds of light-years and scores of stars. But it wasn't. "That's because the heliosphere of any star is well beyond the places where jump points are found or hypernet gates are constructed," Geary explained. "The heliosphere of any star is well out in the dark between stars, in the places where human ships never go. Or rather, where they long since stopped going."

"All right. Why does it matter now?"

"The heliosphere of Sol sets the limit for Sol Star System," Geary said. "That's the region where Sol's solar wind predominates."

"Yes," Desjani said with exaggerated patience as she read the results of her query. "In the case of Sol, the heliosphere extends out about twelve light-hours," she quoted. "Or about one hundred astronomical units. What the hell is an astronomical unit?"

"A very old way of measuring distance. You know, like a parsec."

"A what?"

"Never *mind*," Geary said.

"Fine," she replied. "This is the line you were talking about? The edge of the bubble that defines the heliosphere for Sol? But it's way past *anything*. Nobody goes that far from a star in real space. Why would they? There's nothing there but dead, wandering rocks."

"Tanya, once upon a time, people couldn't use hypernet gates or jump points to travel to other stars. The missions to the first stars reached by our ancestors had to cross that line, physically cross it in real space. It meant something very important. It meant humanity had left the star that had given birth to us and humanity was now reaching into the universe."

"It was important to our ancestors?" Tanya regarded the display over Geary's desk with new respect. "Yes. Of course it was. That marked the point where a ship and the people on it left Sol."

"Exactly. They had a celebration. And even after we discovered jump technology and no longer had to physically leave and enter the heliosphere, ships still used to mark when they crossed that line. Any other star's heliosphere didn't matter. But Sol's did. It was a very big deal to say you're a Voyager."

"A... Voyager?"

"Once you've crossed the line, you can call yourself a Voyager," Geary said. "That's the tradition."

"Our ancestors did this?"

"Yes."

Desjani nodded. "Then we should. How did you happen to remember this? I can't recall anyone ever saying anything about it."

"The fleet used to send a ship back to Sol every ten years," Geary said. "To commemorate the anniversary of the launch of the first interstellar mission from Old Earth's orbit. We only sent a ship at decade intervals because it was a long haul without hypernet capability. I never went, but I talked to some people who did, and at that time the whole crossing-the-line ceremony was still a big deal."

"But during the war, we couldn't afford to send any ships," Desjani said. "I get it. Those early years were desperate. We couldn't have spared a ship for that long in those days."

Geary nodded. "The next ship was supposed to be sent less than a year after the initial Syndic attacks hit. I remember that everyone was wondering who would be selected. It seems strange to think about it now, but wondering which ship would get to make the trip was one of the biggest topics of conversation in the fleet before the fight at Grendel."

Tanya looked back at him blankly. "That was your biggest concern?"

He felt a flush of shame. Tanya, like all of the officers and crew in the fleet, had spent her career, had spent her entire life, worried about the war with the Syndics, worried about life and death and the lives and deaths of those she knew and loved. *How can she imagine a universe where the biggest concern in the fleet was which ship would get to go on a joyride to Sol? How can I ever feel superior to those whose lives have been consumed by issues far more grave than the little things I once had the luxury of being concerned with?*

"Yes," Geary finally said.

"I… guess that was important back then," Tanya said in a way that made it clear she was trying to grasp the concept and failing. "I can understand the crossing-the-line thing," she added. "And commemorating the first mission to another star. That was so big. They actually traveled at sublight speed across the dark between stars. I read about that when I was a little girl."

Her eyes went distant with memory, and she smiled. "The *Ship to the Stars*. I remember the book because I read it so many times. It was about a girl and a boy on the ship. They had been born on the ship because it was a generation ship. The trip would take so long that the crew who had left Old Earth would all die of old age on the way. Their children were brought up to run the ship and continue the journey, and *their* children would actually reach the other star."

Geary smiled, too, recalling the story. "I read the same book. I wanted to be that little boy. Anyone could travel to another star, but only people like him ever crossed the dark between stars. Ever since we discovered how to use jump drives, no one has gone into the Great Dark."

"I talked to Jaylen Cresida about that once," Tanya said in a low voice, her expression saddened at these memories of their dead comrade. "The observations those people and their instruments recorded are still used. Jaylen had studied some of them. We still depend on that data about the nature of space far from any star because no one else has ever gone out there to collect it."

"Really?" Geary looked toward a bulkhead as if he could see through it to the space beyond the bubble of nothing in which *Dauntless* was heading for Sol. "Instruments must have gotten a lot better since then. You would think someone would propose an automated mission to get new data."

Desjani shrugged. "We've been busy," she said.

He wanted to slap his forehead over his boneheaded statement. Busy. With a century of desperate warfare. "I know. Um… there was a ceremony when you crossed the line. This is your ship, so it's up to you, but it is a tradition."

"What sort of ceremony?" She started reading. "Are you serious? That's— All right, we can— No. Not that part. But the rest looks doable. Absurd, but doable. I guess our ancestors had more of a sense of humor than I've given them credit for. Are our Very Important Senators and Not So Important Envoys going to participate in this?"

"It's voluntary," Geary said.

"Meaning I have to invite them?"

"Yeah. You have to invite them."

"Let me make one thing very clear," Desjani had announced to her officers and senior enlisted, her voice taking on all the depth and force of command. "This must remain in fun. We have all been through hard and long years in which fun usually meant short, hectic times on a strange planet or orbital facility between campaigns and battles, the sort of fun that often ended up producing as many injuries to the crew as a battle would have. This is different. You all must ensure that it remains enjoyable. If there is any hint of its becoming something else, any hint of real hazing or real hurt of any kind, you are to step in and stop it before it happens. I will be walking the passageways of *Dauntless* throughout this entertainment, and I expect the same of all of you who are not part of the ceremony. Are there any questions? No? Then go out, have a good time, and ensure everyone else has a good time." Desjani finally relaxed her stern expression, smiling at the assembled officers and senior enlisted. "That's an order."

A number of main passageways had been converted into gauntlets designed to inflict mock injury and real, though slight, humiliation. In one passageway, the deck sailors responsible for much of the routine maintenance aboard *Dauntless* had rigged up devices to spray fake tattoos using dyes that faded within minutes. As Geary walked through it, getting a large and elaborate WHAT WOULD BLACK JACK DO? design emblazoned on the front of his uniform, he noted that the tattoos near him were considerably tamer and less suggestive than those he had spotted emerging from that passageway earlier.

In another passageway, the code monkeys had set up a maze from which you could only escape after figuring out the right pattern.

In a third place, *Dauntless's* food-service specialists were handing out ancient Syndic ration bars the fleet had picked up off an abandoned facility during the fighting retreat from the Syndic home star system. Those who in the past had complained the loudest about the food aboard the ship were forced to gag down a few bites before being allowed to proceed.

Another gauntlet lined the passageway leading to the shuttle dock. The weapons wielded by the sailors and Marines lining that passageway ranged from stuffed bunnies to balloons, with the occasional rubber chicken or a fluffy, fake stobor. Geary walked down the passageway, grinning, as the veterans of countless battles laughed and pelted him with silly, harmless weapons.

The main show was in the shuttle dock, the largest single compartment on the ship, where the unworthies seeking entry into the fellowship of the Voyagers were forced to pass muster before the "rulers" of Sol Star System.

Master Chief Gioninni, playing the role of King Jove, sat on an impressive throne created by modifying a high-g survival seat. His face boasted a long, bushy, fake beard, and Gioninni had somehow acquired an actual trident, an ancient weapon with a two-meter-long shaft and three wickedly barbed points. He wore a crown fashioned in one of *Dauntless's* machine shops, gleaming with gold plating that should have been used in electronics repair. Geary resolved to make sure that gold ended up back in the ship's repair stockpiles and didn't get diverted for any personal uses, then realized that Desjani had surely already seen to that.

The crown had nine points, each bearing a representation of one of the planets in Sol Star System, the largest, in the center, Jove itself. There had been some debate about how many planets should be on the crown, as the ancestors had apparently been unable to decide how many planets there were in Sol's orbit. Throughout history the numbers had fluctuated from nine to eight to twelve, then six, before returning to eight, then nine in the latest official records. Geary had finally chosen the latest number, and nine it was.

On the right side of King Jove sat Queen Callisto (usually known as Senior Chief Tarrini), wearing a crown identical to King Jove's. But instead of a trident, Callisto bore a bow of ancient design. The arrows in her quiver appeared to be just as real and dangerous as the trident Gioninni waved about with a carelessness that was most likely false, but from the way Senior Chief Tarrini held her bow, she looked prepared to use it as a club on the king and anyone else she thought required a little extra discipline.

On Jove's left sat Davy Jones, in the form of Gunnery Sergeant Orvis, the commander of *Dauntless's* Marine detachment. Orvis held a gavel of judgment as if it, too, were a weapon.

"I understand Jove," Charban said from where he stood near Geary, a GROUND APE tattoo with appropriate illustration fading on his chest. "That's the largest planet in Sol Star System. And Callisto is one of the largest moons of Jove and at one time was the largest human colony in the outer star system. They make sense. But who or what is Davy Jones supposed to represent? I looked into it, and there were no early spaceship commanders by that name."

"Davy Jones was a mythical figure," Geary explained, "that sailors on Earth thought ruled over the bottom of the ocean, caused disasters at sea, and took the spirits of dead sailors."

"I see." Charban glanced at the three senators, who had cautiously entered the shuttle dock and were looking about with varying expressions. "That makes sense."

"No, it doesn't," Senator Suva complained. "What do the oceans of Earth have to do with space?"

"We're still sailors, Senator," Geary said. "We sail a much vaster ocean, one lacking in water and all else, but the job is the same."

Senator Costa snorted. "From what little I remember of my ancient history, sailors on the seas of Earth spent most of their time drunk, which probably explains all this. It must have made sense to someone who was three sheets to the wind."

Senator Sakai did not comment. He appeared to be busy studying the Sirens standing to either side of the two monarchs and the judge. The Sirens, one female and one male, had been chosen from among the enlisted sailors and Marines by popular vote. In accordance with the old traditions, the Sirens wore uniforms modified to be alluring. Geary had heard of celebrations in the past in which this had sometimes led to overly enthusiastic modifications that ended up requiring remarkably small amounts of uniform fabric, but Captain Desjani had made it clear that the outfits of any Sirens on her ship had better fit an official definition of alluring and not go one millimeter less than that.

On their left hips, both Sirens wore one of the multipurpose tools known as a Swiz knife. On their right hips, each carried a roll of duct tape. That symbolism, Geary thought, even the Dancers could easily grasp if they saw it. But the aliens probably wouldn't be able to tell that the Sirens not only represented a chance of help when other aid was too far distant, but also the sort of temptations far from home that could create problems in the first place.

An unfortunate sailor had just fumbled his explanation of how the mythical devices called mail buoys were supposedly positioned to relay transmissions between stars. At a brusque gesture from King Jove and an imperious sweep of her bow by Queen Callisto, Davy Jones directed the sailor to stand in a far corner and loudly recite a long, satirical, and risqué song called "The Laws of the Fleet" for the benefit of his fellows before returning for another try.

A roar of welcome sounded as Captain Desjani entered the shuttle dock. She walked past cheering sailors and Marines until she reached Master Chief Gioninni and fixed him with a warning look.

But Gioninni just grinned. "Captain Desjani! Your reputation proceeds you!"

Senior Chief Tarrini nodded. "Queen Callisto can find no fault with Captain Desjani."

"She is judged worthy to enter your realm by Davy Jones," Gunnery Sergeant Orvis added.

Gioninni's smile faded, and he cocked a stern eye on her. "Captain Desjani, you are hereby sentenced to command of the battle cruiser *Dauntless*, the finest ship in the fleet, but one crewed by the biggest band of slackers, misfits, scoundrels, deadbeats, and slovenly sailors ever to sail the stars! Can you turn such a crew into real sailors, Captain?"

Desjani's reply could be heard easily over the laughter following King Jove's sentence. "I already have!"

"Then enter into my realm of Sol Star System, Captain Desjani, and be a member in good standing of the ancient and revered order of Voyagers!"

Amid renewed cheers, Tanya walked out past Geary with a salute and a wink. He returned the salute, then looked over at Charban and the senators. "You're welcome to meet the King and Queen as well."

Charban squared his shoulders with dramatic exaggeration and marched toward the Royal Family of Sol, but Costa and Suva hesitated. Sakai, after a few seconds, shook his head. "This is an event for the military, Admiral. We should not intrude."

"This is an event for anyone who travels in space," Geary corrected.

"We're not… like you," Senator Suva said, her voice tinged with what sounded like regret.

"Are you sure of that?" Geary asked.

The senators looked back at him as if they had never considered that question before.

The next day, they arrived at Sol.

All signs of merriment and celebration had vanished except for a single stuffed bunny that a hell-lance battery had adopted as a mascot. But those weapons were powered down for arrival, as were all other weapons aboard *Dauntless*. The shields were at full strength, because that was a necessary secondary protection against radiation and other hazards to navigation, but otherwise the warship was in as peaceful a configuration as a battle cruiser could be.

"I don't like it," Desjani grumbled for the hundredth time as she sat on the bridge.

"The requirements for entering Sol don't allow for exceptions," Geary reminded her for at least the fiftieth time. "And Sol Star System is demilitarized. There are no weapons and no threats."

"There is no place where humans are that fits that description," Desjani objected.

"Two minutes to hypernet exit," Lieutenant Castries announced.

Near her, the three senators jostled each other for position near the single observer seat on the bridge. Rione and Charban were also on the bridge for the historic moment, but well off to one side where Lieutenant Yuon had made some room for them.

The last minute passed in silence, everyone lost in their own thoughts.

Nothing was abruptly replaced by Everything as they left the hypernet. Off to one side, a distant spark of light marked Sol, the home star of humanity.

But Geary couldn't spare time to sightsee. Instead, his eyes went to another part of his display, where warning signs had sprung to life on a dozen warships of unfamiliar design.

16

"I told you!" Desjani said. "It's a good thing they're too far away to pose an immediate threat!"

"They're not Syndics," Lieutenant Yuon reported, bewildered.

Orbiting half a light-hour past the gate, the strange warships were too distant to attack, but their presence here was inexplicable.

Aside from those ships, all of the other space traffic in Sol Star System looked routine. Merchant ships swung between planets, faster couriers and passenger ships were on flatter trajectories, and near most of the worlds orbiting Sol smaller craft could be seen dipping into and out of planetary atmospheres.

Geary sat, his eyes on his display, letting his thoughts settle as he took in everything, trying not to be distracted by the names of the planets, which had assumed the status of legend. Mars. Jupiter. Venus. Old Earth itself. *Dauntless* sailed among the monuments to humanity's first achievements, mankind's first steps into space. But amidst those fabled names and worlds were warships of unknown origin and intentions. "Does anybody know what we're dealing with here?" he finally asked.

Senator Suva sounded and looked bewildered. "Sol Star System is neutral and demilitarized. Only... only ceremonial military forces are ever allowed here."

"These do not appear to be ceremonial," Rione answered. "You do not recognize them, Admiral?"

"No. Neither do our combat systems." *Dauntless's* sensors were evaluating everything they could see on the mystery warships, but even though tentative identifications of sensors and weapons sites were appearing on their hulls, the SHIP TYPE and ship ALLEGIANCE tags on the displays remained blank.

"Syndics," Costa declared. "They modified some of their designs—"

"Our systems could spot that easily," Geary said, trying not to sound dismissive of the senator. "They are not Syndics."

A virtual window appeared near Geary, revealing Lieutenant Iger. "Sir, nothing matching those warships is in any of our intelligence databases."

"Are they human?"

"Definitely human, sir. Even though we can't identify the ships, there are some design features on their hulls that hint at their origin." Lieutenant Iger looked unhappy as he spoke his next words. "Sol."

"Sol?" Geary did his best not to sound angry at Iger. "Everything human came from Sol. Are you saying these warships *belong* to Sol?"

"No, sir. But they are human in origin."

Geary glanced at the six Dancer ships surrounding *Dauntless*. Iger's information wasn't as useless as it had seemed at first. "That's as near as you can identify them? Just a common origin at Sol?"

"If the design features we see are being interpreted correctly," Iger said, "the design of those warships and the designs we're familiar with diverged *at* Sol."

"There is nothing unusual being broadcast in the star system 'notices to shipping,'" Lieutenant Yuon reported. "The notices provide the same language about the star system being demilitarized that we have in our procedures for entering Sol Star System."

"And yet there they are." Desjani grimaced. "Six of them are big, but smaller than us. Not heavy cruisers, and not battleships. Sort of like those scout battleships the Alliance tried."

"The ones that got wiped out in battle?" Geary asked, even though he knew the answer.

"Yeah, those." She tapped a quick command. "Whatever these are, they're a bit smaller than the Alliance scout battleships. Hard to tell yet what kind of armor they've got."

"We'll have to watch how they maneuver," Lieutenant Iger chimed in. "That will give us some means to calculate their mass. Any mass in excess of a reasonable estimate for that size ship will likely represent armor."

"What about the smaller ships?" Geary asked. His display was rapidly filling in details on the six escorts with the six bigger warships, showing barracuda shapes reminiscent of Alliance destroyers and Syndic Hunter-Killers, but not as large as either. "They've got less mass than even Syndic HuKs."

"Corvettes?" Desjani guessed. "No. They're even smaller than the Syndic Nickel corvettes."

"Who do they belong to?" Senator Suva demanded. "You should know that! How can you not know that?"

427

Geary sighed and rubbed his forehead with one hand. "Senator, wherever these ships came from is not anywhere that the Alliance has current information on."

"Where would that be?"

"I think I know." Everyone's attention centered on Senator Sakai. "I have studied much history," he said. "Including the period when humanity first left Sol. The ships from Sol went in all directions, but there were two main paths. One path led inward along the spiral arm of the galaxy in which we reside. That resulted in the colonies near Sol in that direction, then the Alliance, the other groupings of star systems such as the Callas Republic and the Rift Federation, and beyond that the Syndicate Worlds. The other path led outward along our arm of the galaxy. Some of the earliest human colonies sprang into existence there. Perhaps these ships come from stars on the other side of the expansion from the one we occupy."

Geary tapped in the same queries that everyone else was, seeing an image of the galaxy appear near his display with human-occupied space highlighted upon it. The image gave him momentary pause. *We think we've come so far. In human terms, we have. Hundreds of light-years. Unimaginable distances. But lay out the region of the galaxy that we have explored and occupied, and it is just a small piece of one portion of that galaxy, which itself is but one of countless other galaxies. I'm used to space being huge, but even for me it is impossible to grasp how HUGE the universe is.*

Rione commented first. "I never realized how lopsided human expansion has been. In terms of stars and distance, the vast majority has been inward toward the center of the galaxy. We've spread up and down and inward. I always assumed we started expanding in those directions. But my data says we first started going outward."

"Something stopped us," Costa said, her voice suspicious. "More threats like the enigmas who stopped our expansion inward?"

"How could that secret have been kept for so long and so close to Old Earth?" Rione asked. "The Syndics kept knowledge of the enigmas from us for a century, but that was because their contact with the enigmas was in regions of space far from our own, and the war drastically limited communications."

"And," Charban added, "we had stopped looking for other intelligent species after so many stars and worlds had yielded none. In the early days of human expansion, we expected to encounter such beings at any time."

Geary had his eyes on the increasingly detailed images that *Dauntless's* sensors were creating of the unknown warships. "They look human. The ships, I mean. We have some experience with nonhuman spacecraft designs. I don't see anything on those warships that looks like the differences we saw on ships built by the enigmas or the Kicks or the Dancers."

"What do I do?" Desjani asked him.

"Head for Old Earth," Geary directed. "Transmit the standard arrival message to the Sol Star System authorities there. We'll continue with our mission until something makes us do otherwise."

Had one or more of the senators been ready to put their oar in? But none of them did, perhaps because none of them could think of any other useful form of action right now.

"Those may be human-built ships," Desjani commented after adjusting the course of *Dauntless* slightly, "but look at all that extra junk on them. They look like something from one of those space fantasies. What do you call that stuff?"

Lieutenant Castries answered. "Frippery and furbelows, Captain. You're right. Those ships look like the illustrations to a space fantasy with kings and princesses and wizards. They're crawling with decorative detail. The ship's systems are trying to analyze the purposes of those features, but I don't think they have any other purpose but decoration."

"Is that why the fins on those ships are so big?" Lieutenant Yuon asked. "They've got a lot more height than should be required for sensors and shield generators."

Desjani raised an eyebrow toward Castries. "You read space fantasy, Lieutenant?"

"Not… much… lately, Captain. I mean, yes, Captain."

"Everyone needs some romance," Geary said, while Lieutenant Castries acted as if she were suddenly absorbed in analyzing sensor readings.

"Oh, please." Desjani rolled her eyes. "One of those stories where the beautiful, brainy princess wakes the sleeping Black Jack with a kiss so that together they can overthrow the evil star demon and live happily ever after?"

Geary realized his mouth was hanging open and shut it hastily. "Tell me that you're kidding."

"Nope. Lieutenant Castries?"

"Those are usually pretty good," the hapless Lieutenant admitted. "They don't get you right, Admiral, of course."

"Would you like to see some of the illustrations for those?" Desjani asked.

"No, I would not. If I may get back to the situation we're facing, you're telling me these outer-star ships are extensively ornamented, and not for any useful purpose."

Lieutenant Iger, who had still been listening but wisely refraining from commenting up until now, nodded. "It might not impact their fighting capabilities, Admiral, but it does indicate they have the luxury of investing resources into nonfunctional ornamentation."

Rione shook her head. "I have seen a great deal of nonfunctional ornamentation in my time, and I can say with certainty that not all of it was purchased because the person doing the buying could afford it. We may be dealing with status, appearance, and other issues that have little to do with simple monetary calculations."

Lieutenant Castries spoke up again, sounding excited. "Captain, I asked our systems to evaluate the fins on those ships, adding in variables for nonfunctionality. When asked to do that, our systems have evaluated a high probability that the fins were designed for form rather than strength."

"Ostentation?" Senator Suva asked. "Display? Are we certain these are warships?"

"We have identified some weapons," Lieutenant Iger said. "Not too many, yet, but the ships are definitely armed."

Charban was shaking his head, mouth pursed. "Speaking as an outside observer, I have seen a lot of ships. I have never seen any that look like that which weren't warships."

"Common design ancestry," Senator Sakai said. "That is what our systems analyzed, is it not? These ships came from the same sources as the one we are aboard. We can reasonably estimate function from appearance."

"They've finally seen us," Lieutenant Yuon reported. "They're altering vectors."

Geary watched his display as the unknown warships turned inward toward Sol and began accelerating. "They're coming our way but not directly at us."

"Look at their vector. They first want to block our direct path back to the hypernet gate," Desjani said. "Wait and see. Whoever they are, they are moving to block our access to the hypernet gate. That is not a friendly act."

"Maybe they—" Suva stopped speaking, then shook her head. "It does look as if they're trying to keep us from leaving before warning us off, if that's what they intend."

"They're trying to trap us?" Costa demanded.

Geary looked to Rione and Charban. "Please tell the Dancers we would like them to stay close to us. If they ask about the other warships, tell them we're trying to figure out who they are and what they want."

"You make telling them that sound so simple," Rione commented sarcastically. "We will try our best."

"Captain?" the communications watch-stander called. "We have a message coming in from the unidentified warships. It uses an old format that's standard for comms in Sol Star System and is addressed to our, uh, 'senior superior command supervising authority and controller.'"

"Redundant much?" Desjani growled. "Forward it to the Admiral."

"Let everyone on the bridge see it," Geary ordered. "Envoys Rione and Charban, please wait on that message to the Dancers until we see what these other ships tell us."

An image appeared before him of a man well past middle age seated on a bridge not too different from that of *Dauntless*. No surprise there. The most efficient arrangement of controls and watch stations had been worked out centuries ago. Wherever anyone went in human space, they would find the configuration of a ship's bridge to be roughly similar.

The man wore a uniform with such elaborate design and ornamentation that Geary found himself searching for the rank insignia and unable to sort it out among the many other glittering objects adorning the outfit. The suits of Syndic CEOs were well-known for their intricate and expensive tailoring, but this uniform would have put any Syndic CEO to shame. The man's hair was about shoulder length and as ostentatiously styled as his uniform, the top of the hair formed into a stiff peak that ran back like the plume on an ancient helmet. On the man's right and left breasts, a solid sheet of award ribbons and medals formed a multicolored breastplate reaching from shoulder to waist.

It was all undoubtedly meant to be impressive, but as Geary took in the gaudy image, he heard Tanya Desjani not quite stifle a giggle. Elsewhere on the bridge of *Dauntless*, there were muffled laughs and suppressed sounds of wonderment.

"I am His Excellency Captain Commodore First Rank Stellar Guard of the Fist of the People Earun Tavistorevas, Paramount of the Shield of Sol," the extravagant officer declared in a bored tone of voice. "I condescend to speak to the lowly representatives of the barbarous government of the inconsequential so-called Alliance. You have entered this star system without permission. You have brought with you tramontane creatures whose presence is an affront to the unsullied Earth. Hear my command. You will disable all combat systems. You will graciously welcome security auditors who will board your vulgar craft in search of impurities and render it impotent to do harm. You will surrender the tramontane conveyances to us. Once you have complied with all instructions and requirements, I will permit you to depart upon your plea for clemency. By the authority granted me to ensure the security of all, this is Earun Tavistorevas."

Geary was the first to speak when the transmission ended. "What the hell is a tramontane?"

Rione answered. "I just looked it up. An ancient term which literally means 'from over the mountains.' Newer meanings, and by newer I mean quite a few centuries ago, are 'foreigner,' 'barbarian,' or 'alien.'"

"They couldn't just say 'alien'?" Charban asked. "I assume they are referring to the Dancers."

"Vulgar craft?" Desjani said in a dangerous voice. "Did they call *Dauntless* a vulgar craft?"

Uncharacteristically, Rione answered again, speaking directly to Desjani. "They appear to feel superior to us in all ways."

"How many awards did that clown have displayed on his chest?" Charban, who rarely spoke so bluntly, let his words drip with scorn. "He must be the greatest hero by far in the history of humanity."

"Give me a background shot from that transmission," Geary ordered.

Without the image of the "Captain Commodore" in the foreground, they could much more easily make out the figures of the others on the bridge of his ship. All of them displayed large panels of awards on their uniforms, though none as large and sparkly as that of their leader.

"Make that a crew of amazing heroes," Desjani said contemptuously. "They must hand out medals for getting up in the morning."

"From the looks of it," Geary said, "they may hand out medals for displaying your prior medals properly."

Senator Suva spoke angrily. "Are you all done mocking him? You do realize he ordered us to surrender this ship? And that we are very badly outnumbered?"

"He's over half a light-hour distant," Geary pointed out. "I don't know what velocity he will accelerate to, but his ships seem to be maneuvering comparably to our ships. It's going to take him a while to catch us even if we don't speed up."

"Speed up? Are you talking about resisting his orders?"

Rione sounded more annoyed than angry as she answered. "We have no obligation to follow his orders. Nor do I trust him to abide by his claim that he would let us go after disabling our weapons and after we beg his forgiveness for breaking rules we did not know of and are not required to follow."

"He can enforce those rules," Charban said in a heavy voice. "He has the firepower to do so."

"We cannot fight in Sol Star System!" Suva cried. "Even those who do not consider it sacrilegious would be outraged!"

Geary spoke loudly enough to shut down the conversation. "We don't intend fighting. I'm going to answer that overdressed clown, telling him politely that as a warship of the Alliance we are not subject to his authority in a neutral star system. I will further tell him that the business of the Dancers is with the authorities here, not with his... whatever it is."

"He didn't address his message to you, so you shouldn't

answer it," Costa said sharply. "He specifically said it was for the representatives of the—" She broke off, looking startled.

Sakai nodded slowly. "How did he know this ship carried representatives of the Alliance government?"

"Could someone have gotten here ahead of us?" Costa demanded.

"Someone must have. Someone who left Varandal allegedly en route a different destination came to Sol instead, and left before we arrived." Sakai's face had become as unrevealing of emotion as stone. "Those ships were awaiting our arrival and, immediately upon seeing us, acted aggressively. I wonder what would become of each of us if we surrendered to their demands?"

"Who would want all three of us—" Suva began, then also ceased speaking abruptly.

Sakai nodded again. "Perhaps not all three of us are in peril. Perhaps one, or two, would be released safely. Perhaps not. There may be those who want none of us to come home."

"You know there are," Costa spat. "And some of them have a lot of money. That overdressed buffoon may act contemptuous of the lowly government of the inconsequential Alliance, but I'll bet you he accepted a handsome bribe from... some person." She looked around, half-defiant and half-worried, becoming aware again that others were listening to the discussion.

Desjani's eyes went to Geary. He could read the message in them. *You're the target of this, too. You and* Dauntless.

He nodded back to her in wordless agreement, trying not to let his expression become too grim. Black Jack without a fleet at his back. A single battle cruiser, outnumbered and isolated. The politicians on board might be targets, Costa, Suva, Sakai, and Rione, but were they the primary targets? Or would they and *Dauntless's* crew be more collateral damage of attempts to "stop" Black Jack?

"Why don't we know more about these people?" Rione complained, glaring at her data pad. She had been furiously tapping in search commands and now looked toward Lieutenant Iger's image. "There's nothing here about star systems beyond Sol except literally *ancient* summaries."

Iger made an apologetic gesture. "Everything for the last century has been focused on the Syndicate Worlds. Even before that, I would guess that acquiring new data about star systems so far distant from the Alliance was given a very low priority. They were a long way away. They didn't matter."

"They matter," Senator Suva said angrily, "if they act as some sort of police force in Sol Star System and threaten us!"

"There is no record of that before this," Senator Sakai mused, gazing at his own data pad. "These ships, it is like viewing an alternate version of what we have become. It is remarkable to see living history like this."

"I prefer my living history less well armed and less aggressive," Geary replied.

"I agree," Sakai said. "The last visit here by an Alliance warship was over a century ago, but at that time and prior to that there is no record of encountering outer-star warships in Sol Star System."

"A vacuum of power?" Geary asked. "We weren't here, so someone else came in?"

"And someone else took advantage of their presence here to endanger us?" Rione made an angry gesture. "It's not that simple. Not where Sol and Old Earth are concerned. They are supposed to be separate from politics. They are supposed to be kept free of involvement in disputes. I am very surprised that anyone made such a blatant move to claim some sort of authority here."

"The Alliance built a hypernet gate here," Geary said.

"Yes. Forty-five years ago," Rione said, her eyes on her data pad again. "A serious investment of money and resources at a time when the Alliance did not have any of either to spare."

"Then why did the Alliance build it?" Geary asked.

Apparently unaware of how everyone else was watching her, awaiting an answer, Rione shrugged. "From what I have been told, it was a political ploy. A desperate one, but judged worth trying as a means of possibly gaining external support against the Syndics and as a way to boost morale within the Alliance. Sol is a special place to humanity. The Alliance publicly proclaimed it was building the gate here to benefit Sol and to make it easier for humans to visit the Home of us all. Very altruistic. The actual intent of the hypernet gate was to symbolically tie Sol to the Alliance, even though no one said that, and symbolically tie the Alliance to Sol. The Syndics couldn't play that game since we sat between them and Sol."

"Sol must have approved letting the gate be built," Charban pointed out.

"You don't understand. Sol is still fragmented. There are dozens of different sovereign governments in this star system, and on Old Earth itself, legacies from ancient times. They get along now, having warred to exhaustion centuries ago, but they're probably still debating whether or not to approve letting the Alliance build the gate here. The authorities at Old Earth are the voice of an organization built on the ashes of the last wars here, an organization designed to *prevent* the projection of power by any government in Sol Star System." Rione stopped speaking, looking appalled, then slapped a palm against her forehead so hard that the sound of the gesture reverberated around the bridge. "*Stupid!* We should have realized this would happen!"

"What do you mean?" Senator Sakai asked, while everyone else stared at Rione.

"We caused this!" Rione said. "We built the hypernet gate as a symbol. That's what it is, a symbol whose meaning could provoke others but bring us no certain benefit. Why are these outer-star warships here? Why do they claim to protect Sol Star System and Old Earth? Because the Alliance staked a symbolic claim that other star systems near here could not ignore. They are here because we built that gate even though we should have known that Sol could not stop anyone else from doing what we did, acting unilaterally in the supposed best interests of Sol."

After a long moment, Sakai nodded. "I believe that your reasoning is correct."

"Then," Senator Suva insisted, "this may be a misunderstanding."

"I'm happy to go with that," Geary said. "But we have to convince those outer-star people to laugh it off as well."

"They're not going to accept anything that we say!" Rione replied. "As far as they are concerned, we planted a flag here, in Sol Star System. They are going to assert their own authority to counter our claim. Even if they haven't been bribed, they would contest our presence here. If they have been paid to ensure we don't leave this star system alive, it would only reinforce their own agenda of keeping the Alliance out. For all we know, whoever tipped them off that we were coming also claimed that we were coming to establish a permanent military presence here."

Costa grimaced. "I'd like to tell them to eat ground glass, but they outnumber us considerably."

"We must consider the appropriate course of action," Sakai agreed. "For safeguarding the interests of the Alliance, for the safety of the mission, and for the safety of all aboard this ship."

"Nothing must be done until the governmental representatives on this vessel reach a decision," Suva said, her eyes on Geary. "Our lives are on the line here as well."

Geary could feel the fleet personnel on the bridge stiffening at the words, but before he could speak, Rione did, her tone serious and agreeable.

"You are right, Senator," Rione said. "This must be debated and discussed. We must come up with a policy to address these unanticipated circumstances, and we should begin that discussion immediately."

"You have no vote in the matter," Suva said with disdain.

"Actually, I do. Senator Navarro gave me his proxy before we left."

"He—!"

"But I don't wish to use that proxy in haste. We need to talk about this. About who might have tried to ensure the failure of this mission and the destruction of this ship. About our best course of action. But we must talk in private."

"I don't—" Costa began.

"Of course we need to meet in private," Suva declared, looking around the bridge, then pointedly at Costa. "Senator Sakai?"

"Of course," Sakai echoed.

"Admiral Geary," Rione said, "until we return with further guidance, you are to adhere strictly to the instructions the government already gave you."

"Yes!" Suva agreed. "Strictly adhere to them, Admiral."

"I will," Geary said, trying not to smile. Rione was keeping a straight face, and if she could, so could he.

Charban watched the three senators leave, then gave a rueful look to Geary. "Not being actually elected to anything, or holding any proxies for anyone who was, I have no role in the debate. I will instead attempt to pass your earlier message on to the Dancers, unless you believe it should be changed."

"Please do, General." Geary indicated the Dancer ships on his display. "The Dancers still need to be told to stay well clear of the outerstar warships. But in light of that message we received, tell them there is some sort of misunderstanding that we need to work out, and until we do, it would be dangerous to approach those other ships."

"I will do my best to get the message across, Admiral," Charban said. He paused, then saluted with a wry smile before leaving the bridge.

Geary glanced at Desjani, who was staring stiff-jawed at her display. "What's the matter?"

She turned her glare on him. "They tied your hands. Or did you miss that?"

"No, they didn't. I was told to continue to follow previous instructions. Rione made sure that was emphasized before she and the others departed."

The glare shifted to realization. "And your previous instructions allow you to act as you see fit in unanticipated circumstances."

"Right."

"Damn!" Desjani seemed even more upset now. "I hate it when that woman does that!"

"Does what?"

"Does something that's... not evil. It makes me wonder what she's actually up to." Desjani settled back, her expression becoming thoughtful. "What will you do?"

"I could talk to them," Geary said.

"That didn't work with the enigmas or the Kicks. It has rarely worked with the Syndics. And as much as I don't want to agree with anything those politicians said, it is very suspicious that those ships knew we were coming and who would be aboard. If they knew that, and have taken the actions they already have, they're not going to listen to anything we say."

"That's a point. How about if I talk to them in a way they might understand? I'll avoid admitting there are any Alliance governmental representatives aboard. That might confuse them. While we're talking, we'll keep heading for Old Earth."

"And if they're after you?"

"I'll let them know we won't roll over without a fight."

He took another long look at the image of the flashy, overdressed, and over-medaled commander of the outer-star warships, then hit the reply command. "Captain Commodore Tavistorevas, this is Admiral Geary of the Alliance fleet. As I am sure you understand, this warship is a sovereign extension of the Alliance itself. I cannot permit this battle cruiser to be boarded by a foreign power operating in a neutral star system. I am also charged by my government to safely escort to Old Earth the ships carrying emissaries from the alien species we know as Dancers. The Dancers are the only intelligent alien species with which humanity has yet managed to establish friendly relations. In accordance with my orders, I must protect them from any interference or harm, and I will do so.

"Should you wish to issue a formal objection to the actions of the Alliance, please send it to me and I will ensure it is forwarded to appropriate authorities upon our return to the Alliance.

"To the honor of our ancestors, Admiral Geary, out."

Desjani shrugged. "That can't hurt. Hmmm. They're pushing their velocity up to point two light. They're definitely not just out to block us from leaving. They want to catch us."

"Admiral?" Lieutenant Iger's image had reappeared. "Our systems have had a chance to evaluate how those warships maneuver. Their estimate is that the, uh, Shield of Sol warships have no armor."

"No armor?" Geary questioned.

"There's a small margin of possibility that light armor might be in place around critical areas," Iger said.

"What about weapons? I'm still just seeing a few weapon sites and types identified on my display."

"Those are all that have been confirmed or labeled as high-probability," the intelligence officer explained. "All of the ornamentation on those ships could be concealing a lot of other weapons, but we're doing pixel-by-pixel analysis of high-resolution scans. If there are more weapons, we'll spot them."

"As soon as possible," Geary emphasized, then gave Desjani a disgruntled look as Iger's image vanished. "There have to be a lot more weapons on those ships. We need to have a better idea of what we might have to fight."

"No armor," she mused. "But they're not faster than us. Good. And unless I miss my guess, from the look and sound of Mister Medals, they have highly centralized command and control. If we can take him out, it might be a lot easier to handle the rest."

Geary looked at the formation of the other warships, a shallow tube longer than it was wide, with one of the megacruisers and two of the corvettes inexplicably spread out from each side. "Mister Medals is probably in that center warship. He won't be easy to get to."

"No," Desjani agreed. "Not without taking heavy fire from all sides, and *Dauntless* isn't built to take that kind of punishment."

He didn't answer, feeling increasingly gloomy as the situation sank in. *Dauntless* was alone. She had to look out for the six Dancer ships, but even without that handicap, the Alliance battle cruiser faced a difficult situation, badly overmatched in numbers and firepower. Moreover, the enemy was an unknown quantity in many ways. What sort of tactics did they use? How good was their fire control? How powerful were their weapons? Was Mister Medals a good commander or the sort of aristocratic buffoon that he appeared to be? If he was really good, then the buffoon act might be totally misleading, designed to cause others to underestimate him.

How much had the enemy been told about *Dauntless* by whoever had told them of the Alliance governmental representatives aboard her?

Too many questions. Not nearly enough answers.

And guessing wrong could be fatal, not just for *Dauntless* but for whatever hopes rested on humanity's relationship with the Dancers.

17

Old Earth was much farther distant than the "Shield of Sol" warships, so it was no surprise that they had not yet heard anything from Sol Star System authorities when a reply came from the outer-star forces.

The gaudy commander of the outer-star warships, whom Geary found himself unable to think of except as Mister Medals, this time acted not only bored but also how-dare-you imperious. "I am *His Excellency* Captain Commodore *First Rank Stellar Guard of the Fist of the People* Earun Tavistorevas, *Paramount of the Shield of Sol.* You are to use my *full title* when communicating with an officer of my position. I have no interest in whatever orders you received from the vulgar leaders of your barbarous society. You will comply with my orders. If you do not immediately reduce velocity and power down all offensive and defensive systems, I will destroy you as well as every tramontane impurity you have brought into our Home."

"I don't think they want to negotiate," Desjani said, as the transmission ended. Her words sounded light, but her expression was dour.

Geary knew why. The Shield of Sol ships had kept closing on *Dauntless*. Having upped their velocity to point two three light speed, the other warships were only a couple of hours from overtaking the Alliance battle cruiser. Of the many other spacecraft in Sol Star System, all of them civilian ships, the ones whose tracks would have brought them anywhere near the tracks of *Dauntless* and the other warships had all altered course to stay well away. They obviously expected the worst. The Dancers had stayed with *Dauntless*, but was that for the best? Wouldn't they be safer if he told them to scatter, to head for the hypernet gate and home? But what if they didn't listen? How could he protect them? How could *Dauntless* be saved? In an attempt to distract himself, Geary spoke loudly. "Does anyone have any idea why he keeps using terms that have to do with purity and vulgarity?"

Everyone on the bridge shook their heads, so Geary repeated the question to Lieutenant Iger.

"No, sir. They seem to think they are somehow special."

"I had already gathered that on my own," Geary said, breaking the call to Iger with an abruptness he knew was unusual. Something was bothering him. Something that loomed just beyond his conscious awareness like a huge beast staying out of his sight but close enough that he could tell it was there.

He stared at his display, feeling an unusual tightness in his guts. He could feel his breaths becoming quicker and shallower. A strange object seemed to be stuck in his throat.

"Admiral?"

He had been here before. He hadn't been good enough that time. "*Admiral.*"

Desjani's tone broke through Geary's fixation on his display. He looked over at her.

She was watching him with first surprise, then appraisal. "What's the matter?"

He tried to answer, and that effort finally caused him to understand what had rattled him so badly. *Why now? I can't have a flashback now. I thought I was past this.* Whatever was impeding his breathing also kept him from saying anything.

Desjani was leaning close, her voice very low and fierce. "Dammit, Jack, *what's the matter?*"

He met her eyes and managed to say one word. "Grendel."

"Grendel?" Tanya eyed him, puzzled, then her expression cleared. "Grendel. You, one ship, against bad odds, trying to protect a convoy. This is the first time you've faced that situation since you fought there."

He nodded. *Thank our ancestors that she understood, that I didn't have to try to explain something I don't entirely understand. This isn't Grendel.*

"This isn't Grendel," she said on the heels of his own thought.

Words broke from him in a sudden rush. "Tanya, I had my ship blown apart around me. Most of my crew killed. If that happens again—"

"This is *my* ship, Admiral. If *Dauntless* gets blown apart, *I* will be on her bridge fighting her to the last."

Geary stared at her. "Is that supposed to make me feel better?"

She actually reached across and grabbed his wrist, the sort of physical contact they normally avoided to keep anyone from gossiping about the admiral and his wife the captain. "Listen. If I die here, it won't be just your fault. It'll be mine, too. This is my ship. I will stay with her until the end. And you will get everyone you can off of her, if that is our fate. We've been blessed with each other for a time far too short. But we never should have met at all. You should have died a century ago. You didn't, and I won't now."

"Tanya—"

"Listen. I am certain that I can drive *Dauntless* better than any of those pretty boys and girls on their fancy ships. One-on-one, I'd kick their butts. But we're up against a bunch of them, and I need somebody looking at the overall situation, outthinking and outguessing Mister Medals. Together, we can do this. But this is no time for stress memories to throw you off. If that happens, if you go jelly on me, we're dead. Will you go jelly on me?"

"No!"

She bared her teeth in a grin that was half snarl. "Damn straight. You never have, and you never will. Throw it off or bury it or whatever you need to do until we've beaten these guys. Can you do that, or do I need to call a doc up here to give you some head meds?"

"Yes." He realized only after saying the word how calmly and firmly it had come out. "I can do that. But get a doc here anyway. Everybody up here can tell I'm rattled, and I want them to see I'm dealing with it smart. Thanks to you. What did I ever do to deserve you?"

"Not enough. I'll let you know if you ever get there. But this is my duty, Admiral. Don't forget that I'd be doing this no matter who was sitting in that seat." Desjani released his wrist and settled back in her seat, tapping one of her internal comm controls. "Sick bay, we need a head check on the bridge. Nothing critical, just some safeguards."

Geary rubbed his chin and cast discreet glances around the bridge. As he suspected, everyone was pretending not to have noticed anything unusual regarding the admiral and their commanding officer. Being able to pretend you hadn't noticed a superior officer's behavior was one of the essential survival traits in the fleet, and probably in any military throughout human history. "All right. We've got a couple of hours even if we don't accelerate to reposition." He had learned to say such things the right way. The fleet, scarred by a century of war and fixated on honor, did not retreat, and it did not flee pursuit. It repositioned. "We've got some advantages."

"Right. We're faster." Desjani waved at her display. "We've got more mass than those megacruisers, but even bigger main propulsion relative to that, so we've got a better thrust-to-mass ratio. Assuming their inertial dampers are no better than ours, we can outturn and outaccelerate them."

He frowned at his own display. "Anything else?"

"They've got even less armor than we do." She frowned at her display. "In terms of weapons, it doesn't feel right at all. They've got to have more weaponry than we're seeing. I can't call that an advantage. Maybe they don't have a null-field generator, but we'll have to get awful close to use that, and they might have something different but just as deadly."

"Not much good there," Geary commented. "What else?"

"We've got you."

Geary actually felt himself smiling. "And you. Best damned ship driver in the fleet."

She grinned. "And my crew," she added. "Been there, done that. We know our job."

He paused to think, only to be interrupted by the communications watch-stander. "Captain, we have a message from Sol Star System authorities."

"Route it to the Admiral and me," she ordered.

Geary watched intently as the comm window popped into existence near him. He had somehow expected the people of Old Earth to look different. Older. Wiser. Smarter. But the two women and one man who looked out at him didn't seem any different from anyone else he had ever talked to. Perhaps there was a tinge of fatigue around their eyes, a sense of age beyond the years their faces revealed. Their clothes were nothing like the ornate uniforms on the warships, instead being simple in design, the colors evoking a sense of brightness faded but still strong.

"Greetings to the ship *Dauntless* of the Alliance," one of the women said. "We are excited beyond measure at the news you bring of contact with a nonhuman intelligence, and at the possibility of meeting the ambassadors from that species you have escorted here.

"Unfortunately, as you must have already discovered, Sol Star System has been occupied by a military force from the Covenant of the First Stars, which claims to be protecting us. We have protested their actions and have been trying for the last two decades to reach agreement on procedures for attempting to assemble a coalition of other nearby powers to expel the Covenant warships from Sol. However, that effort has been complex due to the special status of Sol and worries about provoking aggression from the Covenant against other star systems. There have been no wars in this region of space for several decades, and no major conflicts for the last two centuries."

"They've been trying for two *decades*?" Desjani said. "Two decades spent arguing over whether to do anything?"

"Yeah," Geary agreed. "Rione was right about how Sol Star System does things. Or doesn't do things. It prevents aggression but also defense. So much for the idea that Sol is a unique oasis of peace and harmony among the stars of human-occupied space. Still, it looks like there hasn't been much actual fighting."

The woman from Old Earth was still speaking. "We can offer you no assistance against the Covenant military force. Because of that, we urge you to act in whatever manner you deem best, keeping ever in mind that you are at the Home of Humanity. It is better that you, and these representatives from another species, be safe than that you run unnecessary risks.

"This is Dominika Borkowski, for the people and the Home, end."

Geary rubbed his nose, grimaced, then nodded to Desjani. "Please have your people forward that message to our senators and envoys."

She gave the orders, then turned back to Geary. "What do you suppose they'll do with it?"

"I don't know. Debate what to reply. What can we do with it?"

"They gave us a free hand," Desjani pointed out.

"That's because they didn't know they were talking to Tanya Desjani," Geary replied dryly.

A medical assistant came onto the bridge, did a brief scan of Geary, offered him a tailored med patch that his equipment had ejected, and Geary slapped it on as the assistant checked with the others on the bridge. The actual effects of the meds would take a couple of minutes to manifest, but he felt better just from the psychological results of knowing relief was on the way and would not cloud his judgment.

"All right," Geary said. "I am going to send an answer to the Sol Star System authorities." He straightened, got a quick appraisal of his appearance from Tanya, then tapped the reply command. "This is Admiral Geary of the Alliance Fleet, senior military commander aboard *Dauntless*. Thank you for your reply and your warning. The representatives of the Alliance government aboard *Dauntless* are crafting an official response, but for now we would be very grateful for any information you can provide us regarding the Covenant and any details regarding the Covenant warships. Those warships are blocking our return to the hypernet gate, and moving to intercept us and the ships of the Dancers, which we have vowed to protect, so we may be unable to avoid taking necessary actions to defend ourselves and the Dancers. Your information may be of great assistance in our efforts.

"Our actions will take into account this star system and its special status. Unlike the Covenant, we do not seek violence here.

"To the honor of our ancestors, Geary, out."

He sat back, eyes on his display, not really aware for the moment that everyone else on the bridge was watching him, waiting for what Black Jack would come up with to save *Dauntless* and the Dancers, and to beat a little humility into Mister Medals and the ships of the Covenant. "Tanya, let's assume our government representatives will be tied up indefinitely debating what to do. I am pretty certain that Rione will do her best to keep them occupied and out of our hair. I think we should tell the Dancers to continue on toward Old Earth while we turn to engage those Covenant ships."

"Good plan," she replied. "Except... I know it's unusual for me to worry about diplomatic junk, but maybe this one time it might be a good idea to make sure they fire first."

"So we're unquestionably acting in self-defense? Do you have any suggestions on how we can bring that about, Captain Desjani?"

"As a matter of fact, I do, Admiral Geary." Desjani moved her hands to illustrate her words as she outlined her plan. "We brake *Dauntless's* velocity to point zero five light and let the Dancers continue on toward Old Earth at point one light while the Covies overtake us a lot faster. The Covies keep telling us to drop our shields and we keep telling them it's not going to happen in ways that will make Mister Medals even more unhappy with our attitudes. When we get in range, Mister Medals opens fire, *Dauntless* lights off full acceleration, and we avoid their first volley of missiles. Then we kick their butts."

"An interesting plan," Geary said. "The last part is a little vague, though."

"We'll have to improvise."

The meds had definitely kicked in. The lurking beast had gone from his mind. Geary studied his display with a mind clear and focused, the past only something that he could use to help figure out tactics to employ here and now. "It's risky. We don't know how good their missiles are."

Desjani brought up, floating between her and Geary, an image of the Covenant formation. "Did you look at this? Watch." She waved in another command, and curved lines connected the warships, the lines forming—

"A bird?" Geary said, not believing what he was seeing. "They're arranged that way because it makes a pretty picture?"

"Yes. Those four corvettes and megacruisers on the sides? We couldn't figure out why they were there because we were evaluating the formation in terms of functionality in battle. But if you look at that formation in terms of show, the two corvettes and single megacruiser on either side form the wings."

"Ancestors preserve us. They're getting ready to fight us in a parade formation?"

"That woman from Old Earth," Desjani pressed, "said there hadn't been any fighting around here for decades and nothing serious for centuries. Imagine our own fleet headquarters without any actual combat issues or experience or demands to influence their decisions. Decade after decade of that, the emphasis on how good things look rather than how well they work, while weapons and designs are evaluated in bureaucratic terms rather than whether they work or not and officers get awards for how fancy their hair is done up."

"Mister Medals." He looked at his display using new eyes. "But there are a lot of them and only one of us. What if they send a pursuit after the Dancers?"

"Those clowns *cannot* catch the Dancer ships unless the Dancers let them," Desjani said.

"True. We'll have to assume the Dancers will stay clear of trouble. That leaves Old Earth and the other historical sites throughout this star system. We can't risk anything's happening to those places."

She stared at him. "You don't think they'd fire on Home?"

"I don't know." He let his own gaze settle again on the blue-white orb shown on his display. "You and I look at that and can't imagine doing it harm. But the craters on the surface show that in the past other humans have dropped rocks on the Home of all of us. What humans have done once, they can do again. That's why we can't afford to string this out using the distance to Old Earth's orbit. The farther we go in-system, the closer we get to places like Home, and Mars and Venus, as well as all of the shipping near those planets. We'll have to get this done out here, where space is emptier, and we'll have to keep the attention of the Covies focused on us."

It had worked at Grendel. Well enough, anyway.

If Dauntless *dies here, if Tanya stays with her to the end, so will I. What the hell, I had a good run. But I lost everything once. I won't lose everything that matters to me now.*

Ancestors, what if she dies in the battle, and I don't?

It must not happen. I will keep it from happening.

"Very well, Captain Desjani. We'll follow your plan. Wait a couple of minutes, then reduce the velocity of *Dauntless* to point zero five light speed." Geary tapped an internal comm control. "Envoy Charban, are you having any luck?"

Charban shrugged. "I can't tell."

"*Dauntless* is going to be slowing considerably, but we want the Dancers to continue on toward Old Earth without us. Can you get across to the Dancers that the other warships are enemies who are likely to attack us, and will attack them if the other warships get within range?"

"Brother enemies," Charban said. "The Dancers understand that concept. I'll tell them to keep on keeping on, and we'll hope they do that."

Maneuvering thrusters fired on *Dauntless*, pitching her bow up and over so that it faced back along her track, toward where the

Covenant formation was coming on steadily. The main propulsion units fired to reduce her velocity, though Geary noticed that Desjani was only using half of the main units for that task. If the Covenant ships evaluated *Dauntless's* maneuverability based on that, they would seriously underestimate her actual agility.

With the closure rate increasing dramatically, the time to contact began rapidly decreasing. "Forty minutes until the Covenant warships will be able to fire upon us if their missile ranges are equivalent to ours," Lieutenant Yuon said.

Geary nodded absently, his eyes on the Dancers. They had matched *Dauntless's* pivot, but were now pivoting back and moving onward without reducing speed. *So far, so good.* "Tanya, when we get into the estimated range envelope of the Covenant missiles, I'm going to leave when and how to maneuver *Dauntless* up to you."

"Thank you, Admiral." Desjani looked back at her watch-standers. "Bring *Dauntless* to full combat status, but I do *not* want any sound of that to reach the senators aboard this ship. Keep their compartment silent."

Geary nodded in an exaggerated manner. "We don't want to interrupt their discussions. Those are very important."

"Uh… right. Get the word out, people."

Passageways and compartments that the day before had been filled with laughter and celebration would now be filled with officers and sailors racing to their combat stations. Real weapons would be powered up, real targets would be selected, and neither Jove's trident nor Callisto's bow would decide the result.

"All departments, report full combat readiness," Lieutenant Castries said.

The image of Master Chief Gioninni appeared near Desjani. "Captain, as senior enlisted officer aboard the ship, I wish to suggest that you explain what's going on. There are a lot of rumors flying, and with this being Sol, people are worried about different things than usual."

"That's a good suggestion, Master Chief," Desjani approved. "Admiral Geary will address the crew."

I will?

"Thank you, Captain." Gioninni's image vanished.

"Whenever you are ready, Admiral," Desjani said, smiling at him.

"Thank you, Captain," Geary said, deliberately echoing Gioninni. "Do you have a copy of what I was going to say? Because I seem to be having trouble recalling what it was."

"No, but I remember the gist of it," Desjani replied confidently, giving no hint that she was making it up as she went along. "Something about defending Sol and Old Earth against aggressors who have already targeted us."

"Was that what it was?" Geary took a few moments to compose his thoughts. "The odds against us are awful, Tanya. How do I give the crew hope when they must be aware of that?"

"We don't need hope," she replied. "None of us hoped to survive the war with the Syndics, and none of us hoped to see the end of that war. We could hope to win each battle, but we'd fight like hell whether we thought we had a chance or not. Hope is for people who expect to see a better future. We stopped believing in that a long time ago and learned how to fight without that belief. Until you came. Haven't you figured that out?"

He took a few seconds to reply. "I guess not."

"Just tell everyone we didn't choose this fight, but we're going to win it."

"All right." Geary gestured to the comm watch-stander to have his voice broadcast everywhere on the ship except in the compartment where the senators were debating with each other and Rione. "This is Admiral Geary. As you may have heard, upon our arrival in Sol Star System, we discovered that one of the minor powers located in nearby star systems had violated the sanctity of Sol by stationing a flotilla of warships here. Those warships have threatened the people of Sol, and they have demanded that we surrender to them.

"The people of Sol have told us that they cannot defend themselves. We are being attacked, and those attacking us are also threatening Sol Star System and Old Earth. We did not seek a fight. We did not choose a fight. But because the aggressor warships here are blocking our route to the hypernet gate, threatening the Dancers, threatening Old Earth itself, and moving to intercept us, we have no choice but to fight. The odds do not favor us, but since we have to fight, we're going to win."

He could only hope that the bold shouts and cheers within *Dauntless* could not be heard by the senators, and if so, that the senators would think they were somehow related to the crossing-the-line celebration of the day before. "I guess that was good," he told Tanya.

"It would have been better if you just said what I told you to say."

"What I said was close to that."

"You are *not* my editor, Admiral." She tapped the arm of her chair lightly. "Half an hour to contact. The senators are probably going to notice when we start combat maneuvers."

"Probably." He left it at that.

"Another message from the other warships," the comm watch-stander said.

Mister Medals appeared to be annoyed and a bit baffled, in the manner of someone who was so unused to being crossed that he didn't quite know how to handle it. "You are quickly running out of time to comply with your instructions. I am not in the habit of repeating my directions. You are to drop your shields now and reduce your velocity now, or I will take any measures required to preserve the security and safety of Sol."

Geary tapped his reply command. "I am not in the habit of accepting orders from a minor commander of minor forces representing a minor collection of star systems. You are to cease all offensive activity in this star system and you are to immediately change vectors to remove your ships from this star system by whichever means you choose. Sol cannot defend itself, but we can and will defend Sol as well as ourselves. Geary, out."

Desjani gave him a grin. "I don't think the senators would approve of that language."

"No, they wouldn't." Could Rione keep them occupied until *Dauntless* was committed to the fight? The odds against them would get even worse if someone interfered with the plan they had come up with. "I just realized something."

"Good or bad?"

"Good. With Rione having a vote, that means four votes. Left to themselves, those three senators might have settled on a two-to-one result after a little infighting. But with four votes, Rione can shift every time a majority starts to develop and keep everything stymied at two to two. Senator Navarro must have known she would be able to do that if he gave her his proxy." *Navarro, weary as he is of the ugly politics afflicting the Alliance, was canny enough to figure out how to frustrate any attempted interference with me. But if he anticipated the need for that, did he think I might face this situation? Did he know someone might try to set up this ambush at Sol? Or did Navarro just plan for the worst in case it was needed?*

"Ten minutes to entering estimated threat envelope," Lieutenant Yuon said.

"Are you going to keep your bow pointed at them?" Geary asked. *Dauntless* had been going backwards at very high speed ever since pivoting around to slow her velocity.

"Until I guess their missiles are launching," Desjani confirmed. "I want my strongest weaponry and shields facing them."

The remaining minutes passed with the usual slowness they acquired when waiting for a critical event. When *Dauntless* entered the missile threat envelope, there would be only a few seconds to react, but Geary sat back with every sign of calm confidence as he waited for Desjani to make her decision.

For her part, Desjani no longer seemed aware of him, her focus locked on the display before her.

"Entering—"

Lieutenant Yuon broke off as *Dauntless* pitched downward and accelerated at the maximum capability of her main propulsion units, then rolled into a skidding turn tens of thousands of kilometers wide as the thrusters on her port bow fired at full power.

Geary braced himself against momentum forces strong enough to leak past the inertial dampers. A low groan of straining metal and composites rose around him as *Dauntless* herself protested the stresses on her hull. On his display, red danger symbols marked a volley of missiles bending around in pursuit of *Dauntless*.

"They fired first," Desjani said. "Request permission to return fire."

Not only had the Covenant ships fired first, but they had unleashed a volley of missiles instead of a single warning shot. Any question about whether they sought *Dauntless's* destruction had now been answered. "Permission granted. Take all necessary actions to defend *Dauntless* and the Dancer ships."

Geary's comm alert pulsed urgently. The senators had noticed the last maneuver, probably when it pitched them from their seats. "Yes?"

Senator Costa glared at him from a virtual window. "What is happening?"

"We have been fired upon by the warships of the Covenant flotilla, Senator. They opened fire without provocation, using sufficient force to have destroyed *Dauntless* if we had not maneuvered to evade their attack." *Don't ask. Don't ask. Don't ask.*

Geary's silent plea was answered. Costa didn't ask what *Dauntless* was doing now, her image vanishing without another word. She doubtless assumed that the battle cruiser was simply avoiding the attack and getting clear of danger.

On Geary's display, the Covenant missiles were still closing on *Dauntless*, whipping through tighter turns than the battle cruiser could manage, the long arcs of their intercept vectors curving toward the place where *Dauntless* would be if she maintained her current course and speed.

But under Desjani's command *Dauntless* bent her path upward and to starboard. The missiles had to react, swinging through wider arcs, burning their propulsion furiously as they sought to compensate for the battle cruiser's latest maneuver.

"Admiral?" Lieutenant Iger's image had appeared beside Geary. "Sir, the numbers of missiles in that volley match the number of missile launch points we had previously identified on the Covenant ships."

"Good, that's— What?" Geary moved his hand against the strain of Desjani's latest maneuver, calling up data. "That's all? On that many ships? That means the big ones only have two launchers apiece?"

"And the small ones have none," Iger confirmed.

Geary stared at the statistics. "These ships have armament roughly comparable to our own auxiliaries. They're a little better armed, but not much. Why the hell would anyone build a warship that big, that expensive, and that elaborate and put so few weapons on it?"

"I... don't know, sir."

Tanya was right. These people forgot about war-fighting when designing their ships. "Captain Desjani, your estimate about the firepower on these warships was correct."

"Thank you, Admiral. That's all I need to know."

The threat symbols on Geary's display were winking out as Covenant missiles ran out of power and went zooming off on their last vector, unable to maneuver and heading into endless, empty space. Desjani had brought *Dauntless* up and over and was now arcing back downward and to port as the Covenant formation raced to pass beneath her, making final adjustments in her track as the other warships stuck stubbornly to their own vectors.

"Targets designated," Desjani said, her voice loud and almost unnaturally clear. "I want these, ladies and gentlemen. Make your shots count." *Dauntless* whipped through the outer edge of one wing of the Covenant formation, the other warships there and gone too fast for human senses to register, the battle cruiser still shuddering slightly from having unleashed every weapon that would bear.

Encounters in space often happened far too quickly for humans to react, but automated systems could track and fire at the proper instants, choosing just the right millisecond to unleash weapons at where another ship would be when the weapon passed through that same spot. Now *Dauntless's* sensors were evaluating the result of that firing pass while Desjani brought her battle cruiser sweeping back to starboard to come up behind the Covenant warships.

One wing of the Covenant formation had disappeared. Three of the little corvettes were simply gone, their power cores overloaded by *Dauntless's* barrage of hell lances and grapeshot, and the megacruiser on that wing had been broken into several large pieces, which were tumbling in the wake of the Covenant formation.

The Covies had fired back, but *Dauntless* had taken most of the hits on her shields, only one penetrating to damage the hull. "Get that grapeshot launcher back online," Desjani ordered. She sounded frustrated, not triumphant. "We didn't get enough of them, and now we're the ones in a stern chase," she grumbled to Geary as *Dauntless's* main propulsion units pushed the battle cruiser to ever-higher velocity.

"We'll get them," he said with more confidence than he felt, one eye on the hull-stress meters, which were edging into red danger zones as Desjani's maneuvers pushed the battle cruiser to the limits of what her hull could withstand even with the help of the inertial dampers.

A sudden commotion behind him marked the return of the senators to the bridge. "What is going on?" Senator Suva demanded.

"We're defending ourselves and the Dancers in accordance with the orders given to me by the government," Geary replied, while Desjani studiously ignored the presence of the politicians.

"Then the weapons which this ship fired were defensive?" Senator Sakai asked, his tone as mild as usual.

"Absolutely."

"We are in a combat situation," Rione said. "Our presence on the bridge is disruptive."

Costa and Suva rounded on her, but before they could speak, Sakai did. "Envoy Rione is correct."

"She is not," Suva insisted. "This hero has started another war while she kept us tied down with debates!"

Rione met Suva's eyes with cool resolve. "Who fired the first shot, Admiral?"

"They did," Geary said. "A volley of missiles as soon as we were within range. We had no alternative but to defend ourselves against a force that the authorities in Sol Star System have told us is unwelcome and uninvited."

Lieutenant Yuon cleared his throat apologetically as he interrupted the debate. "At our current closing rate, we'll be within range of the rear of the Covenant formation in forty-two minutes, Captain."

"We're chasing them?" Suva asked, disbelieving. "If they want to kill us, why aren't we just avoiding them?"

Geary called up the display at the observer's seat. The Covenant formation, one wing gone, had continued on a long, shallow trajectory that crossed the path of the Dancers much farther inside the star system. "They are still pursuing the Dancers. They're on an intercept course with them. They have indicated an intent to attack the Dancers, too. What would you have us do, Senator?"

Suva covered her eyes, then nodded. "I am not a fool, Admiral. Our discussions with the Covenant commander have been even less fruitful than those with my companions on the grand council. Too many minds are set too firmly in opposition, and some of those minds will not stop at debate. Do what you must to save all of us. We'll try to sweep up the mess afterwards." She sounded defeated and worn-out.

Costa glared at her. "Now you see why our earlier decisions were necessary to ensure the safety of the Alliance—"

"You would talk of those decisions here?" Sakai asked, his voice still calm but somehow easily cutting across Costa's.

Senator Costa jerked, looking around as if she had indeed again forgotten where she was. "I... no." Her gaze fastened on Rione. "Some individuals may have a voting proxy, but they do not have authorization to know everything that the grand council has done for the Alliance."

"I count myself lucky in that respect." Rione sounded amused, but her voice had an iron edge under the humor. "Or do you mean everything the grand council has done *to* the Alliance? I might know more of that than you think, Senator. Many people may know more of that than you think."

Costa, very obviously not looking at Geary now, stomped off

the bridge, followed by Suva, who gave Rione a questioning look different from her customary hostility as the envoy followed Suva. Behind them came Sakai, his feelings as usual masked.

Assorted lieutenants and other watch-standers watched the politicians go, their eyes wide and their mouths wisely shut.

"Back on task, everyone," Desjani ordered. Even though she had not turned around or apparently paid attention to the politicians and the argument, her command came the instant the hatch sealed behind them.

Geary did his best to put the senators out of his mind as well, focusing back on the situation. "We should get within range of them slightly before they catch up with the Dancers." At that point, though, coming up from behind, they would face the firepower of the entire Covenant formation again, without the same ability to dodge missiles unless they turned away and failed to engage the other warships.

A sudden intake of breath by Tanya was followed by her pointing at her display. "No, we won't catch them before that. Look. The Dancers have turned back toward us. They're going to run into those Covenant warships long before we catch up."

18

"Charban! Tell the Dancers to avoid the Covenant formation!"

"They're a few light-minutes distant!" Charban protested, "and if I read this space display properly, they're going to encounter the other warships very quickly because they're accelerating toward them!"

Geary stared at his display. Unfortunately, the former ground forces general was reading his display right. The Dancers had not simply reduced their velocity to allow the Covenant ships to close on them more quickly. Instead, the Dancers had come around and kept accelerating, killing their own velocity in one direction and building it in the direction facing the oncoming enemy. The vectors on the Dancer ships led straight into the heart of the Covenant formation. "Did they acknowledge your warning to stay clear of those ships?" he asked, feeling an agony of frustration.

"Yes. Very clearly. *Understand*. I don't know what they're doing." Charban sounded very unhappy and upset as well.

Desjani didn't say anything, her eyes fixed on her display, her expression bleak. *Dauntless* was accelerating as fast as her main propulsion units could manage. There was nothing more she could do, nothing more any of them could do, but watch.

"Captain," Lieutenant Castries reported, her voice awed, "the acceleration on the Dancer ships is exceeding our estimates of what their hulls could sustain. If they continue at their current rate, it will have them going point one one light speed when they reach the Covenant formation."

"Thank you—" Desjani began, then stared at Castries, then at Geary. "The Covenant ships are going point two four light. The combined velocity when they meet will be more than point three five light."

Maybe there was a chance. "Unless those Covenant fire control systems are a lot better than ours, at point three five light they won't have much chance of scoring any hits."

"And the Dancers are small targets," Desjani said. "And the Covies don't have nearly as much firepower as we'd expected." One of her hands had formed into a fist, which was slowly, softly, rhythmically, hitting one arm of her seat.

"One minute to contact between the Dancers and the Covenant formation," Castries said.

Geary blinked as the two groups of ships swept through each other. At the last moment before contact, the Dancers had narrowed their own formation, sudden changes of vectors by the Dancer ships that would have rendered impossibly hard what had already been a very difficult fire control problem for the Covenant ships. The Dancers had torn by the central Covenant ship in the formation close enough to freeze Geary's breathing for a moment even though the Dancers were there and past before he could grasp what they were doing.

"I know we can work with them," Desjani said in an outraged voice, "but those Dancers are *crazy*." She slapped her controls, throttling back *Dauntless's* main propulsion units slightly.

Ahead of them, the Covenant ships had pivoted and were braking, trying to reverse course in place rather than maneuver the formation through a wide turn. "They've got too much momentum to shed," Desjani complained. "And they're wasting it all."

"A turn-in-place maneuver looks sharper than a formation swing," Geary commented.

"So a peacetime fleet got used to doing it that way? Idiots. All right, everyone, we're going to intercept them a lot faster. Let's see if we can knock off that bird's other wing."

With the Covenant ships reducing their velocity rapidly, the time to contact was shrinking very quickly as well. Desjani adjusted *Dauntless's* vector to aim for the still-intact side of the Covenant formation.

"You're giving them a lot of warning where you're going to hit them," Geary murmured.

She lowered her brow at him. "No, I'm giving them a lot of warning as to where I want them to think I'm going to hit them. I've been watching this guy Black Jack. He does that a lot."

But he still doesn't know when to keep his mouth shut. "Sorry."

Desjani carefully designated targets for the ship's fire control systems as the last minute before contact began running down. "Hang on," she advised her crew, then whipped *Dauntless* onto a slightly different vector. The difference had been a tiny one, but given the distances involved and the relatively small size of the Covenant formation, that bob to one side meant *Dauntless* tore through the already whittled-down wing of the Covenant flotilla rather than hitting the opposite, untouched wing.

Geary barely caught the alerts as Covenant missiles aimed at where *Dauntless* had been going strove to compensate for the change in her track and failed, as Covenant particle beams and grapeshot tore through empty space.

The targets of *Dauntless*, though, hadn't changed vectors, making them sitting ducks as the battle cruiser poured fire into them during the fraction of a second while they were in range before the Alliance warship was through the Covenant formation.

Desjani had ignored the corvettes this time. Most of her fire had hit one of the megacruisers, which was now rolling out of formation, all systems dead. The remaining shots from *Dauntless*, including the null-field generator, had hit a second megacruiser, which was still with the formation but was now riddled with damage. The hole eaten into the megacruiser by the null field made it look as if a giant had taken a large bite out of one side of its bow.

Under the push of her maneuvering thrusters, *Dauntless* was swinging up, to port, and around again, aiming once more for the undamaged wing of the Covenant formation. For their part, the Covenant ships had finally killed their velocity in the original direction and were now accelerating back toward the Dancers, who were engaging in a complex pattern of interweaving maneuvers among themselves as they headed back in the direction of the hypernet gate. But the Dancers had stopped accelerating, holding their velocity at a rate that would allow the Covenant ships to catch them again.

"They're acting as bait," Geary said in wonderment. "They're dancing in front of the Covies, just out of reach, taunting them." And the Covenant commander, enraged, unable to come to grips with the Alliance battle cruiser which had been his original target, was locked on trying to strike the mocking alien ships dancing just out of reach.

What had Charban complained about? He thought the Dancers were withholding something, were not admitting how well they could communicate with humans. *It's the same sort of thing, isn't it? Dangle the objective just out of reach of whoever you're dealing with. Is that what the Dancers are doing to us in a different way? But why? Because that's how they do things, and they may not even realize they're doing it when it comes to talking with us? Or are they doing it deliberately, to get us to pursue some goal they'll keep just beyond our grasp?*

"They're just holding formation." Lieutenant Yuon sounded baffled.

It took Geary a moment to realize that the lieutenant was talking about the Covenant ships. It was true. Even though the Covenant flotilla had lost nearly half of its ships, the remaining ships had stayed rigidly in formation, a now-lopsided bird with only one wing.

Desjani spoke with dawning realization. "This is the opposite of what we were like, isn't it? We were fighting without regard for formation, just slugging it out, before you reminded us how good formation fighting could multiply our effectiveness. But these guys are acting like they can't imagine breaking formation. They haven't even adjusted the formation to compensate for their losses or form a more effective defense. It's like there's a spot they have to be in relative to the guide ship, and they aren't going to move from that spot even if the living stars showed up and said go."

Dauntless had swept through her turn and, instead of continuing on toward the undamaged wing of the Covenant formation, was lining up on the center of that formation. Desjani clearly intended to take out the flagship this time. Geary didn't question that targeting decision.

The Covenant ships did not pivot to face the oncoming Alliance battle cruiser, instead continuing to accelerate at their best rate toward the Dancers. Still moving fairly slowly relative to *Dauntless*, they fired weapons that could bear aft and down, scoring several hits this time as Desjani bored in on her target.

Specter missiles leaped away from *Dauntless*, the entire volley aimed at one of the megacruisers, then the battle cruiser tore through the Covenant formation again, hammering the megacruiser from which Mister Medal's transmissions had come.

As *Dauntless* began another wide turn, her thrusters pushing her down and to starboard this time, Geary watched the Covenant flagship explode. Near the site of the flagship's destruction, the megacruiser targeted with specter missiles had taken multiple hits on its stern and was spinning wildly away from the formation.

"One more run ought to do it," Desjani said.

"Captain!" Lieutenant Castries called. "Escape pods are launching!"

"From which ship?" Desjani asked sharply.

"Um… all of them."

Once again, Geary found himself watching his display in disbelief. The megacruiser badly hurt on the second firing run was spitting out escape pods, as was the megacruiser that had lost propulsion on this attack run. But so was the so-far-untouched last-surviving megacruiser, as were the three remaining corvettes. "They're panicking."

"They're... ?" Desjani gave him the look that meant his words made no sense to her.

"Their commander is dead. They may not even have known why he attacked us. Most of their ships have been destroyed. They know they're outmatched in firepower, maneuverability, and tactical skill. They're panicking."

"What?" Desjani repeated. "That— *What?* They've taken losses, so they're giving up?" She sounded far more confused than Yuon had been earlier.

Looking around the bridge, Geary saw the same incomprehension on the faces of everyone else. "They've never fought a real battle," he said, speaking slowly. "Just practice fights, against fake enemies who probably always lost. Because no commander wants to lose, and in practice battles senior commanders always place themselves in charge of the ships playing their own side. This is the first time they've faced an enemy who didn't cooperate with them, an enemy who wouldn't roll over and play dead because that's what the plan called for, an enemy experienced in real combat who played for keeps. This is the first time they've seen ships destroyed in battle, the first time they've seen comrades die, the first time their training and their weapons haven't worked the way they were supposed to. Everything they've been told was right has turned out wrong, their officers probably have no idea what to do when things don't go exactly according to plan, and discipline has simply disintegrated on those ships as everyone tries to save themselves."

Desjani shook her head. "The next time they want to fight,

they'd better be ready for a real fight. We could walk over these guys, couldn't we? An Alliance fleet could wipe them out while they were still fainting at the sight of blood." She sounded angry as well as contemptuous.

"If we wanted to," Geary said. "Do you want to?"

"Hell, no. People who bail out of perfectly good warships aren't worth the energy needed to put a hell lance through their escape pod."

He could understand how the crews of the Covenant ships felt, their escape pods spreading out and away from the abandoned warships that plowed onward and, unless boarded by crews from some of the Sol shipping farther out toward the edge of the star system, would keep traveling outward until they were lost in the deep dark between stars. He could also understand how Desjani and her crew felt, hardened veterans who had sailed with Death too long to be shocked or surprised at his appearance among them. They knew war. The Covenant crews had known only parades and drills and practices with foreordained results. *Dauntless* had been built for war. The Covenant ships had been built for peace even though they had the outer shape of warships. When the crews and ships of the Alliance and the Covenant had met, the result had been inevitable.

Geary looked away from his display, wondering if this was indeed the last fight between the Alliance and the Covenant. "Envoy Charban, please ask the Dancers to rejoin us. We will be proceeding toward Old Earth as originally planned. Senators Suva, Costa, and Sakai, Envoy Rione, the engagement is over. Sol Star System is no longer menaced by an occupying military force, and the threat to the Alliance governmental representatives has been eliminated." He threw that in just to remind the senators that they had been targets, too. "We will continue en route Old Earth."

The Dancers were already coming back toward *Dauntless*, their ships moving in a pattern that might have meaning to the aliens but remained incomprehensible to humans.

"They want to go to the surface," Rione said. She was leaning back in her seat in the conference room as if she didn't have the endurance left to stand.

"The surface," Geary repeated. "The Dancers went to send someone down to the surface of Old Earth."

"Yes. Sol Star System authorities say they'll have to debate and discuss the issue and asked us to wait. The government controlling that portion of Old Earth where Kansas is located, though, has invited us to land. They're eager for the prestige of being the site of the arrival of the Dancers." Rione looked at the image of Old Earth slowly rotating above the conference table. *Dauntless* and the Dancer ships were in orbit about that fabled planet, looking down on white clouds, blue oceans, and large continents that every human had seen images of but relatively few alive had actually gazed upon in person. Few lights showed on the parts of the globe experiencing night, but that was normal. Light sent outward and upward served no purpose but waste. Of more importance were the full-spectrum images that showed cities and towns in a density that was shocking to those from worlds where the human presence had come much later.

But many of those cities were patched by dead sections. Areas destroyed in war and still not reclaimed, or areas once populated when the number of humans on Old Earth had peaked, then depopulated during the bad times that had followed. Old Earth still had an impressively large population, but one that it could now sustain over the long term.

In some places, ancient cities along the coasts were girdled by berms and barriers to keep out waters that must have risen about them. In other places, less fortunate cities were marked by leaning, decrepit towers rising from shallow waters that had submerged lower structures.

"It's amazing, isn't it?" Senator Suva said. "They survived so much. The scars are there, but the people of Old Earth are slowly bringing her back."

Geary nodded. "Someone recently told me that we had learned to live without hope for a better future. But I don't think that was entirely true. Hope always lived here. Old Earth survived her trials and still managed to send out the first colonies to other stars. Those colonies gave birth to others, until humanity has spread across hundreds of star systems."

"Old Earth," Charban noted with a smile, "is invoked not just as Home, but as an example that where life remains and resolve does not fail, victory, or at least survival, may always be possible."

"But possibly at great cost," Rione added.

"Speaking of victory," Senator Costa said acidly, "you will doubtless be happy to hear, Admiral, that the people of Sol Star System are of conflicting opinions about our liberating them from the occupying force from the Covenant." Now that the battle was done, and the Covenant warships eliminated, Costa had embraced the engagement without any hint of her previous misgivings. "They're glad enough to be free of the occupiers, but they aren't thrilled with the fighting or our own continued presence."

"What did they say about the threat to you and the other Alliance senators?" Geary asked.

Costa's smile stretched wide and sardonic. "No reply on that. No curiosity or questions, either. None at all. It's enough to make you wonder if someone at Sol wasn't involved in the matter."

"We will make what contacts we can and perhaps learn more about what happened," Senator Sakai said. "Admiral, we have gained agreement under Sol Star System tourism regulations to allow every member of the ship's crew to visit the surface, one-third of the crew each day for three days. Old Earth will send up shuttles and take groups to different cities. The ancestors of those on this ship came from many different spots on Old Earth, and the people here will try to accommodate the wishes of our people to visit the places that mean the most to them. The Alliance government will cover the cost of those shuttle runs."

"Sol didn't offer to cover the cost?" Geary asked.

"That would have required special debate and procedures," Sakai said. "I assumed we did not have decades to wait while those matters were resolved. There is another issue we must discuss. The authorities on the portion of Old Earth containing the region called Kansas would like a much clearer indication of where the Dancers wish to go. Kansas is a large area on the surface."

Charban tapped a control, causing an image of angular letters to appear. "The Dancers sent me this when we reached orbit. More of that ancient text that said *Kansas*. These letters spell a word that might be pronounced Lee-on or Lie-ons."

"We will send that to the authorities below," Sakai said. "Perhaps they will be able to tell us where that is."

"Have they explained why humanity expanded so much farther inward along the galactic arm than we did outward?" Geary asked. That issue had been bothering him ever since it was pointed out.

Was Sakai's small smile tinged by darkness? It was hard to tell. Even his voice only *might* have carried a cutting edge. "The first colonies outward made that happen. In the outward direction, the first colonies were obsessed with their own profit and security. Worried that even newer colonies beyond them might surround them with potential enemies, or compete with them economically, they clamped tight controls on movement through their star systems and created barriers to further exploration and colonization. Since jump technology required anyone going beyond them to pass through them, they successfully prevented any threats to their security, prevented anyone else from exploiting the star systems farther outward from them, and became an isolated, forgotten backwater relative to the rest of humanity."

"So, they won?" Geary asked sarcastically.

"They thought so."

Geary stepped off the shuttle ramp, feeling the soil of Old Earth itself under his feet. *The last time I actually stood on a planet was when I was on Kosatka with Tanya. Before that… a century ago, though it feels much shorter to me. And now Tanya and I are here. Home. The place all ancestors of all humans came from.*

He blinked against the bright sun overhead and the strong, cold wind blowing across this land, carrying fine particles of dust and grit with it. The parched dirt had formed ridges and small dunes sculpted by the breezes.

Nearby, a battered tower of dark stone rose from the remnants of a larger structure, broken window openings gazing out blankly. The shuttle had landed in an open area surrounding the remains. Watching the landing area on the way in, Geary had seen that the open area had formed a square about the large building. Here and there, flat segments of concrete, the remains of roadways, were visible beneath the drifting soil.

Around the open square were some other dark stone ruins or just low mounds that marked the buried remnants of smaller structures, the mounds set in straight lines that marked the boundaries of the ancient roads. Buildings had been here, but centuries of abandonment had led to their collapse, time and weather eating away at the works of humanity.

He took a few steps, seeing that here the concrete road had given way to brick. A small patch of brick lay beneath his feet, the paving still intact though badly cracked. This section must have been buried for some time and only recently exposed by the unrelenting winds.

A few stunted trees grew amid the scrub grass that formed patchy oases among the dusty dunes. Large old tree trunks lay partially buried, their crumbling remnants testament to how fertile this land had once been.

Tanya had come to stand beside him, looking around curiously. "This is where the Dancers wanted to go? I've seen bombarded worlds that were in better shape."

"It must have been a nice town, once," Geary commented. "I don't see signs of destruction. It must have been abandoned." He pointed to some of the buildings. "You can still see signs of repairs. Some people must have hung on here as long as they could, even when the area turned into a desert."

An atmosphere flier had come to rest nearby, the occupants walking out to stand amid the desolation. "Earth once endured orbital bombardments, and many other ills," one of them said, her face saddened. "This is the place where Lyons, Kansas, once stood. Like many such towns, it could not survive the great changes in climate, the wars, and the many other troubles Old Earth has endured. People stayed and tried to keep this place and many like it alive, but in time their efforts were not enough. Here you see what became of the dreams of many people because of the folly of many people."

"Such places are not disturbed, except by natural processes," a man from Earth added. "They are a reminder, and a monument."

"Like living in a graveyard," Desjani muttered in Geary's ear.

Another woman smiled and knelt to touch sprigs of brighter grass that were springing from the side of a mound. "We've finally managed to reverse the climate processes that led to this area's becoming so dry. It was hard, reaching agreement with everyone on this world, but the steps have been taken to slowly bring the planet back into balance, avoiding the sort of shocks inflicted upon us in the past. The rains are coming back. They will bring back the rivers and the creeks and the lakes, then the trees and the animals of the plains will return. In time, so will the people. Perhaps they will build new homes here and rebuild this town," she added with a sharp look at the man who had spoken of not disturbing such places. "This is a living world, not a museum."

"We shouldn't argue this in front of others," the man replied, looking cross.

"If they're not going to repeat all of our mistakes, they need to know all about those mistakes and how we're dealing with them." The second woman straightened, brushing dust from her trousers. "Though from what I hear, there have been a lot of mistakes made among our world's children. Has the never-ending war between the Alliance and the Syndicate Worlds indeed finally come to an end?"

"Yes," Geary replied. *Mostly*, he added silently. "Seeing this, actually grasping how many people died on Old Earth, I wonder how we survived long enough to reach other stars."

"Survived to repeat the same follies," Senator Suva said, her eyes tragic as she scanned their surroundings.

"I am certain that we would recognize both the follies and those who pursued such policies," Senator Costa added in a caustic voice as she gazed meaningfully at Suva.

"I am certain that we would," Suva said, with a scathing glance at Costa.

"We may lack for answers," Rione said, as if commenting to no one in particular, "but we have a great deal of certainty, don't we?"

"Do we have to carry our quarrels to this place?" Dr. Nasr asked before either Suva or Costa could lash out at Rione or each other again. "Your ancestors, my ancestors, may have lived here, may have visited this very spot. Do not their memories deserve respect rather than discord?"

Geary looked around, seeing that Senator Sakai and Charban had also joined him outside. "What do you think?" he asked them.

"Home is the worse for wear, isn't it?" Charban remarked.

"We were fortunate," the woman from Earth who had first spoken said. "The lessons we learned and the technology we developed in making Mars habitable played a large role in helping this world recover from the damage we inflicted upon it. And what we learned about a functioning ecology in order to build crewed ships that could carry generations of people to other stars during voyages lasting more than a century in normal space has guided us in repairing the ecologies of the Earth."

"Ironic, isn't it?" another of her companions added. "Only by leaving our Home could we find the means to save our Home. You should come to other places. See our forests, our cities. Not all of Home is like this, and even here the scars of the past will soon be covered by new life."

"A living world," the woman agreed pointedly, with another look at the man who had spoken of leaving all undisturbed. "A tired world, but still living, and not every person here is tired. The restless ones often go off world, though. The stars are an important safety valve for us."

Nice for you, Geary thought. *But that leaves us to deal with whatever those restless people want to do when they get out among the stars.*

He had noticed that none of the people from Earth had brought up the fight with the Covenant warships and those warships' deliberate attack on an Alliance ship. They were deliberately avoiding any discussion of that matter.

Any further conversation was forestalled as one of the Dancer shuttles, a smooth ovoid similar in shape to their ships though much smaller, came to rest on the ancient roadway near the human shuttles. Everyone watched the gleaming Dancer craft, which balanced gently on the soil like a ballerina poised on one foot.

Geary's skin prickled slightly. He looked around and saw Dr. Nasr nodding in approval.

"The people here set up an isolation screen around this whole area," Nasr explained. "They have activated it as a precaution against contamination."

"What is to happen?" one of the people from Earth asked.

"This is the Dancers' show," Rione replied. "We'll have to see what they do."

A circular opening appeared in the side of the Dancer craft, expanding from a tiny point to a large access. From the bottom of the opening, a short and broad ramp extended to touch the ground.

"Has this happened before?" another of those from Old Earth asked. "And how often? Or is this the first time an intelligence not our own has set foot to the soil of humanity's Home?"

"They picked an odd place for it," Senator Costa grumbled.

"Out of any place on Earth, they picked *our* land," a woman from Earth declared proudly.

"But why would that matter to these aliens?" the first man asked pointedly.

"The Dancers always have their reasons," Charban said, "even if those reasons don't always make sense to us. I see something moving inside their shuttle."

Two of the Dancers came out onto the ramp, wearing protective suits that helped mask their hideous-to-human-eyes appearance.

Like a giant spider mated with a wolf was how most people described the Dancers. This was the first time Geary had seen one in person, and he was grateful for their wearing the protective gear even as he felt ashamed of that reaction.

The Dancers were carrying something between them, walking with a curious slowness.

It was an oblong container, made of some clear substance, about two meters long and perhaps a meter wide and deep.

Inside it...

"Ancestors preserve us," Senator Suva gasped. "A human?"

Dr. Nasr walked up to the container as the Dancers lowered it to a level patch of ground with the same slow, careful movements. He looked down, then pulled an instrument from his belt and studied it. "A human who died a very long time ago. The body has been protected inside that container and thus preserved by natural mummification. The body is wearing some sort of protective suit. There is no sign of trauma. I cannot say how they died, but this person was not slain by violent means."

Another Dancer came forward, holding out a much smaller container, this one opaque.

Dr. Nasr took the box with a slight, respectful bow, then looked inside. He reached in and held out some small objects. "Does anyone recognize these?"

One of the Earth representatives came forward and took them gingerly. "Ancient data-storage devices. Even if these have been protected and stored properly, it's very unlikely the data on them still exists in readable form after so long. We might be able to recover something, though."

"What of this?" Dr. Nasr held up a metal pin that glinted with color in the bright sun.

More of the people from Earth came forward, studying it, then one held it out toward Geary and the others from the Alliance. "In the old form of the language, it says *Operation Long Jump*."

"What was that?" Geary asked, looking at the pin but not touching it. It didn't seem right to mar this object from history with the touch of his fingers.

"I'm checking." Another Earth representative was consulting a data pad. "There is little here. Secrecy in the old days and destruction of records since then have cost us much information. What our historians have pieced together is that Operation Long Jump was one of the earliest attempts to use jump space to reach other stars. Several of the experimental ships were lost, some automated and some with human pilots. Subsequent experience proved those jumps were aimed too far, beyond the ability of jump drives of that time to work properly."

"They didn't come out of jump," Desjani said, her voice filled with horror. If there was one thing that could seriously rattle any sailor, it was the prospect of being trapped in jump space. "They died in jump. May the living stars have mercy on them. All the way to Dancer space? Decades, maybe, in jump. This person must have died long before coming out of jump space. There couldn't have been enough food, water, and life support on their ship to survive a fraction of that time, even if being alone in jump space that long didn't drive him or her insane."

"There is no sign of violence," Dr. Nasr repeated. "Self-inflicted or otherwise. Perhaps oxygen or other critical life support failed, bringing as peaceful an end as this poor pilot could hope for."

"But the ship carrying this pilot did come out of jump eventually," Charban said. "How?"

"Who knows?" Desjani said. "Why would anyone want to conduct experiments that involve tossing something into jump space when there isn't any expectation it would come out again? No human would agree to that, once they understood what was going on, and why waste automated ships?"

"Perhaps the ship accidentally came close enough to a jump point much farther along than its original destination, and it popped out," Geary speculated. "Or maybe jump space will eventually eject anything that doesn't belong there if the object gets close enough to a gravity well. But who was this person?"

"Perhaps this will tell us," Dr. Nasr said, holding up a small rectangle of metal with tiny letters and numbers embossed on it.

"The same old form of the language," an Earth representative said, taking the tag and tilting it to catch the light of Sol. "It is hard to read. It says, 'Maior... Paul... Crabaugh. 954... 457... 9903.' That first word must be Major. Rank and name and a personal identification number used back then."

"This is the last object in the box," Dr. Nasr said. He had in his hand another piece of metal, this one about half the size of the palm of a hand, rectangular, and with an enameled decoration on one side. The ancient enamel still shone brightly in the sunlight.

As the Earth representative took the object, Geary craned his head to see the decoration. There were big letters on it, easy enough to read, over a scene of fields of bright green vegetation heavily dotted with large flowers bearing vivid yellow petals.

"The large word says Kansas," the man from Earth read. "The small word says Lyons. This place. A souvenir. Perhaps from his family. Made when this town still lived and such plants grew here, as they will again. He took this into space with him, to remind him of home."

"Now we know why the Dancers wanted to come here," Rione said. "They were bringing him back."

For a long time, no one spoke. The Dancers waited silently near the hatch to their shuttle. The wind sighing through the ruins of the town was the only sound.

"Why didn't they tell us why they needed to come here?" Desjani finally asked.

"How would they have explained it?" Charban replied. "Apparently, they felt an obligation to return the body here. If they had told us at Varandal that they had him, we would have wanted him given to us at Varandal. If they had then refused to turn over the remains for reasons they couldn't convey to us, what would we have done?"

"Totally misinterpreted things," Rione said.

Dr. Nasr knelt by the container holding the remains of Major Crabaugh. "I see no signs of autopsy or other invasive procedures. If they examined his body, they did so only by noninvasive means."

"They respected him," Costa said, sounding angry. But as she glared at the other humans, it was clear her anger was not aimed at the Dancers. "They didn't take him apart, they didn't desecrate the body, they didn't treat him like some strange animal cast up on their doorstep. Instead, they treated his remains as if he were…" She struggled for words.

"One of theirs," Dr. Nasr finished for her. He stood up but continued looking down at the remains. "They did not know who he was, or what he was, or where he had come from. His appearance was very different from their own, perhaps as hideous in their eyes as the Dancers appear to us. But they looked at the artifacts with him, they looked upon him, and they saw a creature who must be like themselves in many ways. A creature whose remains deserved respect. A creature with a family and a home, both of which might be waiting for his return. They looked upon him and did not see the differences. They saw what this human must have in common with them, and when they could, they brought his carefully protected remains back to his home."

"They have shamed us," Senator Suva said. She was standing very straight, tears running down her face. "They have shamed us. We would not have done as well. We never have, and even after so many centuries of supposed progress, we still look at each other and see only the differences between us."

"I will not be shamed by something that looks like that," Senator Costa muttered, then gave Suva a challenging look. "I won't be less than them. What they can do, I can do."

Suva hesitated, then nodded. "We can try."

Standing beside Geary, Senator Sakai spoke softly. "For so many years we searched for them. For someone like ourselves, yet different. When we found them, we thought we could learn from them, that whatever they were they would see things in us that we did not. It seems the philosophers were right. But will knowing this be enough to overcome human folly?"

"We don't even know if we're interpreting their actions here correctly," Geary said in a very low voice so only Sakai and Desjani could hear. "But I don't think I want to bring up that possibility. Maybe what we think we're seeing is best left unexamined for now."

Tanya reached out and squeezed Geary's wrist. "Those sorts of questions are way above my pay grade. We got the Dancers here, and the Dancers did what they wanted to do. What do *we* do now?"

Geary looked around at the crumbling ruins of this town, at the remains of Major Crabaugh, brought home at last, at the Dancers in their armor, and the humans from the Alliance and from Sol. At the new grass springing up nearby, grass that matched that in the ancient decoration. The past lay heavy on Old Earth, yet the living were looking to the future.

"Let's go home," he said. "Once the crew finishes visiting Home, once our senators finish their talks with the authorities here, and once all the ceremonies are done, we'll go back to our own home. We have work to do."

AUTHOR'S NOTE

There have been a few changes around here.
CAPTAIN TANYA DESJANI

Way back in the twentieth century (the late 1960s to be exact), I lived for a few years on Midway Island in the center of the Pacific Ocean. In those days satellite TV was, well, science fiction. The only TV we had on the island came from a single local station that broadcast old programs for a few hours a day. Even white sand beaches, a beautiful lagoon protected by a coral reef, and the antics of the gooney birds wear thin at times. When that happened, I could read, and most of what I read in those days was history.

But there was another diversion available at the base movie theater. On Saturdays and Sundays, it would show matinees consisting of a one-hour TV show like *Mission: Impossible* or *The Big Valley*, and a one-hour episode of *Star Trek* (the original series, of course). While the rest of the world watched Kirk, Spock, and

McCoy on their small TV sets, I got to see their adventures on the big screen.

When I started writing I found that those influences showed up in my stories. History offered many ideas, and the original *Star Trek* had shown me how SF could be exciting, thought-provoking, and fun. It had also impressed upon me how important the characters were. The spaceships were cool, but the stories wouldn't have been the same without people in them whose actions mattered and who tried their best even against seemingly impossible odds.

A lot of other things went into the Lost Fleet series. At its core lie those basic influences, but when a writer creates characters they can start influencing the story, telling you what they would and wouldn't do, telling you they would make a different decision than you had originally planned. As I've told Black Jack's story, he has surprised me more than once. He has found friends and allies, overcome a wide variety of enemies, and developed a very close relationship with a certain battle cruiser captain. When the opportunity arose to take him to new places and face new challenges, I was glad to carry on Geary's story in the Beyond the Frontier series.

While I wrote about Black Jack Geary, I also wrote about his opponents, and foremost among those foes has been the Syndicate Worlds. In every challenge that he's faced, Geary has done his best to hold to his duty, to simple truths, and to real honor grounded in how he acts. Against that, the Syndics have followed practices opposed to all that Geary believes in. Those characters could have been simple: people who were evil because they were evil. But that would have short-changed the story because no enemy is monolithic, no foe is unvarying from person to person, with every man and woman marching in lockstep. The people of the Syndicate Worlds are human. Some are committed to the system that gives them power or have vested all of their faith in believing that only this system can maintain order. Others see the flaws in the system and work against it. Yet others have been turned against the system by the injustices they see or personally experience.

Many readers asked to know more about the Syndics, so I wanted to show this other side of the Lost Fleet saga. What about the Syndics who had believed their system was the best, until it failed spectacularly, with the Alliance triumphant? What about those who had long ago stopped believing in that system but saw no alternative while war still raged? The Syndicate empire is falling apart, the central government trying to hold on to as many star systems as it can while revolt and rebellion break out. And if revolution succeeds, what replaces the old way of doing things?

When the Alliance fleet returns to Midway near the end of *Invincible*, it discovers that the Syndicate Worlds is no longer in control. There has been fighting on the inhabited world and in space, and the two leaders of the star system now call themselves president and general. *The Lost Stars: Tarnished Knight* tells the story of the revolt at Midway. CEOs Gwen Iceni and Artur Drakon have had enough of the Syndic way of doing things, but it's the only way they know. They can't trust each other, they can't trust *anyone*, because that is how politics and everything else works in the Syndicate Worlds. But Iceni and Drakon need each other as they fight to not only defend their own star system but also carry the battle to neighboring star systems wracked by internal fighting and Syndic counterattacks. Two people who have long since ceased trusting in anything have to find something to believe in. If they can live long enough.

It has been great to see how well the Lost Fleet saga has been received by readers. There is no better reward for a writer than for people to want to read the stories he creates. In turn, I want to offer more to readers, more stories about more parts of the Lost Fleet universe. The Lost Stars series takes us to a part of that universe where a lot is happening, where new characters face tremendous challenges and the shadow of Black Jack looms large.

The Lost Stars: Tarnished Knight
is now available from Titan Books.

ABOUT THE AUTHOR

John G. Hemry is a retired US Navy officer and the author, under the pen name Jack Campbell, of the *New York Times* national bestselling *Lost Fleet* series (*Dauntless, Fearless, Courageous, Valiant, Relentless,* and *Victorious*) and the follow-on series *Beyond the Frontier* and *The Lost Stars*, set on a former enemy world in *The Lost Fleet* universe. Under his own name, John is also the author of the *JAG in Space* series and the recently reissued *Stark's War* series. His short fiction has appeared in places as varied as the last Chicks in Chainmail anthology (*Turn the Other Chick*) and *Analog* magazine (which published his Nebula Award-nominated story 'Small Moments in Time' as well as most recently 'Betty Knox and Dictionary Jones in the Mystery of the Missing Teenage Anachronisms' in the March 2011 issue). His humorous short story 'As You Know Bob' was selected for *Year's Best SF 13*. John's nonfiction has appeared in *Analog* and *Artemis* magazines as well as BenBella books on *Charmed*, *Star Wars*, and *Superman*, and in the *Legion of Superheroes* anthology *Teenagers from the Future*. John had the opportunity to live on Midway Island for a while during the 1960s, then later attended the US Naval Academy. He served in a variety of jobs including gunnery officer and navigator on a destroyer, with an amphibious squadron, and at the Navy's anti-terrorism center. After retiring from the US Navy and settling in Maryland, John began writing. He lives with his long-suffering wife (the incomparable S) and three great kids. His daughter and two sons are diagnosed on the autistic spectrum.

ACKNOWLEDGMENTS

I remain indebted to my agent, Joshua Bilmes, for his ever-inspired suggestions and assistance, and to my editor, Anne Sowards, for her support and editing. Thanks also to Catherine Asaro, Robert Chase, J. G. (Huck) Huckenpohler, Simcha Kuritzky, Michael LaViolette, Aly Parsons, Bud Sparhawk, and Constance A. Warner for their suggestions, comments, and recommendations.